THE END OF

AMERICA'S WAR

IN AFGHANISTAN

TED HALSTEAD

Books by Ted Halstead:

The Second Korean War (2018)
The Saudi-Iranian War (2019)
The End of America's War in Afghanistan (2020)

All three books, including this one, are set in a fictional near future. Some events described have happened, and others have not.

For example, American troops did leave Iraq, only to return several years later. American troops did not leave Afghanistan, only to return later.

Yet.

To my wife Saadia, for her love and support over more than thirty years.

To my son Adam, for his love and the highest compliment an author can receive- "You wrote this?"

To my daughter Mariam, for her continued love and encouragement.

To my father Frank, for his love and for repeatedly prodding me to finally finish my first book.

To my mother Shirley, for her love and support.

To my granddaughter Fiona, for always making me smile.

All characters are listed on the very last page, because that's where I think the list is easiest to find for quick reference.

Chapter One

Karachi, Pakistan

The bomber's boss had told him to do precisely what Mullah Abdul Zahed said.

The problem was, he didn't like anything he was being told to do.

Mamnoon Sahar prided himself on targeting only enemies of the Taliban. Well, one woman targeted in this job was indeed married to a Pakistani soldier.

But that soldier was stationed here in Karachi on the Arabian Sea coast, about as far from fighting the Taliban as he could get and still be in Pakistan.

Plus, he was an ordinary enlisted man, not even an officer.

Even worse, Abdul had told him to make sure the bomb didn't go off when the soldier was home.

Then, Abdul had insisted the bomb had to destroy the neighboring house as well. The bomber had checked, and the man in that household was an auto mechanic.

So, he would be killing two women, nine children, and a man who fixed cars.

Enough was enough. Either Mamnoon got the explanation Abdul had so far refused to provide, or he wouldn't do the job, no matter what his boss said.

Mamnoon looked at Abdul doubtfully. He wore the usual low white turban and had a matching full white beard to go with it. Abdul's face was lined and worn, as was to be expected of the last living member of the Taliban government that had ruled Afghanistan during the years before the Americans came.

His friends and his many enemies would agree Mamnoon was a dangerous man, both with a bomb and a blade. Thin and wiry, he stayed clean-shaven so he could move freely in parts of Pakistan where a full beard on a young man might attract unwanted attention.

Mamnoon had taken on many men who wished to kill him, and he was still here.

This old cleric should pose no challenge. But something about him made Mamnoon nervous.

No matter, Mamnoon decided. He had lived by certain principles for many years. He wasn't going to throw them away for this old man, cleric or no.

"You realize what you are asking me to do will kill many innocents, women and children. The number of deaths will draw a great deal of police and maybe even military attention to my work," Mamnoon said.

Abdul nodded. "Can you make the explosions look like an accident, as we discussed?"

"Well, yes," Mamnoon replied. "The compressed gas bottle used to provide fuel for cooking is just outside the soldier's home, as usual. The idiots who designed the neighbor's house you also wish targeted, placed the kitchen so that it is nearly adjacent to the one in the soldier's home. So, the gas bottle for one home is only a couple of meters away from the other."

Mamnoon paused. "But you knew this when you asked that I target both homes."

Abdul shrugged but said nothing.

"So, my question to you is simple. Why do these people need to die?" Mamnoon asked.

Abdul pursed his lips and considered his reply. Finally, he said, "One of them has betrayed the Taliban. The others must die so that if somehow it is discovered this was no accident, it will be more difficult to focus the investigation on our real target."

Mamnoon frowned, and considered Abdul's answer. He knew it was the best he would get.

Just as he was about to tell Abdul it wasn't good enough, the cleric lifted one finger.

"Before you reply, Mamnoon Sahar, know that I wish you and your family in Rawalpindi nothing but the best of good fortune. However, if this mission is not a success, I have many followers who would be sorely disappointed."

Mamnoon did his best to keep his expression impassive, which was difficult when he felt as though he'd just been punched in the gut.

His boss would have never told Abdul his actual name. It was his most carefully guarded secret.

Well, next to his family's location.

The fact that Abdul knew both meant he indeed had no choice, especially after that business about "his followers." Abdul was telling Mamnoon that killing him wouldn't solve his problem.

Worse, now Mamnoon knew he risked being eliminated along with his family as soon as he finished this job.

The only way Mamnoon could see to avoid that was doing this job so well that Abdul would see him as worth keeping alive.

His instincts had been right. This old cleric was a threat, and if he wasn't managed correctly could end up killing him and his entire family.

All this flashed through Mamnoon's thoughts in an instant.

Aloud, he said, "I understand. I will set the charges."

Mamnoon had a van with the removable logo of a gas cylinder company, and work clothing with the same logo.

He need not have bothered. No one challenged him or took any notice of the time Mamnoon spent next to the first cylinder, and then the other.

Mamnoon next drove the van two blocks away to a small parking garage, and when he was sure he was unobserved, removed the logo from the side of the van. Then he pulled the logo patch from his shirt. Both went deep into a fetid dumpster behind the garage.

Next, Mamnoon walked the short distance back to the small neighborhood mosque where he and Abdul were staying. As a cleric, Abdul's right to stay there overnight was a given, and the same went for his young "servant."

Abdul and Mamnoon took turns standing watch. Their small room had a window that let them observe both homes.

Mamnoon sighed internally. He knew that if this mosque had not been handy, Abdul would have found another way.

But he was certain without asking that Abdul saw the mosque's location as yet another sign that he was doing God's work.

As it turned out, they didn't have to wait long. Only a few hours after Mamnoon had set the charges, the last person being targeted in the two homes arrived, probably just in time for the evening meal.

The auto mechanic.

Abdul was the one who saw him arrive. He nodded towards the radio detonator Mamnoon had attached to his belt, and said, "It is time."

Mamnoon pressed the button.

The resulting explosion was not only incredibly loud. It shook the small mosque hard enough that for a moment, Mamnoon feared he had done his job too well.

But only for a moment. The shaking stopped, and the mosque was still there. There were no cracks or other damage Mamnoon could see, at least in their room.

Probably the best indicator was that the glass in the room's only window was unbroken.

Abdul went to it and looked down the street.

Mamnoon didn't like the look of the smile that spread across Abdul's face.

Abdul turned to Mamnoon, who thought to himself that he liked the unholy gleam in Abdul's eyes even less than his smile.

Abdul's happiness came from the fact that with the illumination provided by the fires, even in the night, he could see that both homes had been completely leveled.

"Excellent work! Tell me, how did you do it with such small explosive charges?" Abdul asked.

Mamnoon kept reminding himself that his safety, and more importantly, his family's, depended on keeping Abdul happy.

Abdul had insisted on seeing the explosive charges Mamnoon planned to use, probably because he knew their residue would be the most definite sign that the explosions had been no accident.

"I added compressed gas to both cylinders until they were not only full but slightly over-pressurized. Not enough for them to rupture, but enough that . . . well, you see the results. There shouldn't be enough explosive residue left to be noticed, and the same should be true for the radio trigger receivers," Mamnoon said.

Not long ago, Mamnoon wouldn't have been able to say that with such confidence. But the shrinking size of electrical and radio components in recent years had indeed been a blessing for men like Mamnoon.

"It's not often that my expectations are not only met, but exceeded. Tomorrow you will go with me to another job. I will tell you more about it on the way. For now, we should both get some sleep," Abdul said.

Mamnoon nodded and went to one of the two small cots. Just as he closed his eyes, he heard Abdul say softly, "Now that you have proven yourself, I will tell you that you are playing a part in a great plan. One that has been many years in the making, and that has much time still left to go. But at its end, the Americans will be forced to leave Afghanistan forever."

Mamnoon gave the only reply possible before turning over to sleep. "God be praised," he said.

Mamnoon's last thought before he fell asleep was that his skills had bought him and his family a reprieve.

He wondered how long it would last.

Khyber Pakhtunkhwa (KPK), Pakistan

Mullah Abdul Zahed pounded his right hand on the carved wooden table that dominated the room so hard the men sitting next to him involuntarily jerked from the sound.

"This plan is the only way we will get the Americans out of Afghanistan and Pakistan for good, and it will only happen if you give me the men and weapons I need! You all know me, and you know I would never say this if it were not true!"

The room was large, but it was still packed with leaders from both the Afghan Taliban, which included Abdul, as well as Pakistan's Tehrik-i-

Taliban (TTP). Such meetings were extremely rare because of the danger of drone strikes, but Abdul's demands were so high that every Taliban leader involved insisted on hearing the reason for them personally.

Abdul had thought he could convince the others based on his considerable reputation. After all, he was the last surviving member of the Taliban government that had ruled Afghanistan until 2001.

Looking at the faces of the men around him, though, Abdul could see his reputation alone wouldn't be enough.

Abdul wasn't surprised that the next man to speak was Khaksar Wasiq from the Pakistani TTP. He had known coming into the meeting that Khaksar, as the head of the largest TTP faction, would be the least enthusiastic about committing his resources to an attack he could only watch from a distance.

Khaksar was at least as old as Abdul, but his hair and beard were still jet black, with only a few strands of grey. Thickly and powerfully built, he looked like an aging wrestler. It had been years since he had participated in an attack against the Americans, but he still kept saying he planned to lead his men into battle at least one more time.

"We know you believe what you've said is true. But you are asking for our best, most experienced fighters, and all of our most advanced heavy weapons. If your attack fails, it may be years before we can mount a meaningful offensive in either Afghanistan or Pakistan."

Khaksar paused. "You have said you cannot tell us the details of the attack or even its goal because word might reach the enemy. I understand this. But you must tell us something that will help us understand why this is a risk worth taking. For example, you said we wouldn't believe how long you have been planning this attack. How long, exactly?"

Abdul was seething, but he knew he couldn't just refuse to answer. Once he opened the door, though . . . .

Looking at the faces around him, Abdul could see he had no choice.

"Since 2002," Abdul said flatly.

Looking at the varying expressions of shock around the table, Abdul experienced some satisfaction but knew more questions would follow.

Khaksar nodded. "Many here were only children then. If you first planned it so long ago, surely others were involved as well?"

Abdul knew where he was headed, and decided to answer first since it would do Khaksar no good. Abdul quickly rattled off three names.

Khaksar looked grim and responded, "All great men, who died many years ago. Yet all three were known to at least one of us."

Khaksar then pointed at two men from the Afghan Taliban, as well as one from the Pakistani TTP. All three nodded.

Khaksar then turned back to Abdul. "So, you can't share the details of the attack with all of us. But the four of us knew the men who planned it with you. Tell us, and the others here will accept our decision if we agree to proceed."

Both Abdul and Khaksar could see that many of the other leaders were not, in fact, happy with their exclusion. But everyone could see it was the best solution.

And no one was eager to linger in this meeting spot a minute longer than necessary.

Quickly, the other leaders filed out until only Abdul, Khaksar, and the other three leaders remained.

Abdul scowled and shook his head. "First, you have to remember how bad it was when the Americans and their allies first came in 2001. We thought we could crush the Northern Alliance traitors with tanks left over from the Russian occupation before the Americans arrived in real numbers. Then, a handful of their 'Special Forces' soldiers hid and used lasers to guide bombs to our tanks. Many of our best-trained men died for nothing."

Abdul sat quietly for a moment, clearly collecting his thoughts.

"Then, at the end of 2001, there was the battle at Tora Bora. The Americans dropped bombs containing seven thousand kilos of explosives they called 'daisy cutters.' The bombs came down for days, and then their soldiers followed. More good men gone."

Khaksar nodded. "I talked to one of the men who fled Tora Bora with Bin Laden. He said the bombs sounded like the end of the world."

Abdul shrugged. "Yet worse was to come. In early 2002 what the enemy called 'Operation Anaconda.' We lost hundreds of our best men. Hardly any enemy were killed. In fact, the enemy competed to set records over the greatest distance they could kill us."

Khaksar shook his head sympathetically. "The Americans have been difficult opponents for many years."

Abdul glared back. "The two snipers setting records for killing our men at distances of over two kilometers were Canadian!"

Khaksar winced but said nothing, and the other three Taliban leaders silently shook their heads.

Abdul sighed. "I could go on. American paratroopers dropped onto one of our fortresses at night, killing or capturing every one of our men. Their casualties? One sprained an ankle. You start to see why we were ready to think about a new approach."

Khaksar shrugged and nodded, but asked nothing. It was apparent he had decided to let Abdul tell the story his way.

Abdul looked thoughtful and then continued. "Continuing to resist the foreign invaders was never a question. We beat the British, and we beat the Russians. Every great empire has believed they could rule us, but all have failed. These invaders would be defeated as well."

All the other men present nodded. There was very little every man who called himself Taliban could agree on without question. What Abdul had just said might have been its sum total.

Abdul scowled. "But, how long would victory take? After the wars that brought American troops to Germany, Japan, and Korea, they stayed for over half a century. Yes, we would keep fighting even then. But what would Afghanistan look like after generations of American occupation?"

Khaksar stirred, and it looked like he was about to object, but then he settled back and remained quiet.

Abdul smiled grimly. "You were going to talk about Vietnam. Yes, indeed, Americans were there in real numbers for only about a decade before they abandoned the fight. And there were clear similarities between that conflict and ours. A superpower that risked turning the population against it when its massive firepower inevitably killed civilians. A nearby country where freedom fighters could find sanctuary. Other countries secretly willing to help them."

The other men all smiled and nodded, but were also clearly puzzled. Why give up hope that they could have the same success as the Vietnamese?

Shaking his head, Abdul said quietly, "Nearly sixty thousand Americans died in combat in Vietnam. We have not killed even three thousand, in over twenty years of fighting. But that is not the greatest difference between the two wars."

Looking each of the other men in the eye, Abdul said, "Every American who came to fight us in Afghanistan was a volunteer. And none of them have forgotten the crimes of that madman Bin Laden that brought them here."

Now several of the other men looked displeased but said nothing.

Abdul nodded and said, "Yes, I know many of you have been taught that the attacks on the Americans in 2001 were a great victory. But all they accomplished was to kill people in planes and buildings who had nothing to do with us, and to leave the country fielding the most powerful military on earth with an endless appetite for revenge."

Khaksar nodded back. "It is true. Some of their soldiers here were not even born in 2001. They fight like men who have not forgotten."

Abdul shrugged. "And so we come to the greatest difference. There were years of mass demonstrations against the Vietnam War. Thousands of Americans fled to Canada to avoid being drafted to fight in Vietnam. Afghanistan? Today we are rarely even discussed by the Americans in their news and their politics. All this is exactly what we feared in 2002, and why we decided we had to take radical action if we were to be free of the Americans."

Abdul paused. "You all remember how the Americans left Iraq at the end of 2011?"

Everyone nodded.

"And how, when ISIS was nearly within sight of Baghdad, the Americans returned in 2014?"

Everyone nodded again.

"In 2019, the Americans invited us to Camp David. When they agreed in advance to exclude the puppet government in Kabul and to let us once again call our country the Islamic Emirate of Afghanistan, we knew these were actually surrender talks. Of course, the talks were canceled. But it wasn't long before the American President came to Afghanistan, and we were invited again," Abdul said with a smile.

The other men smiled too, but like Abdul's, the smiles were tinged with sadness.

"We finally won. But then the Americans returned. And they've stayed ever since."

Abdul shook his head. "So, we don't just need to force the Americans to leave. We must also convince them never to come back."

Now it was clear Abdul was struggling with his next words.

"Even though I know it is finally time, it is hard for me to speak of the plan we devised. The other men who worked on it with me are long dead. I have feared every day for more than two decades our enemies would learn of our plan, and end our last best hope. But now I see that no one man can reach such an important goal alone. So, here is what we did."

The other men were all leaning forward, and were absolutely silent.

"Pakistan tested its first nuclear weapon in 1998. In Taliban-ruled Afghanistan, we watched, we were interested- but we knew there was no chance the Pakistani government would ever share even a single nuclear weapon with us. We also knew there was no chance we would ever be able to steal one. After all, the Pakistani government had built them as a counter to India's nuclear weapons, which were seen as a mortal threat. What could be more closely guarded?"

Now the other four men set back in their chairs, clearly disappointed, but still silent.

Abdul grinned fiercely, and said, "You think you are going to hear the dreaming of an old man. We did much more than dream. We developed a plan to get someone working for us inside Pakistan's nuclear program."

Khaksar couldn't help himself. "How?" he asked.

"You all know that throughout the fighting in Afghanistan since 2001, over a third of our soldiers came from Pakistan," Abdul said.

The other four men nodded, their expressions showing they were all curious to see where this story would lead.

"We recruited female relatives of those fighters to marry Pakistani soldiers. Over several years, we were able to succeed with about three dozen."

Khaksar asked, "Why soldiers? Did you expect to recruit them, or to learn anything useful from them about Pakistan's nuclear program?"

Abdul shook his head. "No. But that was never our intention, and none of the soldiers were involved with Pakistan's nuclear weapons. Instead, once the wives gave birth to a son, we planned for these new mothers to recruit their sons to help us. These sons would be bound to the Taliban cause from birth."

At first, the other four men all stared at Abdul in disbelief.

After a moment, though, Khaksar nodded. "You thought that since the son often follows in the footsteps of the father, nobody would suspect it was their mothers urging them to join Pakistan's military. To help us. And when a background check was run on the parents, they would find a soldier and a housewife. Their son would be easy to clear for any duty, including with nuclear weapons."

Abdul was delighted with Khaksar's statement. "Exactly! I'm pleased you understand our thinking. Yes, the plan required many years to show results. But, here we are well over two decades later, finally ready to reap its rewards."

Khaksar next asked the most obvious question.

"How many of their sons finally succeeded in joining Pakistan's nuclear program on our behalf?"

Abdul answered quietly, "One."

Khaksar shook his head. "What happened to all the others?"

Abdul shrugged. "Some of the wives died. Others had no sons. Many had sons that had no interest in becoming soldiers. As you know, Pakistan has never had a draft, so the sons had to be willing to volunteer. Several other sons became soldiers, but so far have had no assignment anywhere near Pakistan's nuclear program."

Now Abdul grimaced with distaste. "Of course, none of the wives dared tell their Pakistani soldier husbands about our plans. However, two of the wives told me they had changed their minds about helping us, and I had to eliminate them. The man who helped me do it turned out to be disloyal, so he had to be dealt with as well."

All of the other men nodded. There was only one way to deal with betrayal.

Abdul continued, "Our great good fortune is that one son became not just a soldier, but as a university graduate, became an officer. Not just an officer, but one of the small number trained to work directly with nuclear weapons. He has been able to learn of the transport schedule for a shipment of nuclear weapons from Pakistan's production facility at the National Defense Complex in the Kala Chitta Dahr mountain range west of Islamabad."

Abdul paused and looked at the others solemnly. "I plan to capture eight of these weapons. I am also going to launch attacks as distractions for the American 'special forces' that will be sent to get them back. You will have many questions about the timing and details of these attacks. For now, there is just one question, which you must answer before the Americans have one of their drones end our conversation. Will you give me the men and weapons I need?"

Khaksar glanced at the other three men and could see from their expressions that they thought as he did.

"Yes. Yes, we will. And before the attack, this group will meet again to discuss how you will capture these eight weapons, and what we will do with them."

Abdul nodded. "Agreed. We must do all we can to kill only the Americans and their Afghan servants, or our countrymen will be right to turn against us, and make all our work and sacrifice over more than twenty years pointless."

CHAPTER TWO

Peshawar, Pakistan

Ibrahim Munawar looked around the room nervously. The four men sitting on the other side of the table were all looking at Ibrahim and his laptop with frank curiosity. Like the man who had invited Ibrahim and was seated next to him, Mullah Abdul Zahed, everyone else in the room sported a full beard and was at least double Ibrahim's age.

Ibrahim was clean-shaven and looked like the recent university graduate he was. He was so pale several of the other men in the room had the same unspoken thought—one of the British colonizers might have figured among his ancestors two or three generations back. Brown hair that was already thinning and gold-colored, wire-frame glasses helped contribute to that impression.

Abdul could see how nervous Ibrahim was but could think of nothing he could do to help. Abdul knew that Khaksar Wasiq and the other men who had approved his request for men and weapons could still change their minds if they didn't like what Ibrahim had to say, and so felt a bit nervous himself.

Best to get this over with as quickly as possible. Here in one of Pakistan's largest cities, they might be safe from American drone strikes. Arrest or worse by one of Pakistan's many law enforcement or intelligence agencies, though, was always a risk.

Abdul had a far-away look in his eyes as he began to speak.

"I have had a dream for many years. It has one of the missiles you have all seen the Pakistanis roll down the streets in their military parades. In my dream, the missile is flying through the air towards an American airbase, still carrying its original Pakistani markings. I remember thinking to myself, why take the time to repaint the missile, when the Americans would never see it?"

There were a few uneasy chuckles, but it was clear Abdul's audience was mostly confused.

Abdul smiled and now looked directly at his audience. "There are always a few steps involved in translating a dream into reality. There will be no missile falling on a base from above. But make no mistake. The Americans will taste the nuclear fire that so far they have only brought to others."

Abdul gestured towards Ibrahim, and said, "Ibrahim is the one we have to thank for telling us when and where nuclear weapons will soon be transported, and vulnerable to capture. He has also developed a plan to carry out the attack. He will now explain its details."

Ibrahim lifted the laptop's lid, revealing a screen displaying a large truck holding four missiles.

"This is the Nasr launch system. It has two main components. The first is a transporter erector launcher or TEL for short. That is the vehicle that transports and launches the missiles. The second is the missiles. You can see that there are four."

Ibrahim tapped the image on the screen.

"The most important thing to remember is that this TEL, and the one I'll show you next, cannot be damaged in the attack. For reasons I'll explain in a minute, we have to move these TELs away from the attack site, and even a single blown tire would make that impossible."

Ibrahim paused and looked at the four men on the other side of the table. They were paying close attention, but their expressions so far revealed nothing.

"The destructive power of each Nasr missile is relatively low, equal to a little under one kiloton of TNT. By comparison, the bomb that destroyed Hiroshima equaled about fifteen kilotons. Nasr is a system designed for tactical use against invading Indian forces, which means they would detonate within Pakistan. Obviously, for that purpose, the Pakistani military doesn't want a city-destroying missile."

Khaksar and the other men nodded. Then, Khaksar asked, "What is the missile's range?"

Ibrahim shook his head and answered, "It doesn't matter, because we won't be firing the missiles."

Seeing the surprise and confusion on the faces of Khaksar and the others, Abdul could see they hadn't understood his earlier comment and interrupted. "This operation is complex and will need some time to explain. Once Ibrahim is done, that will be the best time to ask questions."

Ibrahim looked at Abdul gratefully. "There are several problems with trying to use the Nasr as designed by the Pakistani military. First, the TEL's control console won't allow launch without a code issued by Pakistani military headquarters. Second, even if we could somehow obtain a code, no target we want to hit is anywhere within its sixty-kilometer range. Finally, the TEL is huge and slow. We'd have no chance of hiding it long enough to aim and fire a missile at a target before more Pakistani forces arrived and either destroyed or recaptured it. Before I explain what we're going to do with it, let me show you the other weapon we plan to seize in our attack."

Ibrahim touched a few keys on the laptop and then turned it back to face the other men. It now had another TEL on the screen with four missiles, which was even larger than the first.

"This is the Babur cruise missile system. The Babur's warhead is much more powerful, and at ten kilotons is capable of destroying a small to medium-sized city. It has a longer range than the Nasr system, but the need for a code we don't have and can't get, make it impossible to use as-is. Plus, it's even bigger and more impossible to hide for any length of time."

Ibrahim could see that the men on the other side of the table were becoming impatient, and didn't blame them. It was time to explain the plan.

"Once we seize both TELs, we'll move them a short distance away to the equipment we'll have set up at a warehouse we've already rented that's big enough to fit both TELs inside. That equipment will let me remove the missiles from the TELs, and then take the warheads out of each missile. We will then put each of the eight warheads in a separate vehicle, which we will drive in eight separate directions."

Ibrahim paused, and pressed a few more keys on the laptop to bring up another image, this time of a large truck towing a trailer covered with antennas.

"We stole this R-330ZH electronic jammer from the Pakistani military a few days ago, and one of our men knows how to use it. Once it's turned on, nobody in convoy with the two TELs will be able to call for help. That will give us some time before more Pakistani military forces arrive, but not much. At best, when the convoy fails to arrive on schedule at their planned destination, the alarm will go out. However, they may be scheduled to check-in at regular intervals. Someone may try to reach them en route after we start jamming. So, we'll have to hurry to remove the warheads and get them out of the warehouse as soon as possible."

Next, Ibrahim pressed keys that brought up an image of eight vehicles. Four of them were vans of different models and colors, and the other four were medium-sized trucks that had nothing in common except that their cargo beds were covered in cloth. All of the vehicles had the logos of various businesses on their sides, ranging from a plumbing contractor to a fertilizer supplier.

"These vehicles are already in place at the warehouse. The vans will transport the Nasr tactical nuclear warheads. The trucks will move the larger Babur cruise missile warheads. There are several small to medium-sized cities less than a thirty-minute drive north, south, and east of the warehouse. All of the vehicles will separate as quickly as possible, and attempt to reach the hiding places we have prepared. These range from an auto repair shop for one van to another, much smaller warehouse for one of the trucks."

Khaksar frowned and shook his head. "Will the Pakistani Army give us the time we need to do all this? We will certainly lose men attacking the convoy. I doubt we'll have enough left to take on the kind of force that is surely ready, waiting, and trained to respond to a threat to their nuclear weapons."

Ibrahim nodded. "You're right that we may not have enough time to escape with all eight warheads. However, removing the warheads may take less time than you think. Both the Nasr and Babur missiles were designed to allow the use of either nuclear or conventional warheads. That means they were both designed to allow swapping out warheads easily and quickly. It also means the warheads are even easier to remove, and not replace."

Ibrahim paused, and pointed at himself. "I used to be one of the technicians who placed the warheads in these missiles, so I know exactly how to remove them. I have already trained many of our men in how to carry out this task. We will work on two missiles at a time. As soon as we remove a warhead, it will be in a vehicle and on its way."

Abdul smiled, and interrupted. "Ibrahim, though, remains the only person who has already successfully worked on these missiles. But that is not the only reason that keeping him alive during this mission is a high priority."

Ibrahim shrugged. "I will not argue with the proposition that keeping me alive is important. In particular, because while warhead removal is fairly straightforward, creating a functioning nuclear weapon with these warheads is not. I have sketched out possible weapon designs using both the Nasr and Babur warheads and given them to Abdul. However, in spite of my best efforts, I'm not sure whether our men are capable of turning these designs into working weapons."

Khaksar and the other three men looked at each other with alarm. "Then, wouldn't it be better to leave you out of this mission until we have the warheads? If you've trained others in how to remove them, do you need to be there?"

Ibrahim nodded. "Yes. There is a danger I haven't yet mentioned. As I said, the nuclear warheads cannot detonate without a code. However, each warhead contains a core with nuclear material surrounded by conventional explosives. A mistake in removing the warheads could result in the detonation of those explosives. For the Nasr, the result would be to kill most of our men. There are enough explosives in the larger Babur to level the warehouse. So, I must oversee the warheads' removal, at least at the beginning."

Khaksar was still concerned but finally shrugged. "Agreed. If we don't succeed in removing the warheads, you'll have nothing to use to build a weapon."

Ibrahim and Abdul both nodded.

Khaksar then asked, "So, if everything in this plan works, where will we use the weapons?"

Abdul frowned. "First, I'll point out that it's doubtful we'll end up with eight working nuclear weapons. We don't know how many warheads we'll have time to remove. We don't know how many will make it to their hiding places. We don't know whether Ibrahim's designs will work with both the Nasr and Babur warheads."

Glancing at Ibrahim, Abdul quickly added, "No offense."

Ibrahim laughed and said, "None taken. What you're saying couldn't be truer."

Abdul continued, "So, I propose just two targets. If we're lucky and end up with more than two working weapons, so much the better. But I think the destruction of the two targets I have in mind will be enough to make the Americans leave Afghanistan, and once they go, their only real reason for interfering in Pakistan will disappear."

Khaksar nodded. "Agreed. And the targets?"

Abdul said, "If Ibrahim can create a weapon based on the Babur warhead, we should use it against Bagram Airfield. It has one of the largest concentrations of Americans in Afghanistan, and is critical to their interference in our affairs."

Khaksar frowned. "All you say is true. Do you think we can destroy the airbase while avoiding the destruction of the nearby town of Bagram, and Parwan prison?"

Abdul spread his hands and shook his head. "There is no way to know for sure. We're still not certain how powerful the finished weapon will be, and how . . . delicate. Maybe we can avoid destroying the town and the prison. But that may be a price we have to pay."

Khaksar looked grim but finally nodded. "I know many of the men locked up at Parwan. All of them deserve a better fate. But if they have to die so that the Americans can finally be forced out, I know every one of them would gladly make that sacrifice."

Abdul looked at the other three men and could see that all of them agreed with Khaksar.

"Very well," Abdul said. "If Ibrahim can make a weapon from a Nasr warhead, that should be used to destroy everything in the Kabul Green Zone. That is where many Afghan traitors work for their so-called government, and the Americans and all their allies have their embassies."

Khaksar and all the others looked at Abdul in alarm. Khaksar then said, "There is no way you can be sure the weapon's impact will be limited to the Green Zone. What is the point of forcing the Americans from Afghanistan, if we no longer have a capital from which to govern?"

Abdul shrugged. "As you heard earlier, Nasr is a tactical nuclear weapon designed for use on the battlefield within Pakistan. Remember that the Green Zone in Kabul was recently expanded to over five square kilometers. Getting the weapon we make from the Nasr warhead as close as we can to the center of the Green Zone will be a challenge. If we can do that, though, Ibrahim believes damage and casualties outside the Green Zone will be limited."

Khaksar turned to Ibrahim with a scowl. "How limited?"

Ibrahim looked back at Khaksar impassively. "I don't know for sure. In particular, variable prevailing winds on the day make casualties from fallout impossible to guess. However, this weapon was designed for use against Indian forces that had just crossed the border into Pakistan. Unlike some parts of Pakistan, like the region bordering Iran, there are towns and cities all along the border with India. This weapon, in short, will certainly not level Kabul the way the Americans' first atomic bomb destroyed Hiroshima."

Khaksar turned his glare back to Abdul. "Thousands of Afghans live and work in the Green Zone. Do you think we will be forgiven for sacrificing them to be rid of the Americans?"

Abdul met Khaksar's glare with a look of contempt. "Have you forgotten that any Afghan in the Green Zone is either a traitor themselves, or living with one? When have we ever shown mercy to traitors to the Afghan people?"

Abdul and Ibrahim could both see from the reaction of the three men sitting next to Khaksar that Abdul had scored a hit, much to Khaksar's fury.

Visibly reining in his temper, Khaksar asked, "What will you do if the weapon is impossible to place near the middle of the Green Zone?"

Abdul shook his head. "I have no other ideas. The Green Zone and Bagram are where nearly all the Americans still in Afghanistan live and work. We must succeed in delivering the weapons to these two targets. If God truly wishes us to be rid of the Americans, we will find a way."

Khaksar reluctantly nodded. "And what will we do with the other weapons?"

Abdul smiled. "First things first. We don't yet know how many warheads we'll be able to remove from the missiles, how many we'll be able to transport and then hide, and how many Ibrahim will then be able to make into functioning weapons."

Ibrahim grunted. "I am . . . highly motivated to do my best. But a single mistake could immediately end weapon production, and though I've tried, there is not enough time for me to teach someone else how to make one and be sure of success. Besides, if I fail, none of my students are likely to succeed."

Abdul then added, "But if we do somehow produce more than two weapons, we should keep them in reserve. Russia, China, India, and Pakistan are all interested in the rare metals that were recently discovered in

Afghanistan, and any of them could try to replace the Americans once they're gone. If we have at least one remaining weapon, it could help discourage such a move."

Khaksar looked doubtful but finally nodded. "Agreed. Do you need anything else from us?"

Abdul looked at Ibrahim, who shook his head. "No, I think we've done all we can to prepare. Soon we will see whether it will be enough to let us reach our common goal—forcing the American invaders to leave Afghanistan forever."

Abdul paused. "One last thing. I plan to accompany the weapon going to Bagram Airfield. Ibrahim will go with the one targeting the Green Zone in Kabul."

Ibrahim said, "My weapon will use a more complex design that needs a trained technician to check and trigger it. My leader will be going with a weapon using a simpler design, that may be slightly less powerful than it could be, but will be easier for a non-expert to set off."

Turning to Abdul, Ibrahim added, "No offense," and arched one eyebrow.

There was a second of silence, and then Khaksar roared with laughter, quickly joined by all the others at the table.

Abdul put his arm around Ibrahim's shoulders, and they stood together as the men's laughter turned to cheers and applause.

Yes, soon they would both die. But for now, this was the happiest moment in their lives.

FSB Headquarters
Moscow, Russia

Anatoly Grishkov and Mikhail Vasilyev both sipped their strong black tea thoughtfully. They were each looking over the single sheet of paper that their host, FSB Director Smyslov, had placed in front of them as soon as he ushered them to the sturdy red leather sofa that dominated his office. Reading the update didn't take long. Grishkov and Vasilyev already knew nearly everything the Russian government had learned about the Taliban's plot to force the Americans out of Afghanistan. Vasilyev had personally collected most of that intelligence, at no small risk.

As Grishkov aged, he looked more and more like his father, who had also been a policeman. Like him, he was shorter and more muscular than the average Russian, with thick black hair and black eyes. His wife Arisha used to say that his face gained more 'character' every year. After his narrow escape during his last mission, she had stopped saying that and started going to the small Orthodox church a short walk from their Moscow apartment. His son Sasha was thirteen, and his other son Misha was eleven. Though both had black hair, otherwise they thankfully looked more like Arisha.

Grishkov had worked together with FSB Colonel Alexei Vasilyev, Mikhail's father, on his last two missions. Before that, he had been the lead homicide detective for the entire Vladivostok region, but after the success of their first mission together, Director Smyslov had put him on "indefinite special assignment" as a Captain in the Moscow Police Department. After Alexei Vasilyev's death in their second mission, Smyslov had assigned his son Mikhail as Grishkov's new partner.

This was no coincidence. Smyslov knew that Grishkov was close to insisting on a return to police work after his second mission, simply because he thought his luck was unlikely to last for a third encounter with rogue nuclear weapons. He also knew Grishkov was not concerned for himself, but that he felt a strong responsibility to Arisha and his two sons.

Grishkov had only agreed to volunteer for this latest mission because of the deep respect he had even now for Alexei Vasilyev and his nearly superstitious belief that his son Mikhail would help Grishkov survive it. Like his father, Mikhail was in excellent physical condition, and like him, Mikhail was a firm believer in the value of hand-to-hand combat skills. Mikhail was only a bit taller than Grishkov but was even thinner than his father. His full head of dark brown hair, as well as his perpetual air of detached amusement, had helped Grishkov recognize Mikhail immediately as Alexei's son.

That recognition had come only after Alexei's death. Alexei had been worried that knowledge of Mikhail's existence would be used against him by the many enemies he routinely encountered in his assignments abroad, a worry which only intensified once Mikhail defied him and also began working for the FSB.

Smyslov immediately reminded nearly everyone he encountered of the stereotype of the Russian bear, with his stout frame and full dark beard. Normally he was jovial when he briefed his agents, particularly ones he liked as much as Grishkov and Vasilyev.

But not today.

Frowning, Smyslov said, "I'm sorry not to give you a proper meal before sending you off on such a mission. Unfortunately, Grishkov, your pilot was very specific about the need for you to avoid both food and alcohol before your flight. It seems turbulence is expected during your trip to the 201st Military Base. While the MiG-31 is an excellent choice for getting an agent somewhere quickly, it is not so good for passenger comfort."

Grishkov nodded. "And being a good host, you felt that you and Mikhail could not feast in front of a starving man."

Now Smyslov did smile. "Yes, just so. Now, as you will see in your orders, 201st Military Base is in Tajikistan, a short distance from the Afghan border. Though primarily an Army base it has an airstrip for its five SU-25 ground attack aircraft, so you will not have to parachute from your MiG-31." With that, he handed Grishkov a slim folder containing his orders.

Grishkov's eyebrows flew upwards. "Good. As you know from my file, I qualified as a paratrooper before I served in Chechnya, but did not particularly relish the experience."

Smyslov grunted. "Understood. I have always thought jumping out of an otherwise functional aircraft more akin to insanity than bravery. Yet, your next step will be nearly as dangerous. You will travel into Afghanistan with one of our local agents to meet with our sole remaining contact in the Taliban leadership."

Grishkov stared at Smyslov, astonished. "Remaining? You mean . . ."

Smyslov nodded. "Yes, exactly. Though we have maintained contact with a few other Afghan leaders since we left in 1989, this man is the only one in a position of real power and influence within the Taliban."

Vasilyev looked thoughtful. "I wondered how you had been able to confirm my report that the Taliban was planning to steal eight nuclear weapons. So, why is it necessary for Grishkov to meet this man in person, and with such urgency?"

Smyslov scowled. "Because in exchange for the exact time and place of the attack that will target the Pakistani nuclear weapons, he wants ten million American dollars in cash. He calls it his 'retirement plan' and says if we don't hurry, it will be too late for both him and us."

Vasilyev smiled and pointed at Grishkov. "He's small, but I don't think he'll leave enough room in a MiG-31 cockpit for a bag with ten million American dollars. Unless we can hang the bag from a weapons pylon?"

Smyslov sighed and shook his head. "Yes, your father's sense of humor. A small cargo plane carrying the cash and two armed guards is already en route to 201st Military Base. Though much slower, with its head start it should get there before Grishkov's arrival."

Vasilyev nodded. "And I will be in another MiG-31?"

Smyslov shook his head. "No. You will meet later. First, you need to travel to Islamabad with Neda Rhahbar. You will be flying there from Domodedovo Airport via Doha, and should get to Islamabad tomorrow morning."

Vasilyev was startled by the news. "So, this is why you had me brief an FSB trainee on what I learned about the Taliban's plans on my last assignment in Pakistan. What will her role be in this mission?"

Smyslov frowned and said, "Critical if the theft of Pakistani nuclear weapons cannot be prevented. She speaks Urdu, can pass for Pakistani, and is a nuclear physicist familiar with nuclear weapons design. At my direction, she now knows everything our military intelligence colleagues at the GRU do about Pakistan's nuclear weapons."

Grishkov, who had been reading his orders, now looked up. "Does that include disarming them? Speaking as a husband who would like to return to his wife and children, I think that should be our priority."

Smyslov leaned back in his chair and rocked his right hand back and forth. "Yes and no. Pakistan's nuclear weapons require codes to both arm and disarm them. Our information says that the Taliban have no access to these codes, and so will have to remove the warheads and use them to construct new weapons. We hope that upon examination, Neda will be able to disarm whatever new weapons the Taliban can build."

Vasilyev grinned at Grishkov. "Of course, I'm hoping you'll be able to join us by then."

Grishkov smiled back, grimly. "Sure, me too."

Vasilyev's smile faded, and he turned to Smyslov. "Do we have any idea what locations the Taliban might target with these weapons?"

Smyslov pointed at Grishkov. "As Anatoly has already seen in his orders, he is authorized to pay our Afghan contact an additional two million dollar bonus for that information, if he can obtain it by the time they meet. Of course, we can already make an educated guess."

Vasilyev nodded. "The Green Zone in Kabul, and Bagram Airfield."

Grishkov shrugged. "No other targets make military sense. Destroy those, and you kill most of the Americans still in Afghanistan. So, let's suppose I am successful in obtaining the information on the planned theft of Pakistani nuclear weapons. Why not then warn the Pakistani and American governments, sit back and wait to receive their well-earned gratitude?"

Smyslov smiled. "I see by the way you asked the question you understand it is not so simple. First, I think we should warn the Pakistani government if we obtain detailed information on the planned attack in time, even though our alliance with India may make them question the source. You are going via MiG-31 because while we may not find out quickly enough, it will not be for lack of trying. Whether we warn the Americans depends at least in part on whether our information is specific enough to be useful."

Smyslov paused and sighed. "The President has told me he will make these decisions personally. He has to consider whether the Pakistanis can overcome their doubts of a warning provided by an ally of their mortal enemy, India, in time to prevent the attack. Also, he wants no chance of the Americans thinking we had anything to do with the theft of these Pakistani nuclear weapons. Or even worse, their use by the Taliban against American troops and diplomats in Afghanistan. Otherwise, he believes we could face American retaliation if the Taliban attack is successful."

Grishkov scowled but finally nodded. "If such misplaced retaliation is even a remote possibility, I understand we must avoid it."

Smyslov grunted. "But, there are other factors that must also be considered."

Vasilyev nodded. "As I noted in my report if the Taliban can build more nuclear weapons than they need to eliminate the American presence in Afghanistan, they might make one or more available to their allies. So, a weapon could be detonated in Israel, provoking a general Middle Eastern war that could draw us in as well as the Americans. The Chechens could use one against a Russian city. The possibilities are endless and all unpleasant."

Smyslov nodded agreement. "All true. However, the President surprised me by pointing out that this crisis also represents an opportunity. It is well known that Afghanistan has mineral resources worth over one trillion American dollars if the security situation allowed their extraction."

Grishkov shook his head. "But didn't I read that there is already a long line of countries with huge mining companies waiting to dig them up?"

Smyslov smiled. "Yes, not just a 'simple soldier' as you like to say. You are right. But the Chinese appear to have lost their place at the head of that line by locking up over a million Muslim Uighurs in so-called re-education camps. If we can take credit for preventing a nuclear attack on their country, the President believes in spite of our unfortunate history in the 1980s the Afghans might be willing to include Russian mining companies among those extracting their rare metals."

Vasilyev nodded. "And leaving all other considerations aside, we do have one direct interest. Russia has a sizable Embassy in Kabul's Green Zone."

Smyslov grimaced with distaste. "Yes. And the President has already told me that under no circumstances will he evacuate it. If the Taliban attack is prevented, evacuation will be unnecessary. If it is not, evacuating in time would be seen as proof of complicity."

Vasilyev frowned. "While on assignment, I have worked with many of the men and women at our missions overseas. Sacrificing an entire Embassy would be a heavy price to pay. However, I understand that to avoid retaliation for a nuclear attack, it may be unavoidable."

Vasilyev then paused and pointed at Grishkov. "Speaking of sacrifice, what's to keep our Afghan friend from shooting Anatoly and driving off with his twelve million dollars? Surely he could bring far more men and firepower to the rendezvous than we can."

Smyslov nodded. "Quite true. He has been reminded that the Americans are not the only ones with armed drones and that one will be overhead during their meeting."

Vasilyev shook his head. "I don't think that will be enough. I know we have armed drones, but they are nothing like as capable as the American models, and in spite of them, the Taliban are still very much in the fight in Afghanistan."

Smyslov smiled. "Agreed. Anatoly, you have finished reading your orders?"

Grishkov nodded. "Yes. I am to inform the Afghan selling us details of the attempted theft of Pakistani nuclear weapons that I am holding a dead man's switch connected to a device in the container with his money. I presume the device contains dye packs."

Smyslov and Vasilyev looked at each other, and then simultaneously roared with laughter. Grishkov could do nothing but look at them in astonishment.

Finally, gasping for air, Smyslov said, "My dear Anatoly, sometimes I forget that you spent far more time as a policeman than as an FSB agent.

The device contains about ten kilos of PVV-5A plastic explosive, enough to not only destroy the money but to ensure the death of anyone close enough to shoot you."

"Ah," Grishkov said weakly. "Well, I'd already planned not to drop it."

Smyslov smiled and looked at his watch. "Anatoly, a helicopter is waiting to take you to Kubinka Air Base. By the time you arrive, your MiG-31 should be ready. Mikhail, a car will take you and Neda Rhahbar to Domodedovo Airport. The driver is one of my assistants so that you may speak freely about your mission to Neda. She has been told little about the specifics of this mission yet. Only that she is traveling with you to Islamabad. How much she needs to know will be up to you."

Smyslov stood up, quickly followed by Vasilyev and Grishkov. Smyslov pounded each of them on the back as he walked them out of his office.

"Best of luck to both of you," he said. "I know I'll be hearing from you soon."

CHAPTER THREE

Kubinka Air Base, 65 Kilometers West of Moscow, Russia

Anatoly Grishkov grunted as the MiG-31's pilot tightened the strap crossing his chest. The pilot was standing on a service cart adjacent to the MiG-31. "Cozy?" the pilot asked with a grin.

Grishkov's right hand was still free, but he quickly thought better of his first impulse and nodded.

From the pilot's answering laugh, he had seen Grishkov's hand twitch, and then his decision not to follow through with the gesture.

"As your reward for not saying or doing anything rude, you get this special helmet," the pilot said, handing one to Grishkov.

Grishkov noticed that the service cart did indeed have a selection of helmets of different sizes and slightly different shapes.

"Notice the small piece of plastic here towards the bottom of the helmet. If you press against it with your chin, you will be able to speak with me during the flight, which even at the speed we'll be going will take some time. The only time I'll ask you not to speak to me is when we're refueling," the pilot said.

Grishkov nodded. "And where will we be stopping to refuel?" he asked.

The pilot laughed. "Stopping? For a special passenger like you, there is no stopping. We will be refueling in mid-air, and as a bonus will be doing so at night."

Grishkov stirred uneasily in his seat. "Which you have done before, yes?"

The pilot grinned at him as he finished checking Grishkov's flight harness, and the fit of his helmet. "That's why I'm flying you. Many MiG pilots have experience with mid-air refueling, but only a few have done so at night. We don't do it unless it's essential."

The pilot climbed into the cockpit, and a crewman drove the service cart clear of the plane. As his hands blurred over the MiG's controls, the pilot said, "When you have time someday, you can look up a video the Defense Ministry uploaded to the Internet showing how it's done. Sadly, you can't see it's me in the clip. I've been told I'm quite photogenic."

Grishkov was spared having to reply by the canopy closing, followed immediately by the roar of the MiG-31's two turbofan engines.

En Route to Domodedovo Airport

Neda Rhahbar frowned as she finished reading the one-page summary, but said nothing.

Mikhail Vasilyev's eyebrows rose, and he asked quietly, "Anything additional you'd like to know?"

Neda's gaze moved to the driver in what was a silent question.

Vasilyev nodded approvingly. "You are right to check with me before speaking. However, in this case, I can tell you that the Director himself has approved our driver and intends us to use this time to discuss the mission. So, feel free to ask questions."

Neda shrugged. "From what I see here, if Grishkov is successful in obtaining information on the Taliban's planned theft of Pakistani nuclear weapons, it may be possible to prevent their capture. In that case, there will be no need for my expertise. So, I think it would be best to avoid telling me more about our mission than is on this page until we hear from Grishkov."

Vasilyev looked at Neda with new respect. "So, let me guess. My namesake is still training at the Academy."

"Yes," she nodded. "He was also called Mikhail, but he was much older than you. He said one of the reasons the USSR lasted as long as it did was that its spies knew how to keep their mouths shut."

Neda paused. "I believed him."

Vasilyev smiled. "I know your training was cut short by this mission's timing, but I'm pleased you have already learned the most important lesson. Still, do you have any questions about this mission that do not relate to its objectives?"

Neda frowned and pulled out her passport from her purse. "I was surprised to see that I am traveling to Pakistan on a new passport issued by the Iranian Embassy in Moscow under my real name. Don't agents normally travel under an assumed identity? Also, wasn't it difficult to get an Iranian passport for someone who recently defected from Iran?"

Neda had gone to the Russian Embassy in Tehran earlier the same year. It had been to inform them that her husband, who had been in charge of Iran's nuclear weapons program, was planning to make three nuclear test devices available for an attack on Saudi Arabia. She had then barely escaped Iran with the help of two Russian agents, Alexei Vasilyev and Anatoly Grishkov.

Vasilyev smiled. "I will address your last question first. Remember, there has been a change of government in Iran since your defection. Only a few people at the top of that government know of your role in recent events, and they plan to keep it that way. So, if someday you wish to return to Iran, I believe it would be safe for you to do so, as long as you also remain quiet about your defection and the reason you left."

If Neda noticed how intently Vasilyev was watching for her reaction, she gave no sign.

"No, thank you. Maybe someday many years from now I will go to see my parents and my sister if they refuse to visit me in Moscow. For now, though, Tehran only holds bitter memories."

Vasilyev leaned back, satisfied. He did not doubt her sincerity.

"Now, to answer your first question. Since you had traveled to Pakistan before under your real identity when you were a university student, it is much safer to have you fly in using that identity. All travelers arriving at Pakistan's international airports are checked through facial recognition, and due to your earlier trip, your photo is probably in their database."

Neda frowned. "Really? Pakistan is not a rich country. How is their entry screening so sophisticated?"

Vasilyev shrugged. "The cost of facial recognition technology has dropped substantially as many countries, cities, and even companies have started using it routinely. And remember that we are talking about a country willing to spend billions on nuclear weapons in the name of security. The primary target of facial recognition in Pakistan is Indian spies, just as their nuclear weapons are aimed at the Indian military."

Neda shook her head. "But your name in the file is not your real name, and it says your passport is Pakistani!"

Vasilyev grinned. "Well, it helps that thanks to my mother, my complexion is a bit darker than the average Russian's. As for my dark brown hair, I'm sure you must have seen it before on your last trip to Pakistan. The British were there for a long time. Of course, my identity has been thoroughly backstopped, including the false birth certificate listing my late father as British. A shame he never acknowledged me, or I might have obtained a British passport."

Neda shook her head even more stubbornly. "None of that explains how your name can be different, and mine cannot."

Vasilyev nodded. "The name in my current passport is identical to the one I used on my first trip to Pakistan, and on every trip since. You see, no country has access to a worldwide database that can verify the identity of every traveler. All a country can do with facial recognition is force a person to keep using the same identity every time they travel to that country. Unless that is, they are willing to answer some uncomfortable questions."

Neda was clearly not convinced. "Can't facial recognition be fooled by wearing glasses and a wig, for example?"

Vasilyev smiled. "You can make the software's job harder. However, facial recognition works by reducing the dimensions of a face to a mathematical expression. It might be possible to change measurements like the distance between the pupils of your eyes."

Now his smile widened. "But, I'll bet it would hurt."

Neda shivered. "Very well. One final question. The reasons for traveling together as a married couple are obvious. But have you considered that questions may be asked about our age difference? I must be at least five years older than you, which is unusual in both Iran and Pakistan."

Vasilyev nodded. "Six years older, actually. But your looks explain how I came to marry you in spite of that."

Neda blushed and for once had nothing to say. Vasilyev could hear a poorly concealed snort of amusement from the driver.

"I apologize for my poor choice of words," Vasilyev said. "It was not . . . professional. I didn't mean to embarrass you. But in this work, beauty is like strength or any other attribute. It is a tool to be used in accomplishing the mission. In this case, I am confident it will protect us from questions that might have been raised by our age difference."

Neda shrugged, clearly still uncomfortable, but at least less so.

Vasilyev said with relief, "And it is good that was your last question," as he pointed out the car window at the airport terminal building. "It will be some time before we are in a location where it will be safe to ask another."

En Route to 201st Military Base, Tajikistan

Grishkov wasn't aware of it, but he was doing his very best not to move or breathe. An IL-78 "Midas" aerial refueling tanker filled the canopy in front of him, and a part of his brain was insisting the pilot was trying to fly inside it. In spite of this, a lifetime of first military and then police discipline had kept Grishkov's chin off his helmet's radio switch.

Instead, Grishkov tried but failed to follow the dialogue between the pilot and the tanker coming over his helmet headset. The few clipped words were Russian, but meant nothing to him. He took some comfort, though, from the calm and professional tone of the exchange.

Finally, with a distinct "thunk" the tanker's refueling equipment detached from the MiG-31 and began to return to the IL-78. After a few minutes, the MiG-31 began a gentle bank to the right, and within seconds the tanker was no longer visible.

Grishkov realized as air flowed into his lungs just how tense he had been. His first reaction was annoyance, as he thought to himself he'd been in many more dangerous situations. After a few more moments, he realized that the difference this time was that his survival had depended totally on the pilot's skill.

As though he were reading Grishkov's mind, the pilot's amused voice now came over his helmet's headset. "See, I told you I did this before! You did remember to start breathing again back there, right?"

Grishkov remembered to press his chin against the helmet's talk switch. "Yes. A good thing I was wearing a mask feeding me oxygen."

The pilot's laugh echoed in Grishkov's ears. "Very good! I'm glad to have a passenger with a sense of humor."

Then the pilot's voice lowered and became more serious. "I would, of course, never ask what you will be doing after you finish this ride. To satisfy my curiosity, though, I will ask you one question. In your opinion, not your bosses, is all this effort worth it?"

Since Grishkov had spent the hours before the tanker appeared mentally reviewing his mission to prevent the Taliban from obtaining Pakistani nuclear warheads, he didn't hesitate for a moment.

"Yes," he said.

The pilot grunted with satisfaction. "Good. I can hear in your voice that you mean it. I talked recently with an American diplomat who was visiting Kubinka Air Base, and can tell you that sometimes risks like nighttime midair refueling are taken without real cause."

Grishkov knew the pilot expected him to ask but was also curious. "And what would an American diplomat know about unnecessary risk in military operations?"

The pilot laughed and said, "Well, this diplomat told me an incredible story about being part of a group of military officers and civilian officials visiting a U.S. Marine base. One of the many items of military equipment he saw demonstrated was the Harrier Jump Jet."

Grishkov nodded, but then realized the pilot couldn't see him. "Yes," he said, "I have heard of it. It can go straight up like a helicopter, then fly at high speeds like a plane, and come straight down to land."

"Correct," the pilot said. "However, a Harrier pilot seldom uses the 'straight up/straight down' capability because it has a high fuel cost. Instead, vectored thrust allows for very short takeoffs and landings, and the use of roads as runways."

"Interesting," Grishkov said. "I can see how that could be very useful in combat operations. But, just a moment. Why was this group at a Marine base?"

"A good question," the pilot replied. "They were attending a U.S. military academy. They had been selected because they were thought likely to reach General's rank or for the few civilians the equivalent in their agency. The idea was to make them aware of what each military branch could do, and so they visited a base representative of each service in turn."

"A worthwhile concept," Grishkov said. "So, I imagine the 'unnecessary risk' came from the demonstration?"

"Indeed," the pilot said, "The Harrier would land on a two-lane blacktop road cut through a pine forest on the base, while the visiting group would observe."

"Observe from where?" Grishkov asked.

"From either side of the road, lined up a couple of meters away from the edge," the pilot replied.

"Efficient," Grishkov said dryly. "That way, no matter whether the jet veered slightly right or left on landing, you could still be assured of having a wing slice through half of the group."

The pilot laughed. "I couldn't have put it better myself. The diplomat told me he started to think the demonstration might not be altogether safe when he noticed one of his classmates edging back from the road until he had nearly reached the trees. He then recalled that his classmate, named 'Tom,' was himself a Harrier pilot. When the diplomat asked Tom what he was doing, he replied, pointing at the rapidly approaching Harrier, 'I don't know this guy' and moved back a little farther."

Grishkov laughed in turn. "But if he told you this as an amusing story, I presume the landing took place without incident."

"Yes," the pilot replied. "Then this diplomat told me something interesting. He said that the most impressive military capability he had seen demonstrated was at an airbase in Oklahoma. He was taken inside a structure he was told covered more acres than any other on earth, and required the use of electric carts to see any significant portion."

Grishkov grunted. "And inside this huge structure?"

The pilot said thoughtfully, "Aircraft in the process of refurbishment. He saw more aircraft than he could count, many stripped to the fuselage. He told me this brought home to him the real strength of the U.S. military- a logistical capability no other country could match."

CHAPTER FOUR

Islamabad International Airport, Islamabad, Pakistan

Neda Rhahbar looked around her in amazement as they walked to the terminal exit. "It is so much nicer than the last time I was here. I can't believe it's the same airport."

Mikhail Vasilyev smiled. "It's not. The new airport for Islamabad was opened in 2018, not so long ago. Companies based in France, the UK, the U.S., and Singapore all had a hand in its design and construction. I agree that the result is very impressive."

It was only a short walk from the airport exit to the attached parking garage. Neda exclaimed with dismay when Vasilyev stopped in front of a small white, boxy car that appeared to have been built in the 1980s.

"Surely, this is not our car!" Neda exclaimed.

Vasilyev laughed and replied, "Yes, I'm afraid so. Let me get our luggage put away, take a look around the car, and I'll explain as I drive."

Not long after they had driven clear of the airport, Vasilyev said, "Now, to help you get oriented, we'll be going most of the way down Kashmir Highway, and then once we're in the city we'll turn off on Khayaban-e-Suhrwardy. Our temporary quarters are within walking distance of the Russian Embassy. The whole drive should take less than an hour, as long as the traffic cooperates."

Neda was scowling. "Never mind that. You were going to tell me why we have this terrible car."

Vasilyev grinned and said mildly, "Well, I've driven worse, even in Russia. This is a Suzuki Mehran, retired from the European and Japanese markets in 1988, but sold in large numbers in Pakistan until 2019. That's why we're driving it, and why its color is the most popular for a car sold in Pakistan- white. This car is as close to anonymous as possible, which is an excellent thing for people like us."

Neda's frown, if anything, deepened. "I am looking for any sign of airbags, which even in Iran most cars possessed."

Vasilyev nodded. "You won't find them. Or antilock brakes, shock absorbers, seat belt warnings, or for that matter, rear seat belts. Everything, including transmission, ignition, doors, and windows, is manual."

Neda shook her head. "We didn't have to get a car this bad to be anonymous. Remember, I was here before, and I saw plenty of Toyota Corollas, and they are much better cars."

Vasilyev smiled. "You're right. In spite of Corollas costing more than twice as much as Mehrans, by 2019, they were outselling it, one reason the Mehran was finally retired in Pakistan. But you're a scientist—how could the systems in a modern car be used against us?"

Now Neda's frown changed from annoyed to thoughtful. "I've seen videos of stolen cars being remotely disabled by police, and the doors locked to prevent the escape of the thief."

"Correct," Vasilyev nodded. "Even more cars are vulnerable to hacking that would allow a built-in GPS to be remotely monitored, or even fed false data. You are right that police have some access to these tools. However, we are more likely to be targeted by ISI, which has the technical capability to do far more. You are familiar with them, yes?"

"Of course," Neda snorted. "I'd heard of the Inter-Services Intelligence Agency even before my last stay here. Every Iranian knows about them, just as every Pakistani does in this country. Governments come and go in Pakistan. ISI is always here."

Vasilyev smiled. "Quite right. So, avoiding their attention is a high priority for us. I've been watching since we left the airport, and have seen no sign that ISI or anyone else is following us. Of course, if we were a high priority target, detection would be almost impossible."

"Yes," Neda said, "I remember that point from my training. Either in a vehicle or on foot, all an experienced team needs is enough cars or people to switch off frequently enough that you can't spot them. Unless they make a mistake."

"Very good," Vasilyev said with an approving nod. "Now, what do you think I was looking for when I examined this car back at the garage?"

"Either a bomb or a tracking device," Neda replied immediately.

Vasilyev laughed as his eyes continued to flick intermittently between his side and rearview mirrors. "Well, primarily tracking devices. ISI could arrest, question and execute us if they decided we were a threat, and would not want the messy spectacle of a bombing in an airport garage plus the danger of collateral damage."

Neda shook her head. "But what about the Taliban? If they found out foreign agents were coming to interfere with their plans, a bomb would work quite well."

Surprised, Vasilyev glanced at Neda, who he saw was looking at her side mirror. "Well, you're right. If they were capable of obtaining intelligence on the movement of Pakistan's nuclear weapons, who knows what else they might have learned? Now, did you notice the small instrument I was using to examine the car?"

"Yes," Neda said, "I remember it from training. It is designed to detect the electronic signals emitted by either a tracking or explosive device.

But I noticed that you were looking very carefully, and not relying on the device."

"Correct," Vasilyev said with a smile. "Many such devices attached to a car are designed to remain inert until the car is in motion. Also, an explosive device with a simple trembler switch would never emit a signal at all. You were right to remind me that one could always be there."

Neda looked around the car, still obviously unwilling to accept it. "And what if we need to outrun a pursuer? Please don't tell me you think this is the car for that task."

Vasilyev laughed. "Well, no. It's a three-cylinder, and its top speed of one hundred forty kilometers per hour could be easily bested by any vehicle used by either the ISI or the Taliban. But on this drive from the airport to our quarters, the ISI is a much more likely opponent. With the resources they can bring to bear here in the capital, even a Ferrari would be unlikely to save us."

Neda said nothing in response, but when Vasilyev glanced her way, he could see that silence did not equal agreement.

Then Vasilyev added mildly, "Did I mention that we will be switching this vehicle with another once we reach our quarters?"

Neda's answering glare could have cut glass. "So why not tell me that, and avoid this discussion?"

"Precisely because I believe it has been helpful for both of us," Vasilyev replied with a smile. "Now that we're getting into the city proper let's see how much you recall from your last stay. Point out significant landmarks as we approach our quarters."

Neda gave a resigned sigh and was about to begin when she paused. "Don't you think I should continue to help you look for pursuers?" she asked.

Vasilyev shook his head. "I noticed that up to now you've been doing so, and appreciate the backup. However, if we were a target of interest at the airport, I believe it would be obvious by now. Or an ISI follow team is on us with resources we'll never spot. Either way, checking your situational awareness is more important."

"Very well," Neda said with a shrug. "We're just passing the Federal courts. Up next are many other government office buildings, plus if I remember correctly two hospitals."

"Excellent," Vasilyev said with a nod. "Do you recall the hospital names?"

Neda frowned with concentration. "KLR and . . . Ali. So, I suppose it is sometimes useful for agents to know hospital locations?"

Vasilyev grinned in response. "Yes, but let's hope it doesn't come to that. Let me know when we start to pass embassies."

Ten minutes later, Neda began calling out the embassies in turn as they passed them, "France, Thailand, Malaysia, the Netherlands, Italy, America . . . Russia."

Vasilyev nodded. "Good. Next, we pass the embassies of Kuwait and Qatar, and then make the turn for our quarters."

A few minutes later, they pulled up in front of a small, white two-story residence that looked enough like its neighbors to have been built from the same blueprint. A solid metal fence rose three meters high, with a portion cut off and mounted on a hinge to make a gate large enough to admit a car.

Vasilyev opened an app on his phone and tapped in a code. A few moments later, the gate silently swung inwards, and Vasilyev turned their car into the driveway. The gate closed behind them just as quietly.

At the end of the driveway, a large, new black SUV was waiting for them. Neither of them, though, was focused on their replacement vehicle.

Vasilyev and Neda looked at each other, and though both remained silent, they were both thinking the same thing. Despite the absence of any visible sign, both felt that something was wrong.

They walked together to the front door of the house, where Vasilyev pointed silently at the handle. Neda nodded her understanding. Their briefing papers included a description of the nearly invisible telltale that had been attached to the handle. Its absence almost certainly indicated that someone had entered the house.

And might still be inside.

Vasilyev used hand signals to tell Neda that he was going to circle to the back entrance and that she should wait for him out front. As soon as she nodded her understanding, Vasilyev silently disappeared around the corner of the house.

Seconds later, the front door opened, and a large bearded man who appeared Pakistani stepped out directly in front of Neda, much to his evident astonishment. He quickly collected himself, and his right hand moved inside his jacket.

Though many aspects of Neda's training had been rushed, she had been given the full course in two separate martial arts used by FSB agents. The first was SAMBO, a Russian acronym translating to "self-defense without weapons." The second was "Systema." It included both a different style of hand-to-hand fighting as well as the use of edged weapons and firearms. There was nothing formal or stylized about either one.

Neda's first move was to strike the man's windpipe with the edge of her hand. In training, she had practiced on a dummy with a sensor where she was supposed to hit. It had taken her two days of practice to finally be rewarded with the tone telling her she had struck with sufficient force. Neda had been brought back to the dummy at irregular intervals again and again until finally real dislike for the mannequin helped to propel her blows.

Today the training paid off as the man reflexively moved his right hand away from his jacket and towards his throat while gasping for air.

This left him open to Neda's next move, which was to kick him between his legs as hard as she could.

The man cried out in pain and doubled over, only to find his head held down by Neda's right hand while her right knee drove upwards.

A sickening "crunch" and a scream of pain said that the man's nose had almost certainly been broken. He slumped into the doorway in a heap. As far as Neda could tell, he was unconscious.

Vasilyev appeared behind the man, and pulled him back into the house, gesturing at Neda to enter as well before closing the door. Vasilyev checked the man for weapons, quickly discovering the 9mm pistol he had been reaching for when he first saw Neda. Reaching into his jacket, Vasilyev pulled out two zip ties and made sure the man would remain immobile.

Still using hand gestures, Vasilyev indicated he planned to search the rest of the house, and that Neda was to stand guard over the intruder. As soon as Neda nodded her understanding, Vasilyev moved off.

Keeping one eye on the still figure of the zip-tied intruder, Neda looked at what she could see of the house. From the entryway, she could only see the living room, hallway, and what she was sure was the door to the kitchen.

The furniture and layout of the house were a perfect match for the solidly middle-class homes Neda had visited when she had been in Pakistan before as a university student. Each time she had been invited home for dinner by one of her fellow female students.

Neda had been sure each time of her friends' motives. Their parents were another matter. All were genuinely curious since Pakistanis in the capital rarely encountered Iranians. One mother, though, had seemed actively suspicious. Neda wasn't sure whether it was because she was Shi'a, Iranian, or both.

Neda had found her year at university in Pakistan interesting and had never regretted deciding to go. As she reviewed the memories brought back by this house, though, she realized she also didn't regret the decision not to extend her stay.

Vasilyev returned, and Neda was relieved to see him immediately make an "all clear" hand signal. Next, he held up his cell phone, so Neda could read a coded text exchange that she immediately knew meant help was en route.

A few minutes later, Vasilyev's cell phone buzzed, and after checking the still unconscious man's restraints, he nodded towards the front door.

This time, Neda observed, if anything Vasilyev was more thorough in examining the large black SUV. She correctly assumed this was because of the possibility the intruder had attached a monitoring or explosive device before entering the house.

Vasilyev's search was both exhaustive and quick, even including wedging his entire body under the SUV's chassis. A few minutes later, he gestured for Neda to enter the vehicle. Vasilyev had parked the Mehran far enough to the side of the driveway that there was just enough room for their new SUV to exit.

As they exited the driveway and the gate closed shut behind them, Neda saw a similar SUV approaching, and Vasilyev's cell phone buzzed again. Without even slowing down, Vasilyev pointed their vehicle north as the gate opened behind them, and the other SUV entered.

"So, other agents will question my attacker," Neda said flatly, her tone making it clear she would have preferred to do so herself.

From the amused glance Vasilyev gave her it was clear he had understood that tone. "Yes, since as you know we have more important business. They will pass on whatever they learn, which hopefully will have nothing to do with us."

Neda frowned. "Nothing to do with us?" she repeated with obvious annoyance. "That gun he was reaching for felt very personal."

Now Vasilyev couldn't help but laugh. "I understand it felt that way, but anyone he had encountered would have received the same treatment. I think it's likely he was a contractor hired by ISI. One of the terms of his contract was ensuring nobody knew what he'd been hired to do. So, eliminating you was simply part of the job."

Neda's frown now deepened to a scowl. "So, why do you think he was a contractor, rather than an ISI agent?"

Vasilyev nodded and said, "As I think you've guessed, because of how easily you incapacitated him. Don't misunderstand me—I was very impressed with your technique. I have seen less capable performances from far more experienced agents."

Slightly mollified, Neda asked, "So then why are you so sure he was a contractor?"

Vasilyev shrugged. "Because there's not a mark on you. ISI takes training its agents just as seriously as we do. He would have known better than to reach for his gun and leave himself completely open to attack if he'd had even rudimentary instruction. Of course, even most ISI contractors would know better. I think he underestimated you so badly simply because you're a woman."

Neda gave Vasilyev a thin smile. "I doubt he'll do that again."

Vasilyev's eyebrows rose, and he replied, "I'm sure you're right."

"Why do you say it that way?" Neda asked with a frown. "What will happen to him?"

Vasilyev took his right hand off the steering wheel and rocked it back and forth. "I can't say for sure. But if I'm right that he's a contractor and knows nothing of value, he'll be eliminated. The ISI will be unlikely to object, or for that matter, even acknowledge his existence."

Neda shook her head. "I don't like being responsible for another person's death."

Vasilyev snorted. "Consider the alternative. He was certainly ready to kill you. If we released him instead, your full description plus a high-quality sketch of your face would be in the hands of every ISI agent in Pakistan later today."

"I know," Neda said quietly. "I understand everything you've said, but I still don't like it."

"Good," Vasilyev replied. "That means you're human. The FSB doesn't recruit psychopaths, and I have no desire to work with one."

"Why do you think he was in the house?" Neda asked.

"A good question," Vasilyev replied. "I'm hoping that because it had been rented just before our arrival, ISI was having audio, and perhaps video surveillance installed. ISI often does this to monitor rental homes near embassies, but it usually takes longer. That's probably why they used a contractor to step up the pace. If my guess is right, ISI knows nothing about us specifically, and running into their contractor was just bad luck."

Neda frowned. "We said nothing while we were in the house, but if there were cameras, ISI would know what we look like."

Vasilyev nodded calmly. "Yes. But the odds are with us. Video monitoring is more expensive, much easier to detect, and usually reserved for a high-priority target. The agents who came to collect your attacker will do a thorough sweep of the house and let us know for sure."

Neda looked out the window. "We're on our way out of the city. Where are we going?"

Vasilyev grinned. "Another good question. There's always a Plan B. Compromise of the safe house was always a possibility, and if that happened, we would have to go elsewhere. That will be a small lodging not far from the facility that manufactures Pakistan's nuclear weapons.

There's a good chance the attack will happen somewhere in that area, so we'll wait there for word from Grishkov."

Neda looked puzzled. "That makes sense, but then why didn't we go there in the first place?"

"Because the Taliban hitting the weapon transports before they've gone far from the manufacturing facility is only one possibility. If they are tactical nuclear weapons, then they're probably headed for deployment at the southern stretch of Pakistan's border with India. If the Taliban have learned of the weapons' destination, they might be planning to attack in that area. In that case, we'll have moved in precisely the wrong direction," Vasilyev replied.

"But you don't believe that," Neda said flatly.

Vasilyev grinned and glanced at her, and wasn't surprised to see she was smiling too. "No, I don't. The Taliban have to know this attack will be their only opportunity to steal nuclear weapons. The Pakistani military may have relaxed a bit after moving their weapons around the country without incident for well over twenty years. After an attack, the military would increase security to the point that the Taliban would never get another chance. So, the Taliban might strike weapons transports with a mix of tactical and strategic nuclear weapons. I don't think they'll use their only opportunity on ones with only tactical nuclear devices."

Neda frowned. "So, until we hear from Grishkov, all we can do is make our best guess and hope we get lucky?'

Vasilyev nodded soberly. "In this business, that's often the best we can do."

CHAPTER FIVE

Peshawar, Pakistan

Mullah Abdul Zahed tried hard to keep his real thoughts and feelings from reaching his face as he looked at Hashmat Mohebi. His thinning white beard, emaciated frame, and gaunt features made him look one short step from the grave.

It was hard for Abdul to accept, but in one respect, Hashmat was perfect. From a distance, Hashmat's white beard, turban, and overall size and height were a close match to Abdul.

Abdul had been in hiding for several years while preparing the final stage of his plan to expel the Americans from Afghanistan. Anyone seeing Hashmat from a distance could easily mistake him for Abdul, and think that his illness accounted for Abdul's absence. He had heard that the Americans always liked to get "visual confirmation" if they could, so he had to make sure the bait was credible.

Abdul strongly suspected that Hashmat seeming to be at death's door was true in reality, not just appearance. Hashmat refused to speak about his health, always saying there was nothing wrong with him that a cup of coffee and some rest couldn't cure.

Well, Abdul didn't blame Hashmat for refusing to see a doctor trained in England or America. They would give him drugs that would make him even sicker.

Abdul thought Hashmat probably had cancer. Whatever his ailment, it worked to Abdul's advantage, and that was all that mattered.

Hashmat was almost pathetically eager to still be of use, to make a difference of some kind in the fight against the Americans. Though he had done more than his share of fighting over the years, his days in combat were over.

So Abdul had told Hashmat of another way he could be useful. It was a way that, at first, he had vigorously resisted.

That was good because it was what all the other Taliban leaders would expect. Hashmat, who had fought so hard and so faithfully for so many years, would never sell out his brothers to the Americans for money.

But, Abdul explained, the men Hashmat would be giving to the Americans would be sacrificed for a higher goal. To lay an ambush for the American special forces, perhaps one that would even manage to snare the vaunted SEAL Team Six.

Also, Abdul explained, Hashmat would have a chance to atone for his betrayal and go to God with a clean conscience. Hashmat would play the part of Abdul, and serve as bait for the trap. A trap that, once it snapped shut on the Americans, would also immediately send Hashmat to God's judgment as a hero.

Abdul was careful to praise the men that Hashmat would hand over to the Americans, telling him how much he regretted having to lose them and that he wished there was another way.

Abdul had selected Hashmat's victims carefully from among men who he knew to be opposed to his vision, but who had not spoken openly against him. After all, Hashmat might be feeble, but he wasn't stupid.

Abdul had one other ingenious twist to his scheme. Someone had to take the blame for the betrayals. Those selected to do so came from the same group—opposed to Abdul, but not vocally so.

How to lay the blame at their feet? Here Abdul's experience with moving money, which dated back to his days in the Taliban government, indeed came in handy.

Abdul had given Hashmat instructions on how the Americans were to send payment for information leading to the capture of his opponents. He told Hashmat that the money would go to finance Taliban operations.

And in a way, it did.

All of the men he had selected as victims had ties to Afghanistan's foreign export of narcotics. Since Abdul was known to view the drug trade as at best a necessary evil, this was one of the reasons many Taliban leaders opposed him.

It meant, though, that these men all had foreign bank accounts they could access online.

Ordinarily, Abdul had little time or patience for dealing with technology. When it came to money, he made an exception.

With the financial transactions the Americans had carried out to reward Hashmat's betrayals, Abdul knew precisely how such a payment would look online. Merely getting the account numbers of his victims was easy since, in theory, the money in those accounts was supposed to be available to finance Taliban operations.

Removing money from those accounts required passwords that Abdul didn't have.

But no password was required to send money to the accounts. For someone with Abdul's years of experience, it was child's play to set up a payment account that would make it look like the Americans had sent the money.

After all, Abdul said to himself with a chuckle, in a sense they had.

Abdul had only one real worry about the entire plan. That Hashmat would drop dead before he could be used as bait for the Americans.

Happily, it was now time to spring the trap, and Hashmat was still alive.

Abdul smiled. He knew the Americans could send a different SEAL team, or what they called Rangers.

But for the critical targets, like Osama bin Laden, they always sent the best. And the last remaining member of the old Taliban government counted as "really important."

It would be very satisfying to see the Americans get tricked and trapped for a change.

201st Military Base, Tajikistan

Anatoly Grishkov nodded his thanks to the young lieutenant who punched in the code that opened the door to the base's Operations Center. Once he entered, he was struck by the contrast between the blazing heat outside and the chilly air in the Op Center. The contrast was sharp as well between the dazzling sunshine outside and the dim interior, punctuated here and there by glowing LED screens.

A figure immediately moved towards him through the gloom with an outstretched hand. "Captain Igor Bronstein. I am the only one on base who knows about your mission, and I intend to keep it that way. Let's talk," he said, gesturing towards an office. Though small, Grishkov could see through its open door that the office had been soundproofed.

Bronstein shut the door behind them and said, "I understand you have to leave immediately. I'd ask how your flight was, but having flown a MiG-31 myself know the answer."

Grishkov grunted, and said, "Fast."

Bronstein laughed. "Yes. And for your mission, that counted for far more than comfort. Now, let me tell you about my role."

Bronstein pulled out a slim folder and passed it across the desk to Grishkov. The first picture in it Grishkov recognized as a type of drone, though not one he'd ever seen. He then asked, "Is this what will be protecting me during my meeting in Afghanistan?"

"Yes," Bronstein nodded, "Also, you are looking at its operator. This drone is the Okhotnik, which the Americans call Hunter. A total of three exist, so your mission must have a high priority indeed. I must warn you that all three are still considered prototypes. Though they have performed well in testing so far, equipment failure either on or after takeoff is a possibility, and there is no backup for the Okhotnik stationed here."

Grishkov nodded his understanding. "Payload?" he asked.

Bronstein smiled. "The next photo."

The photo showed a missile, with essential details displayed at the bottom. One figure made Grishkov frown.

"This missile carries a two hundred fifty kilogram warhead?" Grishkov asked.

"Correct," Bronstein replied. "The Okhotnik will carry two KH-38MLE missiles on this mission. It is half the size of the maximum dual-missile cargo because I want to give you some chance of surviving its use against your enemies. However, you will still need to keep some distance between you and your attackers for its use to be practical."

Grishkov grunted. "No chance of loading anything smaller?"

Bronstein shook his head. "No, for two reasons. First, nothing smaller has been tested for use in the Okhotnik. It was designed for ground attack, not close air support of ground forces. Second, nothing smaller has the range we need."

"Why does the range matter? Won't the drone be flying overhead?" Grishkov asked.

Now Bronstein looked uncomfortable. "Well, no. The Americans keep a close watch on the skies over Afghanistan. Our standing orders do not allow us to operate drones there, both to avoid diplomatic complications and to safeguard our equipment, which the Americans would not hesitate to shoot down."

Grishkov stared at Bronstein, not sure whether to be angry or astonished. "Then how is this drone going to protect me?"

Bronstein quickly nodded. "Yes, let me explain. The missile has an operational range of forty kilometers, well within striking distance for your meeting location about thirty kilometers inside Afghanistan. We have been operating our Okhotnik near the Afghan border for months now, and expect no reaction to its use today from the Americans."

Grishkov scowled. "And how will this drone monitor the situation at the meeting spot from thirty kilometers away?"

"It won't," Bronstein said with a shrug. "You will signal that you need assistance with this radio transmitter," he said, handling Grishkov a small metal box with an antenna and a large red button.

Grishkov shook his head. "How can the drone fire on a target successfully from so far away?"

Bronstein smiled. "Not as hard as you might think. You will provide the initial bearing with your radio signal. A laser signal that you transmit will then provide the missile terminal guidance to the actual target."

Bronstein then handed Grishkov another small metal box, this one with a black button and a glass emitter lens at one end.

Grishkov nodded. "Yes, I used similar devices in Chechnya when we were coordinating airstrikes."

"Yes, I know," Bronstein said, tapping a bulky folder in front of him. "I read your file, or at least what I could through all the recent redactions."

"How long will I have to illuminate the target? Which will probably not be holding still, and is likely to be shooting at me?" Grishkov asked.

"Not long," Bronstein replied. "The KH-38MLE flies at Mach 2.2, and so will be on your target very quickly."

Grishkov was still visibly unenthusiastic but finally shrugged.

"Good," Bronstein said, obviously eager to move on from the topic. "Now, let's talk about the man who will accompany you to this meeting," he said, gesturing for Grishkov to move on to the next photo.

The bearded, graying face that glared out from the photo was not one Grishkov was excited about as a traveling companion, as his expression made plain.

Bronstein laughed. "Yes, Amooz is not the most cheerful fellow you'll ever meet. But he's had a hard life even by Afghan standards. He worked with us as a teenager when we were in Afghanistan, and is one of the few men we've stayed in contact with since we left. He's lost his entire family in the decades of fighting since then. Not even a cousin is left. For an Afghan, that guarantees you don't wake up with a smile."

Grishkov was not reassured. "So, why should I trust this cheerful fellow?"

"Because we are all he has left. And because we have kept our promises to him, while he has suffered repeated betrayal at the hands of his fellow Afghans," Bronstein replied.

"I'd still rather do without him," Grishkov said flatly. "I can drive the truck, and I can follow a map. The meeting will be a simple exchange, for which I should need no help."

Bronstein shook his head. "You do need Amooz, for several reasons. First, the border guards know him, and they don't know you. A bribe to let your truck pass the border is not enough. It has to be paid by someone they trust. Next, the meeting may not be as simple as you think, and though the file says the man you'll meet speaks Russian and English, a translator may still be useful. Finally, if you do come under attack at some point, Amooz has proven he is a survivor. I know him, and would trust him to have my back."

He could see that the last point meant more to Grishkov than any of the others. "Very well," Grishkov said. "If a Russian officer vouches for him, that's good enough for me. How long before we can get underway?" Grishkov asked.

"Immediately," Bronstein replied. "I'd normally have insisted you get some rest and a decent meal after being catapulted across Russia in a MiG-31, but it seems there's not a minute to waste. So, sandwiches are waiting for you in the front seat of the truck, and with luck, you'll be able to doze a few minutes before you reach the border. I don't know all the details of your mission, but enough to be sure it's important," he said, thrusting his hand across the desk. "Good luck.'

"Thanks," Grishkov said as he stood and shook Bronstein's hand. "I'm pretty sure I'll need it."

CHAPTER SIX

Approaching Tajik-Afghan Border

Anatoly Grishkov looked at Amooz through half-closed eyes as the truck continued its bumpy, lurching way towards Afghanistan. He was exhausted, having had little luck trying to sleep in the MiG-31's cockpit, and even less on roads that seemed to get worse the closer they came to Afghanistan.

Amooz had said little, and at first, that had been fine with Grishkov as he tried to sleep. As the latest bounce brought his teeth together with a clack, though, he realized he really should sit up and learn something about his driver, translator, and—if things went wrong—fellow combatant.

"So, you are the first Afghan I've met who has been with us since we had forces in Afghanistan in the 1980s," Grishkov said, as neutrally as he could.

Amooz glanced towards Grishkov expressionlessly. "Yes," he said calmly. "I suppose you're wondering why I supported the Russian forces."

Grishkov nodded.

"Well, the last Afghan king was overthrown just six years before Russian forces arrived. His cousin took over, and the only change was that a different bunch of nobles continued to exploit the poor and uneducated, as they had done for centuries. You Russians said you'd gotten rid of your nobles, and could show us how to do it too. Or maybe I just heard what I wanted to hear," Amooz said with a bitter smile.

Grishkov shrugged. "When the Communist Party lost power, and the USSR collapsed, many hoped the grip of the party elite on wealth and privilege would disappear. However, many of the old elite were able to adapt very well to the new Russia."

"Good, you understand me," Amooz said, nodding. "By the time I realized you Russians were in Afghanistan for your own purposes and had no real interest in us and our problems, it was too late. I have lost my family over decades of fighting. I have learned just three things over more than three decades."

Grishkov cocked his head, making it clear he was paying attention.

"First, the Taliban are medieval barbarians, with whom there can be no negotiation. They are determined to impose their will on their women and on anyone in Afghanistan who is not from their Pashtun ethnic group, and will tolerate no foreign interference."

Grishkov nodded his understanding.

"Second, the Americans are fools. They have cast their lot with the Afghan nobility, whether they realize it or not. Afghans will only fight to keep them in control of the major cities as long as the Americans are willing to pay, and to maintain enough troops here to keep their jet fighters, helicopters, and drones flying. I doubt they will stay here forever, and once they go, the Taliban will be back in Kabul in a matter of days."

Grishkov shrugged and nodded again.

"Finally, when a man realizes everything he hoped for is beyond his reach, he's left with just one thing. Honor. That's why, Russian, you can count on me to get you to your meeting."

Grishkov was about to reply when the truck made a sharp turn on the road, and the Tajik border post was before them.

"No matter what happens, keep quiet!" Amooz hissed in a fierce whisper.

Grishkov sat still and looked straight ahead as their truck pulled up to the border crossing. Though he couldn't follow their conversation in what Grishkov guessed was Tajik, Amooz seemed like a different person. Laughing and joking with the border guards, who he clearly knew, Amooz eventually slid an envelope through the truck's window that quickly disappeared in the hands of the border post's commander. Moments later, they were on their way.

Once they turned around another bend in the winding road and were out of sight of the Tajik border post, Amooz pulled the truck off the road. Grishkov looked at him questioningly and got a fierce scowl in response.

"Something's wrong," Amooz said flatly.

Grishkov shrugged. "Everything seemed to go well, and they didn't search the truck. What makes you think there's a problem?"

If anything, Amooz' scowl deepened. "I didn't like the smile Mahmoud had on his face when we left. It's a smile you give when you know something the other person doesn't."

Grishkov nodded. "I'm guessing Mahmoud is the border post commander?"

Rather than answer, Amooz appeared to make a decision. "I'll be able to see the Afghan border post from the top of that hill. At least we can find out what's waiting for us. Stay here with the truck, and lift the hood. If anyone stops to help, tell them a tow truck is on the way. I won't take long, so you probably won't see anyone. We picked this route because it's not too busy."

With that, Amooz pulled a pair of Komz 8x30 binoculars from the glove compartment. In response to Grishkov's raised eyebrows, Amooz said, "I took these from a Russian officer who no longer needed them."

Grishkov nodded. Since they were about to be used in support of a Russian mission, he could hardly object. In fact, he found it oddly comforting that one of the highest quality items produced by the old USSR was about to help him reach his objective. Komz, like many Soviet enterprises, had significantly benefited from captured German equipment, technology, and even technicians.

Grishkov thought to himself with a frown that the Soviet Union had paid dearly in blood for everything it took from the Germans. By the time he'd completed the thought, Amooz was out of sight.

Lifting the truck's hood, Grishkov looked down the road, which was as empty as Amooz had promised. Except for a few hills, the land around him was flat and featureless, with only occasional patches of grass and shrub punctuating long expanses of bare dirt and rock.

Grishkov wiped his forehead with his sleeve. Even at mid-morning, it was already a hot day under a clear blue sky.

Amooz was true to his word, and before any other vehicle had appeared on the road was back. One look was all Grishkov needed to know the news wasn't good.

Climbing back into the truck Amooz nearly spat a single word, "Dushkas!"

Grishkov frowned. More than one was very bad news. The DShK-1938/46 heavy machine gun fired 12.7mm x 108mm ammunition roughly equivalent to the American .50 caliber round at a rate of six hundred rounds a minute. Designed primarily as a weapon against low-flying aircraft and light armor, it would have no trouble chewing through their truck. Over a million had been produced, and it was very good at its job.

Even worse, a poorly trained gunner only had to point a Dushka in the right direction inside a kilometer to be nearly sure of a hit with a target as large as a truck. A competent gunner could do even longer ranges.

Grishkov knew that "Dushka" came from the acronym "DshK." Anytime he thought about it, though, he couldn't imagine a less fitting nickname for this killing machine than the Russian word meaning "Sweetie."

"How many?" Grishkov asked.

"Two," Amooz answered. "Two too many. One is pintle-mounted and static. The other is triple mounted on a GAZ truck."

Grishkov nodded. "How many do they usually have?"

Amooz just stared at him. "Do you think I'd be going anywhere near those by choice? They normally have zero Dushkas. Ordinarily, it looks like the Tajik border post we just passed, five or six soldiers with AK-74s, and nothing heavier. Those Dushkas are for us."

Grishkov grunted agreement. Bronstein might have been required to coordinate with the Tajik government, and someone there saw an opportunity. Or Bronstein had turned them in himself, in return for a cut of the millions in the truck. Thinking back on his encounter with Bronstein, Grishkov doubted that was the answer.

Well, one way to find out for sure.

Aloud, he said, "I'm going to take a look for myself. Stay here with the truck until I get back. And pass me those binoculars."

Amooz didn't like that at all. "Those Dushkas aren't going away, no matter how many people look at them. We need to take another way to your meeting, and you need to tell them you'll be late."

Grishkov looked at him calmly. "I won't be long," he said, holding out his right hand for the binoculars.

Muttering and shaking his head, Amooz finally did just that.

Grishkov climbed up the same hill he'd seen Amooz on just minutes before and made his way the last meters to the top at a crawl. First, he poked his head over the hill's crest to get his bearings and had no trouble spotting the border post. Even without the binoculars, he could see one of the Dushkas.

As he focused on the second Dushka with the Komz binoculars, Grishkov gave thanks to both German optical engineering and Russian craftsmanship. The other Dushka was now as plain as day, and happily not far from the other one.

Grishkov pressed the radio transmitter button and then aimed the laser target designator midway between the two Dushkas.

As he waited prone on the crest of the hill, Grishkov reflected that what happened next would answer many questions. Had Bronstein betrayed them? If not, was he willing to destroy an Afghan border post? Had Moscow made it clear this mission had the highest priority?

Grishkov pressed himself even more firmly in the ground as a roar that seemed to pass directly over his head answered all of his questions. It took every bit of his concentration to keep the target illuminated. Then Grishkov pressed his head into the earth as a brilliant flash, and an earth-shaking explosion announced the KH-38MLE's arrival at its goal.

Grishkov slowly lifted his head and shook it, trying to get his eyes focused after being dazzled by the flash of the explosion. After a few moments, he was able to bring the binoculars to his eyes so he could confirm the destruction of both Dushkas, as he fully expected from a strike by a two hundred fifty kilogram warhead.

His expectations were exceeded. At first, Grishkov thought he was looking in the wrong place, or that his eyes were still playing tricks on him. He shortly realized that his first impression was correct. The border post was gone.

Grishkov had seen both artillery and airstrikes in Chechnya and thought he knew what to expect here. After a moment, he realized that he had never seen an impact from a missile traveling at over twice the speed of sound. Also, since they were right at the border, the weapon would have only burned a small percentage of its fuel. That left the rest to contribute to the explosion.

That was all to the good. Not good was that the explosion had to have been heard by the troops at the Tajik border post. Those troops wouldn't cross the Afghan border, but they would come to investigate at least as far as Grishkov and Amooz were right now.

They needed to get moving.

As soon as Grishkov turned around and looked down the hill towards their truck, he saw a scene that at first made no sense to him. A battered white pickup truck was parked just behind their truck, and what looked like two bodies were on the ground beside it.

Grishkov hurried down the hill as fast as he could, pistol in hand. As he approached the truck, he heard a dry chuckle from Amooz.

"You can put that away," Amooz said. "I've already dealt with our un-invited guests." He was sitting as before in the truck's driver's seat, and the engine was already running.

As soon as Grishkov climbed into the passenger seat, Amooz put the truck into gear, and they began moving towards the flaming debris that had once been the Afghan border post.

In response to Grishkov's questioning look, Amooz said, "Just as you reached the top of the hill, they showed up and started asking questions. I guess you were so focused on the border post you didn't hear them. I was just wondering how I was going to take out both of them when you were good enough to provide me with a distraction."

Amooz then nodded towards what little remained of the border post, which they were now passing on the left, and asked what had destroyed it. Grishkov thought to himself absently that it was lucky the missile's strike had left the road intact and next that they should still be able to make it to the rendezvous on time.

Then Grishkov realized with a start that Amooz had been right. The arrival of the pickup truck and Amooz's dispatch of its two occupants had happened without his notice. Yes, he'd been focused on guiding the missile to its target. Yes, the subsequent explosion would have distracted even the most alert person.

But now Grishkov couldn't deny that lack of sleep was affecting his performance.

Bronstein had been right too. He did need Amooz.

With that, he focused on the question Amooz had just asked about what had destroyed the border post.

Shaking his head vigorously and willing himself awake, Grishkov finally said, "A drone. The Americans are no longer the only ones who have them."

This statement earned Grishkov the first smile he had seen on Amooz's face. It looked like the first that had been there for a long time.

"So, will our guardian in the sky be with us for this meeting?" Amooz asked.

Grishkov nodded. "Yes, but it only has one missile left."

Amooz shrugged. "Just as well. If more than one is needed, I would rate our survival chances as low anyway. We'll want to keep as much distance from our attackers as we can."

Grishkov was pleased to see Amooz had realized this on his own and nodded.

"I'm driving a bit faster than I'd like on this road to make up some of the time we lost back there. I still think we can make the rendezvous on time, but it's going to be close. Help me keep an eye out for potholes or debris in the road. We don't have time to change a tire," Amooz said.

Grishkov grunted agreement and leaned forward in his seat. Then he swore as the truck hit a pothole, and only his seatbelt kept his head from hitting the dashboard.

Amooz made a gesture that Grishkov correctly interpreted as meaning, "What can you do?" Then he added, "Sometimes this road has so many potholes, you have to choose between them and pray."

Fortunately, they didn't have far to go. As they rounded yet another curve on the winding road, Grishkov spotted a Lada Niva 4x4 SUV waiting for them, painted in Army green. Well, he thought to himself, if any Russian vehicle were going to survive this long after we left, the Lada Niva would be it. At least it wasn't big enough to hold an overwhelming force.

Grishkov's military experience told him this was a lousy spot for a rendezvous. The low hills to their right didn't precisely overlook the road, but they were within comfortable automatic weapons range for competent troops. Rocks and brush on the hilltops provided plenty of cover for anyone lying in ambush.

Grishkov scanned the hilltops for any sign of movement but saw nothing.

As they drew closer, the two front doors of the Lada Niva opened, and two men in Afghan dress emerged. One was carrying a folded piece of paper, and the other had an AK-74, which he slung over his shoulder.

Grishkov's utility coveralls had plenty of pockets. He now checked to be sure that the dead man's switch was in one of them, and then put his right thumb firmly on the trigger. That done, he pressed the smaller switch on the handle that armed and disarmed the device.

It felt a bit ridiculous to be using a switch connected by radio to a large explosive charge in the truck to guarantee the security of the exchange, now that he knew there were only two people in the SUV. Grishkov then chided himself. More shooters could still be hiding in the back of the vehicle. Plus, who knew how many shooters were hiding in those hills, and whose side they might be on.

And, of course, orders were orders.

Amooz had been paying close attention, as Grishkov had expected. Jerking his head towards the approaching Afghan men, Grishkov said, "Cover me."

Amooz nodded and exited the truck with his AK-74 in hand, taking up position so that the body of the truck gave him some protection. As Grishkov left the vehicle, holding up the switch in his hand, he could hear Amooz say in a low voice, "Don't trip."

The two Afghans had spotted the dead man's switch because their pace slowed noticeably. However, they still moved forward. In just over a minute, both men were standing near Grishkov a few meters in front of the truck.

The man holding the map matched the description Grishkov had been given—tall, and despite his grey hair and beard, still alert. He said, "I am Baddar. You speak English, yes?"

Grishkov nodded. "Yes, I do."

"Good," Baddar said. "Here is a map showing the location for the planned attack on the nuclear weapons transports. You will see right below it is written when the ambush will happen. You don't have much time."

Grishkov asked, "Were you able to find out where the weapons will be targeted if the attack is successful?"

Baddar nodded. "Just before I left to come here. Bagram Airfield, and the Green Zone in Kabul."

Grishkov looked at the map, and then folded it and put it in his pocket. Baddar was right. They didn't have much time to stop the attack.

Jerking his head towards the truck, Grishkov said, "The keys are in the truck. If your Lada is empty, I think we'll wait for our ride there."

Baddar shrugged. "There is no one in the Lada, and the keys are in it too. I think you can put that switch away now."

No sooner had Baddar finished his statement than the sound of automatic weapons fire made all of them dive for the ground. It only took a few seconds for Grishkov to realize that it was coming from the hills he'd spotted earlier.

"Everyone, back to the truck," Grishkov said.

Baddar reached over to the man who had accompanied him, and who was now motionless on the ground. He had said nothing, and now never would.

Taking the man's AK-74, Baddar quickly moved with Grishkov to the other side of the truck, gouts of earth rising around both of them as the shooters on the hilltops tried but failed to kill them as well.

Amooz had once again saved Grishkov from likely death, by forcing the shooters to attack under fire. Grishkov saw with approval that Amooz had set his AK-74 to single shot, and was taking careful aim at each target. He saw at least two unmoving dots on the nearby hilltops that testified to Amooz's skill with the weapon.

Now Baddar took up a position about two meters away from Amooz and began adding his fire as well. Grishkov bent down and carefully turned the dead man's switch to "safe" and put it into one of his pockets.

"Just keep them busy," Grishkov said, as he reached into another pocket and pulled out the small device that would call in the drone strike.

In response to Baddar's questioning look, Grishkov said, "I'm calling for help."

Baddar shrugged and continued to fire back at their attackers.

Remembering how quickly the first missile arrived, Grishkov pulled out the laser target designator and illuminated a point on the hilltop that appeared to be the midpoint between the shooters.

Grishkov heard a soft grunt behind him but had to stay focused on il-luminating the target.

It wasn't long before the second missile's arrival, with an impact no less spectacular than the first. Grishkov was dimly aware of Baddar drop-ping down beside him as they both instinctively sought shelter from the blast. His eyes were again dazzled by the explosion, but as soon as they re-gained focus, he looked for Amooz.

He hadn't gone far.

Amooz was just a couple of meters away, slumped against the right rear tire. Blood was seeping through a wound in his chest, and his breathing was labored. Grishkov pulled out the medical kit from the truck and hurried to Amooz's side.

As Grishkov opened the kit, Amooz shook his head. "No. This is my time." Weakly gesturing towards Baddar, who was still groggy and shak-ing his head, Amooz said, "Ask him to see that I am properly buried here in my homeland."

Grishkov nodded. He hesitated and then thought to himself that sometimes humanity was more important than orders.

"That man just gave me information on the planned theft of Pak-istani nuclear weapons by the Taliban. They intend to use them here in Afghanistan. Thanks to your sacrifice, we still have a chance to stop them," Grishkov said.

Amooz nodded and whispered, "Good," and closed his eyes.

He didn't open them again.

To his side, Grishkov heard Baddar saying something rhythmic in a language he didn't understand, and correctly guessed it was a prayer for Amooz.

Grishkov stood up and looked at the hilltop where the shooters had staged their attack. Its top was noticeably shorter than before, and smoke was still rising from burning shrubs and grass. He couldn't see anything recognizable as a body, but there was no gunfire greeting his appearance, and he was willing to take that as proof the missile strike had been successful.

Grishkov pressed the button on the device that would hopefully summon a Mil-8 helicopter. Bronstein had said that the Mil-8 could fly under American radar coverage for a short distance. He had also warned it would not linger.

Then Grishkov turned to Baddar.

Gesturing towards Amooz's remains, he asked, "Can you take Amooz with you for burial?"

Baddar nodded. "It will be my honor. He fought with courage. Please help me move both Amooz and Mohammed into the truck."

Grishkov saw that Baddar was gesturing towards the body of the man who had accompanied him to the meeting. Well, now he knew his name, at least. They worked together, and it didn't take long until they had secured both remains in the truck bed for their last trip.

"I'm sorry about your friend Mohammed," Grishkov said sincerely.

Baddar nodded. "And I for your friend Amooz. Good luck with making the men responsible pay for their crimes."

Grishkov could hear the rapidly approaching flutter of the Mil-8's rotors, and so just nodded in response as he checked to make sure the map Baddar had given him was still secure. Then he shook Baddar's hand and, bent low, rushed to meet the Mil-8 as it touched down a dozen meters from the truck.

As soon as he passed through the helicopter's open doorway, Grishkov felt an arm press him against the seat, and heard a voice yell, "Go, go, go!" As Grishkov fumbled with the flight harness, he could feel the Mil-8 lurch skywards.

CHAPTER SEVEN

201st Military Base, Tajikistan

Less than half an hour after he had boarded the Mil-8, Anatoly Grishkov was back in Captain Igor Bronstein's office. Though only hours had passed since he left for the meeting with Baddar, it felt like days.

"Was your mission successful?" Bronstein asked.

Grishkov nodded, pulling out the map Baddar had given him, showing the place and time of the planned attack and handing it to Bronstein.

"Excellent," Bronstein said. He pressed a button on his desk, and a lieutenant rushed in. Bronstein handed the map to the lieutenant and ordered him to have it scanned and transmitted to headquarters. The lieutenant saluted and hurried out even faster than he'd arrived.

"That information will be in the hands of the decision-makers in Moscow very shortly. Now, did Baddar know which targets the Taliban hopes to strike with these stolen weapons?"

Grishkov nodded tiredly. "The Green Zone in Kabul, and Bagram Airfield."

Bronstein grunted. "If it had been up to me, we'd have paid Baddar nothing extra for that information. Both targets are obvious for the Taliban. But still, I suppose it helps to be sure. We, as well as the Americans, have been surprised by the Afghans before."

This time, Grishkov just nodded.

"I'm sure you're past exhausted. The good news is that soon you'll be able to get some sleep. That Mil-8 is refueling and will take you on a short flight to Dushanbe. There you will take a charter flight to Islamabad. You will be on board as a Tajik government courier to their Embassy in Islamabad."

Bronstein handed Grishkov a Tajik diplomatic passport, which Grishkov saw had a Tajik name next to his picture. Grishkov recognized the photo from his induction to the FSB the previous year. He'd looked a lot younger, he thought wryly.

"We kept your actual date of birth, so all you have to remember is the name in the passport. There shouldn't be any other questions, because of your status as a diplomatic courier. All of the luggage we are sending with you is protected from search, for the same reason," Bronstein explained.

"The 'luggage' contains weapons?" Grishkov asked.

"Yes," Bronstein confirmed. "The best part is that even if the Pakistanis violated diplomatic procedure and searched the cases, they'd have no reason to object. All diplomatic missions in Islamabad are expected to arm their security personnel. Even though you aren't Tajik, the diplomatic passport is, and that's all that matters. The Tajik Embassy will confirm your identity and that your 'luggage' is genuine and authorized if asked."

Grishkov nodded. "Very accommodating of our Tajik friends. Is this something we often do?"

"Often, no. But it's not unprecedented. Over half of Tajikistan's national income comes from remittances sent by Tajik citizens working in

Russia, so when we ask for a favor, the answer is usually yes," Bronstein replied.

"How long will it take to get me to Islamabad?" Grishkov asked.

"Not long. I think your real question is whether you'll be able to get to the attack site in time to join the other agents assigned to preventing it. The answer is, maybe. The main unknown is driving time from Islamabad to the attack site, which is fortunately not very far away," Bronstein replied.

Then Bronstein hesitated. "You should also be aware that neither you nor the other agents may be involved at all. The information you obtained may be handed over to the Pakistani authorities. We're sending you to Islamabad as a contingency, not because it's sure you will go on to attempt to prevent the attack."

Grishkov shrugged. "It always seemed to be more sensible to leave this up to the Pakistanis. After all, they have far more resources, and with a prior warning should make short work of any force the Taliban can assemble."

Bronstein said nothing and just nodded.

Grishkov sighed. "But you don't think that's what will happen. We discussed some of the problems with leaving response up to the Pakistani authorities before we left Moscow."

"I'm only guessing," Bronstein said. "But the Pakistanis have a complicated relationship between the civilian and military authorities, due to many previous coups where the military took power by force. If we give this warning the proper, diplomatic way to the civilian politicians, notice may well not reach the nuclear transport force in time. If we warn the generals directly, the politicians may be . . . unhappy. But there's a more serious problem."

Grishkov nodded. "Our alliance with India."

"Correct," Bronstein said. "We have been aligned with India for decades. They have bought billions of dollars worth of our weapons exports, and we even jointly developed the very capable BrahMos PJ-10 anti-ship cruise missile. The Pakistanis would treat any warning from us with suspicion. Great suspicion."

Grishkov shrugged. "And if we attempt to prevent the theft, fail, and are then captured alive by the Pakistani authorities?"

Bronstein winced. "Yes. If the Pakistanis then identified you as Russian agents, our long alliance with India might make them think the attack was an Indian plot supported by Russia. Truly, our President has many factors to consider."

"But you're sending me to Islamabad anyway," Grishkov said.

"Yes," Bronstein said, standing up. "There are many reasons we should stay well clear of this business. But I think the President will decide the prospect of a nuclear-armed Taliban outweighs all of them, and that is why you are going. Good luck!"

Grishkov stood and shook Bronstein's outstretched hand.

At least on the charter flight, he could finally get some sleep.

Taxila, Pakistan

Neda Rhahbar looked at the hotel room's single bed and sighed. "I'll take the couch," she declared.

Mikhail Vasilyev raised one eyebrow and shook his head. "That will not be necessary for either of us. Recall your training."

Neda first frowned, and then flushed as she remembered. "When two agents are sharing accommodation on assignment in a location where threats are present, one must stand watch while the other sleeps on a mutually agreed schedule."

Vasilyev nodded. "And if we had any doubts about whether threats are present, your encounter with the intruder at what should have been our residence in Islamabad settled them."

"So, this location is close to what we think would be the starting point for the nuclear weapons convoy?" Neda asked.

Vasilyev rocked his right hand back and forth. "More accurate to say it represents our best guess at a starting point. Both missiles and their launchers are produced here in Taxila. However, other locations such as Fateh Jang are also known to produce launchers."

Vasilyev paused and then shrugged. "More important is that the Pakistan Ordnance Factories near Wah are only about fifteen kilometers from here. Near one of the factories are six earth-covered bunkers inside a heavily guarded multi-zone security perimeter, which we suspect is used for nuclear warhead storage. To maintain that level of security as long as possible, the last step before transport would be attaching the warhead to the missile and then mounting the missile in its launcher. At any rate, that's how we've always done it."

Neda frowned. "Something's been bothering me since you said the name of this city. It sounds familiar for some reason that has nothing to do with nuclear weapons."

Vasilyev smiled. "Now you've hit on the other reason we picked Taxila as the backup location to wait for news from Grishkov. The city is a UNESCO World Heritage site that has over a million visitors a year. There are ruins dating back to before Taxila's conquest by Alexander the Great, museums packed with Buddhist and Hindu sculptures and artifacts, and much more. In many other places in Pakistan, two strangers, including one Iranian, would attract notice. Not here," Vasilyev said, shaking his head.

"Yes!" Neda exclaimed. "Now I remember one of my classmates suggested a trip here, but I was a young university student free of my parents for the first time. Of course, the relatives I was staying with watched what I was doing, but not nearly as closely as my mother. I didn't want to waste that limited freedom visiting ruins and museums. Hearing you describe Taxila, I think maybe I was shortsighted."

Vasilyev shrugged. "I wouldn't mind walking in the footsteps of Alexander the Great. Late in life, my father developed an interest in history and would talk to me about the people and events that captured his imagination. Maybe it's not a surprise that someone with 'the Great' as part of his name was one of them. Anyway, we'll be staying in this hotel room until we hear from Grishkov. It should be a matter of hours."

"I heard about your father during my training. I know he died very recently, but I never had a chance to express my sympathies to you. The only other thing I heard about him was that he died a hero, but nobody I asked knew any details," Neda said, her voice trailing off.

If Vasilyev picked up on the implied question, he completely ignored it. "Good," he replied. "I'm pleased to hear you're not the only one paying attention to the other Mikhail's advice about keeping your mouth shut."

He paused and then added, "I'll take the first watch."

Neda said nothing more and went to bed fully clothed, taking off only her shoes. As she put her head on the pillow and turned her back to Vasilyev, she had just one thought before exhaustion claimed her.

"This job is hard enough. I'm glad I don't also have to live up to a legend."

Islamabad International Airport, Islamabad, Pakistan

Anatoly Grishkov grunted with satisfaction as he recognized the model of the large black SUV waiting for him in the airport parking lot. Its presence meant his request for weapons in addition to the ones in his diplomatic cases had been approved. He was particularly hoping that one very special weapon was in the SUV's hidden compartment but would have to wait for a less conspicuous location to check.

Everything had gone well so far. Grishkov had finally been able to sleep on the plane, and the diplomatic passport had worked like a charm. Grishkov and his luggage had been waved through customs and immigration.

Now, Grishkov scowled, if the President would make a decision. For now, his orders just said to rendezvous with Vasilyev and Neda, and await further instructions. That was fine as far as it went since the attack on the Pakistani nuclear weapons convoy was going to happen not far from Taxila.

The problem was time. There wasn't much left. It was now to the point that it depended on traffic whether Grishkov would be able to make the rendezvous and then the attack location.

It would make much more sense for Vasilyev and Neda to head to the ambush site, and for Grishkov to meet them there. But they couldn't do that without orders, and so far, only Grishkov and the President knew the attack location.

It wasn't like the President to hesitate over a decision. Grishkov had undoubtedly disagreed with some of them, but "vacillating" wasn't a word he'd ever heard used in describing the President.

The choices on hand weren't great. Do nothing, and take the chance that the Taliban would succeed in obtaining nuclear weapons. Warn the

Pakistani authorities, and if the warning came too late, perhaps be blamed for the theft.

Or take a chance that two Russian agents and one brand-new female Iranian recruit could help the Pakistanis foil the Taliban's planned ambush. And if they were killed and their bodies identified, perhaps have Russia accused of complicity in the trap.

Grishkov shrugged as he put the SUV in gear. All he could do was drive, and hope that the President made the right decision in time.

Chapter Eight

Neda Rhahbar felt a curious mixture of excitement and annoyance when the phone buzzed in her pocket. Excitement, because it almost certainly meant news from Grishkov. Annoyance, because while she was now well-rested, Mikhail Vasilyev had only been asleep for two hours.

She wasn't sure why that bothered her so much.

Neda hesitated between reading the message and immediately waking Vasilyev. This dilemma was quickly solved when Vasilyev woke, pulled out his phone, and began reading in a series of movements so rapid and fluid that Neda took a step back.

She didn't envy anyone who attempted to attack Vasilyev in his sleep.

Whatever Vasilyev was reading, Neda could see it evoking an emotion she hadn't yet seen from him.

Anger.

Visibly collecting himself, Vasilyev glanced at Neda and said, "We leave immediately. You'll find your purse is a bit heavier after a gift I put there while you were sleeping."

Neda looked inside her purse. What she found there made her smile, because it was apparent Vasilyev had read her file.

The PSS-2 was the culmination of a KGB quest begun in 1980 to develop a genuinely silent pistol. Instead of a suppressor, which never did more than reduce the sound of a gunshot, the PSS-2 used a unique 7.62 x 43 mm SP-16 cartridge with an internal piston to nearly eliminate the sound of its discharge. Weighing less than a kilogram fully loaded, it was less than 165 mm long, including the 35 mm barrel, making it easy to conceal.

While most of Neda's firearms instructors had been men, a woman had trained her on the use of the PSS-2. She had emphasized that "your male opponents will not expect you to be armed," and taught her a grip taking advantage of Neda's long fingers to help conceal the small pistol from view.

With an effective range of just twenty-five meters, the PSS-2 was only useful at close quarters. Neda had practiced with the weapon almost obsessively until her instructor finally pronounced her not only qualified but the best shot with a PSS-2 she had ever trained.

Neda closed her purse and hurried after Vasilyev.

20 Kilometers North of Islamabad International Airport, Pakistan

Anatoly Grishkov finally saw a promising opportunity to assemble the special weapon he'd requested unobserved and took it. The dirt road turnoff was framed with trees on both sides, and there was a clearing a short distance to the right. The clearing had no trees but was overgrown with tall grass and low brush, so that once his SUV entered it, it would be effectively invisible from the paved road.

At first Grishkov had been unsure about spending the time required to assemble the weapon, but finally decided its capabilities made it worth the extra few minutes. After all, new orders could come at any time, redirecting him from the Taxila rendezvous with Vasilyev and Neda to go instead directly to the ambush site.

First, Grishkov pushed down the rear seats. Next, though the remote he held had only the standard door and trunk buttons, pressing them in the correct coded sequence caused the entire rear two-thirds of the SUV to lift to the ceiling, revealing a cavernous storage compartment.

Grishkov was pleased to see the Chukavin SVCh-308 sniper rifle had been packed with a German Schmidt and Bender scope as he'd requested. Opening another case, he was astonished to find an American-made Harris bipod stand, laser designator, sound suppressor, and a barrel-mounted flashlight.

There was only one possible explanation for this fantastically expensive collection of sniper hardware. This was the actual rifle that the previous Russian President had fired years ago on national TV, hitting a target at maximum range three out of five times.

FSB Director Smyslov had told Grishkov that the current President had been pleased with his performance on his last two missions. As he assembled the rifle, he thought to himself that this gift had done more than awards and cash to convince him Smyslov had meant it.

The Chukavin came in three versions, one firing the same round as the Dragunov sniper rifle it replaced and another the Western equivalent .308 Winchester. The third version was what Grishkov had received, the high-powered .338 Lapua Magnum. He'd asked for it because the Lapua-chambered version had a longer effective range of nearly one and a half kilometers.

There was also an assortment of submachine guns, grenades, and ammunition in the vehicle. For now, though, Grishkov decided to leave those in place.

Grishkov hesitated but finally made his choice. After assembling the rifle, he lowered the storage compartment and put the rear seats back in place. Then he put the assembled gun on the floor of the back seat, covering it with a black tarp designed to match the rest of the SUV's black interior. It would fail all but the most cursory inspection, but at this point, he didn't imagine stopping short of his goal.

Whether that goal was to rendezvous with Vasilyev and Neda, or to go straight to the ambush site, Grishkov wasn't going to let anything stand in his way.

30 Kilometers Outside Taxila, Pakistan

Neda Rhahbar finally couldn't resist. "I can see that something about our orders upset you, but I've read them on my phone and don't understand why. Is there something I should know?"

Mikhail Vasilyev relaxed his grip on the SUV's steering wheel and glanced towards Neda. Finally, he nodded.

"Yes, and I should have told you sooner. There is an excellent chance we will be too late to stop the attack. I'm angry because though Grishkov did his part and got us the ambush's time and location, the President took too long to decide to send us."

Neda, at first, said nothing. Then, slowly, she said rather than asked, "Your message gave you more details than I received."

Vasilyev shrugged. "Yes. When one agent is more experienced than the other, this is standard practice. We are all given only the information we must have to do our job. But there is some good news. I've also been told that Grishkov is on his way to meet us."

Neda smiled. "I'm glad to hear that. As you know, he helped me escape Iran, and I have great faith in him. Will he be able to join us in time?"

Vasilyev scowled. "Maybe. I don't know anything for sure, which is why I probably seem so angry. Difficult odds I have faced and overcome before. Uncertainty is what I dislike above all."

Neda looked at the car's GPS unit, and then asked, "What do you think we will find ahead?"

Vasilyev nodded. "A good question. Standard Pakistani military procedure for nuclear weapons transport calls for the use of well-paved secondary roads, not highways. A 'rolling roadblock' stops traffic a fixed distance ahead and behind the transports. It's easy to break down and reset the roadblocks because the transports rarely go even as fast as their top speed of fifty-five kilometers per hour."

"So, when we come across this roadblock, what do we do?" Neda asked.

Vasilyev grinned and gave Neda the answer she was dreading. It was the three words she had heard most often in training.

"Assess and improvise."

As Vasilyev said those words, Neda could see the roadblock ahead. She reached into her purse, removed her pistol, and rolled down her window. Next, she lowered her veil until only her eyes were visible, and folded her hands over the PSS-2 in her lap.

Vasilyev nodded approval and rolled down his window. His weapon was in a hidden compartment in the lower driver's side door. A tap of his knee at the right spot would reveal a GSh-18 pistol, with an eighteen round magazine. The compartment's placement put it out of easy view of a man standing outside the vehicle, and it was a fact that untrained opponents tended to fixate on their target's right hand.

There was a good reason for that, Vasilyev had to admit. His initial belief that learning to shoot left-handed would be easy had been . . . mistaken. Only dogged persistence and many hours of practice had finally allowed him first to meet and then exceed qualification standards. It helped that unlike many pistols, the GSh-18 had a reversible magazine release for left-hand shooters.

Vasilyev had been particularly annoyed to find that his new ability to shoot left-handed failed to translate to any other field. His mediocre tennis skills, for example, had not benefited at all from his weapons training. Unless amusing his opponent counted as a "benefit."

As he examined the soldiers coming into view, though, Vasilyev counted the training time that would let him make use of the hidden compartment as well spent. The GSh-18 pistol was one of the few capable of firing the armor-piercing 7N31 9 x 19mm round. All of the soldiers were wearing vests, and though headshots were preferable, they weren't always possible.

An angry red light winked on the satellite phone attached to a dashboard mount halfway between Vasilyev and Neda. Seeing Vasilyev's reaction, Neda had to ask.

"Does the light mean there's a problem with the phone?"

Vasilyev nodded. "Yes. There's a jammer nearby capable of blocking satellite as well as cell phone reception. To do that, the Taliban would need a truck-mounted system, probably a R-330ZH. It means the Pakistani soldiers, including the ones at this roadblock, won't be able to call for help."

Vasilyev would have much preferred talking his way through the roadblock but rated his chances as low. It's not that his cover story was so bad. There was a hospital about ten kilometers ahead, it was the only one close by, and he was going to claim his "wife" desperately needed medical attention. He was even going to suggest soldiers in one of the several vehicles manning the roadblock escort them to the hospital.

A close look at the soldiers at the roadblock changed Vasilyev's assessment of their chances of avoiding violence from "low" to "none."

Some of the soldiers' uniforms were too loose, and one was too tight, and several soldiers were poorly groomed. None of this was likely in the elite troops that the Pakistanis would assign to guard nuclear weapons in transit.

And Vasilyev's sharp eyes also spotted two soldiers with small dark patches on their uniforms. Their particular shade could have come from only one source.

Dried blood.

The attack was already underway. This roadblock was manned by Taliban fighters wearing the uniforms of the Pakistani soldiers they had killed, probably just minutes earlier. They were here to make sure no one interfered with the Taliban's assault on the nuclear weapons transports further up the road.

In a low voice, Vasilyev said "Zasada" in Russian to Neda.

Ambush.

The "soldiers" all had their rifles leveled at Vasilyev and Neda. There were five that Vasilyev could see, two on his side and three on Neda's. Poorly groomed they might be, but they all held their rifles like men who had used them before. And not on paper targets.

The tallest Taliban fighter approached Vasilyev slowly with his rifle aimed and his finger on the trigger. He said in Urdu, "Exit your vehicle with your hands raised. Slowly."

Vasilyev nodded rapidly. "Yes, officer. Please, my wife is very sick. Can you please direct us to another way to the hospital?"

The only response was a quick jerk of the rifle pointing away from the SUV to return a second later to its previous position pointing straight at Vasilyev's head. The meaning was unmistakable.

Out. Now.

Neda used her left hand to lift her veil, revealing both her face and the makeup she had applied on their way from Taxila. She hadn't worn makeup at all since leaving Iran since it would have looked ridiculous during her firearms, close-quarter fighting, and other FSB training.

Now, though, it served its purpose perfectly. Attractive even without makeup, with it Neda rivaled many of the actresses popular in Pakistani cinema.

Doing her best to appear both alluring and helpless, Neda asked, "Please, can't any of you help us? All we ask is directions."

Neda could see the three men closest to her having the same thought almost simultaneously, and then they glanced at each other to see if the others had been thinking the same thing.

The woman didn't have to die. At least, not right away.

With that thought, three rifles lowered almost involuntarily, as the men gripping them each thought about how they wanted Neda to spend her final minutes. Each of them also moved closer to Neda's side of the SUV.

Neda had often wondered during her FSB firearms training whether she would do as well shooting at people as at paper targets. After her lone female firearms instructor pronounced her qualified with the PSS-2 pistol, Neda had finally asked her the question.

The woman had shrugged and said, "Nobody knows for sure until they are in the moment. I think, though, if it is a question of survival for you or another agent, you will not fail."

Survival would have probably been reason enough. Neda was sure, though, that her steady aim and lack of hesitation were helped by the thoughts she could see in the faces of each of the men approaching her door.

When the tall Taliban fighter confronting Vasilyev heard three clicks in succession, followed by three impacts on the ground on the other side of the SUV, his head turned while he tried to understand the sounds. Was there a sniper? Had his men been shot, or were they seeking cover?

The brief distraction was all Vasilyev needed to retrieve his GSh-18 pistol from its hidden compartment. Vasilyev relieved the man of his confusion, and his life, with a single well-placed shot.

Before the other Taliban fighter on Vasilyev's side of the SUV had a chance to react, he had been killed by two shots. To Vasilyev's annoyance, his first shot only hit the man in the shoulder, though he did release his grip on his rifle. This gave Vasilyev the leisure to aim his next shot more carefully.

Vasilyev had no idea why he then had a sudden overwhelming impulse to duck and to pull Neda down low with him. But he obeyed it.

An instant later, both his driver's side window as well as Neda's side of the windshield exploded and showered them with glass fragments. Almost immediately afterward Vasilyev heard the distinctive "*craaak*" of a high-powered sniper rifle.

Neda tried to crouch even lower as the window in her car door disintegrated, followed immediately by most of what remained of the windshield. This time, though, even Neda, with her limited experience, recognized the round as coming from an ordinary semiautomatic rifle.

Of the type held by the men she had shot.

This thought was immediately followed by Neda's hearing movement outside her door. Indeed, though she had killed two of the three men she had targeted, the third had now regained consciousness. Neda's bullets were not armor-piercing, and so had failed to penetrate the third man's vest.

Another round from her side punched through the car door and passed just over Neda's head. A metal shard from the door sliced across her right cheek, covering her face with blood.

As Neda balled up her scarf and pressed it against her wound, she had just one thought. With shooters firing on both sides of their SUV, how could they survive?

CHAPTER NINE

29 Kilometers Outside Taxila, Pakistan

Anatoly Grishkov had finally received orders to proceed directly to the ambush site just before turning onto a highway that would have sent him in the wrong direction, which made him feel better about his decision to stop and assemble the sniper rifle.

Grishkov turned around a bend and spotted the roadblock up ahead. He could barely make out that a black SUV had been stopped there, and guessed the vehicle might contain Mikhail Vasilyev and Neda Rhahbar.

Grishkov considered accelerating forward as quickly as possible and instantly discarded the idea. He could never reach the roadblock in time.

Instead, Grishkov immediately pulled off the road at a sharp angle, pulled out the Chukavin sniper rifle, and flipped open its bipod. Then, he placed the gun on the hood of his SUV.

This was not a particularly busy road, but it did have some traffic. Only seconds after Grishkov had the rifle placed, another vehicle approached behind him.

The vehicle immediately slammed on its brakes, as soon as its driver saw what he was doing. Next, he reversed and executed an impressive J-turn that kept his car moving away from Grishkov.

Grishkov's briefing papers had included a reference to a Swiss study ranking Pakistan as the world's fourth-highest country in per capita civilian firearms ownership, with an estimated forty-four million guns in private hands. So, he wasn't surprised that most Pakistani drivers could be counted on to make the right decision when coming upon a man with a sniper rifle.

Grishkov also thought it was likely that the man could be relied on to warn other oncoming drivers, and to alert the authorities. The red light on Grishkov's satellite phone told him he wouldn't be able to, even if he hadn't been busy with other matters.

While he had these thoughts, Grishkov had been focusing his scope on the roadblock. He saw five armed men approach the SUV. The professional soldier in Grishkov made him shake his head at their poor tactical awareness.

Then Grishkov realized these were not soldiers at all. They must be Taliban, he thought to himself.

No sooner had Grishkov had this thought than all five Taliban fighters were down. Grishkov's relief changed to horror in an instant as a sniper round blasted through the driver's side door, and more bullets hit the SUV from the passenger side.

So far, Grishkov hadn't been able to spot the sniper. But the Taliban fighter who had picked himself up on the passenger side was another matter. A round from Grishkov's rifle put him back down, this time permanently.

Why hadn't the sniper fired again? With a target the size of the unmoving SUV, he could hardly miss.

Because he's an experienced sniper, Grishkov realized, probably one of the best the Taliban have. No sniper would live long enough in Afghanistan to become experienced if he stayed in the same spot while he fired multiple rounds. Moving after shooting would be an ingrained routine.

And, Grishkov thought to himself with a grim smile, his presence here proved that the practice had a purpose. You never knew who else might be out there.

So, if I were a sniper on the move, I would be heading . . . there.

No sooner had Grishkov completed the thought than the view in his scope included a bearded man lining up a shot on the SUV.

A shot Grishkov never gave him the chance to take.

Grishkov swept his scope around the roadblock but saw nothing else moving. Including inside the SUV, he thought with a frown. He could see it had taken damage, though not whether it was still drivable.

Well, nothing for it but to check for survivors. With that, Grishkov quickly put the rifle back in the SUV and gunned it towards its counterpart at the roadblock ahead.

Grishkov stopped well behind the other SUV and called out, "Vasilyev! It is Grishkov. Are you and Neda OK?"

The damaged SUV's driver's side door opened, and several glass fragments spilled out as Vasilyev emerged pistol in hand, his head swiveling side to side. Seeing no more Taliban fighters, he gestured for Grishkov to bring the other SUV closer.

Once the SUVs were side by side, Vasilyev jerked his head towards the cargo compartment of Grishkov's SUV. "Bring your medical kit," he said to Grishkov.

"Just curious," Neda said. "Don't we have one in this SUV?" As she asked this, she continued to press her scarf against her cheek, which had slowed but not stopped the flow of blood from her shrapnel wound.

Vasilyev nodded. "We do. But only Grishkov's kit contains the medication you need at this point."

Before Neda had a chance to ask more questions, Grishkov was at her side. Removing the scarf from her hand, Grishkov first did his best to clean and disinfect the wound. Then he quickly used an alcohol swab on her arm and injected her with a syringe.

"What's . . ." Neda started to ask. Grishkov shook his head. "Stitches first," he said firmly, taking the equipment he needed from the medical kit.

Neda grit her teeth as Grishkov began stitching her wound but was surprised that there was little pain. After he finished, Neda smiled and said, "Thank you. You're good at this."

Vasilyev did his best to suppress a smile, but not well enough to escape Neda's notice. "So, why is that funny?" she asked.

"It's not that Grishkov isn't an excellent medic. He learned the basics of combat medicine by necessity while serving in Chechnya, and certainly did a better job of stitching your wound than I could have. But that's not why you didn't feel much pain. There, you have the injection to thank," Vasilyev said.

Neda shrugged. "So, a painkiller of some type."

Now Grishkov intervened. "Yes, a strong one, coupled with a stimulant that is just as potent. You've lost some blood, and would soon feel faint and weak otherwise."

Neda started to frown, and then made herself stop as the pain from her stitches forced its way through the medication. Who knew frowning included cheek muscles? "But how long will these effects last?"

Grishkov rocked his hand back and forth. "I'm not sure, but probably about an hour or two. When I prepared the syringes, I had to guess dosage reduction due to your low weight."

Grishkov held up the empty syringe so that both Vasilyev and Neda could see it. The letter "N" had been written with a black marker on its side.

"There is one more syringe marked for you in case it's needed later in this mission. But you will get no more doses today. There is a price to pay, of course. After that hour or two, your body will shut down, and you will sleep for many hours," Grishkov explained.

Vasilyev gestured at the road behind them, and asked Grishkov, "Did you see anything suspicious on your way here?"

Grishkov shook his head. "No, so whatever weapons the Taliban managed to obtain must have taken another route. It's also possible the Pakistani military is still trying to hold them off since this roadblock was still in place."

Vasilyev turned to Neda. "Do you think you can continue? I must be honest and say our chances are not good. If the Taliban could leave this many men to guard their rear, they are likely to have many more up ahead."

Neda gave a small smile, even though she knew it would hurt. "Nuclear weapons in the hands of men like this?" she asked rhetorically, nodding towards the bodies of the Taliban fighters who had been leering at her a few minutes earlier.

"It will take more than a few stitches to stop me."

Vasilyev nodded soberly. Turning to Grishkov, he said, "Help me assemble the weapon I'm carrying. It should help even the odds at least a little."

The storage compartment in Vasilyev's SUV worked the same way as Grishkov's, and seconds later, its contents were revealed.

Vasilyev had never seen a smile so broad on Grishkov's face.

"They sent another one! After the rear echelon incompetence we had to put up with in Chechnya, I got used to expecting little and getting less. I'm starting to think we may have a chance." While he was saying this, Grishkov was removing pieces of the weapon from the compartment with Vasilyev's help.

"What makes this so special?" Neda asked.

Grishkov was still grinning. "This is the M133 Kornet anti-tank weapon. Since the launch tube is a little over a meter long, it had to be cut in half to fit in this compartment. This metal bracket fits the two halves together," Grishkov said, tapping the bracket.

Vasilyev added, "As you have probably guessed, our friend has used this before. Do you think it can stop something the size of the TELs that are being used to move the nuclear weapons?"

As he lifted the now assembled launch tube and examined it, Grishkov replied, "That depends. What kind of warhead came with this?"

Vasilyev smiled. "Thermobaric," he said.

"Then yes," Grishkov replied immediately.

Just as quickly, Neda asked, "Do I understand correctly that 'thermobaric' means this warhead will explode with substantial force once it strikes the TEL?"

Grishkov nodded. "Yes. 'Kornet' means 'Comet' and when you see a round impact you'll know why. Could I end up detonating one of the nuclear weapons it carries?"

Neda shrugged. "Probably not. The Pakistanis would have put safeguards in place against accidental detonation, including against something as simple as a highway accident. However, as Goldsboro showed, safeguards aren't perfect. You should aim for the TEL's rear compartment, as far from the warheads as possible."

Grishkov nodded. "I'd already planned to aim for the fuel tank, which is at the extreme rear of the vehicle."

Seeing Neda's horrified reaction, Grishkov smiled. "Unless you think that would be a bad idea."

Neda looked thoughtful and finally shrugged. "You might be able to disable the TEL just by shooting out one of its tires, but who knows? They might have a way to replace a tire. Or they might be able to remove the warheads from the missiles."

Then, she shook her head decisively. "No. We can't take a chance. Aim for the fuel tank. In the unlikely event a warhead does detonate, better it happen in this wilderness than in a city full of innocents."

Grishkov nodded and said, "If we live through this, you'll have to tell me what happened at Goldsboro."

Turning to Vasilyev, Grishkov said, "I know from your file that you're at least as good a shot as I am with a sniper rifle. Take Neda, the rifle and my SUV and get as far forward as you can without being spotted. I will follow with the Comet, which leaves no room for other passengers. I will use the Comet on a TEL as soon as I see an opportunity."

Next, Grishkov looked appraisingly at Neda, who returned his look with a defiant stare and raised chin. Nodding, Grishkov said, "Your file says you demonstrated an outstanding throwing arm on the grenade course. Were any of the grenades live?"

Neda mutely shook her head.

Grishkov shrugged. "Well, your training was abbreviated. Ready to join me up ahead and complete it?" he asked with a grin.

In spite of herself, Neda laughed. "Yes. And I know the stakes. Our lives, and the lives of thousands who could be killed if the Taliban is able to steal these weapons."

Grishkov nodded soberly and said, "Good luck to us all," as he carefully placed the Comet's launch tube diagonally so that one end rested in the front passenger seat and the other stuck out of the SUV's lowered rear window.

Vasilyev and Neda hurried to Grishkov's SUV and set off on the road ahead. Vasilyev looked back and saw Grishkov had been able to get their

SUV moving behind them in spite of the bullets that had removed most of its windows.

"Goldsboro?" Vasilyev asked, his gaze sweeping from side to side but so far seeing nothing.

Neda replied, "An incident in America in the 1960s. One of their planes that carried two thermonuclear bombs crashed near a town called Goldsboro. One bomb was destroyed in the crash. The other deployed its parachute and survived. It had four safeguards against accidental detonation."

Vasilyev sighed. "Let me guess. Three failed."

A look from Neda was all the confirmation he needed.

"Understood," Vasilyev said, glancing at the sniper rifle lying in the seat behind them. "Avoid shooting the warheads."

Chapter Ten

34 Kilometers Outside Taxila, Pakistan

Neda Rhahbar heard the distant crackle of gunfire first. She was about to tell Mikhail Vasilyev when he nodded. He heard it too.

"It appears the security force assigned to the weapons continues to resist," Vasilyev said. "Our chances of success have just gone up considerably."

As he said this, Vasilyev spotted a turnoff to a dirt road on the left. He couldn't be sure, but it appeared to lead to some hills overlooking the battle ahead.

Of course, if that were true, the Taliban would hardly have failed to notice it as well. He had only an instant to decide.

Vasilyev wrenched the steering wheel to the left and glanced behind him. Grishkov had made the turn as well.

It was a poor road, and as they bounced up and down its many potholes, Vasilyev was grateful for both the SUV's reinforced suspension and its four-wheel drive. Vasilyev guessed, correctly, that the road had been created only to remove logs from the area. Regrowth had proceeded far enough to obscure the road ahead, which twisted and turned its way up the route of least resistance.

A loud "*craaak*" up ahead told Vasilyev that the Taliban had indeed recognized the value of this location in their ambush, and immediately slowed. It wasn't easy, but Vasilyev was then able to find a gap in the trees off the road to his right large enough to wedge the SUV. He just had to hope that no Taliban were following, since the SUV was still clearly visible from the dirt road.

A few minutes later, Grishkov had pulled over as well and came striding up with the Comet slung awkwardly over his shoulder. He looked at Vasilyev and shook his head.

"They've probably put their best man on this hill. And unlike the sniper I took out, this one probably has a spotter to watch his back," Grishkov said in a low voice.

Vasilyev nodded. He'd had the same thought. Just as quietly, he replied, "I wish there were another way, but I don't see one. I'll have to work my way up the hill as silently as possible, and hope I see them before they spot me."

Grishkov shrugged. "Agreed," he said. His eyes narrowed, and he looked thoughtfully at Neda.

"How are you feeling?" he asked quietly.

"Fine," Neda replied, in a level voice that implied there was no need to ask.

"Good," Grishkov said with a smile. He handed Neda the case containing the Comet's single thermobaric round, plus their grenades. Then he draped a strap over her shoulders attached to the Comet's launch tripod.

"Believe it or not, this tripod is made out special metals, and the legs are partially hollow to reduce weight. It's intended for only one use. Still, I know it's not exactly light. But to lug this launch tube close to the

TELs, I'm going to need both hands free." Grishkov then pointed at a barely visible trail headed downhill. "Another set of eyes will come in handy as well."

Neda's response was to nod and put a fresh clip into her PSS-2 pistol.

In less than a minute, Grishkov and Neda were both far enough down the wooded trail that Vasilyev could neither see nor hear them. He hoped they were as hard for the Taliban to spot.

Vasilyev saw no trail leading conveniently uphill. So, the challenge was to locate the sniper and—probably—his spotter before they saw him.

Or Grishkov and Neda.

The road was clearly out of the question. That left the trees and brush on both sides of the road. It appeared a bit less dense to the left.

Vasilyev made his decision. Speed was paramount, so left it was.

Common sense said the sniper was at or near the top of the hill, an assumption confirmed by the evidence of Vasilyev's ears. The fact that so far he had heard only a single shot supported his guess that this was an experienced sniper.

Only fire when you are sure of your target. Remember that every shot helps the enemy fix your position. Staying in a single spot is the best way to help your widow collect an early pension.

Everything Vasilyev had learned in sniper school ran through his head as he laboriously made his way up the hill.

One other fact about the sniper's position was undeniable. It had to be on the side of the hill overlooking the enemy. And now he was moving straight as an arrow to the other side.

On the one hand, this would make his shot more difficult. On the other, a spotter would tend to focus on the most direct route up the hill.

Finally, Vasilyev judged that he had moved far enough up the hill to have a chance of spotting the sniper through his scope. No sooner had the thought formed than another "*craack*" warned him that time was short.

A reduction in the volume of fire below suggested that the transports' defenders probably wouldn't be able to resist much longer.

Vasilyev now faced the classic sniper's dilemma. He wanted a clear field of view. But he also needed concealment from the spotter he could feel in his bones was out there.

As he decided and took up his position, Vasilyev knew that this choice and mere seconds would separate success from failure.

Vasilyev found the spotter almost immediately because he had the good luck to have started searching just after the sniper had made his last shot. The spotter was on the move, and almost certainly, the sniper was too.

But Vasilyev couldn't see any trace of the sniper.

Patience, Vasilyev told himself. Once the spotter takes up position . . .

There! Vasilyev still couldn't see the sniper, but he could barely make out the end of his rifle barrel. And from that could work his way backwards to . . .

The spotter's gaze, augmented by binoculars, had begun sweeping across the hill as soon as they took up their new position. Now that gaze settled on . . . him. He'd been found!

There was no time for thought. Vasilyev pulled the trigger, and the spotter went down.

But the sniper had vanished.

Vasilyev knew he couldn't have gone far. He also knew that unless he abandoned his rifle, the sniper couldn't move fast. Would one of the Taliban's best snipers leave his gun, probably one he'd used for years?

No.

Holding his rifle, the sniper certainly wouldn't move down the hill towards the fighting. He probably wouldn't run towards the man who had just shot his spotter.

Human nature suggested moving in the opposite direction from an unknown threat, down the other side of the hill. If the sniper had done that, he was probably already out of Vasilyev's reach.

But what if the spotter had been a friend? Someone the sniper liked and trusted?

Then he might move down the hill directly away from the fighting, and try to flank Vasilyev.

All of these thoughts went through Vasilyev's mind in an instant. He then took what he knew was a wild guess about the sniper's position and fired.

If Vasilyev had hit him, there was no sign.

Now what?

With regret, Vasilyev carefully placed his rifle between a distinctive tree and a bush, which had overhanging branches making the rifle impossible to spot from a distance. Then he pulled out his GSh-18 pistol and made his way up the hill towards where he guessed the sniper was headed.

It was a straightforward race. If the sniper found a new perch quickly offering at least some concealment and a clear field of view, he could probably pick off Vasilyev before he was able to reach pistol range.

But if Vasilyev could find the sniper before then, at close range, his pistol would be far more effective than a sniper rifle.

Darting from one tree to another, Vasilyev tried to make as little noise as possible, while still keeping up a brisk pace. Though he managed this task reasonably well, Vasilyev thought with near despair that a marching band would have been quieter.

So, it was with astonishment that Vasilyev spotted the sniper prone on the ground, just bringing his rifle up to begin searching for him.

Vasilyev did not let him complete the motion. Three rounds from Vasilyev's pistol were enough for the sniper to drop his rifle and lay still.

When Vasilyev reached the body, he was grateful that his pistol had been loaded with armor-piercing rounds, since the sniper had been wearing a ballistic vest. He also saw a bloody gash on the sniper's leg that he knew hadn't come from his pistol rounds.

It explained how Vasilyev had won the race. His guess about the sniper's location had been sufficient to graze the Taliban fighter with the last round he fired from his rifle, and slow him down just enough.

Vasilyev picked up the sniper's rifle. He wasn't surprised to see it was a Dragunov rifle with a standard PSO-1 telescopic sight. Though inferior to the Chukavin sniper rifle he had been forced to abandon, it was still a capable weapon.

Vasilyev ran towards the front of the hilltop overlooking the battle below, thinking to himself that if Grishkov and Neda were still alive, they might be within Comet range by now.

He was sure they would appreciate some help.

Chapter Eleven

Anatoly Grishkov was impressed. He'd known plenty of men who would have had trouble keeping up with the pace he was setting through some fairly dense woods, particularly with the load Neda Rhahbar was carrying.

Even after a wound that had led to significant blood loss, Neda was matching him step for step, and was also taking care to make as little noise as possible. Based on his experience with his wife, Grishkov had often said to anyone who would listen that women were just as tough and capable as men if allowed to prove it. A pity, Grishkov thought, that few Russian men agreed.

As they drew closer to the scene of the ambush, Grishkov noticed that the combatants' rate of fire had started to slow. It could mean that one or both sides were beginning to run low on ammunition. Or men.

Grishkov mused that the Taliban had felt confident enough to leave a half-dozen fighters behind at their roadblock. So, more likely that the Pakistani defenders were about to be overwhelmed.

There! Grishkov had just spotted the paved road that had to mark the ambush site through a gap in the trees.

Grishkov lifted his hand and stopped, and was pleased to see that Neda followed suit immediately and silently. He gestured towards the case Neda was carrying, and she responded by putting her hand on one of the clasps that secured it and looking at him inquiringly. Grishkov nodded.

Neda carefully opened the case, revealing the single Comet round, as well as four grenades. Grishkov pointed at the grenades and gave Neda an enquiring look. She nodded vigorously.

Good. Grishkov was pleased to see Neda appeared confident. He had doubted whether the Taliban would give him the leisure to throw all of the grenades on his own.

Grishkov gestured for Neda to close the case, and they resumed their quiet and steady pace towards the ambush site. Finally, they were close enough to the road that Grishkov could see several vehicles. All were damaged, and one was burning.

And bodies. At least a dozen were lying on the road that Grishkov could see. Most were wearing Pakistani military uniforms, but some were Taliban.

Grishkov carefully laid down the Comet, and through gestures, communicated that Neda was to remain with the weapon while he scouted ahead. Neda nodded her understanding.

At first darting from tree to tree, Grishkov covered the last few meters crawling on his belly. He drew in his breath as the scale of the battle in front of him became clear. Grishkov had thought from the outset that an ambush would have been possible only if the Pakistanis had carelessly provided their nuclear weapons with a small escort.

Looking at the number of bodies he could now see strewn on and near the road, Grishkov had to admit he'd been wrong. If he'd been planning the transport operation himself, he wouldn't have assigned more men.

As he counted the number of Taliban bodies, Grishkov shook his head. How had they been able to assemble a force this size inside Pakistan? How did they know exactly when and where to strike?

A final flurry of gunfire about two hundred meters up the road brought Grishkov back to his present dilemma. The silence that followed it told Grishkov the battle was over. The handful of men he could see still moving . . . weren't wearing Pakistani uniforms.

Grishkov lay stock still as other Taliban fighters emerged from several different spots- including the forest on either side of him. All of them went to where the fighting had just ended.

The focus of the fighting had been a transporter erector launcher (TEL). Due to a bend in the road and an overturned vehicle obstructing Grishkov's view, it was only now that he could see even part of the massive vehicle.

So, unless the remaining Taliban were obliging enough to catch the two grenades Grishkov planned to throw their way, he was unlikely to remove enough of them on his own to let him set up the Comet for a clear shot at the TEL.

Even worse, he could see only one TEL. Unless the other one was so far ahead he couldn't spot it, the Taliban had already been able to hijack one of the TELs carrying nuclear weapons.

Grishkov made his decision. He could think of only one slim chance.

A few minutes later, Grishkov was back with Neda. His lips almost touching her right ear, Grishkov whispered his plan to Neda. Her eyes widened as she realized how unlikely it was to work, and then Neda shrugged acknowledgment.

Grishkov and Neda moved through the forest at the edge of the road towards the TEL. The challenge was balancing the need for speed against

THE END OF AMERICA'S WAR IN AFGHANISTAN · 117

the disastrous consequences of detection. Fortunately, this close to the road, there were few trees, and mostly brush that was reasonably easy to pass through, while still providing excellent concealment. Also, luckily, the attention of the surviving Taliban was focused on the TEL.

As Grishkov and Neda moved closer, they could hear the Taliban yelling to each other, and though Grishkov couldn't understand a word, it was apparent they were frustrated. Seeing his puzzlement, Neda tapped Grishkov's shoulder and gestured for him to stop and move closer.

Then Neda whispered in his ear, "They can't get it to start."

Grishkov grunted. That might give them a few more minutes.

It also tracked with what he saw several Taliban doing—looking through the pockets of dead Pakistani soldiers near the TEL.

Grishkov held up his right hand, and they both stopped. Peering through a gap in the brush Neda could see why. Not far ahead, the Taliban had expanded their search to the edge of the road.

Where they were now would have to be close enough.

Grishkov gestured for Neda to open the case. First removing the Comet round, he then handed two grenades to Neda and kept two for himself.

Next, Grishkov pointed to the Taliban on the roadside, the closest to their position. His finger then flicked to her.

Neda just smiled.

One of the Taliban on the side of the road triumphantly held up a bunch of keys he'd found. No doubt, Grishkov thought, thrown there as a last desperate gesture by a Pakistani soldier knowing they were about to be overrun.

The two other Taliban who had been searching the road's edge converged on the man holding the keys, laughing and pounding him on his back.

Grishkov lifted three fingers. Neda knew from her training what this meant. Throw on three.

Grishkov's expectations of Neda's grenade throwing skills were low. After all, she had only received abbreviated training and had no combat experience.

So, when Neda quickly threw the first grenade and then the other almost precisely in the center of the three nearby Taliban, he was pleasantly surprised.

The same could not be said for the three Taliban. Nor for the four Taliban near the TEL who had been the targets of Grishkov's two grenades.

Seconds later, Grishkov looked up. As far he could see, all of the Taliban who had been visible were down. Dead or wounded was impossible to tell at this distance, but he just needed them to stay down for another minute.

Grishkov then set up the Comet's tripod, attached the launch tube, and loaded the thermobaric round. His previous setup record in Chechnya had been forty-five seconds, and though he didn't bother to time his performance today, he beat it by two seconds.

Grishkov aimed the Comet at where his briefing had indicated the TEL's fuel tank should be located. As his hand reached for the trigger mechanism, he heard behind him, "click, click, click."

Grishkov wheeled around to see Neda in a two-handed firing stance, as well as two prone and unmoving Taliban fighters. Her concentration was absolute, Grishkov saw with approval, as her gaze and pistol swept the forest behind them.

Like anyone who had lived with firearms his entire life, Grishkov had believed there was no such thing as a genuinely silent pistol. It seems, he mused, the FSB has proved me wrong.

Though his first impulse was to say something encouraging to Neda —her performance so far had been outstanding—Grishkov's stronger instinct was to hurry up and fire the Comet. So he turned back around, to do just that.

Where the first thing that greeted his view was a tall, heavily bearded Taliban fighter lifting an AR-74 to eye level. Apparently, one of his grenades' victims had only been wounded. At his range, there was no way the Taliban fighter could miss.

As Grishkov's right hand moved towards a pistol he knew he would never reach in time, all he could think was how much he wished he could wipe that man's arrogant smile from his face.

"*Craack*," Grishkov heard an instant after a distant rifle shot threw the Taliban fighter backward onto the road.

"Well, apparently Vasilyev is still with us," Grishkov thought to himself, at the same moment that he pulled the Comet's trigger.

In a move he'd already planned, Grishkov turned around and tackled Neda, sending both of them to the ground. Once he had turned, Grishkov was propelled towards Neda by what felt like a giant hand on his back. Both of them were pressed together against the grass a bit harder than he'd intended.

Shrapnel whistled over their heads, and a wave of intense heat and pressure made Grishkov worry they might not be far enough from the explosion to survive.

Grishkov's concern only lasted a moment, though, and he was once again able to breathe. He rolled off of Neda and stood up, and was pleased to see her stirring.

"It appears the warheads did not detonate," Grishkov said, looking Neda over carefully as she slowly sat up.

Neda brushed her hair back from her face with her hands, wincing as she accidentally touched one of her stitches. Grishkov could see that the shot he had given her was beginning to wear off.

Neda shook her head tiredly. "We're not out of danger yet. It's true that if the safeguards were going to fail, it would have probably happened during that explosion. But one or more of the warheads may be intact and cooking as we speak," she said, gesturing towards the flaming debris that had been the TEL.

Grishkov grunted acknowledgment. He knew from experience that warheads and fires did not go well together. But he saw no way to do anything about it.

"How are we going to get out of here?" Neda asked.

Grishkov nodded. A good question. "I think Vasilyev is still alive, and given time, I think would retrieve our less damaged SUV and pick us up. But as you've noted, I think we should leave sooner if we can."

Neda shakily rose to her feet. "I suppose we should check to see if any of these vehicles are drivable." Looking around at the closest ones, she saw they were overturned, on fire, or riddled with bullet holes.

Grishkov nodded. "Yes, I think that's our best chance. I see nothing on this side of the TEL that looks promising. If we can get to the other side of it, though, maybe we'll see something that can still drive."

Neda shrugged acknowledgment.

Grishkov almost said something about the need to stay alert for danger, both from fire and secondary explosions, as well as any remaining Taliban fighters. One look at Neda's grim expression and the way she was carrying her pistol, though, convinced him that wasn't necessary.

Grishkov and Neda edged their way around the remains of the still-burning TEL, finally emerging on the other side of the smoke to see several vehicles. All but one were as heavily damaged as the ones on the other side.

Grishkov guessed, correctly, that this undamaged vehicle had brought many of the Taliban fighters who were still living when he had arrived on the scene with Neda. It was dirty, at least a decade old, and covered with the dents and scratches that marked any vehicle regularly exposed to Pakistani traffic.

Grishkov thought it was one of the most beautiful things he had ever seen.

As he walked towards the vehicle, Grishkov saw movement near one of the heavily damaged Pakistani military vehicles nearby and raised his pistol.

Grishknov lowered it when he saw that the motion had come from a man wearing a Pakistani uniform. But he remembered the roadblock Vasilyev and Neda had encountered manned by Taliban fighters wearing Pakistani uniforms, and so kept the pistol ready.

As Grishkov walked towards the man, he saw him try to play dead. Grishkov thought wryly that the man didn't have to play too hard, as the pool of blood from his wounds testified. Once Grishkov came next to him, the man abandoned the attempt and lunged for his nearby rifle.

Which Grishkov kicked away, saying cheerfully, "Is that how you say hello to your doctor?" He didn't think about it at the time, but Grishkov said this in Russian.

Turning to Neda, Grishkov said, "Ask him what happened here. Keep your pistol on him while I look in here for a medical kit."

The exchange that followed took only a few minutes and was finished by the time Grishkov emerged from the vehicle holding a medical kit. As he opened it, Neda said, "He says it happened just as we thought. An ambush with overwhelming force, and total surprise. They couldn't radio for help because all the frequencies were jammed."

Grishkov was already tightening the first of several bandages he'd need to stop the man's bleeding. "And he is a genuine Pakistani soldier?" he asked Neda.

Neda smiled. "Either that or the world's greatest actor."

Grishkov nodded. Good enough. He quickly finished bandaging the man and stood up. As he did, the man spoke rapidly, and Grishkov looked inquiringly at Neda.

"He says thank you, and wants to know who we are," Neda translated.

Grishkov shrugged. "Tell him if he wants to thank us, he'll forget we were here. Also, that we'll notify the authorities to send help as soon as we're out of jamming range."

But the man's eyes had already closed.

Neda leaned down and then stood back up with relief in her expression. "He's still breathing," she said.

"Good," Grishkov said. "These soldiers fought bravely against terrorists, and at least one should survive to tell their story."

Grishkov then gestured for Neda to come with him to the lone undamaged vehicle. As they drew closer, Grishkov could see it was a sizeable Japanese model SUV. He mentally crossed his fingers as he opened the driver's side door, which was conveniently unlocked.

Neda had never seen Grishkov smile with such genuine warmth. The source of his pleasure immediately became apparent.

"They left the keys in the ignition!" Grishkov said, and if anything, his smile broadened.

Neda looked puzzled but nodded and said nothing. Now Grishkov laughed.

"I know we've both been trained in starting this or any other car without keys. But it's a good omen that we don't have to bother," Grishkov said.

Grishkov pressed a button on the dash that caused the rear door to rise upwards. "Let's see if the owners left behind any presents," he said, moving to the SUV's now open back door.

Just moments later, Grishkov held up an AK-74 in triumph, which he passed to Neda. Then, he pulled out another AK-74 for himself. "These could come in handy if we run into more Taliban," he said.

Neda shrugged tiredly and sat down heavily in the front passenger seat, holding her AK-74 at the ready.

Grishkov placed his AK-74 carefully within arm's reach in the back seat, making sure the safety was engaged.

As Grishkov started the SUV, Neda asked, "Wouldn't all the Taliban have been here, at the site of the ambush?"

Grishkov shook his head as he carefully maneuvered the SUV around the other disabled and burning vehicles, finally emerging onto unobstructed roadway.

"Remember the roadblock you ran into before. There may be another in the other direction. Also, the radio jamming vehicle is around here somewhere and is sure to be guarded. I'm hoping that the Taliban found somewhere off this road to hide it, and we can drive out of its range without either of us seeing the other," Grishkov said.

Neda looked visibly unhappy but nodded.

Grishkov shook his head and laughed. "Truly, it's any Taliban ahead who should be worried. Just think of the odds we've overcome so far!"

Neda gave Grishkov a thoughtful look and finally smiled. "You're right," she said.

"Besides, it's time to give you some good news. Once we're out of jamming range, I'm going to call for a helicopter to get us out of here. By the time it arrives, I'm hoping that Vasilyev will have caught up to us," Grishkov said.

Neda knew better than to ask why she hadn't been told this previously. As the most junior team member, she was only told what she needed to know for security. Security . . .

"Why did you take the time to save that Pakistani soldier? Didn't it increase the chance that we'll be intercepted before we can get to the helicopter? Isn't it likely he'll describe us to the authorities?" Neda asked.

Grishkov glanced at the satellite phone display before he answered. Still no bars.

"Everything you have said is true. I'm expecting to hear it again, in more detail, from Vasilyev. I do regret putting you at risk, as well. But there is no way I could have let a fellow soldier bleed out when I could help," Grishkov said and then paused, clearly gathering his thoughts.

"Besides, you saw the bodies. If he and the other soldiers hadn't stood their ground and fought hard against nearly two to one odds, we would have had no chance of success against the Taliban fighters who remained. Put simply, we owed him," Grishkov concluded.

Neda shrugged. "When you put it that way, I have to agree."

Grishkov smiled. "Good. And it looks like we may get out of here after all. I have a bar," he said, pointing at the satellite phone display.

Lifting the phone from its cradle, he punched the single button programmed to call for extraction. "Yes, we are ready," Grishkov said and ended the call.

Neda lifted one eyebrow but said nothing.

Grishkov smiled. "It's not so complicated. The pilot will home in on the satellite phone's location, as fixed by GLONASS. So, we can keep driving away from the ambush site, and the helicopter will still have no trouble finding us . . ."

Grishkov's voice trailed off as he looked at the obstacles and signs blocking the road ahead. At least, he thought they were signs from their size and shape, but whatever they said was only printed on one side. The side facing away from them.

A paved road similar to the one they were on turned off to their right. With a bit of maneuvering, Grishkov was able to move the SUV off the road. Then, he took it around the obstacles that had been set up to stop traffic to the ambush site from this direction.

Grishkov was puzzled. From what he knew of people, there were always ones who ignored signs, including detours.

"Neda, please translate the signs," Grishkov asked.

Neda replied. "Detour. Road Construction. Explosives In Use."

Grishkov grunted. "Whoever set up this ambush was no fool. Those are signs that would not only turn away almost anyone but would help explain any sounds from the fighting that might carry this far."

Grishkov then turned right. It wouldn't hurt to change direction away from the ambush site.

"Does the FSB have helicopters on call in every country?" Neda asked, her tone making it clear she knew the answer.

Grishkov laughed. "I asked Vasilyev the same question. I will shorten his answer. Basically, in countries like this, where Russia has a significant interest, front companies are set up—doing things like renting helicopters. These companies carry on regular operations most of the time, and only a few people at the top know who finances and controls the company. They are called on for help only when truly necessary."

Neda frowned. "But isn't that expensive?"

Grishkov shrugged. "Not according to Vasilyev. He says that many of these front companies, including this one, actually turn a profit. It seems having a sponsor with deep pockets to back you is a real advantage in business."

Neda pointed at the satellite phone's display, and asked, "Are you sure the GLONASS system you're using instead of GPS can be counted on outside of Russia? I thought I read that after the Soviet Union's collapse, it had become unreliable."

Grishkov scowled. "Yes, the 1990s was a dark time for us in many ways. However, in the following decade, much money was spent to bring GLONASS back to worldwide coverage."

Grishkov paused. "Both as a soldier and police officer, I used it frequently, so I've been interested in GLONASS for a long time. It now accounts for a third of Russia's space budget. Maybe the best testimonial is that so-called GPS devices in the West also draw on GLONASS satellites to improve accuracy and reliability."

Next, Grishkov touched a button on the satellite phone, and the display showed three dots.

Tapping the display, Grishkov said, "The center dot is us. The fast-moving dot at the edge of the screen is the helicopter. The closer and slower dot is Vasilyev. Now that I know he made it out, we will find a good spot to pull off this road and wait for both him and the helicopter."

Neda smiled. "I was going to ask you how Vasilyev would know to make the turn onto this road. He has one of these phones too."

Grishkov nodded absently; his attention focused on the road ahead. Just minutes later, he saw a dirt road turnoff that looked promising. As he had hoped, less than a kilometer down the road, the trees and brush that lined the paved road gave way to a clearing with dirt, small rocks, and occasional tufts of grass.

And Grishkov was confident it would be large enough for the helicopter to make a safe landing.

Grishkov looked again at the display, and said with satisfaction, "Vasilyev made the turn. He should join us about the same time as the helicopter."

No sooner had he said this than both of them could hear sirens approaching the turnoff they had used moments before. The sirens didn't hesitate and continued.

Straight to Vasilyev.

Neda looked at Grishkov and asked, "What should we do?"

Grishkov grimaced and replied, "I follow the Russian Orthodox faith, and I understand you are Muslim, yes?"

Neda whispered, "Yes."

Grishkov shrugged, and said thoughtfully, "I suggest we both pray."

The dot on the screen representing Vasilyev stopped. Long minutes passed, and the dot stayed right where it was.

And then finally began to move towards them again.

Neda pointed at the dot and exclaimed happily, "He's OK!"

Grishkov shook his head. "Possibly. But they could have taken him into custody, and sent his vehicle back with one of their officers to be searched at their station."

Grishkov paused. "Or they might have found Vasilyev's satellite phone and be using its display right now to track us."

Now Neda looked angry. "You know the stereotype of Russians is that you're always gloomy. I think you enjoy proving them right."

Grishkov first looked startled, and then laughed. "Well, from childhood, we're taught to expect the worst and be pleasantly surprised if we're wrong. Long winters, decades of Stalin and his gulags, followed by decades of threatened nuclear war—maybe it's no surprise our outlook is not so cheerful."

Neda cocked her head. "I think I hear the helicopter," she said.

Grishkov listened intently, and said, "I don't . . ." just as they could both see the helicopter appear in the distance. A few seconds later, Grishkov could hear it as well.

"Well done," Grishkov said. "A talent that will serve you well in this business."

Neda frowned. "What if Vasilyev is in that car, and doesn't get here in time? Isn't the pilot likely to insist that we leave right away?"

Grishkov shrugged. "I'm not concerned. I'm sure we can get him to listen to reason."

Neda looked at him, and her eyes narrowed, but Grishkov said nothing further.

"I was expecting you to do something dramatic, like pulling out your gun," Neda said as she looked intently at the dot on the screen showing the position of Vasilyev's vehicle. It would arrive after the helicopter.

Grishkov shook his head. "You've been watching too many American movies. Violence only makes sense in response to violence. After all, if policemen like me shot every suspect, what would be left for lawyers and judges to do?"

Neda's tart reply was drowned out by the sound of the helicopter as it landed in the clearing less than a hundred meters away.

Grishkov said calmly, "Go to the helicopter and tell the pilot I'll be just a minute because I have to gather our belongings. And his bonus."

Neda was about to ask a question. Then, she looked at Grishkov's smile and instead gave an exasperated sigh and bent over to walk towards the helicopter.

At least Grishkov hadn't insulted her intelligence by telling her not to hurry.

Grishkov looked at the satphone display as though he could force Vasilyev's vehicle to move faster.

It didn't work.

Grishkov opened the door and walked to the back of the battered SUV. Lifting its rear hatch, he pulled random items from the trunk to look like he was "gathering their belongings."

Then he kicked himself. Hard. He called himself a policeman!

It had never even crossed his mind to do a thorough search of the vehicle, rather than just a quick look for weapons. A car that had been used by Taliban terrorists.

Of course, over the past forty-eight hours, Grishkov had only slept on the two-hour flight from Tajikistan. That thought never even crossed his mind, consumed as it was with self-criticism.

A map. Covered with notes. And Grishkov had come this close to leaving it behind.

Grishkov hurriedly emptied the rest of the trunk but found nothing else remotely useful.

There was nothing in the backseat. The glove compartment was empty.

Grishkov's breathing slowed. OK, he thought to himself acidly, at least I almost missed just one incredibly vital clue.

Vasilyev's SUV pulled into the clearing, and Grishkov was relieved to see that Vasilyev was the driver and the vehicle's only occupant.

Grishkov was about to blame himself again for letting himself be distracted by the search for clues when he shook his head. Pointless, and if the car had been full of Pakistani soldiers, all he had to stop them with was one rifle anyway.

Vasilyev and Grishkov ducked low and ran together to the helicopter.

CHAPTER TWELVE

Pakistan Secretariat, Islamabad, Pakistan

Hamza Shadid still looked like what he had been for most of his working life. A handsome actor with a neatly trimmed beard and mustache, who had played many roles in dramas and action movies for over two decades.

Making the transition to politics had been done before in many countries. In Pakistan, where a cricketer had already made it to the Prime Minister's office, it had not been so difficult.

The stern and forbidding expression that had looked out from a million movie posters was now trained on the General standing at attention before him.

Hamza had not offered General Ehsan Monir a seat. Nor, given the news he brought, was he going to do so.

"So, General, let me see if I understand your report correctly so far. The Taliban have destroyed four of our Babur nuclear cruise missiles. Four of our Nasr tactical nuclear missiles have been stolen, and we have no idea where they are. Every soldier in the missile's security detail but one was killed, and he was severely wounded. Does that sum up the situation?"

Ehsan hesitated, and said slowly and carefully, "Yes, four Babur missiles were destroyed, but maybe not by the Taliban. We think the Taliban did steal the four Nasr missiles. I was going to explain this next."

Hamza scowled and gestured for him to continue.

"We found evidence that someone attacked the Taliban force besides our security detail. A roadblock the Taliban set up well apart from the fighting had all of its members killed, but none of our soldiers' bodies were anywhere near. A Taliban sniper and his spotter were both killed. Again, far from where our soldiers were fighting to defend the missiles. But the most telling evidence is a Russian missile launcher we found hidden not far from the destroyed Babur missiles and their launch vehicle," Ehsan said.

"What is so special about this missile launcher? Surely the Taliban have many Russian weapons. So does our military," Hamza observed.

"Yes, sir," Ehsan acknowledged. "However, this one had been specially modified. Our experts believe only a small number exist and are only available to Russian special forces."

Hamza's scowl deepened. "So, you believe Russian soldiers destroyed four of our most capable nuclear weapons? In cooperation with the Taliban?"

Ehsan shook his head. "No, sir. What we've been able to piece together so far suggests they did it for another reason. Most likely, to keep the missiles out of the hands of the Taliban. Especially because of the number of dead Taliban around the destroyed missiles, with injuries that make it clear they were caught up in their explosion. And there is the testimony of the lone surviving soldier."

Hamza was startled. "I thought he was near death. He has regained consciousness, then?"

Ehsan nodded. "Yes, sir. The doctors have upgraded his condition, and now believe he will survive. They also say he would not have if it weren't for the medical care he received before the relief force arrived."

"So, what did the soldier have to say, General?" Hamza asked.

"He said that the man who bandaged him was Russian. He says he knows this because he used the Russian term for 'doctor.' He says that's the only word of Russian he knows because his doctor when he was a child, was given that as his nickname. The doctor did his medical training in Moscow," Ehsan replied.

Hamza grunted. "Wasn't he in shock from blood loss at that point?"

Ehsan shrugged. "Yes, sir. One other detail. He says that there was a woman with the Russian."

Hamza stared at Ehsan. "Really?" was all he could manage through his astonishment.

Ehsan nodded. "Yes, sir. A beautiful woman with fresh stitches across one cheek, who spoke Urdu with a Baloch accent. He said she could have been either Pakistani or Iranian."

Hamza leaned back in his chair and looked thoughtful. "If it was a hallucination, it was a remarkably detailed one."

"Yes, sir, we thought so as well. Finally, our doctors say that the bandages applied to our soldier saved his life, but were not done by a trained doctor or nurse. They say the treatment was the sort they would expect to see from someone specifically trained in combat medicine, like a soldier. However, none of our other soldiers survived," Ehsan said.

"Very well, General, let's say you're right, and these were Russians trying to stop the Taliban attack on our weapons. Why would they bother? And why not warn us instead?" Hamza asked.

Ehsan shrugged. "Sir, I can only guess. But I can't imagine the Russians would be happy at the prospect of a nuclear-armed Taliban that might share those weapons with other terrorists like the Chechens. As for warning us, would we have listened?"

Hamza frowned and was silent for a moment while he thought about Ehsan's points. He was probably right that the Russians would see a Taliban with nuclear weapons as a threat. And if the Russian ambassador had come to him with a warning, wouldn't he have looked hard for an ulterior motive from a long-time Indian ally?

And probably waited too long to pass the warning to the military? Hamza was suddenly glad that the Russians hadn't tried to warn him, and made him directly responsible for this disaster.

Aloud, Hamza said, "Well, let's leave the Russian question aside for the moment. What are we doing to get back the stolen nuclear weapons?"

"We have set up a search perimeter based on the speed of the vehicle transporting the missiles, and when we believe they were captured. I have put in command my best and most experienced officer in such matters. That officer will be assisted by one of the head technicians at our nuclear weapons production facility. We will continue until every one of the weapons is recovered," Ehsan said confidently.

Hamza frowned. "And what is to stop the Taliban from using the weapons immediately?"

Ehsan shook his head. "All of our experts assure me that is impossible. A code is required to fire the missiles. That code did not travel with the missiles, either in writing or in the head of anyone accompanying the weapons."

Hamza looked far from convinced. "The Taliban are not fools. Why would they go to so much trouble and lose so many men if they couldn't use the missiles?"

Ehsan nodded. "You are even more right than you know, sir. It's not just that our escort was outnumbered by two to one. We have been able to identify most of the Taliban dead because they are in our leadership files. These were the best men they had, and many were from the Afghan Taliban. Losing them will be a heavy blow."

Hamza's shoulders slumped. "So, there must be a way to use the missiles."

"Yes, sir. Our experts say there is, but it would mean removing the missiles' warheads, and then rigging a different means of detonation. That would require a substantial amount of technical knowledge and practical training in how these weapons work," Ehsan said.

Hamza paled. "General, have any of our nuclear technicians failed to report to work?"

Ehsan smiled grimly. "An excellent question, sir. When I asked it, at first, I was relieved that the answer was no. Then I asked if any of the technicians were on previously authorized leave, and was told that two were on vacation. We located one with his wife and children visiting his parents. The other is nowhere to be found."

Hamza nodded. "And is there any way this man could have obtained information about the timing and route of this convoy?"

"He was on the team that prepared these missiles for transport, so it appears the answer is yes," Ehsan replied.

"How long do we have before they can make use of the warheads?" Hamza asked.

Ehsan shook his head. "I'm not sure, sir, but if they have prepared well, I'm told it could be only hours before they remove the warheads, and then they will become much harder to find. That's why we're making a maximum effort to find them now."

Hamza nodded. "Who else knows about this?"

"The two I mentioned who are leading the search. Also, the troops who responded to the attack and secured the scene. I have confined those troops to base until we recover the weapons. I've also closed the affected road until we have time to remove all evidence of the attack. I'm sure there will be rumors, but there always are, and we can deny them," Ehsan replied.

"What is our cover story?" Hamza asked.

Ehsan shrugged. "I believe it's always best to stick as close to the truth as possible. Our troops have been told they are searching for stolen missiles with conventional warheads, and to be careful not to shoot at them. Since many of our missiles can be fitted with either conventional or nuclear warheads, even after we find them, nobody will be able to prove any different," Ehsan said with a smile.

"General, you seem very confident of success," Hamza said with a scowl.

Ehsan's smile didn't waver. "Yes, sir. I told you I put my best people in charge of the search. They've never failed me before, and with the stakes this high, I know they're not going to start now."

Hattar Industrial Estate, Pakistan

Colonel Azita Kamar was the highest-ranking investigator reporting directly to the Judge Advocate General (JAG) Branch at the Ministry of Defence. Pakistan was the only Muslim country with a significant number of high-ranking female officers as well as female soldiers in combat. Azita had served in combat against the Taliban and received the Sitara-I-Jurat (Star of Courage) for rescuing two wounded soldiers under heavy Taliban fire after being wounded herself.

No matter how much grim determination she applied to her physical therapy, Azita's injuries left her with a stiff left arm that required her to transfer out of a combat specialty. She had accepted the transfer to the JAG Investigations Branch, and applied the same zeal there that had served her well in battle.

Azita's severe haircut and perpetually stern expression had not stopped several of her fellow officers from attempting to strike up a relationship with her. After all, no matter how hard she tried to disguise it, Azita was remarkably attractive.

And nothing, it seemed, could prevent her mother from ambushing her with "suitable men" at family dinners. Or showing her photos of other "suitable men" who would love to meet her.

Azita had gone on a few dates, but the truth was none of the men she'd met held the slightest interest for her. No man was going to give her orders once she had finished with duty for the day. No matter how pleasant her suitors might be at first, once married, she knew that was inevitable.

When General Ehsan Monir had called Azita a few hours ago, she'd thought it would probably be about another theft of military equipment of the sort the officers she supervised had investigated successfully many times before.

Azita quickly realized that for the first time in many years, she would need to oversee the investigation of this theft in person. Also that failure would not only end her career but could result in the deaths of thousands of innocent men, women, and children.

And that if she could only manage almost to catch the thieves, so she was nearby when one of the warheads detonated, one of those thousands could include her.

For all these reasons, Azita was highly motivated. Enough so that when she had been called at home, she had gone straight to the industrial estate in her personal car, an unremarkable dark green Japanese sedan.

So far, it was evident that motivation wasn't there for the man in front of her. Maybe it was because Senior Technician Nasir Cheema had spent too much time with his weapons, and become too comfortable with them. Whatever the reason, Azita had to change his attitude, and quickly.

Azita looked over Nasir with barely disguised contempt, to which Nasir appeared utterly oblivious. She considered Nasir a prime example of what happened when there was no military draft, as there had never been in Pakistan. Men like Nasir had never learned discipline of any kind.

Yes, she would have given a lot to put Nasir and the other Pakistani men like him through boot camp. Maybe then he'd have avoided the excess kilos he carried around in his belly and his perpetual slouch. It probably wouldn't have helped with either his need for thick glasses or the premature baldness in his 30s.

In fact, Azita's exasperation was rapidly giving way to anger.

"Look, you've got to help me narrow down our search. There are over four hundred companies in this industrial estate, almost all with multiple buildings, scattered across over four square kilometers. Even with all the men I have looking, it will take too long to find the TEL if we have to look everywhere," Azita said, visibly trying to rein in her temper.

Nasir shrugged. "That TEL is pretty big. The launch tubes were covered with canvas for transport, so it's true nobody would have any reason to think it was carrying missiles. But somebody must have noticed something that size. I'm sure it will turn up. They can't fire the missiles without the codes anyway."

Azita could have put Nasir on the ground as quickly as she could tie her shoes, and for a second, actually imagined how pleasant that would be. For her, anyway.

But it wouldn't help Azita accomplish her mission.

Then a realization hit her.

"Were you briefed before you came here?" Azita asked.

Nasir shook his head, puzzled. "No, they just told me someone had stolen a TEL carrying Nasr missiles and threw me in a car to take me to you. I figured I'm just supposed to make sure the missiles weren't damaged after you find them."

Azita nodded. "So, nobody told you about Ibrahim Munawar?"

Nasir frowned. "What about him? He's on vacation."

Azita smiled grimly. "No, he's not. He's working with the Taliban on these missiles."

Now Nasir drew himself up indignantly. "That's ridiculous! He's one of our best new technicians! Very hard working, always asking questions . . ."

Nasir's voice trailed off, and he looked like someone had just punched him in the stomach. Then he looked off in the distance and mumbled, "Oh no, that's why he wanted to know . . ."

Nasir's gaze then settled on Azita, and she was gratified to see that it was wide-eyed and close to panic.

That was the appropriate attitude for their current situation.

"This is very bad! Ibrahim is going to remove the warheads! Then he can rig another means of detonation! He won't need the codes!"

OK, Azita needed him near panic, not in shock.

"I understand," Azita said, in her best attempt at a soothing voice. "I have dozens of men here looking. All I need from you is a better idea of where to focus the search."

Nasir nodded and was now finally concentrating on doing just that. "They have Geiger counters?" he asked.

Azita nodded.

Nasir shook his head. "They won't help much. When the warheads are removed from the missile casing, you might get a reading, but from outside a metal building maybe not even then . . ."

His voice trailed off, but Azita could see he had a new thought.

"OK, you need to search for buildings that have a ground floor ceiling clearance of ten meters or more."

Azita frowned. "OK, but why? I've seen the specifications for these TELs, and they're not nearly that tall."

"Because the missiles are clamped and locked into their launch tubes when they are horizontal for transport. They are unlocked automatically when the launch tubes are elevated for firing," Nasir explained.

Azita nodded and pulled out her radio, quickly giving new orders to her men.

Once that was done, she asked, "When you need to remove the missiles for maintenance, do you have to elevate the launch tubes?"

Nasir shook his head. "No. The maintenance facility has an access code specific to each TEL that will unlock the tubes' interior clamps."

Azita frowned. "Then why not require a code to elevate and unlock the tubes?"

Nasir shrugged. "That was proposed but rejected. Remember that a code is required to launch the missiles. The clamps are present primarily to keep the missiles from shifting inside the tubes while the TEL is moving up and down hills during transport. Not to keep the missiles from being stolen."

Azita shook her head. "It still seems like an elementary precaution."

Nasir smiled. "Well, imagine you're in command of the TEL when war with India starts, and you get the order to fire. You know the Indians have satellites dedicated to tracking our TELs, and Indian bombers are on their way to take you out before you can launch. A code is already necessary for you to fire. Would you welcome another code just to elevate your launch tubes?"

Azita grunted. "I see your point."

"Besides, they're going to need a hoist with some serious weight capacity and plenty of room to work in first to remove the missile from its launch tube, and then remove its warhead. Until you told me about Ibrahim, I didn't understand why anyone would even try. Rigging a new detonation mechanism for a tactical nuclear weapon isn't something I'd have thought any terrorist could do," Nasir said.

"But you think this Ibrahim can," Azita said.

"Oh, yes," Nasir said bitterly. "I was one of the technicians who helped train him. He worked very hard, and asked lots of questions, including many I didn't understand at the time. Well, now, I do. If he has enough time, Ibrahim will be able to rig the warheads for detonation. But he'll have one big problem."

Azita cocked her head. "What's that?"

"Accidental detonation. He won't be in a government lab with the latest equipment. Instead, he'll be using short cuts and 'whatever works.' Oh, he knows enough to rig the warheads to explode. Getting the warheads safely to their targets before they do? That will be a lot harder," Nasir said, with a look of grim satisfaction.

Azita winced but said nothing. Nasir might be happy that Ibrahim was likely to fall victim to his work.

But she was much more worried about who else might happen to be in a random blast zone.

CHAPTER THIRTEEN

The Kremlin, Moscow

"Thank you for seeing me on such short notice, Mr. President," Smyslov said.

The President nodded, and gestured for Smyslov to have a seat on the ornate antique sofa across from his equally expensive chair. This was his official office, designed to impress visitors. The fact that they were here told Smyslov this would be a short meeting.

"I always have time for the FSB Director. As you know, I have great respect for the position."

This was a reference to the fact the President had occupied the job himself not so long ago. And kept a gimlet eye on its current occupant.

As it happened, though, Smyslov had no political ambitions. The President knew this. It was one of the main reasons, along with unquestioned competence, that Smyslov had his job.

"You have seen the report from our agents in Pakistan," Smyslov said flatly.

The President simply nodded.

"So, we were able to destroy the four most powerful nuclear weapons before they could be stolen by the Taliban. The same Tajik courier plane one of our agents used to enter Pakistan has safely removed all three of our agents to Dushanbe, and they are now en route to our base near the Afghan border. The question, Mr. President, is what we should do next," Smyslov concluded.

The President frowned. "Do next? Surely we have done enough already. I had grave misgivings about intervening at all, and only the prospect of a Taliban armed with nuclear weapons finally made me do."

Almost too late to matter, Smyslov thought to himself silently. Aloud, he said, "Four tactical nuclear weapons still remain in Taliban hands. It is of course up to the Pakistani authorities to recover them. But if they fail, and the Taliban are able to move the weapons out of Pakistan, I think we should be ready to take action."

If anything, the President's frown deepened. "By 'out of Pakistan' you mean Afghanistan, since nowhere else makes sense for the Taliban. Surely, that is a problem for the Americans."

Smyslov looked at the President levelly. "You know we have a capability the Americans lack."

The President leaned back in his chair and sighed. "Yes. You and I are among the very few who knows it exists. And if we help the Americans, we may reveal it to them."

Smyslov nodded. "We cannot prevent their suspicions. But if we keep our own agents in play, we can claim they are the source of the information."

The President shrugged. "I've always thought an FSB Director must be . . . ruthless. But putting the same agents into Afghanistan so soon after Pakistan? On the other hand, we certainly want as few people as possible to know anything about this."

"Precisely, Mr. President. And who knows? They may get lucky."

Smyslov and the President smiled at each other.

Creech Air Force Base, Nevada

Air Force Lt. Colonel Emmanuel Wainwright was not happy. Far from being unusual, for years, it had been Manny's natural state.

He had never cared for either Emmanuel or Manny. He liked the call sign his Air Force Academy classmates awarded him, Weasel, even less.

After a promising early start, over the past decade, his career progress had first slowed and then stalled. Now only one more performance review stood between Wainwright and compulsory retirement.

With two children in college and a hefty mortgage payment due every month, Wainwright had no idea how he could pay his bills if he was forced out of the only job he'd ever had.

For most pilots like Wainwright, the answer would have been easy. Go to work flying for an airline. Though not impossible, that choice had been made much more difficult by his decision years ago to make the career switch from manned to unmanned aircraft.

Wainwright had seen the move as the best way to restart his slow career progress. Instead, it had stalled it completely.

The problem was simple. Early in Wainwright's career as a pilot, he had been judged strictly by his skills in the air, and in fact, he was a natural aviator.

When he was promoted to command over other pilots, though, he needed a completely different set of skills. That Wainwright didn't have.

However, Wainwright refused to believe that lack of what his evaluations called "leadership ability" was the problem. Instead, he thought he was being held back by the increasing emphasis on drones by the Air Force. So, he switched to that field.

It turned out that Wainwright's friction with the young drone operators was even worse than with his fellow pilots. Rather than providing a restart, his career stalled altogether.

Worse, years out of the cockpit put Wainwright at a disadvantage in the fierce competition for pilot positions with the airlines flying out of Las Vegas' McCarran Airport. His mortgage was more than his house was now worth. So, if the Air Force made him retire, he would have to compete for a job at that sole airport.

The truth was, Wainwright didn't blame the airlines for preferring the many Air Force pilots with much more recent experience, including some who were leaving the service after one or two tours and so were far younger.

Retraining a military pilot to fly a commercial jet cost airlines serious money. Why spend it on a pilot who hadn't flown in years, and who didn't have many flying years left?

Wainwright had pulled every string he had left to get the job he had now, commanding drone operations at Creech Air Force Base. He believed his best chance of getting promoted was, above all, to avoid serious errors being made by anyone under his command. That meant doing things by the book.

The officer standing at attention in front of him, Captain Josh Pettigrew, embodied everything Wainwright hated. Pettigrew had spent most of his time in the Air Force as an NCO. Then he had been accepted to Officer Candidate School (OCS).

So, not an Air Force Academy graduate. For Wainwright, strike one.

Pettigrew had been forced on Wainwright as his deputy over his preferred candidate for the position. Strike two.

Pettigrew's performance file had redactions during the time he served in Korea and Saudi Arabia, so on paper, he was largely an unknown quantity.

Wainwright had spoken to his few remaining friends about Pettigrew's career. Twice he had been told bluntly to stop asking if he knew what was good for him.

The third time Wainwright was told that Pettigrew had broken every rule in the book in Korea but that he had escaped punishment because of his successful performance in combat.

The same friend told him that nobody would talk on the record about Pettigrew's time in Saudi Arabia. But there was a rumor that the Commander in Chief himself had ordered Pettigrew's assignment to OCS, and then seen to his subsequent promotion to Captain. No doubt, friends in high places had also landed Pettigrew his job as Wainwright's deputy.

That much was a rumor. Wainwright's friend said he knew for a fact that the General in command of U.S. forces in Saudi Arabia had been relieved and subsequently forcibly retired because of Pettigrew.

But he didn't know why.

At that point, Wainwright had heard more than enough. A very emphatic strike three.

Keeping his expression as neutral as possible, Wainwright welcomed Pettigrew to the base and told him the high priority he placed on following all Air Force rules and regulations to the exact letter. Wainwright also encouraged Pettigrew to see him if he was ever in doubt on that point.

Pettigrew had said he understood, looked forward to serving under Wainwright's command, saluted and left. On the surface, it seemed everything Wainwright had been told was wrong.

Wainwright was willing to bet it would be just days until his friend was proved right.

CHAPTER FOURTEEN

Hattar Industrial Estate, Pakistan

Colonel Azita Kamar knew in her bones that this search was taking too long, as she stood watching one of her teams knocking down yet another warehouse door. She didn't need the increasingly agitated Senior Technician Nasir Cheema at her elbow to tell her so.

But Nasir didn't seem to understand this.

"By now, he's had time to remove at least one of the warheads. He's probably working on the second one right now," Nasir said. It was clear from his expression that he imagined the process underway while he spoke.

Partly to distract Nasir and partly from genuine curiosity, Azita asked, "How exactly will Ibrahim remove the warheads?"

Nasir shrugged. "They are designed for easy removal if you know what you're doing. And Ibrahim does. Most of our missiles are designed to fit either conventional or nuclear warheads to keep the Indians guessing. We switch out the warheads from time to time for the same reason —to make it that much harder for the Indian enemy to know which missiles are worth targeting."

Azita frowned. "It all sounds very complicated. Is it really necessary?"

Nasir's head bobbed up and down emphatically. "Oh, yes. India has far more nuclear weapons than we do and is building more faster than we can. If we don't use every trick in the book, pretty soon you and I will be speaking Hindi."

Azita arched one eyebrow upwards but said nothing in response.

Another thought occurred to her, one she knew Nasir wouldn't like.

"What could Ibrahim do to speed up the warhead removal process?"

Nasir frowned. "Well, if he had space, he could put hoists on both sides of the TEL and remove two missiles at a time. But he would need a lot of help. Plus, he'd have to have trained at least one person up to his level of competence in missile handling and warhead removal. No easy task."

Then he gnawed on his lower lip. "But if anyone could manage the task, it would be Ibrahim."

Azita nodded. "What are we looking for, then?"

"The bigger the building, the better for Ibrahim. If he has two hoists and two crews, one on each side of the TELs for missile removal, plus men ready to start removing warheads two at a time as soon as the missiles are out of the tubes, he's going to need . . . a lot of room."

Azita grabbed her radio and walked away from Nasir, speaking rapidly. A few minutes later, she was back and gestured for Nasir to sit in her car as she started its engine.

"I've put the search priority on the largest buildings here, instead of trying to search for any building Ibrahim could be using more methodically. We're going to gamble that he's trying to remove the warheads two at a time," Azita said.

Nasir shook his head. "If that's what he's doing, he could be almost done removing all four warheads by now."

Azita didn't respond, but instead asked, "You've told us that we should avoid firing near the end of the TEL furthest from the driver's cab since that's the end holding the warhead. Any other area we should avoid?"

Nasir's eyes widened. "Yes, yes! Avoid hitting the TEL's fuel tank, below the driver's cab. We wanted to armor it, but couldn't because of the weight."

Azita nodded. "The biggest building here is occupied by a cement factory, and their main warehouse door is wide open, so we can see that's all it is. We're now arriving at the second largest. It's locked up tight, and nobody's answering their phone."

Then Azita grinned fiercely. "We're not going to knock."

The Talha armored personnel carrier Azita had requested nearly an hour before had finally arrived. She had been told by the officer in charge not to expect it sooner since its top speed was only forty kilometers per hour.

However, what the APC lacked in speed it made up for in sheer mass. Since the Talha weighed over twelve tons fully loaded, the warehouse door would be . . . no real obstacle.

Azita walked up to the squad leader and passed on Nasir's warning about the TEL's fuel tank. The caution was quickly conveyed, and the APC rolled towards the warehouse door at its top speed.

The door crumpled like tinfoil.

Inside it was the TEL, two hoists, and four missiles laid out on makeshift tables. Azita could immediately see that all four were missing their warheads.

There were also over a dozen men inside, who had been preparing to leave. Besides several who had been knocked flat by the collapsed warehouse door.

Azita's troops gave the men no chance to reach their weapons. None of the Taliban tried to surrender.

Minutes later, the Taliban fighters were all either dead or injured. Azita had ambulances ready for the injured, which included only a single one of her soldiers.

Azita would question the Taliban survivors, but based on her past experiences doubted she would learn anything worthwhile. The Taliban were big believers in giving information only to those needing to know it. And even those who knew something would die rather than betray their "brothers."

Azita spoke rapidly into her radio and then gestured for Nasir to exit her car, where she had told him to stay during the assault.

"Based on what you told me before about the size of the warhead, I've told my men to search all vehicles trying to leave this industrial park the size of a large van or a truck of any size. Do you agree?"

Nasir stared at the warehouse interior and nodded miserably. "They have all four warheads! Will you be able to find them all?"

Azita shook her head. "I doubt it. I didn't have enough men even to attempt blocking all the roads leading out of this industrial park as well as search it. All we can do is try."

Creech Air Force Base, Nevada

Air Force Lt. Colonel Emmanuel Wainwright handed the folder across the desk to Captain Josh Pettigrew. As always, he kept his subordinate standing in front of him. Best to remind junior officers who was in charge, he thought.

And that went double for this jumped-up NCO, he thought.

"I want to stress how important this mission is, Captain," Wainwright said. "This is the first time we've ever had intelligence on Mullah Abdul Zahed's location in time to send in a team to capture him. I've already personally briefed the airman who will pilot the drone for this mission."

Pettigrew nodded impassively, but in fact, he was surprised. Usually, he would have briefed the drone pilot. But Wainwright certainly had the right to do so if he wished.

Wainwright continued, "I want you to oversee this mission, and make sure everything is done by the book. Now, you supervised the loadout for the drone we'll be using. Is everything in order and ready for mission success?"

"Yes, sir," Pettigrew said. He couldn't resist adding, "Mullah Abdul Zahed, sir. The only member of the deposed Taliban government still active in the field. How good do you think the intel is that says he'll still be there when we arrive?"

In spite of himself, Wainwright was impressed. He hadn't known off-hand who Mullah Abdul Zahed was, and he'd been dealing with Afghanistan a lot longer than Pettigrew.

Well, time to impress this Captain.

"One detail you won't find in this file is that our intel source has been proven reliable before. He's already given us the location of a couple of lower-level Taliban leaders, and each time they checked out. I guess now he's looking for a bigger payday," Wainwright concluded with satisfaction.

"Yes, sir," Pettigrew said, while thinking to himself that this all sounded too good to be true. He had an immediate mental image of a fat, juicy worm wriggling on a sharp, shiny metal hook.

"Dismissed, Captain," Wainwright said.

Pettigrew collected the mission file from the top of Wainwright's desk, saluted, and left.

CHAPTER FIFTEEN

201st Military Base, Tajikistan

Colonel Igor Bronstein's three guests barely fit in his small sound-proofed office. He handed Anatoly Grishkov, Mikhail Vasilyev, and Neda Rhahbar each a slim folder.

"I have been ordered to do three things. The first is for all of you. I am to pass on congratulations from your superiors for whatever you did during your mission. The second is for you, Grishkov. You are reminded that you are an FSB agent, not a medic," Bronstein said, shaking his head.

Grishkov shrugged, while Vasilyev and Neda both smiled with obvious amusement.

Bronstein expected no explanation and didn't get one.

"Finally, I have briefing materials for you on a new mission. Pakistani authorities are searching intensively for the four stolen nuclear warheads and may still recover some or all of them."

Bronstein paused and looked at them thoughtfully.

"However, if it appears the Taliban have taken them into Afghanistan, we have offered to work with the Americans to locate the warheads and either recover or destroy them."

The reactions on the three faces in front of him ranged from "concern" to "dismay."

"Before we continue, review the briefing materials in your folders. Vasilyev, one marked detail was provided only to you and me. It is up to you to decide whether the mission requires you to share it with the others on your team."

Bronstein stood, opened his office door, and pointed to a vacant desk in the base Operations Center that surrounded his soundproofed office.

"When you are ready with your questions, let me know."

With that, Bronstein left and closed the door behind him.

It didn't take them long to read through the slim folders. Grishkov was the first to speak.

"OK, I'll admit I was wrong, and we did make a difference in Pakistan. But Afghanistan is another matter. The Americans may have fewer troops there than they used to, but the three of us can't do anything they could do as well or better."

Vasilyev nodded. "Normally, I'd say you're right. But we'll have two things the Americans don't. Experts in Moscow have analyzed that map you found, and they show the routes the Taliban are planning to use to transport the weapons to their targets. Also, we have technology the Americans lack."

Grishkov grunted. "I suppose this is the part you're not supposed to tell us?"

Vasilyev shrugged.

"Remember, Colonel Bronstein said it was up to me. I've decided you both need to know."

Pointing at Grishkov, he said, "You will recall the drone that covered you when you were in Afghanistan. The same drone will be fitted with an equipment package that gives us the ability to detect radioactivity to help locate the stolen warheads."

Neda frowned. "I'm sorry, but are you sure that the Americans don't have the same or better technology? No offense, but isn't their scientific equipment generally better than what is produced in Russia?"

Vasilyev nodded. "I had the same reaction. However, in this case, we pulled ahead years ago, thanks to superior motivation. Chernobyl was not our only nuclear accident. Also, in several instances, our nuclear weapons were ... not where they were supposed to be. So, we put more resources into this technology than the Americans, and came up with better equipment as a result."

Vasilyev paused. "And it's worth remembering that for many years we were the only country able to get American astronauts into space. It's not enough to have a theoretical capability. You must also make the right decisions, and set the right priorities, to get the proper result."

Grishkov shook his head. "So why not simply hand over what we learned from the map and what we will learn from the drone to the Americans?"

Vasilyev shrugged. "I've just explained that this tracking technology is one of the few areas where we have an advantage over the Americans. The technology is highly classified, and will certainly not be shared with the Americans or anyone else."

Grishkov looked stubborn. "OK, so what about the map?"

Vasilyev nodded. "Moscow may rethink that decision if the Taliban can bring more than one warhead out of Pakistan. For now, as you saw from the briefing papers, we have asked the Americans to let us operate in coordination with their special forces, with the understanding that we will inform them if we locate a stolen warhead."

"I still don't like it," Grishkov said. "Something else is going on here we're not being told about."

Neda nodded in agreement but said nothing.

Vasilyev looked at both of them and then said with quiet exasperation, "I've told you everything I know. Do you want me to guess?"

Grishkov made a "give it to me" gesture with his hands that brought a smile from Neda.

"Very well. I think Moscow would like very much for us to get the credit for saving Kabul from a Taliban nuclear weapon. We've talked before about Afghanistan's fantastic mineral wealth. Russia has one other card to play in the competition to extract those minerals."

Vasilyev paused, clearly weighing his words.

"Russian companies are not as . . . concerned . . . about security issues as Western companies. The ruthlessness that our security contractors will bring to protecting their operations, as long as it is solely directed at the Taliban, will be welcomed. Ironically, the not altogether undeserved reputation we acquired for brutality during our occupation of Afghanistan may work in our favor in this case."

Grishkov looked thoughtful. "I don't think that's a bad guess. But what about Bagram Airfield?"

Vasilyev nodded. "That's why I said if the Taliban get more than one warhead out of Pakistan, Moscow might reconsider. Realistically, three agents have only a small chance of detecting and stopping one warhead. That drops to near zero if we have to split up."

Vasilyev paused, again thinking over his next words carefully. "If we are told that either two or three warheads have crossed the Afghan border, I am going to recommend to Moscow in the strongest terms that we pursue only the warhead destined for Kabul's Green Zone. Also, that we should give the Americans the information we gained from the map at a minimum. I hope Moscow can also figure out a way to share drone radiation detection data with the Americans without compromising that capability."

Vasilyev spread his hands. "I agree with you that the Americans are more than capable of protecting themselves. In fact, they may decide just that, and refuse our offer of assistance."

Then Vasilyev paused. "But not to make the offer, to stand by and give the Taliban even a small chance of success?"

Vasilyev shook his head. "More than I could stomach," he said soberly.

Grishkov and Neda both nodded. Grishkov spoke first.

"All you have said is sensible. Let's hope the bosses in Moscow agree."

Neda said softly, "I'll never forget the look on the faces of those men at the roadblock when they thought we were their helpless victims. When we started this mission, I was ready to die if necessary to stop the Taliban from using nuclear weapons against innocent people."

Neda unconsciously fingered the fresh scar on her cheek.

"I'm twice as ready now."

Hattar Industrial Estate, Pakistan

Colonel Azita Kamar snarled an oath into her radio handset that she saw Senior Technician Nasir Cheema was visibly shocked to hear coming from a Pakistani woman.

Azita thought to herself with grim amusement that he would have been even more shocked by her conduct in combat. There was a reason she was still breathing, while many Taliban who looked far tougher were not.

"Lieutenant, I don't care how many officials tell you that we have to start letting vehicles out of here without being searched. If they won't listen to you, arrest them. Tell them you are acting on my orders."

Azita signed off and returned to her review of a map of the industrial park. It dated back to shortly after the park opened and was missing dozens of structures as well as several roads. As she had received reports and observed details herself, she had made additions to the map by hand.

Now, as she looked at the map, she was trying to put herself into the shoes of men trying to escape with a nuclear warhead.

Azita knew they were nearby. One, two, or even three warheads might have escaped before she was able to ring the industrial park with troops. But not all four.

At least one warhead was still here. Azita could smell it.

But time was not on Azita's side. She could ignore local officials. Eventually, though, the powerful business owners with assets here would get through to politicians in Islamabad. Politicians with authority to give orders to her superior officers.

Azita's fingers traced over the map, lingering on the roadblocks she had set up on every road. Her eyes narrowed as she saw a wide gap between two of the barriers and remembered driving through the area. There had been nothing in that gap but the burned-out hulk of a chemical factory.

And behind it, flat land that eventually led to the main road. Perhaps drivable by a small truck with four-wheel drive.

Would the remains of the chemical factory be enough to obstruct the view of the soldiers at the roadblocks from an escaping truck?

Azita had a sudden rush of anger. Maybe, if the officers at those roadblocks were being distracted by busybody local officials.

Azita radioed the commander of the Talha armored personnel carrier to tell him to proceed to the field behind the ruins of the chemical factory, and that she would meet him there.

Thanks to being both closer and faster, Azita reached the factory first.

Just in time to see a small truck setting out over the field behind factory.

Azita had carried the same Hechler & Koch G3P4 assault rifle since she joined the Army. It had served her well over that time, and she only had one complaint about it today.

Its effective range was about four hundred meters, and the truck had already traveled about that far. The way it bounced up and down testified to the fact that the land wasn't really flat, and that it was a four-wheel-drive vehicle. Following it in her sedan wasn't an option.

And it also made it a devilishly hard target to hit. Just one round in a tire . . .

But no matter how many carefully aimed rounds she sent towards the truck, it kept getting smaller and smaller in her view.

The Taha APC rolled next to her, and its hatch flew open. The officer pointed towards the fleeing truck, and Azita just nodded and waved towards it.

The Taha's speed might not be so impressive on paved roads. On the open country, though, its treads easily outperformed the small truck's wheels. Long before overtaking it, the Taha's 12.7 mm machine gun had stopped the truck's forward movement.

Azita spoke rapidly into her radio handset, and the Taha rolled back towards them. Minutes later, Azita and Nasir were crammed inside the APC, which then went at full speed towards the small truck.

The truck still wasn't moving.

Azita didn't think for a second that the Taha's machine-gun fire had killed everyone on board and told the APC's commander so.

His only response was to smile.

Azita smiled back. Yes, it was obvious. But sometimes you had to be sure that your troops didn't forget the obvious.

Azita pulled Nasir to the side of the APC, facing away from the truck. Then, she had him hunch down beside her. Keeping the technician alive was a top priority, with—Azita hoped—a recovered warhead to examine. Otherwise, she would have commanded the assault on the truck herself.

Instead, the eight soldiers who had been inside the APC were led by its commander towards the truck. The gunner remained behind to cover them with the Taha's 12.7 mm machine gun, and its driver to move the APC if necessary.

It didn't take long before Azita's prediction that there were survivors proved accurate. Several automatic weapons inside the truck opened fire at the same moment. Still, the soldiers' quick reflexes as each hit the ground, coupled with their ballistic armor, prevented any severe casualties.

A short burst from the Taha's 12.7 mm machine gun silenced the Taliban fighters' rifle fire. At the APC's current range against a stationary target, the Taha's gunner literally couldn't miss.

The Pakistani soldiers advanced cautiously towards the truck, but there were no more surprises. Just a few minutes later, the voice of the APC's commander crackled over Azita's radio with the single word, "Clear."

"We're up," Azita said brightly to Nasir, who appeared anything but enthusiastic. However, he knew there was no avoiding the task, and dutifully followed Azita to the truck.

The Pakistani soldiers had already rolled back the canvas covering the truck's bed and its metal rear frame, revealing multiple unmoving Taliban bodies, and what Azita recognized as one of the missing warheads.

Azita watched approvingly as Nasir's attitude immediately changed to one of intense professional interest. After about fifteen minutes, Nasir looked up.

"If Ibrahim trained someone else to do the warhead removal, he did a great job. I doubt we could have done better back at the lab," Nasir said.

"So, this warhead is intact and could have been rigged for successful detonation by someone with Ibrahim's knowledge?" Azita asked.

Nasir nodded. "Absolutely. If the other stolen warheads are in the same condition as this one, that will go for them as well. He'll need to remove the nuclear cores to get maximum yield from a new device, but he knows how to do that too."

Azita frowned. "Very well. I have another task for you. As you did back at the warehouse . . ."

Nasir's mouth twisted with distaste. "I understand," he replied and quickly examined each of the bodies in the truck bed and cab.

Nasir shook his head. "He's not here," he said flatly.

Azita wasn't surprised and nodded. As the only person the Taliban had capable of building a working bomb with the stolen warheads, Azita had thought it likely Ibrahim had left with the very first warhead to be successfully removed.

Nasir had gone back to looking at the warhead. But now there was a small and unpleasant smile on his face.

"So, what could possibly be amusing about this situation?" Azita asked, with genuine curiosity.

Nasir looked up absently, with the disturbing smile still on his face. "The answer to that question is classified above your level. I will only say that though Ibrahim may indeed have done well to get this far, getting farther may be harder than he thought."

Azita looked at him thoughtfully and then shrugged. "Well, I hope you're right. I don't know if you've realized it, but you and your organization have more at stake than anyone else in Pakistan."

Nasir looked startled. "What do you mean? The Taliban won't want to use these warheads against our nuclear weapons production facilities, or for that matter, anywhere in Pakistan. I'm sure they'll use them against the Americans in Afghanistan."

"I'm sure you're right," Azita said. "Now, ask yourself this. If the Taliban succeeds, what do you think the Americans will do?"

"Well, obviously, punish those responsible . . ." Nasir said, his voice trailing off as he realized what Azita meant.

"Yes," Azita said. "And could we say with a straight face that didn't include us? The Americans would never attack our cities, full of innocent women and children. Our already produced nuclear weapons are scattered and mobile to prevent an Indian first strike."

Azita paused. "But our nuclear weapons production facilities? I guarantee the Americans know exactly where they are. But if the Taliban succeeds in attacking the Americans with our weapons, I'm certain they won't be there much longer."

For once, Azita saw with satisfaction, Nasir had nothing to say.

CHAPTER SIXTEEN

Creech Air Force Base, Nevada

Senior Airman Tom Evans considered himself lucky to have his hands on the controls of a Predator C Avenger. It had a total payload capacity of nearly three thousand kilograms, split almost evenly between its internal weapons bay and external hardpoints. It could carry virtually any weapon in the Air Force inventory.

Best of all, this Avenger was going to support a combat mission. According to the brief, he shouldn't have to fire a shot and only relay sensor data to the SEAL team that would carry out the assault.

Evans' job was to pilot the Avenger. There were also two sensor operators, who were responsible for both collecting sensor data and flagging anything that might require action during flight. He'd flown with them both before, and knew they were highly competent professionals.

Ordinarily, Evans would have had no chance to pilot an Avenger with his limited experience and low rank. But his performance in piloting unarmed drones had been outstanding, and his last glowing evaluation made promotion this year a near certainty. It had also led to this assignment.

Evans knew he was balancing right on the edge of what had been the limit for enlisted men piloting drones. It had only been a few years since piloting drones had been opened up to airmen like Evans. Now, after another policy change, he had just been trained on every aspect of the Avenger's systems and weapons and even assigned to support a combat mission.

But only as long as he was expected to use nothing but the Avenger's sensors.

Well, Evans would take what he could get. He was confident that if he just kept his head down and followed orders, the time would come when he'd be able to take on any mission with the Avenger, including ground attack.

Getting briefed by the CO himself had been a little unnerving, but Wainwright had been pretty clear about what he wanted. Follow orders, and only fire a weapon if requested explicitly by troops on the ground.

Simple enough.

Evans was roused from his internal monologue by the arrival of his immediate superior, Captain Josh Pettigrew. A quick look at the clock confirmed it.

Game time.

"Good morning, Evans. Any questions about today's mission?" Pettigrew asked.

Evans shook his head. "No, sir. Seems straightforward. I keep the bird flying straight and level, while these guys keep an eye out for anything unusual," he said, gesturing towards the two sensor operators.

They both grinned and touched two fingers to their foreheads in mock salute.

Pettigrew nodded and smiled back.

Evans concluded, "If they spot anything, you let the guys on the ground know."

Pettigrew smiled. "Good summary. The CO's already given you the mission brief, right?"

"Yes, sir," Evans said.

"Well, one thing he probably didn't tell you is that the man those SEALs have been sent to capture has been on the run for over twenty years. But somehow, we're asked to believe that he's in this compound in the middle of nowhere with just three other men. And he's staying put for nearly two full days. What does all that make you think, Evans?" Pettigrew asked.

"Sir, what you're saying makes it sound like a trap. But didn't the intel guys think all that through?" Evans replied.

Pettigrew nodded. "Yes. They discounted the obvious, though, because their source has a perfect track record handing over Taliban leaders for cash. Plus, they really want him."

"OK, sir, so what should I do?" Evans asked.

Pettigrew waved his hands to include Evans and both sensor operators.

"All three of you should keep your eyes as wide open as you can. You should expect trouble because I sure do. And Evans, be ready to use your weapons if the troops on the ground request it. I know you expect this to be an observe and report only mission, and with luck, that's what it will be. But remember, there's a reason an Avenger was assigned in support of this mission, not an unarmed recon drone," Pettigrew said.

"Yes, sir," Evans responded. Well, that all made sense, he thought. Even better, none of it contradicted what he'd been told to do by the CO.

A light lit up on the console in front of Pettigrew.

Pettigrew lifted the console's handset for the communications check with the SEALs signaled by the lit indicator. One of his many pet peeves, when he'd been a drone operator himself, had been officers who put the distant troops on speaker, and had a loud conversation with them while he was trying to fly.

When Pettigrew had unexpectedly been offered a slot in OCS, his first resolution had been that he'd never repeat any of the things he'd complained about officers doing.

So far, he thought he was succeeding.

After a brief and quiet conversation with the SEAL team commander over his handset, Pettigrew said, "Looks like the SEALs' helicopters brought them to the target right on time."

"To the target" wasn't entirely accurate. The helicopters would always bring the special forces troops as close as possible without their noise alerting the target. One of the many reasons SEALs and Rangers needed to be in top physical shape was the need to cover the distance between drop off and target quickly while carrying a heavy load of weapons and equipment.

The Avenger was now collecting data from within the compound that was supposed to be housing Mullah Abdul Zahed. The sensor operators quickly flagged several factors that appeared unusual.

Only one man appeared to be standing guard outside the main structure in the compound. So far, they weren't detecting movement inside the structure.

There was also a large truck parked just behind the main structure, between it and the back wall of the compound.

Pettigrew frowned. Just how big was the truck?

When he pulled up the sensor data, he gave an involuntary hiss of dismay. It was the kind of truck ordinarily used in Afghanistan for just one purpose. Movement of large quantities of produce to market.

It would do just as well, though, to transport a large quantity of explosives. Say, the type of bulky, relatively cheap explosives based on the ammonium nitrate fertilizer sold worldwide. Including Afghanistan.

Hold on, now, Pettigrew thought. Maybe I'm making too much of this.

And then he realized that they could check.

"Evans, I want you to drop altitude five thousand feet so we can check out a truck near the target with that new chemical sensing pod we just installed on the Avenger. I want to be sure it's not filled with explosives before the SEALs hit the compound," Pettigrew said.

"Uh, sir, our orders state we're not to go below our current altitude to minimize our chance of detection," Evans replied hesitantly.

"OK, you're still going to be flying too high for anyone on the ground to see or hear you. The Taliban don't have radar, and even if they did, the altitude change wouldn't make a difference to their ability to detect you. It will make a difference, though, to whether that chemical sensing pod works. Carry out my order," Pettigrew said, with growing impatience.

"Yes, sir," Evans muttered.

The truth was Pettigrew understood Evans' reluctance. The Avenger was many things, but agile wasn't one of them. Dropping altitude quickly while maintaining both control and relative position to the target wasn't so simple.

But Pettigrew was convinced it had to be done.

To his credit, Evans did drop altitude at least as quickly as Pettigrew could have himself.

But the SEALs had almost reached the compound.

One of the sensor operators was quick to report. "Sir, I'm getting a strong ammonium nitrate signature."

Pettigrew picked up the handset in front of him.

"SEAL team, sensors show a large enemy bomb deployed directly to your front. Abort mission, I say again, abort mission."

There was nothing but the hiss of static on the other end of the line in response.

Every Avenger mission came with a dedicated team of specialists in support. One, Sergeant Alonzo Johnson, was for communications.

"Johnson, get Bagram, or anyone else you can on the line who can reach that SEAL team. They're walking into an ambush!" Pettigrew said.

Just a minute later, Johnson replied.

"Sir, Bagram has been trying to raise them already after they missed a comms check. No joy. It looks like signals in the area are being jammed."

Pettigrew pointed at Evans. "Pilot, use your Hellfire R9X and take out that truck!"

Pettigrew had ordered the loadout of this Avenger himself. Along with the AGM-114P Hellfire II the Avenger typically carried, it also had a Hellfire R9X with a kinetic warhead designed to reduce collateral damage. It relied on the energy built up from its descent, and whatever fuel was still on board at impact to destroy its target.

The R9X had initially been designed as an anti-personnel missile, so just before impact it deployed six long blades through its skin, which would shred anything in its path. This gave it the nickname, "The Flying Ginsu."

Since the R9X had no explosive charge, the truck was behind the main structure and the SEAL team was approaching from the front, if there was no bomb in the vehicle, there should be no danger to the attackers.

Pettigrew hoped.

Evans didn't see it that way.

"Sir, at this range, don't we risk friendly casualties? And don't our orders say we're forbidden to fire without a request from the troops on the ground?"

Pettigrew thought for an instant about trying to convince Evans to follow his order, and just as quickly rejected the idea.

There was no time.

Pettigrew stood next to Evans and said formally, "Senior Airman Evans, you're relieved. I will take over piloting."

For a moment, it looked like Evans was going to object, and then he rose and left the room.

Pettigrew had a pretty good idea where he was going, but there was no time to worry about that now.

As he sat down and put his hand on the drone's controls, Pettigrew also looked at the monitor displaying data and images from the sensor operators.

And paled. The SEAL team was about to enter the compound.

It only took seconds to select the Hellfire R9X, lock it on the truck and fire.

"Hellfire launched," Pettigrew announced.

As he waited for the missile's impact, Pettigrew's eyes were glued to the monitor showing the SEAL team's advance.

Pettigrew had a moment to hope that the truck had just been carrying ammonium nitrate fertilizer to some farmer's fields, and the SEAL's communications problem was due to coincidentally faulty equipment. Sure, he'd take some heat for the truck's destruction warning the target, and unnecessarily relieving Evans, but he'd be okay with that.

This fantasy didn't last long.

The SEALs were just entering the courtyard when the missile hit the truck.

There was immediately a massive secondary detonation that destroyed the main structure.

Yes, there had been a bomb on board the truck. A really big one.

One of the sensor operators quietly confirmed what Pettigrew saw on the monitor.

"Structure believed to have contained target has been destroyed. Thermal bloom and smoke from the explosion make verification of SEAL team status impossible at this time. Image quality should improve shortly."

"Johnson, get Bagram and let them know what's happened. They'll need to send at least two medevac choppers," Pettigrew said.

Johnson nodded and began speaking quietly into his headset, simultaneously typing a report rapidly on his keyboard for Pettigrew's approval.

Then he stopped typing.

"Sir, I've relayed your message to Bagram, and they've acknowledged. I've got a transmission from the SEAL team to Bagram. It looks like whatever was jamming their signal was destroyed in that explosion. Give me a moment, and I'll get the transmission routed to your console."

Pettigrew shook his head. "Just put it on speaker," he said.

At first, it seemed that he was going to object, and then Johnson said, "Yes, sir."

The transmission began in mid-sentence. ". . . missile landed practically on top of us! I'm going to get on the first plane I can find Stateside, and when I find whoever did this to my men, I'm going to . . ."

"Cut it off," Pettigrew said quietly.

Johnson's hand must have been hovering over the cutoff switch because the speaker went silent instantly.

Well, Pettigrew thought, there's at least one survivor.

One of the sensor operators spoke into the awkward silence that had followed the SEAL team leader's transmission.

"Images show several SEAL team members are mobile and appear to be assisting others who are injured. There is no movement in or near the main structure."

Pettigrew could see that on the monitor. In fact, there was no longer a recognizable structure there at all.

"Johnson, advise when we have a casualty report from Bagram," Pettigrew said.

"Yes, sir," Johnson said. "Bagram has just advised two medevac choppers are five minutes out from the SEAL team's location. Luckily, they were already on standby."

Pettigrew nodded but was thinking that luck probably had nothing to do with it. Instead, it was proper planning by someone there who hadn't believed Mullah Abdul Zahed could be that easy to capture.

He was glad to see he wasn't the only skeptic.

Pettigrew concentrated on circling the Avenger around the target area, while the sensor operators looked for any remaining threats. So far, it didn't look like there were any.

And trying to ignore the sick feeling in his stomach and his mind racing to think of something he could have done differently.

And how long it would be before Wainwright showed up.

The answer, it turned out, was "not long."

The door to the drone command center swung open, admitting Lt. Colonel Emmanuel Wainwright, flanked by two military policemen.

Evans followed behind them. Pettigrew was surprised that instead of the smile he expected Evans to be trying unsuccessfully to conceal, he appeared unhappy with the result of his trip to the CO.

Good, Pettigrew thought. There's hope for him yet.

"Captain Pettigrew, these men are here to place you under arrest for violating your orders, leading directly to the death or injury of American soldiers. You stand relieved. Senior Airman Evans, take over command of the active drone," Wainwright said.

Pettigrew stood up and walked to the waiting MPs, while Evans sat back down at the drone's control station, avoiding eye contact with Pettigrew.

Pettigrew held his hands out, but one of the MPs shook his head. "No need for that, sir. We'll escort you to your quarters."

170 · TED HALSTEAD

Wainwright had looked angry before. Now he looked like he was about to have a stroke.

"He needs to be cuffed and put in a cell! These are serious charges!" Wainwright bellowed.

Neither MP was impressed. "Sir, we have our orders. Our CO doesn't consider Captain Pettigrew to be a flight risk. If you disagree, you need to take that up with him."

Without waiting for a response, one of the MPs gestured towards the door. "Captain Pettigrew, after you."

Pettigrew wasted no time leaving the drone control center, with the MPs right behind him.

He wondered if he'd ever see it again.

CHAPTER SEVENTEEN

Risalpur Export Processing Zone, Pakistan

Colonel Azita Kamar gave a rapid series of orders into her car's radio handset. Senior Technician Nasir Cheema in the passenger seat beside her looked happy not to be the focus of her attention, at least for the moment.

Once she put down the handset, Nasir said, "Thanks for letting me call my wife, and giving me some privacy for the call. I normally work in an office, and adventures that take me driving around the country with a woman my wife doesn't know are not part of my routine."

Azita laughed and replied, "I hope you didn't put it to her like that!"

Nasir shook his head and mumbled, "Of course not."

It was fortunate Azita found his discomfort understandable, Nasir thought to himself. Otherwise, she might suspect the truth. That Nasir was feeling uncomfortable because he had not called his wife or any other relative. He had used the call for a very different purpose.

Pointing at the warehouse set at an acute angle across the street, Azita said, "I've had a tip that suspicious men entered this building within the past hour. We're here because we happened to be closest. I've decided we can't wait for my soldiers to get here to investigate."

"So, when you say 'we,' that means you want me to go in with you to face who knows how many heavily armed men," Nasir said.

Azita nodded sharply. "I'm not expecting you to join me in a fire-fight. I'm going to look for a way into the building that will let us assess the situation. The tip may be wrong, and these men could have nothing to do with our stolen weapon."

Nasir shrugged. "Or the tip may be right about these men being criminals, just not our criminals. That probably won't keep them from shooting as soon as they see your uniform."

Azita grinned. "You have a point." Then to his surprise, Azita reached across him and opened the glove compartment. Next, she pulled out a small pistol.

"My backup weapon. Yours, if you want it," Azita said calmly.

Nasir stared at her. "Are you crazy? I've never touched a gun, let alone fired one. I'd probably end up shooting myself."

"Well, it's your call. If you're smart enough to work on nuclear weapons, I'm betting you can figure out which end of a gun is which. Same for the way it works- point the end with the hole at what you want to kill, and pull the trigger. Oh, and firing it requires you to take off the safety."

With that, Azita demonstrated how to set and deactivate the pistol's safety switch.

Shaking his head, Nasir said, "Fine, I'll take it. For both our sakes, I hope I don't have to use it."

Then he paused and cocked his head. "You said this was the Risalpur Export Processing Zone. Why does 'Risalpur' sound familiar to me?"

Azita smiled. "Probably because Risalpur is the home of our Air Force Academy. It's about a ten-minute drive from here."

Nasir stared blankly at her. "So, they must have troops who could get here before yours!"

Shaking her head, Azita said, "True, but I've been ordered to use only soldiers under my direct command. We can't take any chances about word of the theft getting out."

Looking down at the pistol in his hand, Nasir said, "So instead, your backup will be . . . me."

Azita opened her door and gestured for Nasir to do the same. "Cheer up! We're not the first soldiers to disagree with their orders, and I guarantee we won't be the last. Now, no more talking unless I ask you a question."

Nasir wanted to point out that he wasn't a soldier at all, but had the good sense to follow Azita's last order.

Hunched over, Azita crossed the street and headed for a small door on the side of the warehouse. Nasir looked around nervously as he moved behind her, but saw no activity anywhere near. Dusk was falling. Nasir realized that many of the workers in the area had probably already finished their work for the day.

Azita's hand reached out for the doorknob and then tried twisting it open. Locked.

Next, she slid her hand into a pocket and removed a slim leather case containing small metal tools. Seconds later, the door was open.

Azita bent down and looked inside. Tall stacks of wooden pallets blocked her view of the warehouse interior, but she could hear both activity and several voices. She glanced behind her and saw that Nasir had followed her inside and quietly closed the door behind him.

And hadn't yet shot her or himself. So, not totally useless.

Peering through a gap in the pallets, Azita saw a sight that made her breath catch in her throat. The warhead they were looking for, surrounded by at least six armed men. Too many for Azita to take on herself, even with her trusty Hechler & Koch G3P4 assault rifle.

What were they doing?

First things first. Years before, Azita had worked out a simple series of codes to use in sending texts to her subordinate commanders. Now all she had to do was send the number "4" to a group text address.

Target location confirmed.

Pieces of the warhead's case had been removed, and wires spilled out from it. There were also two cases stacked on a nearby table. Even from this range, Azita recognized the markings on the side of each. They were, in fact, specially designed to be visible from a distance.

Explosives and detonators. Azita could see from his expression that Nasir had spotted them too.

Azita crept to the edge of the cover provided by the pallets and now could just barely hear their conversation.

". . . think it was a mistake to stop here. We should have pushed on to Peshawar."

"You heard the call!" an older and angrier voice replied. "Roadblocks on the M-1. It makes sense to wait them out."

"We could have cut across on the N45 to the N5, and lost hardly any time. We still could," the younger voice argued.

"And if you could figure that out, don't you think the military could too? Just because we haven't been told about roadblocks on the N45 or the N5 doesn't mean they aren't there!" said the older voice.

Well, Azita thought to herself, he was right about that. She'd ordered those roadblocks herself. Too bad the younger man wasn't in charge.

"OK, but we're not just waiting, are we? What's the advantage of trying to remove the nuclear core from the warhead now? I thought that technician Ibrahim was supposed to oversee the removal?"

Now the older voice was clearly angry. "Ibrahim trained me, and I know what I'm doing," he said.

The younger voice was unimpressed. "So, why are you trying so hard to get Ibrahim on the phone?"

Now the older voice switched from anger to worry. "There are too many wires. I don't know what it means, but I'm sure Ibrahim will."

Even from this distance, Azita could see the younger man emphatically shaking his head. "No. We've tried to call him enough times. Let's pack this up, go to Peshawar and ask him in person."

Azita couldn't be sure, but it looked like the older man was crossing his arms across his chest. She was right, and his next defensive words matched the gesture.

"Ibrahim trained me in how to build a weapon, and he gave me the explosives and detonators to do it. If our way forward is blocked, I say we build it here and attack the Air Force Academy," the older man said.

Azita's heart sank, and not only because of the danger to the thousands of Pakistani military personnel in and around the Academy. The schools set up for their children were well known to be the only decent ones in the region, and so students came to them from far and wide.

A successful detonation here would be a national tragedy on an unimaginable scale.

The younger man was still not convinced. "So, if you can't reach Ibrahim, are you just going to guess about what all these extra wires do? Or just cut them all and hope for the best?"

"Mind your tongue," the older man replied, with obviously growing annoyance. "The cell signal is barely able to get through the walls of this metal warehouse. I'm going to go outside and try again."

With that, he headed for the nearest door, obviously to do what he'd just said.

Azita turned towards Nasir and whispered, "If I blow up those explosives, is there any chance of a nuclear detonation?"

As a child, Azita had seen cartoons where a character's eyes seemed to pop out of his head. Nasir's expression immediately reminded her of those old cartoons, but it came nowhere close to making her laugh.

"That would be incredibly dangerous!" Nasir replied in a low and furious hiss. "Since the explosive force would not be applied evenly across the fissile sphere, the full design yield could never be achieved. But some degree of implosion is still possible, with fatal consequences for all nearby."

Azita nodded. "Estimate the explosion's radius," she whispered.

Nasir shook his head and replied in a low voice, "Impossible even to guess. It would certainly vaporize this warehouse."

Azita looked Nasir straight in the eye and whispered, "And how much farther?"

Nasir looked back and paled, as he finally understood what Azita was really asking.

"I'm only guessing. Probably not beyond this industrial district," Nasir said bleakly.

Azita nodded. "Thanks for your honesty," she whispered. "I hope it won't come to that."

Nasir smiled and whispered back, "It may not. If that fool cuts all the wires, the casing is booby-trapped. The charge is too small to cause an implosion, but will certainly kill everyone around the weapon."

Azita nodded and fractionally relaxed. So, this problem might solve itself.

And her men should be here within five minutes. If these idiots would just keep arguing . . .

The older man walked back inside the warehouse, and even from this distance, she could tell he wasn't happy.

"I still can't reach Ibrahim. I've decided to proceed without his help," the older man declared.

The younger man shrugged. Apparently, the argument was over.

Well, if Nasir was right about the booby trap, Azita, and her troops were about to be spared quite a bit of trouble.

Azita had been so intent on listening to the distant conversation that she didn't notice the wrench balanced on the edge of the nearest pallet. Until she brushed against it, sending it clattering to the floor.

All conversation immediately ceased, and every head turned in Azita's direction, though they still couldn't see her or Nasir.

The older man gestured silently to several of his men, who held rifles at the ready as they began moving towards the source of the noise.

Azita.

Now she had a decision to make. Once they killed Azita and Nasir, what were the Taliban fighters likely to do?

Azita knew the answer as soon as she asked herself the question. They'd pack up and leave, maybe quickly enough to escape her soldiers.

She couldn't allow that to happen.

Azita whispered to Nasir, "I need you to move as far away from me as you can that way while staying behind these pallets. When I tell you, put your pistol in one of the gaps in the pallets and start firing. Don't worry about hitting anything. I only need a distraction," Azita said.

"What are you going to do?" Nasir hissed back, clearly terrified.

When he asked, Azita had just removed a model 84-P2A1 grenade from a vest pocket. A Pakistani produced version of the Austrian Arges Type HG 84 series anti-personnel hand grenade, it would send fragments at speed for a radius of about thirty meters.

Azita was confident she could detonate the distant case of explosives if she just had a few seconds to line up her throw.

Azita looked back at him and softly whispered, "Sorry, Nasir. Move off, and when I signal, start firing."

Nasir appeared stunned, but moved as Azita had ordered.

When Nasir had gone far enough, Azita raised her hand.

Nasir lifted his pistol and began firing.

A part of Azita's thoughts included gratitude for Nasir's success in remembering to disengage the pistol's safety, and for providing the distraction she needed.

A bigger part wished she'd seen that wrench.

As Azita had expected, the advancing Taliban fighters had shifted towards Nasir, and begun firing back. So far, no round had hit Nasir, and Azita saw with approval that he was still firing.

Azita pulled the pin from the grenade and immediately darted out from her hiding place at the edge of the pallets. Her arm bent back to throw.

The two closest Taliban fighters shifted their aim from Nasir to Azita and fired. Their first rounds missed, and Azita was able to complete her throw.

The next Taliban rounds didn't miss. But it didn't matter.

A second later, Azita's grenade blasted both the case of detonators and the nearby case of explosives.

A fraction of a second later, Nasir's assessment of a partial nuclear detonation proved accurate. The warehouse, as well as three others near it, ceased to exist. Fire consumed many other buildings, and the explosion's shock wave damaged many others.

The explosion ejected radioactive material for hundreds of meters, and radioactive fallout was produced in a large enough quantity to require decontamination throughout the neighboring area of Risalpur.

However, except for six men working late in two of the nearby warehouses, Azita, Nasir, and the Taliban fighters were the only fatalities.

If Azita had still been alive to ask the question, though, it certainly would have been— How much longer could Pakistan's luck hold out?

CHAPTER EIGHTEEN

Creech Air Force Base, Nevada

The MPs had told Captain Josh Pettigrew that their CO hadn't even ordered him confined to quarters, but did ask that he not leave the base until the investigation of "the incident" was complete. They didn't know what "the incident" was, nor did they care.

One of them had told Pettigrew in a low voice that their CO had only agreed to have him escorted back to quarters to get Wainwright out of his office. Also, to avoid a confrontation between Pettigrew and Wainwright, that might have ended up with no way to prevent immediate charges, maybe against both of them.

It was nice that the MPs and their CO weren't willing to confine him before an investigation had even started. It probably helped that they didn't like Wainwright, or trust his judgment.

But it didn't make Pettigrew feel any better about what had happened. He couldn't stop thinking about the image of those unmoving men on the monitor. How many were wounded and how many dead?

Pettigrew had spent his time after the MPs left flipping from one news channel to another, hoping to find some word of what had happened in Afghanistan. When he finally fell asleep on his couch, he had still heard nothing.

Pounding on his door woke him up at what a quick glance at his window showed was dawn. The same two MPs were at his door.

They said nothing beyond, "Please come with us, sir."

Pettigrew gestured at his unshaven face and wrinkled uniform. They both shook their heads, and one said, "Now, sir."

Though they hadn't cuffed him, Pettigrew thought that his most likely destination was still probably a cell.

So, he was surprised when it became apparent they were going to Lt. Colonel Emmanuel Wainwright's office.

I think I'd prefer the cell, Pettigrew thought bitterly. He wasn't looking forward to a lecture about how badly he'd screwed up.

He'd been giving himself that lecture for hours.

As he walked into Wainwright's office, Pettigrew realized there was no reason it couldn't be both. A lecture followed by a cell.

Except the MPs saluted Wainwright, turned on their heels and left.

The next words from Wainwright were the last ones Pettigrew had expected.

"Take a seat, Captain," Wainwright said. His tone was pleasant, but his face looked like he was sucking on a lemon.

Then Pettigrew noticed the handset lying on Wainwright's desk.

Wainwright continued, "General Robinson is joining us for this conversation by phone. Do we still have a good connection, General?"

"We do," came as a distempered growl from the speaker on Wainwright's phone console.

Pettigrew thought that if Wainwright had any sense, he'd read the tone as meaning, "Get on with it, and stop wasting my time."

As he saw his expression shift, Pettigrew realized Wainwright did—barely—have that much sense.

"I would like to express my regret over your unjustified confinement to quarters when no investigation had even begun. You will return to duty immediately. I would also like to offer you this opportunity to register a formal complaint regarding my actions," Wainwright said.

Pettigrew didn't hesitate. "Sir, I have no interest in making a complaint. I regret that circumstances didn't give me the time to seek your guidance and authorization for acting contrary to orders."

Wainwright nodded. "Very well. General Robinson would now like to speak to you privately."

After the door closed, Robinson's voice rasped over the phone, "Is he gone?"

"Yes, sir," Pettigrew replied.

"OK, Captain, I don't have much more time to spend on this, so you're getting the short version. Four SEALs were injured in that explosion, but are expected to make a complete recovery," Robinson said.

"I'm glad to hear that, sir," Pettigrew said, meaning every word.

That must have come through because after a pause, Robinson finally just said, "Me, too."

"A preliminary investigation team from Bagram has confirmed your belief that the truck you hit was carrying a bomb. Any Seal team members who entered the building would have had no chance of survival once the bomb was triggered. Were you the one who had the Avenger loaded with an R9X, Captain?" Robinson asked.

"Yes, sir," Pettigrew replied.

"Not a standard item for the Avenger, but maybe it should be. The lead investigator says if you had used a Hellfire with a standard explosive warhead, he doubts any of the SEALs would have survived," Robinson said.

"I'm glad the kinetic warhead was effective," Pettigrew said.

"So is the SEAL team commander, Commander Dave Martins. Once he received the preliminary report, Martins told me he would put you in for a commendation," Robinson said.

"Thank you, sir, but please tell him that's not necessary," Pettigrew said.

The answering grunt was partly amused and partly annoyed. "Captain, you haven't been an officer long, so I'll tell you why it's necessary. First, because you will now have a record in your file showing that against orders, you decided to fire a missile practically on top of special forces troops. It would be useful for you to have a document from those troops in the same file saying that it was a good decision. Second, because it will make it much more difficult for your CO to give you the Officer Evaluation Report he is probably mentally drafting right now," Robinson said.

"Yes, sir," Pettigrew replied.

"Good. Now, I've taken the time to sort out this little misunderstanding with your CO partly because my boss has taken an interest in this incident. He also hasn't forgotten your performance in Saudi Arabia. But, more important, there is a new mission tasking coming your way that will be the greatest challenge you've faced yet," Robinson said.

"We're ready, sir," Pettigrew replied. "We've got a good team here."

"Glad to hear it," Robinson said. "Your new orders will be waiting for you back at the drone command center. Good luck, Captain."

"Thank you, sir," Pettigrew said, as the line went dead.

Greatest challenge yet? As he walked out of Wainwright's office, Pettigrew first thought that was fine. After all, he'd joined the Air Force to deal with challenges most civilians couldn't even imagine.

On the other hand, thinking back over the hours of guilt he'd endured after firing that missile, he wondered whether he'd be up to this "greatest challenge."

As he pulled open the door to the drone command center, Pettigrew remembered just hours before having wondered if he'd be back.

Pettigrew realized he was lucky to be standing where he was right now.

He nodded acknowledgment to the chorus of greetings that came from everyone in the room, including Senior Airman Evans.

Yes, Pettigrew thought. I am definitely ready for this.

CHAPTER NINETEEN

Pakistan Secretariat, Islamabad, Pakistan

Prime Minister Hamza Shadid glowered across his desk at General Ehsan Monir, who was standing at stiff attention.

"Report, General," Hamza ordered coldly.

"Sir, two of the four stolen nuclear warheads have now been accounted for," Ehsan said.

It was apparent he was trying not to sound as desperate as he felt.

"So, General, that's how you put it? Do you imagine you are my only source of information? Why don't I say 'Risalpur' and save us both some time," Hamza said contemptuously.

"Sir, from what I've been able to learn so far, one of my officers and a senior nuclear weapons technician were present when one of the warheads experienced a partial detonation. I think it is very likely they prevented a much greater disaster," Ehsan said.

Hamza nodded. "Maybe so, General. We'll probably never know for sure. At least, as you say, the warhead is accounted for," he said with obvious sarcasm.

Ehsan winced but said nothing in reply.

"My sources tell me that the officer you put in charge of the investigation was a woman, a detail you failed to mention," Hamza observed.

"I didn't think it was relevant, sir," Ehsan said.

"Or you thought I might object, and you'd have to assign someone else. Well, though she failed to find all the warheads, I certainly can't question her courage or her devotion to duty," Hamza said.

"Yes, sir," Ehsan replied.

"Unfortunately, I can't say the same for your senior nuclear weapons technician," Hamza continued.

"Sir?" Ehsan asked, obviously puzzled.

"The ISI routinely monitors the movements of all American personnel with diplomatic credentials. Of course, some of them are spies. But, because they have diplomatic status, ISI agents need higher authority to approve any action against them," Hamza said.

Ehsan looked even more confused and said nothing.

"So, once the American left, the ISI agents arrested the Pakistani man he had met. By the time they understood who he was and why he had met with the American, the spy was already safely back at his Embassy," Hamza said bitterly.

Ehsan finally couldn't restrain himself. "Did this man who met the American have something to do with our technician?" Ehsan asked.

"Oh, yes, you could say that, General. Yes, you absolutely could," Hamza growled.

After glaring at Ehsan, who stood stock-still, Hamza continued. "Under intensive questioning, the man revealed that he was your technician's deputy and that he had just come from giving the American spy detailed blueprints of the Nasr missile. He also told him that four Nasr warheads had been stolen, and three were still missing. Of course, this was before one was accounted for at Risalpur," Hamza said.

Ignoring Hamza's sarcasm, Ehsan asked with genuine puzzlement, "Why would he do such a thing?"

Hamza nodded. "A good question. Unlike the fact of his treason, the answer to that question was one the man was eager to provide. It seems your senior technician believed and told his deputy in a phone call that if our stolen weapons were to be used against the Americans, they might decide to strike back at the source of the problem."

More sarcasm. Ehsan, though, was thinking through the implications of this news.

"So, General, was he right? Would the Americans attack our nuclear weapons production facilities? And if so, would the attack use nuclear weapons?" Hamza asked.

Part of Ehsan's thoughts were focused on the realization that one of his questions had now been answered. After he'd heard about the explosion in Risalpur, he had expected dismissal at best, and arrest at worst. This summons to Hamza's office had come as a real surprise.

Now he knew why he was here. It didn't take long for Ehsan to decide how to answer the question.

Truthfully.

"Yes, sir. I think the Americans might hit us, especially if their forces suffer mass casualties. Especially if we don't warn them officially," Ehsan said.

Hamza nodded irritably. "Yes, I'm considering that. Again, will the Americans use nuclear weapons?"

Ehsan looked thoughtful for a moment and finally shook his head. "I don't think so, sir. They have conventional weapons that could do the job. The truth is, we haven't spent much on hardening our production facilities against nuclear attack."

Hamza looked startled. "What! Why not?"

Ehsan shrugged. "Our thinking was that nuclear war with India would either be strictly limited to small tactical devices on the battlefield, or an all-out exchange designed to eliminate each side's weapons and means of both military and civilian production. Years ago, we crossed the threshold for such an exchange resulting in mutually assured destruction. I'm sure you've seen the briefing."

Hamza nodded. It was the first briefing he'd received after becoming Prime Minister. It still gave him nightmares.

"So, your thinking was after an exchange that left nothing else standing, why worry about whether we could make more nuclear weapons?" Hamza said quietly.

"Well, yes, sir. It seemed pointless. And funds we saved by not hardening production facilities could instead be spent on making more weapons now. Improving the balance of power against the Indian enemy is the best guarantee that we'll never have to use the weapons at all. I'm sure you agree that would be preferable," Ehsan said.

Hamza nodded but said nothing. He was thinking, though, that what the General had said was . . . chilling. Hamza didn't like the casual way he had discussed the end of two nations that together were home to over one and a half billion people.

Hamza understood the military had to view these matters with a certain detachment. But maybe it was time for civilian politicians to inject some sanity to the whole issue of nuclear weapons.

Ehsan looked like he wanted to add something, so Hamza said, "Something else, General?"

Ehsan said, "Yes, sir. I should tell you that some officers have suggested we broaden our military alliance with China to include coordination on nuclear weapons policy. The most basic version would be a commitment to use only low yield weapons against targets near India's border with China to minimize the possibility of fallout in Chinese territory. In return, we would expect China to threaten unspecified retaliation if India appeared to be readying a first strike against us."

Hamza looked at Ehsan in disbelief. "And is there another version?"

Ehsan nodded, apparently oblivious to Hamza's reaction. "Yes, sir. Other officers hope that China might go further and coordinate targeting with our forces against our mutual enemies. However, that would depend on progress towards further improvements to the Shaheen missile class. As you know, we were successful in extending the Shaheen 2's two thousand kilometer range to two thousand seven hundred kilometers in 2015 with the successful test of the Shaheen 3. We have just successfully tested the Shaheen 4, which will put several southern Russian cities within range."

Hamza slowly repeated, "Southern Russian cities."

Ehsan barreled ahead. "Yes, sir. Chelyabinsk, Yekaterinburg, and Omsk, with a combined population of about four million. Enough to start negotiating with the Chinese about a shared targeting list, with, of course, more cities to come once the Shaheen 5 comes online."

Hamza looked at Ehsan with an expression that finally appeared to penetrate Ehsan's awareness.

"I had already decided to have you placed under arrest pending trial. Now, I will have to add to that the necessity of interrogation to determine just how many other officers are involved in your mad scheme to embroil us in a multi-country nuclear war."

Shaking his head, Hamza pressed a button under his desk, and two armed soldiers immediately entered and escorted Ehsan out of Hamza's office. It happened so quickly, Ehsan barely had time to react, let alone speak.

That was fine with Hamza. He'd heard enough from General Ehsan Monir.

Now, what was he going to do about the Americans?

United States Space Command, Colorado

Captain Walt Addison looked up from his notes as a monitor in the far corner of his office awoke from sleep mode, accompanied by a harsh buzz designed to attract attention.

Well, it was working, he thought irritably, as he hit a switch, making it go silent. Coupled with the irritation was excitement. Was something real actually happening?

Addison had been promoted to Captain just in time to select his next assignment. When he picked Space Command, he'd been thrilled to find the job of Nuclear Event Watch Officer not only available but easy to get.

He didn't yet have enough experience to ask why it was so easy to get.

Now that Addison only had two months left in his assignment, he knew the answer to that question.

Nothing. Ever. Happened.

At one point, Iran had been sprinting towards nuclear testing. No longer. The same was true for North Korea.

The nuclear missile accident in 2019 that had killed at least seven Russians, and probably many more, appeared to give its leaders second thoughts about a renewed arms race. At least, so far, there had been no more Russian nuclear explosions, accidental or otherwise.

So that left Addison drafting proposals to improve U.S. detection capabilities for events that weren't happening. The U.S. defense budget was big. Some of its detractors had even called it "plump."

Even Addison knew, though, that it wasn't infinite. No officer built a record towards promotion, or even a decent next assignment, on project proposals that would never be funded.

After all, existing U.S. detection efforts weren't cheap. Billions had been spent on detecting nuclear events worldwide, including undersea and underground testing.

The alert Addison had received was from the Integrated Operational Nuclear Detection System (IONDS). While earlier detection programs such as the Vela Hotel program relied on dedicated satellites, IONDS' instruments were placed on the NAVSTAR satellites used to transmit GPS navigation information. This approach both reduced costs and provided genuinely global coverage.

The instrument that had generated this particular alert was a bhangmeter. It searched for the double light flash, with the flashes milliseconds apart, that were the characteristic signature of nuclear bursts.

Walt frowned as he looked over the data collected by the IONDS' instruments. In nearly every respect, they made zero sense.

Great, Addison thought to himself bitterly. A bogus alert set off by either instrument malfunction or some natural phenomenon. Either way, he'd have to identify and explain the problem, along with finding a way to avoid a repeat for whoever was lucky enough to follow him in this job.

OK, so first, let's list the reasons why the instruments haven't identified a nuclear test. Most important, it's in the middle of a populated area called Risalpur.

Addison frowned for a moment as he cross-checked a list of Pakistani military bases, and saw there was one in the Risalpur area. Then he relaxed as he saw it was the Pakistani Air Force Academy. Just about the last place they'd have live nuclear weapons.

In any Air Force, you trained with live nukes only after graduation.

Next, Addison checked to see if the readings could somehow be caused by a problem with a nuclear power plant. No, though Pakistan had five, the nearest one at Chashma was over three hundred kilometers away.

So, it had been decades since Pakistan last tested a nuclear weapon in 1998. The energy produced by that test had been much larger than the tiny yield from this supposed explosion, which the bhangmeter insisted had been nuclear.

What about a non-nuclear explosion?

A quick search of news alerts provided the answer he needed to tie this up. The Pakistani government had just reported an explosion at a chemical factory in an industrial export area, along with an evacuation to clean up chemical contamination. A cross-check confirmed that the site of the explosion detected by the bhangmeter had been at something called the . . . Risalpur Export Processing Zone.

Making the notes he'd need for his report, Addison realized there was just one detail left. Why had the bhangmeter incorrectly reported this as a nuclear detonation?

Addison's best quality was that he was thorough. He'd done the required checks, and any of his superiors would have agreed they showed this was a non-event, probably due to instrument failure. They'd happened before.

There was an optional check left to perform. American imaging drones and satellites only obtained data in response to specific taskings, but in almost every mission, data was collected that was excess to needs.

So, Addison was sure that nobody had asked for image collection of the Risalpur Export Zone. But Pakistan and neighboring Afghanistan were routinely imaged for a long list of reasons. With rare exceptions, only imaging data relevant to a specific tasking was ever reviewed.

Maybe some of those images could help Addison determine with absolute certainty whether or not this had been a nuclear event.

Addison was one of the very few people outside the National Security Agency, Defense Intelligence Agency, or Central Intelligence Agency to have the ability to do a query against those images. He'd never done it before and had to look up the steps.

First, he had to create a Nuclear Event Incident Report record, complete with GPS coordinates. That was fine since he had to do that anyway.

Next, Addison had to enter all of his user details, including clearance level, for system confirmation. Well, he'd been vetted very thoroughly indeed for this job and had the highest level clearance he'd probably ever get in his Air Force career.

Even after all that, Addison found he could request an image search solely for the GPS coordinates in the Nuclear Event Incident Report record. Addison smiled since that was all he wanted. Having the GPS coordinates provided by the bhangmeter pre-populated in the search field even saved him a step.

Addison saw that the time search field had been pre-filled as well from his report, from one hour before to one hour after the incident. Well, that was fine too. He figured he'd need just a few minutes before and after the explosion.

After hitting the "send" button, Addison returned to the notes he'd been working on before the alert. He guessed that soon he'd get the response that no images matched his request, and Addison could include that he'd performed the additional check in his report.

Less than five minutes later, there was a soft chime announcing a response to his search. Addison's eyebrows rose as he saw the answer had a file containing images attached.

Then he frowned as he saw that there were zero details attached to the file. Addison wasn't surprised that the associated mission wasn't included since that was no business of his. He had expected, though, to at least learn which satellite or drone had collected the images.

Addison shrugged. At least now, he might get some answers.

First, he adjusted the image resolution until he could see the buildings that occupied the GPS coordinates. Huh. The structures looked more like warehouses than a factory.

Then Addison shrugged. He was no industrial expert. No reason they couldn't be manufacturing inside warehouse buildings, he supposed.

Addison started to scroll through the image file to get to the detonation but then saw some dark objects zip across the screen that made him slow down.

The image resolution wasn't the best Addison had seen, but not far from it. He zoomed in and saw the men on the screen seemed not to be factory workers reporting to their jobs, since at least some of them appeared to be carrying rifles. Others looked like they were pushing a wooden crate of some kind.

Nothing else happened for the next twenty minutes, so Addison began to speed up the playback again, and so almost missed the next two arrivals. Catching the movement on the other side of the building, he backed up until he saw their vehicle arrive, and then two people emerge and cross the street.

Addison frowned. The first group had walked into the building as if they owned it. These two were moving quickly and making every effort to avoid detection.

One looked like . . . she? . . . was wearing a uniform. Addison wasn't sure why he thought it was a female officer. The fluid way she moved? Quite a contrast with the other person, who was struggling to keep up with her.

Addison slowed down, but nothing else happened. OK, time to speed this up again, he thought.

Realizing that the explosion, even a chemical one, would be bright, Addison was looking away from the screen when the playback reached the time the bhangmeter had reported for the detonation.

The room flooded with light as the expensive, high-quality monitor did its best to reproduce the Nasr warhead's partial explosion.

"Whoa!" emerged involuntarily from Addison's lips at the same moment he said a silent apology to the bhangmeter. It looked like it had been right, but he still needed to be sure.

In spite of looking away from the monitor, Addison's eyes needed a moment to refocus. By the time he was able to look again at the screen, what he saw was a whirling cloud of dust.

OK, to be expected from any explosion. Let's fast forward to when it settles.

When Addison saw . . . nothing. Not smoking debris. Just . . . nothing. Bare ground.

Then Addison expanded the field of view to include the adjoining buildings and caught his breath.

They were gone too.

Finally, once he drew back enough to include the next rank of buildings, he saw ones that had just been damaged. Heavily damaged.

OK, this was no chemical explosion. It was definitely nuclear, but Addison had never heard of a test so small.

Then he shook his head. No, nobody would test a weapon in an industrial district with people in it.

So, not a test. Not a reactor accident. Not a military facility, so not some mistake in weapons' handling made by the Pakistani military.

What did that leave?

Addison shook his head again. It was time to stop guessing and get his boss in here. Maybe he'd have some ideas.

CHAPTER TWENTY

Peshawar, Pakistan

Mullah Abdul Zahed looked over the frantic activity that seemed to occupy every corner of the warehouse and shook his head. All of the work that had led up to this day, and all the work still to come.

And instead of the eight nuclear weapons he'd hoped for, he had just two.

Abdul had hoped that sacrificing Hashmat Mohebi and the other Taliban fighters would have been repaid by the deaths of many Americans. But the trap he had set for the "SEAL Team" had failed.

The American media was better than having spies at Bagram Airfield. Not, of course, that Abdul didn't have those too.

Yes, there had been a rush of hope when his spies had reported the arrival of medical evacuation helicopters at Bagram Airfield. But the twenty-four-hour American cable news networks had an exact casualty count for him long before he heard any further details from his spies.

Four soldiers injured, all expected to make a complete recovery. No fatalities.

Abdul had sincerely hoped to make a real dent in the number of special forces troops sent to hunt for him and his precious cargo. He knew how the Americans worked, and that it would have taken time for their replacements to have arrived in Afghanistan.

Well, Abdul thought as he squared his shoulders, he had other distractions planned. In the meantime, they would have to carry on.

Abdul walked up to his nuclear weapons technician, Ibrahim Munawar, who was standing next to one of the warheads. Abdul noticed that the outer casing had been removed from this warhead, unlike the other one sitting on a wooden table about ten meters away.

Abdul could also see that Ibrahim was writing rapidly on a piece of paper. From where he was, he couldn't read it, but the long column he could see immediately made him think of a shopping list.

Ibrahim looked up, and his gloomy and worried expression was instantly replaced with a brilliant smile.

"My friend!" Ibrahim said excitedly. "I am happy to see you! How many others will be joining us?"

Abdul said nothing. Instead, he shook his head.

Ibrahim's expression switched back to gloom and worry even more quickly than it had brightened.

"Are you sure that no one else made it? Maybe some of them are still hiding!" Ibrahim said, looking every bit as desperate as he sounded.

Abdul shook his head again, even more firmly this time. "No. We have our sources within the Pakistani military. The four larger cruise missiles were destroyed in the fighting, and a Nasr warhead was recaptured as our men tried to leave the industrial park."

Abdul paused. "Another Nasr warhead was destroyed in Risalpur, though I'm not sure exactly what went wrong there. So, I am certain there will be no more warheads."

Ibrahim said nothing and looked close to shock.

Hoping to snap him out of it, Abdul said briskly, "Well, these warheads seem to have made the trip in good shape."

Ibrahim's reaction was . . . alarming. He crumpled over and began quietly sobbing.

The frantic activity around the warehouse ceased, as every eye turned towards Ibrahim.

"Come, come. I'm sure it's not so bad!" Abdul said with all the confidence he could muster. "Just explain the problem to me, and we'll fix it together."

Abdul had to work hard to keep what he was thinking from reaching his face. That the soft middle-class life led by this youth had left him too weak to face a real challenge.

Well, Abdul reminded himself, none of his far more hardened fighters had any chance of landing a blow matching the destruction that would be produced by two nuclear weapons.

Ibrahim slowly pulled himself together, and a quick gesture from Abdul was enough to get everyone else moving again.

"OK, this has to be a long explanation," Ibrahim began. Abdul nodded gravely, though he groaned internally.

Long was never good.

"As I told you before, I have worked on both the Babur and Nasr weapons. I didn't tell you that I only worked on the Babur's warhead component because I didn't think it mattered. Generally, Pakistani nuclear warhead design stays the same from one weapon to another, except for size. Every document I read confirmed this," Ibrahim said.

Abdul noted Ibrahim's defensive tone and was barely able to keep from sighing aloud. They didn't have time for this.

Aloud, he gently prompted, "But . . . ?"

Ibrahim swallowed and said in a rush, "The warhead is the same design. But the control interface is a nightmare! I think what happened is that someone high up was worried about a nuclear weapon this small ending up in hands like . . . well, ours."

Ibrahim waved at the forest of wires leading out of the warhead's core to the rear of the metal casing, where they disappeared from view.

"The Babur's warhead had far fewer of these wires connected to the rear casing. You see, five wires are hanging loose from the warhead. These are the ones that are also present in the Babur, and I know what they do. They transmit information of different types from the control console in the TEL to the warhead."

Abdul nodded. "I see the problem. You think if you try to remove the warhead's core so you can rig an alternate means of detonation, cutting any of these other wires will trigger an explosive charge hidden in the rear of the casing."

Ibrahim spread his hands, taking in the warhead and all the wires spilling out from its nuclear core. "It's the only explanation that makes any sense. I know how to disable these trigger wires, but it will take a substance I don't have here."

Abdul restrained his impatience with difficulty. The Pakistani military's search for the stolen weapons was shifting into high gear, and if they stayed in Pakistan, it was only a matter of time before it succeeded.

Well, if this warhead blew up and took the other one with it, that would be bad too.

Gritting his teeth, Abdul asked, "What is this substance?"

"Liquid nitrogen. It will disrupt the connection between the warhead's core and the trigger sensors I suspect are in the rear casing, but not in a way the sensors should be programmed to recognize," Ibrahim said.

Abdul nodded. "You mean, like simply cutting the wires with a knife."

Ibrahim smiled shakily. "Exactly. And I know where to get some, along with the attachments I've written down on this list. I had a friend who used the supercomputer at GIK, and he told me they use liquid nitrogen to cool it."

Abdul frowned. "GIK?"

Ibrahim shook his head. "Sorry. The Ghulam Ishaq Khan Institute of Engineering Sciences and Technology. It's at Topi. Since GIK is a private institute, it shouldn't be too hard to get through its security."

Abdul grunted but said nothing. Private security guards in Pakistan could be armed, but it was true that security would probably have been tighter at a government facility.

The best news, though, was that Topi was in Khyber Pakhtunkhwa bordering Afghanistan. As the home of the Pakistani Taliban, it should be easy to organize the theft of the liquid nitrogen and its transport. There might even be Taliban living in Topi itself.

Abdul started to reach for his phone but stopped as another question occurred to him.

"How much of this liquid nitrogen do you need?" Abdul asked.

Ibrahim shrugged. "Not much. Tell whoever's taking it to grab whatever container it's in with well-insulated gloves, and to be sure the container remains sealed while it's being moved. Liquid nitrogen will freeze skin on contact."

Abdul shook his head. "Good to know," he said, as he looked up the number of his contact in Khyber Pakhtunkhwa.

Just how many obstacles were going to be placed in their path before final victory?

The White House, Washington DC

President Hernandez sat down at the head of the table in the Situation Room and waved everyone else in the packed room to their seats.

He thought, yet again, that he hated being in this room. It always meant bad news.

Hernandez had been able to avoid dealing with another overseas crisis long enough to get an infrastructure bill passed, which would finally start work on repairing and replacing the nation's crumbling roads, bridges, and airports. He had been looking forward to dealing with education next, but it looked like that would have to wait.

"OK, I'm going to summarize the briefer I read, and you all tell me if I've misunderstood something. The Taliban tried to steal eight Pakistani nuclear weapons and got away with three. That's probably down to two because it looks like one exploded at Risalpur, though it was only a partial detonation. The Pakistanis are trying to pass it off as an industrial accident, but Space Command's report shows it was nuclear. We think the Taliban's targets are Bagram Airfield and Kabul's Green Zone. The Russians have offered to help track down both weapons. So far, the Pakistanis have been able to sell the story that the Taliban stole a couple of conventional missiles. They're using that fiction as cover for their continued search. That sum it up?"

General Robinson, the Air Force Chief of Staff, nodded. "Yes, sir, that sums up the situation at this time."

Hernandez shook his head. "OK, I have a lot of questions. First, why should the Russians want to help us?"

"We can only speculate, sir, but I think the best guess is that the Russians don't love the Taliban any more than we do. A successful attack on us that left the Taliban in charge in Afghanistan would destabilize neighboring Tajikistan, where they have a military base. It might also encourage Muslim radicals in Russia, particularly in Chechnya," Robinson replied.

Hernandez could see that Secretary of State Fred Popel had something to add. "Yes, Fred?"

"Well, sir, the Russians may finally be ready to improve relations with us. When we walked away from the Intermediate-Range Nuclear Forces Treaty in 2019, Russia looked like it wanted to start another nuclear arms race. But they've had one failure after another with their Skyfall cruise missile program, and the price tag for nuclear domination is beginning to look too high. If they help us with this crisis, maybe they think we'd come back to the negotiating table in a more cooperative mood."

Hernandez grunted. "Well, if they really do help us find these weapons, I might indeed be more inclined to trust them. A little, anyway."

After the expected dutiful chuckle died down, Hernandez said, "I'm not sure, though if I'm ready to take on those treaty negotiations until after the next election."

Then Hernandez asked, "What do the Russians want from us in return for the help?"

Robinson looked up from his notes. "Sir, I got this from the Defense Attaché at the Russian Embassy just before the meeting. They're asking for clearance for one of their drones to overfly Afghanistan, and for three of their agents. They say their only purpose will be to help us locate the stolen Pakistani nuclear weapons, and that they will withdraw the drone and the agents as soon as that is accomplished."

Hernandez shrugged. "Three agents and one drone? Not exactly a re-occupation. But to have any hope of making a difference, they must have some information we don't."

Robinson nodded. "Our thinking exactly, sir. I asked the Defense Attaché directly if they knew something we didn't, and he denied it immediately. As I think he'd been told to do."

Hernandez smiled. "That sounds more like the Russia I know. It's almost comforting in a way. So, if they find one of the weapons they'll tell us?"

Robinson frowned. "Yes, sir. Three agents obviously won't be able to take on the Taliban alone. I think the best approach is to have them work with one of our special forces teams since I believe they may prove useful. In particular, the Russians are saying that if we recapture one of the weapons, one of their agents could help defuse it."

Hernandez's eyebrows flew upwards. "Really? Is he a nuclear specialist?"

Now Robinson looked uncomfortable. "In fact, sir, they say she's a woman. An Iranian nuclear scientist, the one formerly married to the head of their nuclear program."

Hernandez frowned. "The one who defected to the Russians? Well, they don't let any asset go to waste, do they? Do we have anybody on the ground in Afghanistan who could do a better job?"

Robinson shook his head. "No, sir, I checked. As you know, we've drawn down our forces steadily, but even at their peak, I doubt we had a nuclear specialist there. Not a threat we anticipated, sir."

Hernandez shrugged. "I certainly didn't think it was possible. Haven't the Pakistanis assured us for years that a stolen weapon couldn't be used without its arming code?"

Popel said, "I just received a cable from our Embassy in Islamabad that may have the answer. We've been given a full readout on the stolen missile type by a Pakistani nuclear technician. He also says a different Pakistani nuclear technician has gone missing, and he thinks that technician knows enough to rig the stolen weapons to explode without the arming code. In return for giving us that information, he asks that we not target their nuclear weapons production facilities."

The room was quiet for the next several seconds.

Hernandez's voice cut through the silence. "So, the threat is real. We'll work with the Russians. Until these weapons are found, this is the top priority for our forces in Afghanistan. Do we tell the Afghans?"

Both Robinson and Popel shook their heads simultaneously.

Robinson said quickly, "Sir, Taliban sympathizers have infiltrated almost every level of the Afghan government and military. All we'd do is tip them off, and maybe even spark a panicked exodus from Kabul. That could be as effective in bringing down the Afghan government as a nuclear attack."

"I agree, sir," Popel said. "We've got to keep this as quiet as we can."

Hernandez nodded dubiously. "I understand and agree to a point. But you know how this is going to look if we can't stop one of the weapons, and it comes out we knew about the threat?"

Robinson replied automatically with a phrase Hernandez knew he had used before.

"Sir, failure is not an option."

Hernandez nodded. He knew he was supposed to be reassured, but he wasn't.

Not even a little.

CHAPTER TWENTY-ONE

Bagram Airfield, Afghanistan

Captain John Rogoff looked across the conference table at the three Russians with frank curiosity. Though the woman didn't look Russian. The file he had said she was probably Iranian.

"My orders say that this Ranger unit is to coordinate with you in recovering stolen Pakistani nuclear warheads. I intend to follow those orders. However, I do have some questions," Rogoff added pointedly.

Mikhail Vasilyev nodded and glanced to both sides. To his right sat Anatoly Grishkov, and on his left Neda Rhahbar.

"Perhaps it would help if I first provided some information that was not already given to you by my government," Vasilyev said.

Rogoff nodded and waited expectantly.

"We were authorized to tell you this just before we boarded the helicopter to come here. We have already provided your government information on the likely location of both targets. For one target, we have obtained a map showing the routes the attackers may use. That target is this base," Vasilyev said, as he slid a map across the conference table to Rogoff.

"OK, well first, thanks," Rogoff said, opening the map and glancing at it briefly.

Vasilyev nodded, knowing what would come next.

"But you know this raises more questions. Where did this map come from? How reliable is it? Do the Taliban know you have it?" Rogoff asked.

Vasilyev nodded again. "We found this map in the trunk of an SUV used by Taliban fighters involved in the theft of the weapons, so we have no reason to doubt its reliability. By the time we took possession of the SUV no Taliban present were left alive, so I doubt the Taliban know we specifically have it."

Vasilyev paused. "But if anyone not involved in the assault knew that a Taliban fighter had this map with him after that fighter failed to return, he could conclude it was now in unfriendly hands. And then decide not to use any of the routes on that map."

Rogoff frowned. "Or the map could have been a plant."

Vasilyev shrugged and nodded.

Rogoff spent a few more seconds studying the map and then shook his head. "Not their style. It's not that they're stupid, far from it. They just consider games like planting maps to be a waste of time."

Vasilyev smiled. "Agreed. I have also been told to tell you all sources available to my government are being used to obtain information on the present whereabouts of the stolen weapons. Any such information will be immediately relayed to me, and I will then pass it to you."

Rogoff smiled back. "I understand. We each have a chain of command. I won't waste your time asking about your sources. I couldn't tell you our sources either. But, we do have the same goal, right?"

Vasilyev nodded solemnly. "Absolutely. My country does not wish to see the Taliban in control of Afghanistan. Some might say we fought a long war to try to stop that from happening in the 1980s."

Seeing Rogoff's eyebrows rise, Vasilyev smiled. "Others might see that history differently. In any case, we certainly don't want to see either the American soldiers here or innocent Afghan civilians in Kabul's Green Zone killed in a nuclear explosion. Not to mention our citizens there at the Russian Embassy."

Rogoff nodded thoughtfully. "But you aren't evacuating your personnel there?"

Vasilyev shrugged. "No more than you are. Mass panic must be avoided."

Rogoff looked at his notes. "Ms. Rhahbar is your nuclear expert. May I ask her a few questions?"

Vasilyev nodded to Neda, who said, "Please ask your questions. And please call me Neda."

Rogoff looked again at his notes. "Where did you receive your training in nuclear physics, Neda?"

"The University of Tehran," Neda replied.

"That's where the head of Iran's nuclear weapons program used to teach, right?" Rogoff asked.

With a thin smile, Neda replied, "Yes, and he was first my teacher and later my husband. I'm sure all that is in your file. I hope the fact that I reported him and his cursed weapons to the first foreign government I could find is there too."

Rogoff nodded. "We had reports, but nothing certain until you told me just now. I've been told to pass on my government's thanks to you for your role in minimizing the casualties caused by your husband's creations."

Neda said, "I'm glad I could help," in a voice as neutral as her expression.

Looking across the table at Vasilyev and Grishkov, Rogoff continued, "We've heard reports that two Russian agents also played a role in keep-

208 · TED HALSTEAD

ing the impact from those three Iranian nuclear weapons relatively low. I'm not going to ask if I'm looking at them, because I'm sure you can't say. I'll add that, if the reports are correct, my government's appreciation would extend to them too."

Vasilyev and Grishkov both looked at each other. Grishkov shrugged, and Vasilyev smiled. Neither said anything.

Rogoff looked at all three agents thoughtfully and then turned back to Neda.

"Neda, how confident are you that you'll be able to disarm one of these nuclear weapons, assuming we're able to secure it?"

Neda's answering laugh was sharp and short and carried a bitter edge.

"I wish I knew the answer to that question, particularly since my survival will depend on it. I've looked over the Pakistani nuclear warhead design documents provided by your government. I can think of many ways I could try to detonate them independent of their original triggering mechanism. Each has advantages and disadvantages."

"Such as?" Rogoff asked softly.

Neda frowned, obviously not appreciating the interruption. Then she sighed and visibly decided this was a point worth explaining further.

"I'm going to grossly oversimplify and say that there are two ways to approach the detonation problem. The first is to concentrate on making sure detonation is successful in achieving the weapon's full designed yield. That means avoiding either a complete failure to reach fission of the warhead's nuclear material or a partial failure where some of the nuclear material is ejected rather than being consumed by the fission event."

Neda stopped and looked at Rogoff, who nodded his understanding.

"Good," Neda said. "Now, the other approach is to focus on avoiding premature detonation. Obviously, the weapon's explosion at a location other than the intended target would be suboptimal. However, there is a tension between the two goals. There are several detonation designs I could imagine that would be excellent for achieving one or the other. So far, I've only been able to come up with two designs that might do both."

Rogoff smiled and said, "Well, that sounds promising. Do you think you could disarm those two designs?"

Neda looked at him soberly. "One, yes. The other, no."

From the way Vasilyev and Grishkov were looking at each other, Rogoff could see this was news to them too.

Neda saw their reactions and shook her head. "Sorry, that's not accurate. At this moment, I know I could disarm one possible design. The other, I have some ideas, but I'm not sure they would work. And I have to be honest. They might come up with a design I failed to anticipate."

Rogoff smiled. "Honesty between us is what we need most of all if we're going to succeed in our mission. I understand that there are no guarantees. But it's good to know that we have a fighting chance."

CHAPTER TWENTY-TWO

Ghulam Ishaq Khan (GIK) Institute of Engineering Sciences and Technology, Topi, Pakistan

As the leader of the largest faction of the Pakistani Taliban, there was a long list of reasons why Khaksar Wasiq should not be leading this raid to obtain liquid nitrogen. Heading that list was that Khaksar was too old to be toting an automatic weapon into a firefight, and would slow down the rest of the squad he had hastily assembled.

Khaksar had dismissed this worry by pointing derisively at their target, which everyone had to agree was far from the most challenging they had ever assaulted.

Next was that it would be disastrous for the Taliban if someone of Khaksar's rank were to be captured. Khaksar dealt with that objection by promising he would never be taken alive.

From the dubious looks that earned him, Khaksar knew more than one Taliban fighter wanted to point out anyone could be wounded and captured while unconscious. Bravery had nothing to do with it.

But, Khaksar knew any response other than accepting his promise would be seen as a charge of cowardice.

So, here he was just after midnight with his squad outside the building housing the GIK's supercomputer. Khaksar had been told the building was always guarded and had researchers using it at all hours.

It turned out "guarded" meant a single unarmed security guard sitting at a desk in the building's lobby, reading a magazine. Which he dropped quickly when a short burst of automatic weapons fire shattered the sliding glass door entrance, admitting Khaksar and his heavily armed squad.

Khaksar yelled, "Hands up!"

The guard didn't listen and instead pressed a button on the desk. In spite of his annoyance Khaksar silently approved of the guard's courage. He had to expect he would now be shot.

Luckily for the guard, Khaksar still needed him and had already told the squad he was not to be harmed.

Khaksar glowered at the guard, who looked back defiantly.

"Come with us, and show us to the supercomputer!" Khaksar demanded.

As Khaksar could see an obstinate look appear on the guard's face, he added, "We are not here to harm you, the researchers or the supercomputer. We only want the liquid nitrogen used to cool it. Once we have it, we will go."

A look of confusion replaced the obstinacy that had been there a second before. The guard was clearly struggling to understand what Khaksar had just said.

Khaksar added, "It would be faster if you used your pass and fingerprints to get us in right now. But if we have to drag your body to the supercomputer door, we will."

The guard shrugged and started walking down the hallway behind his desk, followed by Khaksar and his squad of silent gunmen.

Khaksar smiled grimly at the guard's back. It had been a smart decision. After all, the guard knew help was on the way, and truthfully, what was in this building worth dying to protect?

The guard stopped in front of an unmarked door with a white plastic and metal compartment built into the wall that reminded Khaksar of the ATMs he had seen many times in Pakistan's city centers. Next, the guard swiped his pass in a reader, and then placed his right hand on a flat piece of glass.

A line of light passed from the bottom to the top of the glass. Next, the image of the guard's hand was compared with a database of authorized users. Advanced software used by the reader would have been able to detect that an image was from a hand that had no blood flowing through it, a fact unknown to the guard.

It was just as well since the door would have never stood up to sustained automatic weapons fire.

There was a soft "click" as the door's lock disengaged.

Khaksar pushed the guard through the door in front of them.

Sharp words of annoyance from the two researchers hunched over consoles in front of the supercomputer died in their throat as Khaksar and the other Taliban fighters entered behind the guard.

Both researchers froze.

Khaksar looked them over. They were both a shade of pale that said they rarely ventured outdoors. Khaksar was sure both would be nearly blind without their glasses. He also doubted either man could lift anything heavier than a sack of potatoes.

However, right now, they had information Khaksar needed.

"Where is the liquid nitrogen?" Khaksar demanded.

Neither man said anything. Instead, they stood looking at each other, obviously trying to guess what possible use the gunmen would have for liquid nitrogen.

Before Khaksar had to resort to violence, he saw one of the researchers involuntarily glance towards a door in the room's back right corner. Keeping his gaze and his gun fixed on the researchers, Khaksar ordered two of the squad to check behind the door.

Seeing a glum and rueful look on the face of the researcher who had looked in the direction of the room's corner door, Khaksar was confident they were on the right track.

Khaksar's blood froze as he heard the distinctive sound of an AK-74's arming mechanism being engaged.

Without turning his head, he yelled, "Don't shoot anywhere near where the liquid nitrogen might be. Did you even try the handle?"

Khaksar had told everyone in the squad before they set out on this mission to avoid shooting the liquid nitrogen cylinder since, at best, it would cause the nitrogen to escape. Ibrahim had also told him that depending on the nitrogen's degree of compression, at worst, it might explode.

It was not the first time that a fighter under Khaksar's command had failed to follow orders. It didn't make this time any less frustrating.

Shortly Khaksar heard the sound he had expected. The door opening, with no violence required. It made sense, after all. Was it essential to lock the storage closet door to keep the supercomputer's users from stealing liquid nitrogen and printer paper?

As he kept his gaze on the security guard and the researchers, Khaksar heard an exchange he'd also expected. The Taliban fighter who had not prepared his rifle to fire laughing at the one who had, followed by an embarrassed and rather profane response.

The man felt stupid? Good. Hopefully, he'd be a little less ready to use bullets as a first resort next time. This time, it had nearly cost them the use of two nuclear weapons.

A few minutes later, an odd squeaking noise finally made Khaksar glance backward. What he saw made him grunt with satisfaction. He had been told to have his men look for a metal cylinder with a label containing either the abbreviations "LN2" or "N2" or, more simply, the word "Nitrogen." The label on the cylinder being wheeled towards him on a dolly helpfully had both "LN2" and "Nitrogen."

Even better, several long thin metal tubes with different shaped heads were attached to the cylinder with a Velcro strap. Ibrahim had told Khaksar the bottle would be useless without these since he would need the attachments to dispense the liquid nitrogen safely.

Now maybe they could get out of here before the Pakistani police or military showed up.

Looking at the researchers, Khaksar said, "I don't have to explain why it would be a bad idea to leave this room until long after we're gone, do I? Particularly since this man has already alerted the authorities," he said, gesturing at the security guard.

Khaksar saw with approval that both researchers looked at the guard with new respect. Good. His courage deserved it.

They were also quick to nod and mutter agreement.

Khaksar then looked at the guard but said nothing.

The guard glared back but finally gave a curt nod.

Good. Khaksar had killed many men in his years as a Taliban leader. He was now determined to do so only when truly necessary.

As soon as they left the room, the door closed behind them. Khaksar lifted his rifle. To the other men's surprise, he fired a single round into the station the guard had used to unlock the door. To his satisfaction, a shower of sparks and a wisp of smoke made it clear it was no longer functional.

Khaksar couldn't be sure, but thought it was likely the door now wouldn't open from the other side either.

The van they had brought to carry the cylinder was waiting outside the door, with an SUV behind it holding more fighters for security. Ibrahim had made it clear that without the liquid nitrogen, there would be no useable nuclear weapons, and Khaksar was taking no chances.

They pulled away from the Institute's entrance without incident. However, since only a single road led to and from GIK, Khaksar doubted their luck would last long.

He was right. Flashing lights soon appeared behind them, along with a command over a loudspeaker to pull over.

Khaksar sighed and shook his head. Police. Well, with this van, they certainly weren't going to outrun them.

On the other hand, with the firepower his men had this first round would be no challenge. But could they avoid round two?

As planned, a Taliban fighter thrust his head and shoulders through the SUV's sunroof and began to rake the police car with automatic weapons fire. It immediately swerved off the road, and Khaksar listened hopefully for the sound of a crash or explosion.

He heard nothing and swore. One or both of the policemen in that car had probably survived and just radioed their description back to headquarters. Here near the Afghan border, that would almost certainly be followed quickly by a military response. Could they make the planned switch to another waiting vehicle in time?

In minutes Khaksar had his answer. No.

Two sets of headlights appeared to their right, bouncing up and down on a side road that was probably not as well maintained as theirs. Khaksar couldn't see them yet but was willing to bet they were Pakistani military vehicles.

His heart sank as he saw how rapidly they were advancing, and Khaksar yelled at the driver to increase their already considerable speed. They had to stay ahead of the enemy to have any chance of escape.

Yes! Khaksar's van and the trailing SUV passed the intersection just before the oncoming vehicles.

Khaksar shook his head, though, when he finally got a look at the pursuing vehicles. The Taliban had run circles around the Pakistani military for years because they had stuck with traditional armored vehicles. They had the advantage of being hard to damage but were too slow to keep up with Taliban vehicles such as pickup trucks with pintle-mounted machine guns.

Until finally, a Pakistani frontline officer did the obvious. He used a captured Taliban pickup truck and its machine gun against them. It proved so useful that other Pakistani officers in the combat zone began mounting weapons on many types of small, fast vehicles. None of those vehicles appeared on any list of official Pakistani military equipment.

That didn't prevent two of them appearing behind Khaksar right now.

The men in the SUV trailing Khaksar were some of his best, and they didn't need his orders to act. An arm holding an RPG-7 appeared through the SUV's sunroof, quickly followed by the head and shoulders of one of those fighters. Khaksar was impressed with the man's speed, even though the maneuver was one they had practiced repeatedly.

The man pressed the RPG's trigger at nearly the same instant that machine gun rounds began hitting the SUV. The rocket-propelled grenade was on target, and Khaksar yelled with triumph as the first pursuing vehicle exploded and swerved off the road in a ball of fire.

The cry died in his throat as machine gun rounds reached the SUV's gas tank, and it exploded in turn. It flipped and nearly hit the other pursuing vehicle, but to Khaksar's disgust, it managed to evade the obstacle at the last second.

Without the SUV to shield it, machine gun rounds began striking the van. Khaksar immediately thought- the cylinder! Without a conscious plan, Khaksar wedged himself through the gap between the two front seats and then covered the bottle with his body.

At the same moment, his men kicked open the right side of the van's two back doors and began pouring answering rounds from their rifles. Though they had less firepower, they had one advantage.

Khaksar's men were facing the enemy vehicle's driver. That is where they concentrated their fire.

It worked. Their last pursuer veered off the road, and though the van had been hit multiple times, its tires and engine were intact, so it continued to speed down the highway.

Khaksar had not been so lucky. His last act had saved the cylinder and their mission, but it had cost him his life. Two rounds that would undoubtedly have pierced the cylinder were in his body instead. It was fortunate that the passage of both rounds had been slowed by first passing through the van's metal frame, or his sacrifice would have been in vain.

Only five minutes ahead, the van's driver pulled over next to a nearly new truck bearing the logo of a major supplier of liquid propane to both residences and businesses. The back of the truck was full of propane containers of many different sizes and shapes, including cylinders. It took less than a minute for the truck's driver to attach a new label covering the previous ones carefully so that now the liquid nitrogen cylinder was indistinguishable from all of the other containers the truck carried.

A battered sedan was parked in front of the propane truck, and its driver gestured impatiently for the surviving Taliban fighters to climb aboard.

The van, now containing nothing but Khaksar's body, was left behind. Not from a lack of respect, but because they all knew that would have been what Khaksar wanted. As Muslims, once the van was found either the police or the military could be counted on to give Khaksar a proper burial.

What mattered now was for the surviving fighters to escape so their mission would succeed, and Khaksar's death would have meaning. Thanks to the switch they had just made and the bright lights of a sizable town ahead, that's exactly what would happen, as the propane truck and the battered sedan disappeared into a swirl of heavy traffic.

CHAPTER TWENTY-THREE

En Route to Afghan-Pakistan Border Post

Mikhail Vasilyev had started to snore gently, and Anatoly Grishkov looked at him with frank envy. He wished he could sleep through the noise produced by the Mil-8 helicopter's flight so easily.

From the small smile Grishkov saw on Neda Rhahbar's face, she had correctly read his expression but said nothing.

Grishkov's gaze went back to the map he had been studying, a copy of the one he had found in the Taliban vehicle. This version had expert translations of the notes on the original and had helped them pick the border post they were going to now.

It was still a gamble. Four border crossing points had been marked on the map, two for the weapon going to Bagram Airfield and two for the one going to Kabul's Green Zone.

Grishkov had read all the briefing papers and knew the experts had their reasons for sending them to this particular border post. He still thought it was likely they would come up empty.

He didn't know why, but something made Grishkov shift his view from the map to Neda, without moving his head.

Grishkov knew at once what had subconsciously attracted his attention. Neda was looking intently at Vasilyev, as though she were trying to decide . . . something. But what?

It only took a few seconds for Neda to realize Grishkov had noticed the way she was looking at Vasilyev. Blushing furiously, Neda started to say something, but then stopped.

Grishkov smiled and asked, "His snoring is starting to get on your nerves?"

Neda smiled back gratefully and said, "Yes, that's it."

Both of them knew that wasn't it. But neither of them wanted to discuss what was really happening.

Grishkov would have freely admitted to anyone who asked that he was far from an expert in what he thought of as "romantic issues." Even he, though, had finally realized Neda appeared to be thinking of Vasilyev that way.

Neda keyed her headset and gestured to Grishkov that he should do the same. This would let them speak without yelling over the noise of the helicopter.

"I want to let him sleep while we talk," Neda said.

Grishkov nodded in response.

Neda gestured towards Vasilyev. "You knew his father long before I met you both in Iran, yes?"

Grishkov nodded again. "That's right. We first met when I was in the Army fighting in Chechnya, and he was an intelligence briefer. The only one I ever met there who had information we could really use. Even better, he listened to me when I told him what I thought was going on."

Grishkov paused, clearly thinking back. "It was a huge stroke of luck when I found him again in Vladivostok, on the other end of Russia. Or maybe it wasn't so surprising. Neither of us liked Moscow much, though that's where we ended up after our first mission together."

Neda smiled. "I heard both of you refer to that mission, though I know you can't discuss the details. I remember, though, both of you were surprised you survived."

Grishkov snorted. "That's a considerable understatement. I felt we'd both used up our supply of luck, and was almost relieved when I was later shot on the Iran-Iraq border during our last mission."

Then Grishkov's expression darkened. "As you know, that's the mission where Alexei's luck ran out. My luck actually held, since the bullet only hit my ballistic vest, leaving me with nothing but a bruise."

Neda spoke rapidly, as though trying to chase those thoughts from Grishkov's head. "Well, if there is such a thing as a finite supply of luck, Alexei had been drawing on it much longer than you had. I remember him telling me that I would be astonished by the number of times he had cheated death."

Grishkov smiled sadly. "It's true. He told me many such stories. Here's one that is not classified secret. Alexei was on a commercial flight within South Korea. All such flights are very short because it's such a small country, less than a third the size of Japan. So, such flights are used for training. For example, no sooner had the crew finished the takeoff checklist and reached cruising altitude than it was time to start the landing checklist."

Neda smiled. "I can see how that would make training more efficient."

Grishkov nodded. "But on this flight, the trainee noticed a light was flashing after they were halfway through the landing checklist. He asked the highly experienced captain what the light meant. The captain replied that the light meant they had not lowered the landing gear. The trainee said, ah; then we should lower the landing gear. The captain said, no, we did that already because we're past that point on the checklist."

Grishkov paused and said, "I should note here that we know exactly what they said because they were able to pull the cockpit voice recorder."

"Oh, no," Neda said, breathlessly.

Grishkov shrugged. "The captain and the trainee continued their discussion until the accident investigation established that the captain reached to the side out of the trainee's view and pulled the circuit that was making the warning light flash."

Neda looked at Grishkov in disbelief. "So the plane . . ."

Grishkov nodded. "Landed without lowering its gear. In a stirring endorsement of American engineering, everyone was able to walk away from the plane, which was, of course, a total loss."

Neda shook her head. "Astonishing. What happened to the captain?"

Grishkov smiled. "That was the part Alexei said he found most interesting, next to surviving the flight. There was a lively debate over the airline's decision to fire both the captain and the trainee. Many Koreans argued it was unrealistic to think the trainee would stand up to the captain and hit the switch lowering the landing gear. Alexei sided with the many other Koreans who said that with dozens of lives at stake, nothing less was to be expected."

"So do I," Neda declared emphatically.

"Well, me too. But that wasn't the only time that an aircrew's incompetence nearly cost Alexei his life," Grishkov said.

Neda's eyebrows flew up. "Really? And where was this?"

"On a flight going from Dakar, Senegal to Nairobi, Kenya. That's an entirely overland flight. In a moment, you'll see why that's important," Grishkov said.

Neda shrugged and nodded.

"The airline had just installed a new door to the cockpit designed to resist an assault by hijackers. After the plane had reached cruising altitude and the autopilot had been engaged, the captain left the cockpit to use the restroom. Then the co-pilot left to chat with a flight attendant. The cockpit door closed and locked behind him."

Neda looked at Grishkov, horrified. "You mean . . ."

Grishkov nodded. "Yes. No one but the autopilot was flying the plane. At first, the captain and copilot tried to open the cockpit door without attracting attention, to prevent panic among the passengers. Until several passengers noticed there was nothing below them but water because they had flown past Kenya and were over the Indian Ocean."

Neda shook her head. "So, what did they do?"

"Now that the secret was out, they got the strongest and heaviest passengers together to take a running shove at the cockpit door. It took several tries, but they were finally able to break through," Grishkov said.

"Good," Neda said with relief. "So, that's the end of the story."

"Not quite," Grishkov replied. "You see, the plane no longer had enough fuel to reach Nairobi. After frantic radio calls, they were finally able to get clearance to land at Mombasa Airport, on the Kenyan coast. Even though the runway there was too short for their plane."

Neda smiled. "But since Alexei was still alive to tell you this story . . ."

Grishkov smiled back. "Yes. The front end with the cockpit ended up off the runway, but the landing gear was still on it when the plane came to a stop."

Neda shook her head. "I can see why he felt he was pressing his luck."

She looked again at Vasilyev. "I thought his father was a good man. I think the son is too."

The only response that came to Grishkov's head was nodding, so that's what he did.

So, here was a complication. But there was nothing Grishkov could think of that he could do to address it.

Lahore, Pakistan

Mullah Abdul Zahed frowned, as he immediately saw a change since his last visit to the building where the two nuclear warheads were being detached from their casings. The last time, the warheads had been on worktables far apart. The technician working on the warheads, Ibrahim Munawar, had explained that if something went wrong with the conventional explosive component of one warhead he wanted some chance that the other might survive.

Abdul remembered thinking that this approach seemed entirely reasonable.

But now, the two warheads were side by side, with the nitrogen cylinder obtained at the cost of Khaksar Wasiq's life between them. Why?

The only other difference Abdul saw was that the warheads seemed more . . . disassembled . . . than last time. Certainly, more bare wires were on display. Abdul also noticed that the wires had all been carefully sorted and tied together. However, the order seemed to have nothing to do with the color of the wires.

Abdul shook his head. It was good he had an expert to make sense of all this.

Ibrahim spotted him first and waved him over to the worktables, where four large men were clustered around him. Each of the men was wearing padded gloves.

Now Abdul noticed that next to each worktable, there was a small wooden crate, with styrofoam packing material at the bottom.

"Excellent! You're right on time!" Ibrahim exclaimed, with a degree of cheerfulness that sounded a bit forced to Abdul.

What was wrong here?

"Now, this will be simple. I'm going to apply the liquid nitrogen to prevent the sensors from detecting that the wires have been cut. Then I will cut the wires, and these men will lift out the nuclear cores, put them in the boxes, and take them to the trucks. Carefully, right?"

This last comment was clearly directed to the four men, who nodded in a resigned fashion that told Abdul they had heard this warning from Ibrahim many times before.

"OK, once the cores are secured in the trucks, you will go with one truck, and I will go with the other. We'll meet at the workshop where we've agreed I'll build the weapons."

Abdul nodded but said nothing. Yes, this was what they'd planned. It would be foolish to remain in this location any longer.

Now that he thought about it, though, he wondered why Ibrahim had been so easy to convince. Surely moving everything again would make his work harder?

No, this was simply another symptom of age, Abdul thought. He insisted on seeing problems where there were none.

Ibrahim looked at the four men, now waiting two by two next to each weapon. "You are ready?" he asked.

All four men silently nodded.

"Then here we go," Ibrahim announced, reaching for the dispensing wand attached to the liquid nitrogen cylinder. He then began applying liquid nitrogen to multiple points in both weapons.

A few minutes later, Ibrahim stood back and examined his work. Apparently satisfied, he took a large pair of wire cutters and began to slice through all the wires connecting the nuclear cores to the warheads.

It didn't take long. Less than a minute later, both nuclear cores were free of any connection to the warheads. The minute after that, they were each placed in one of the small wooden crates. Next, they were on their way out of the building to the waiting trucks.

Ibrahim had insisted that the building's air conditioning be set to a temperature Abdul found uncomfortably cool. But he had not argued with Ibrahim, thinking it was probably best to have low temperatures when handling explosives. Of course, it made even more sense once the liquid nitrogen cylinder arrived.

So why was Ibrahim sweating?

Before Abdul could ask, Ibrahim said calmly, "Once those men get the crates in the trucks, we need to follow immediately. I have no idea how long my fix with the liquid nitrogen will work."

Abdul's eyes widened, and he turned to look at the four men, who he could see through the open loading bay doors had almost reached the trucks.

"And why didn't you tell anyone?" Abdul asked in a low, furious voice.

Ibrahim's voice was still calm. "Because I needed those men to move those crates carefully. If they had any idea the anti-tamper explosives in these casings could detonate, they could have hurried and risked dropping the nuclear cores."

Abdul did his best to rein in his fury. Ibrahim's explanation made sense.

"How long do we have?" Abdul asked through gritted teeth.

At the same moment he asked that question, Ibrahim and Abdul could both see the crates had been secured, and the men were entering the trucks.

"Run," Ibrahim answered.

Each of them reached the cab of their truck in a matter of seconds. Since each truck's engine had already been started, they were underway immediately.

As one block away became two and then three Abdul began to breathe more regularly, to the evident amusement of the driver, he saw.

He didn't care. It seemed Ibrahim had underestimated the effectiveness of the liquid nitrogen he had applied.

An ear-splitting roar behind them disagreed with that conclusion. Abdul looked in the truck's rearview window and saw a huge plume of smoke rising behind them.

A second explosion followed almost immediately. And then a third, smaller explosion.

At first, Abdul was puzzled. A third?

Then he realized the answer. The liquid nitrogen cylinder.

Well, at least this solved one problem. He had been planning to have several men go to the building to remove any evidence they'd been there. That was no longer necessary.

Of course, the explosion would be investigated. But this was hardly the first time an explosion had leveled a building in Lahore. They would be well away before anyone could connect the explosion to the nuclear weapons theft.

No, the real problem was that this was all taking too long. The enemy knew what they had, and it wouldn't take a genius to guess where they planned to use the weapons.

Abdul had counted on being able to strike before the Americans could organize to stop them. Now he could feel that time slipping away.

No, he told himself sternly. God would not let them come this far and then deny them victory.

Yes, Abdul said to himself, nodding as the truck ground forward.

He just had to have faith.

CHAPTER TWENTY-FOUR

Afghan-Pakistan Border Post

Anatoly Grishkov squinted as, through the harsh glare of the mid-afternoon sun, he saw a DShK-1938/46 heavy machine gun covering the approach to the Afghan government border crossing. The post was manned by a dozen well-armed Afghan soldiers, who were thoroughly searching every vehicle.

Grishkov smiled grimly. It was remarkable how his feelings about the Dushka had changed, now that he knew it would be pointed at their enemies.

Neda Rhahbar followed his gaze and shook her head.

"I know you like the idea of firing this weapon at the Taliban, but we have to keep the fire from this and all other heavy weapons away from any truck we think might be carrying one of the stolen nuclear weapons," Neda said.

Grishkov shrugged. "You remember the rocket I fired at the missile launch vehicle that was carrying four nuclear weapons. None of those went off, or I think I'd remember."

Neda smiled, shook her head again, and said a word in Farsi that Grishkov remembered translated roughly to "idiot." Or maybe something a little stronger.

"Those were weapons assembled by professionals with all the resources of a government behind them. Since they were mounted on vehicles, the weapons were designed to stand up to the possibility of a highway accident, including falling into a ravine," Neda said, with what Grishkov could see was a bit of impatience.

So he interrupted.

"But what will come to one of these border posts is going to be the work of a single Pakistani nuclear technician we were told went missing. And he's going to slap together whatever he can quickly that will work, without any real safeguards," Grishkov said, looking at Neda for her reaction.

Grishkov was pleased to see that this time, Neda's smile was much more genuine.

"Precisely. We should use as little violence as possible to stop the vehicle holding the weapon," Neda said.

Grishkov nodded. "But we also have to prevent them from setting it off, which I expect they would do if it appeared they couldn't escape. Could they detonate it instantly?"

Neda frowned. "It's impossible to be certain, but from what I've seen of the warhead's design, I would say no. Remember, the warhead was incorporated into a missile. It was only supposed to detonate at the end of its flight. In effect, there is an activation delay built into the warhead's design, even once it is armed. In fact, delay even appears to feature in the design of the nuclear core itself. The delay might be possible to overcome, but from what I've seen, I'm not sure how."

"So, there will likely be a delay to detonation after arming. How long?" Grishkov asked.

Neda grimaced and answered, "I wish I knew for sure. These nuclear warheads were attached to tactical missiles designed to fly a short distance at high speed, so not long. Probably a matter of minutes. At a minimum, long enough for the missile to be out of range of the firing vehicle if something went wrong."

Grishkov grunted. "Yes, I'm sure the soldiers at the launch vehicle would have appreciated that much consideration from the weapon's designers. But even if we could talk to the original designers, we still wouldn't be sure, would we?"

Neda shook her head emphatically. "No, because the technician working for the Taliban has more experience with these warheads than I do. He may be able to bypass the delay somehow. But, there's another factor working in our favor."

Grishkov's eyebrows rose. "Something working for us? Please, let's hear it!"

With a smile, Neda said, "Whoever is going to rig new detonation mechanisms for the warheads must account for the transport of the weapons to their targets. We think the new weapon detonation mechanism is going to be built in Pakistan, and the targets will be in Afghanistan. Say we're right. The Taliban doesn't have access to planes, trains, or boats that can do the job. That leaves trucks, over some pretty bad roads."

Grishkov nodded thoughtfully. "And whatever detonation mechanism that Pakistani technician cooks up for the Taliban might not take too kindly to rough handling."

Neda shrugged. "All I know is that if it were me in the truck and hitting a pothole could start the countdown, I'd want at least a few minutes to try to stop it. Why go to all this trouble only to make a big hole somewhere in the Afghan desert?"

"So, you think that the technician will be in one of the trucks. And someone he's trained in the other one?" Grishkov asked.

"That's my guess, and I'll be honest. These are all guesses. But I do think if we can stop the trucks, we'll have at least a few minutes to disarm the weapons," Neda replied.

Grishkov smiled. "Well, I like your guesses, since they mean we have a chance of living through this mission. A chance is all I ask for."

Landi Kotal, Pakistan

Mullah Abdul Zahed frowned as he looked at what was plainly a cell phone. Yes, it was attached to a tripod, but it was jarring to see it pointed at him instead of the bulky video recorder he'd been expecting.

Abdul's nephew, Afan Malik, grinned at his uncle's reaction. "Uncle, I know you're used to much larger contraptions to record your broadcasts. But believe me, this device will do higher quality video and sound than any you've had before."

Abdul nodded doubtfully. The Taliban had technical experts who he would typically have used for such a recording.

But for this, it had to be family. His wife had died long ago, and he had no children. His brothers had all been killed in Afghanistan's endless fighting.

Afan was the only family he had left. He had just graduated from the University of the Punjab in Lahore with honors. Since it was difficult even to be accepted there as a student, Abdul was sure Afan was capable of performing this task. But . . .

"Maybe. But that thing is also a phone. How can I be sure that what I'm recording won't be transmitted until I'm ready?"

Now Afan's grin disappeared. "That is an excellent question that should always be asked when using a cell phone. I have placed this one in the 'aircraft mode' used to prevent it from transmitting any signals that might interfere with the operation of a plane. That means it won't transmit wirelessly through a Wi-Fi network, Bluetooth, or a cellular network."

Afan's grin now returned. "Uncle, nothing you record is going anywhere until you want it to."

Abdul nodded, satisfied. "Very well. Now, I am going to be recording three messages. Before I do so, I have to explain to you what we are going to do. You must understand because you are the only one I trust to choose the right message to broadcast."

Afan cocked his head, clearly puzzled, but nodded.

"We have stolen two nuclear weapons from the Pakistanis, and will use them to strike a blow against the Americans that will force them to leave Afghanistan forever. One will explode in the center of the Green Zone in Kabul, wiping out both the American presence there as well as the Afghan traitors who work with them most closely. The other will destroy Bagram Airfield."

Abdul paused, knowing that his nephew would have questions.

It turned out, though, that he had just one.

"Are you going with the weapons, uncle?" Afan asked in a near whisper.

Abdul nodded. "Yes, with the weapon that will be used against Bagram Airfield."

Afan stood stock still, clearly overwhelmed with emotion.

After a moment, he said, "Uncle, I am honored to be a part of this historic fight for our country's freedom. Please, tell me what you need me to do."

Abdul smiled. "Your part will be straightforward. Three outcomes are possible, and so I will make three recordings. One will be for a successful strike against Kabul's Green Zone, a second for one against Bagram Airfield, and the third against both."

Abdul paused. "We will try hard to make the strikes simultaneous, since obviously once one weapon is used security across the country will be increased. But we may fail in this, and one will follow the other after some delay. I can only tell you to listen to news you can get from any source, and to use your best judgment as to which recording to release."

Afan nodded. "I will. But I can say now that I think you are right. If one weapon explodes on target, if the other one doesn't within a few hours, I don't think it will."

Abdul shrugged. "Agreed. Now, let's get this started. We don't have much time."

Afan's eyebrows rose, as he saw Abdul's hands were empty. "Uncle, didn't you forget your script?"

His answer from Abdul was a grim smile. "Script? No. I have been practicing these messages in my mind since you were an infant."

CHAPTER TWENTY-FIVE

Afghan-Pakistan Border Post

It was only their second day at the Afghan government border post, but Neda Rhahbar felt as though they had been there much longer. She would freely admit that in part, this was due to her lack of enthusiasm for dwelling in a tent, without the entertainment options she was used to during a life lived in cities.

In part, it was a bit stressful to be the only woman not just at this border post, but she was sure for a considerable radius outside it. Indeed, neither her eyes nor her map gave any hint of dwellings nearby.

Neda would have never complained about the blazing hot sun, the blowing dust in her teeth and eyes, or the endless supply of buzzing and biting insects. After all, it's not as though they didn't exist in Iran.

No, the real problem was the constant, nail-biting tension. Neda knew that nearly any truck or van rolling up for inspection could be carrying one of the weapons they sought.

The tension was increased by the fact that they knew none of the Afghan troops could be trusted. Many could be bought for the price of a good meal in a Tehran restaurant. Some were loyal to the Taliban and were waiting in place for the best opportunity to prove it, even though they knew that proof would almost certainly cost them their lives.

Two factors helped to keep the tension bearable. It was comforting to know that the American special forces soldiers were out there somewhere, with every vehicle that entered the border post firmly within their scopes.

On the other hand, Neda wasn't sure whether to trust the American drone she knew was out of sight far overhead. For so many years, she had associated them with merely killing Muslims who had no chance to fight back. It was more than odd to think of an American drone as on "her side."

She had also seen many pictures of the devastation those drones left behind. If it fired, Neda doubted she would survive the explosion.

Vasilyev's occasional voice coming over her earpiece, though, that was another matter. That was simply and unambiguously ... good. It wasn't just that she trusted and admired Vasilyev. Without understanding how Neda knew that her feelings towards him had become much more personal.

She also knew that under no circumstances was she going to give Vasilyev any hint of how she felt towards him. First, to avoid distractions that could cost both of them their lives, lead to mission failure or both.

Second to avoid embarrassment. Neda was conscious of her age and in Iranian society, a woman marrying a man so many years her junior would never happen. Or if it had, she had certainly never heard of it.

Neda unconsciously fingered the scar on her cheek and sighed. She still remembered Vasilyev's offhand comment about her looks at the start of the mission. Well, that beauty was gone now.

The positions occupied by Vasilyev and Grishkov were only known to Neda because she had helped select them. Like hers, they all offered excellent concealment but were still within comfortable rifle range of the vehicle inspection point even without a scope.

Vasilyev's position was the only one within earshot of the inspection point. That choice was logical since he was the only agent with training in each of the several languages that might be spoken here.

Neda stiffened as she could hear raised voices coming from the soldiers inspecting a large truck. At almost the same moment, Vasilyev's voice came over her earpiece, saying, "An officer is telling his soldiers their inspection is finished, but one of his troops is saying they're not done checking the back of the truck."

Now the voices were even louder, and Neda needed no translation to hear the anger in the words. Vasilyev's voice came over her earpiece again. "The officer is telling the soldier that he is to obey orders, and the soldier responds that the commander of the entire post has told everyone that every vehicle is subject to a complete search . . ."

Neda had a clear view of the officer pulling out his pistol and shooting the soldier in the head. He dropped like a stone.

There was a second of stunned silence after the gunshot.

Then, several things happened in quick succession.

The officer threw down his pistol, raised his hands, and began saying something in a loud voice.

Neda heard a "click" in her earpiece that told her Vasilyev was about to translate the officer's words.

But then he was interrupted as the officer's body was thrown backward by the impact of multiple rounds from weapons carried by the remaining soldiers in the inspection squad.

The truck that had been under inspection rushed towards the closed gate. Neda shook her head. It was evident that even a large truck like this one would be unable to brush aside the solid metal gate and its concrete supports.

But the truck didn't get that far. All four of its tires disintegrated, obviously hit by multiple rounds, and the vehicle came to a shuddering halt.

Vasilyev's amused voice came over her earpiece. "Well, I think one of those rounds was mine on this side, and I'm sure Grishkov managed at least one on his. The other dozen or so rounds came from our American friends."

The truck was very rapidly surrounded by shouting Afghan soldiers. A few seconds later, the three men in the truck were face down in the dirt, their arms being secured behind them with zip ties.

Neda frowned. This was odd. No gunfire, no resistance? No final blaze of glory?

One soldier remained behind with his rifle trained on the prostrate men, while the rest of the soldiers threw open the back doors of the truck and began tossing out everything they found.

Only now did the door to the command post fly open, and a uniformed officer stride towards the truck. Before he was anywhere near, the officer was shouting something Neda couldn't hear. From the silence in her earpiece, Neda guessed Vasilyev couldn't hear it either.

Shouting and cheering rose from the truck. Neda smiled with relief. Whatever the soldiers had found, it was not a nuclear weapon.

Now the officer from the command post was close enough that Vasilyev could hear what he was shouting, and the soldiers' response. His calm voice came over Neda's earpiece.

"The officer is telling the soldiers to get away from the truck. The soldiers are saying it's too late; they already know it's full of money."

Several tense seconds passed, with the officer glaring at the soldiers, who showed no signs of moving from the truck.

Then the officer said something in a much calmer tone, which brought immediate results. The soldiers all exited the truck, with one cradling a black plastic cube in his arms. He went with the other soldiers, who collected the prisoners and disappeared into a nearby building.

A few minutes later, other soldiers moved the truck and the officer's body away, and vehicle inspections resumed.

Then Vasilyev's voice came over Neda's earpiece again. "The officer told the soldiers that of course they must be rewarded for their fine work, and he was authorizing an immediate cash award, to be taken from the drug money they had just confiscated. As you will recall from our briefing, American dollars are smuggled into Afghanistan to pay drug traffickers at the wholesale level. I'm betting that after another hefty deduction for this officer, what remains of the cash in the truck will eventually make it to its original destination."

Neda shook her head in disgust. And this was the country they were risking their lives to protect.

No, that wasn't right, she thought. Corruption was everywhere, and that certainly included Iran.

They were here to protect the innocent Afghan people who would be the victims of the Taliban's stolen nuclear weapons. The greed of these men wearing Afghan uniforms did nothing to change that.

But where were the nuclear weapons?

Landi Kotal, Pakistan

Ibrahim Munawar frowned at the sight of the two small white trucks parked inside an otherwise empty nondescript warehouse. The trucks were nearly identical, and each marked with the dents and scratches to be found on most Pakistani commercial vehicles. There was absolutely nothing remarkable about either one.

Ibrahim turned towards Mullah Abdul Zahed as he walked through the door, but before he could even try to say anything was stopped by a sight he had never imagined possible.

Abdul was completely unrecognizable.

"So, what do you think of my disguise?" Abdul asked.

In one sense, it was simplicity itself. Abdul had shaved off his beard, and removed the turban from his head. That was all.

But it was enough.

"I can't imagine anyone recognizing you," Ibrahim said, with total sincerity.

"Good," Abdul said. "It would be awkward if a soldier realized it was me at a roadblock once we cross the border into Afghanistan. I have paid well, and in advance, to pass those roadblocks without interference. However, the reward for my capture is worth quite a bit more."

Ibrahim shook his head. "Your own mother would not know you."

Abdul laughed, and rubbed his chin. "I hope you're right. The truth is, with my face and the top of my head bare I feel as naked as the day she gave birth to me."

Then Abdul gestured towards the two trucks with a broad smile.

"I want to congratulate you on your success in making these weapons. Without your hard work, we might have never had this chance to repel the American invaders for good," Abdul said.

If Abdul had expected his words to please Ibrahim, he was quickly disappointed.

"I explained the importance of suitable transport for the weapons. Since we're near the Torkham border crossing, I expected we would use large commercial trucks with the weapons hidden in a secret compartment. Thousands of trucks cross at Torkham daily, so they can't give every truck a thorough search," Ibrahim said.

Though Ibrahim hadn't asked a question, his expression made it plain he expected a response.

Abdul nodded. "I considered doing exactly what you just described. If a better method hadn't been available, it's what we would have tried. But before I go on to explain what we'll do, let me explain why I rejected the secret compartment approach."

Ibrahim said nothing but nodded impatiently.

Abdul shook his head. The impetuous nature of all youth.

"The American military has a permanent presence at Torkham. We must assume they know of the weapons' theft and will be on the alert to prevent their transport to Afghanistan. The Americans are not stupid, and know they are the weapons' most likely target."

Ibrahim shook his head stubbornly. "They still can't thoroughly search every truck."

Abdul nodded. "True. But in spite of your belief that we could shield the weapons' radiation signatures from the Americans, what if their technology is more advanced than we know? Maybe they don't have to open and search every truck to find the weapons."

Now Abdul could see he'd scored a hit, as Ibrahim's expression went from obstinate to thoughtful.

"OK, you're right," Ibrahim said. "We don't know for sure what technology the Americans have, and if they'd made major advances in radiation detection, those improvements could well be held secret."

Abdul smiled. "Good. Now, I'll explain our plan. First, I'll point out that we've used this method to transport ordinary explosives into Afghanistan several times, and have never been detected."

Ibrahim nodded and visibly relaxed.

Now Abdul walked up to one of the small trucks, and opened its two rear side by side doors, revealing the interior.

What he saw made Ibrahim gasp in dismay.

"You can't be serious!" he cried. "We're talking about nuclear weapons transport! What amateurs came up with this contraption!"

If Abdul was offended, he gave no sign. In fact, it was the reaction he'd expected. Though he'd never tell Ibrahim, it was nearly identical to his response when he'd been shown "the contraption" about a year earlier.

"The elastic lattice you see here will be adjusted to precisely match the size and weight of the weapon. Once adjusted, it will be impossible for the weapon to touch any of the metal sides of the truck's interior. Also, the energy of any bump the truck encounters will be safely dissipated," Abdul said.

Ibrahim's eyes narrowed. "Bumps? Aren't we crossing at Torkham?"

Abdul shook his head. "No. We will cross the border at night, across open country using the four-wheel drive in these trucks. The location isn't far from here, but well out of sight of the Americans. We will rejoin the main highway once we are north of Torkham."

Ibrahim looked . . . stunned. "Trucks across open country at night? How can you possibly expect that to work?"

Abdul reached inside the truck and lifted what Ibrahim immediately recognized as a glow stick.

"We make these glow sticks ourselves using Chinese kits. The glow agent we use is turmeric, which contains a fluorescent substance called curcumin that glows a bright greenish-yellow color in ultraviolet light. The headlights on these trucks can be switched from UV light to ordinary light once we get back on the highway. So, the glow sticks will light up the route we'll use across the border," Abdul said confidently.

Ibrahim frowned. "Can't these sticks be seen by anyone? After all, I understand these are used at parties!"

Abdul nodded. "That's why we make these glow sticks ourselves. The concentration of curcumin we use creates a glow visible to our drivers using UV goggles, but anyone else would have to be standing on top of them to see their light."

Ibrahim shook his head. "And you've moved explosives this way successfully three times?"

"Yes. Each time we had the sticks picked up afterward to refill them with fresh glow agent since it otherwise fades over time. Of course, it wouldn't do to leave them behind, anyway. Someone might get curious," Abdul said.

"You said we'd cross open country, but all I remember near Torkham is hills. Just how far will we have to drive before we reach the highway north of Torkham?" Ibrahim asked.

Abdul nodded. "Well, to be honest, we'll be driving all night. But as I said, we've done this successfully three times over the past year. I think it makes sense to go with a proven method."

Ibrahim shrugged. "Very well. I want to supervise the process of getting the weapons placed correctly in these lattices of yours. The risk isn't just the obvious one of an explosion. Dislodging one of the weapons' components through careless handling could also cause failure."

"I was counting on your participation. Everyone involved has been told that you're in charge, and to follow your orders to the letter," Abdul said.

As Abdul had hoped, this was exactly what Ibrahim wanted to hear.

"Good. When will we get started?" Ibrahim asked.

"Immediately," Abdul replied.

Ibrahim nodded. "I'm glad. I know this has all taken longer than you expected, and I'm worried that the Americans have had more than enough time to prepare for our attack."

"Don't be too concerned," Abdul replied with a smile. "I've had many years to plan this, and I have a few surprises in store for our American friends."

Chapter Twenty-Six

Landi Kotal, Pakistan

Afan Malik's head was still spinning from the enormity of what his uncle had said. Like many Afghans, he had taken it for granted that the Americans would never leave, just as they had never left Germany, Japan, Korea, and so many other countries.

Afan had fully expected that at some point, he would be called upon to play his part in fighting the Americans. Maybe not as an armed fighter. The Taliban had plenty of those, and not so many like him with university degrees.

But to fight in some way, and either be imprisoned or killed? Afan had genuinely believed that was inevitable.

So, Afan felt sadness for the sacrifice being made by his uncle and many others. He was also experiencing a tremendous feeling of . . . relief.

And with that feeling of relief, came shame. Here Afan had done nothing but press the record button on his cell phone, and he was going to live his life in a free country while so many others died.

Afan had to talk to somebody. He was sitting at a cafe with his glass of tea untouched in front of him, surrounded by other men. But he felt utterly alone.

Of course, he would never tell a soul about his uncle's plans. He would die first.

No, Afan just had to talk to someone he trusted, to let out some of what he was feeling.

OK, he would call Shaan, his best friend at university.

When he took his phone out of airplane mode to make the call, Afan was focused entirely on what he was going to say to his friend Shaan. Even if he had thought about the security of the recording files, he would have believed they weren't going anywhere.

And he usually would have been right. His phone's backup settings had been set to "Wi-Fi only" not because of security, but because of money. Afan was charged by the megabyte for cellular data usage, and the rate wasn't cheap.

However, Afan and his cell phone had been to this cafe before, and the phone remembered its Wi-Fi password. It logged in automatically as soon as he took the phone out of airplane mode, and next searched for files that needed to be backed up to cloud storage.

The phone found three new video files and got right to work. Afan, intent on his call, never noticed.

Even then, as recently as the previous year, the video files would have been safe from prying eyes. They were labeled merely one, two, and three and so in the past would not have attracted attention from any country's monitoring program.

A few months before, though, the U.S. National Security Agency had begun a new data collection program called "Sapphire." The NSA had learned from Edward Snowden's release of information from the

"Boundless Informant" program that it was best to make the names of its collection efforts less colorful and less descriptive.

Sapphire collected data only from areas of high interest to U.S. intelligence agencies. Those included both Afghanistan and Pakistan.

Sapphire had access, some by agreement with companies owning the data and some not, to all cloud storage uploads originating from areas of interest.

A new Sapphire capability was the ability to scan video files and search the associated audio content for preset keywords. Some keywords had a low value because they were in fairly common use, like "Taliban." Higher value keywords included "nuclear," "Green Zone" and "Bagram."

The three video files that Afan had unwittingly uploaded were collected and stored at the Intelligence Community Comprehensive National Cybersecurity Initiative Data Center, better known as the Utah Data Center. They were immediately placed in the analysis queue, but how quickly they would be processed was anyone's guess.

Files matching specific search parameters submitted by an analyst were the top priority.

Ones with a keyword in their title were next, though such files were rare.

The file upload location was also a factor. So, an upload from Afghanistan generally had a higher priority than one from Pakistan. But one from close to either side of the Afghan-Pakistan border had one of the highest priorities, along with other known areas of substantial Taliban activity.

Once processed by the Sapphire program's software, if a file was determined to warrant further review, it was assigned a priority and sent to an analyst's queue. Depending on the priority, it might be anywhere from hours to days before an analyst looked at the file.

In short, it was terrible luck for Afan that Sapphire existed at all. But the sheer weight of the amount of data needing review was on his side.

Afan finished his phone conversation with Shaan, which had helped to calm him. Unfortunately, it had done nothing to resolve either Afan's sadness for his uncle's fate, or his guilt at how he would benefit from Abdul's sacrifice.

Afan was then careful to return the phone to airplane mode. It didn't matter, since he'd talked long enough for the cafe's excellent Wi-Fi connection to send all three video files to cloud storage backup, from where they had gone on to Utah.

Afan had no idea, which was just as well. At this point, there would have been nothing he could do about it.

Crossing the Afghan-Pakistan Border

Ibrahim Munawar looked nervously through the truck's windshield as it bounced slowly forward in the darkness. He had learned to keep his teeth set together since some of the bounces were sharp enough to make them clack together painfully.

To be fair, Mullah Abdul Zahed had warned him. It was just that bad as they were sometimes, Pakistan's roads hadn't prepared him for this experience.

Ibrahim snorted with amusement at his own expense. Road? There was no road.

Only the drivers had the special goggles that let them see the UV glow sticks marking their way. Ibrahim had to admit that Abdul had been right. Once or twice, Ibrahim thought he'd seen one of the glow sticks when he'd looked out a side window, but he'd never been sure.

Ibrahim was confident, though, that nobody would be able to see the glow sticks from a distance. That had been a real worry for him.

As the truck lurched again, Ibrahim winced. That left the worry of whether the elastic lattice cradling the warhead they were carrying could keep it from exploding.

As though in answer to his thoughts, about a kilometer ahead, there was a brilliant flash of light. It was immediately followed by the thunderclap announcing an explosion.

The driver sitting next to Ibrahim in the cab cursed and threw off his UV goggles. A part of Ibrahim sympathized, since he was sure viewing the explosion through the goggles had been painful.

A much bigger part wondered what he would do if Abdul had been killed in the explosion. Then he would have to carry out the rest of this mission on his own with a single weapon. Several minutes crawled by while the driver rubbed his eyes, and Ibrahim thought about what he should do next.

The radio in front of Ibrahim crackled to life, and to his immense relief, the voice that came from it was Abdul's. It said calmly, "One of our escort vehicles had the bad luck to strike a mine. I am sorry to say there were no survivors. I know all of you will join me later in prayer to honor the sacrifice of those brave warriors. Now, though, we must redouble our pace. The enemy may have seen the explosion, and might send troops or drones to investigate."

Abdul had already warned Ibrahim about the danger of mines, but Ibrahim hadn't taken him seriously. Most of them had been planted along the border by the Russians in the 80s. After decades how likely was it that they still worked?

Ibrahim had also noted that if the route had already been traveled three times before, plainly that demonstrated it was safe. Abdul had explained that the glow sticks were laid out by Taliban fighters, not highway engineers. Minor route deviations were to be expected. Also, something as simple as rain could shift the location of mines.

Well, now he knew better than to argue with Abdul, Ibrahim thought bitterly. And if there was one mine, there was a good chance there were more.

Ibrahim looked at the driver, who was still rubbing his eyes. Well, he couldn't do anything about the mines, but he could do something about this.

Lifting his half-full water bottle, Ibrahim gestured pouring it over his eyes. He didn't know why, but he felt it was safer not to talk.

The driver nodded and took the water bottle from Ibrahim and emptied it over his eyes. Blinking rapidly, he then shook his head, sending water spraying everywhere, including over Ibrahim.

Ibrahim used his hands to brush the water off his face but said nothing.

Grunting his thanks, the driver wiped his face with his sleeve, and then put his goggles back on.

With a grinding of gears, the truck was once again on its way.

CHAPTER TWENTY-SEVEN

En Route to Jalalabad, Afghanistan

Anatoly Grishkov looked at Neda Rhahbar's work with frank admiration. Their flight in the Mil-8 was anything but smooth. But the quality of Neda's drawings had not been affected, no matter how much the helicopter bucked and swayed.

The drawings showed how Neda believed Ibrahim could have rigged a new detonation mechanism for the Nasr nuclear cores after they had been removed from their original warheads. She had pushed away a tablet offered by Mikhail Vasilyev for the task, saying it was incapable of showing the necessary detail.

What had astonished Grishkov was that Neda had produced the drawings with nothing more than a sheaf of paper attached to a cardboard backing and two pencils. One she had sharpened to a fine point, and the other she had carefully carved to expose enough graphite to let her do shading.

Neda had insisted they all board the helicopter as soon as it touched down at the Afghan border post, over the objections of its pilot who said it was unsafe for them to be aboard while it was being refueled. Vasilyev had been forced to remind the pilot bluntly that their orders specified he was in command of all aspects of the mission.

As Neda filled page after page with drawings, it had quickly become evident that her mind had not been idle while they had waited in vain for the stolen nuclear weapons to appear. This helicopter represented her first opportunity to share her thoughts freely with her teammates. Neda knew these were points that only Vasilyev had the authority to share with the Americans.

Neda tapped the center of the drawing she had just finished.

"If this is the design he uses, you will need to cut the wire leading to this component first. Forget about colors. The wires could be any color. Also, the component's shape might be slightly different, since several different models could serve the same purpose. But, it will look more like this than anything else you will see. Clear?"

Neda's eyebrows rose, and Grishkov saw that Vasilyev was also quick to nod his understanding. Grishkov had a sudden vision of himself as a student in one of Neda's physics classes, and had to suppress simultaneous urges to smile and to shudder.

Physics had not been Grishkov's best subject, and he'd told Neda so.

"Identifying the component which will have the next wire attached you need to cut will be easier. It must be spherical and must be about the same size I have shown here. However, while the first component must be placed as I have shown in this drawing, the spherical component could be placed anywhere as long as it is the same distance from the fissile core."

Grishkov and Vasilyev both nodded.

Then Grishkov asked, "What if Ibrahim places it under the core?"

Neda smiled grimly. "So, not good at physics, but you can spot problems. Yes, if he wanted to make disarming the weapon difficult, that's exactly where he'd put it. Moving the core wouldn't be so hard. However, touching the core even with lead-lined gloves would result in radiation exposure that would eventually prove fatal."

Grishkov shrugged. "Well, at that point, the alternative would be allowing the weapon to detonate, so not a hard choice."

Neda stared at Grishkov and shook her head. "Russian fatalism. No matter how many times I hear it, it's no easier to understand."

Grishkov and Vasilyev traded grins, much to Neda's obvious annoyance.

"Now, I told you before that I didn't know how to disarm the other potential design. I now have an idea for how to accomplish that, but I must be honest. I'm not sure it will work."

With that, Neda flipped to another set of drawings and looked challengingly at Grishkov, as though daring him to say anything else "fatalistic."

Grishkov just grinned at her.

Exasperated, Neda shook her head. "Yes, I know. Consider the alternative. Very well, here are the steps . . ."

By the time she finished, they were all exhausted. Neda said, "I'm going to try to get some sleep." Grishkov grunted, "Good idea," and less than a minute later, both of them were asleep.

Tired though he was, Vasilyev found himself picking up Neda's drawings and looking through them. The detail was so well rendered that he felt as though he could reach out and touch the weapon. He wasn't thinking about Neda's instructions. Instead, he was admiring the drawings as art.

They reminded him of sketches done by Rembrandt he had seen in a museum in Amsterdam. Except he thought these were better.

It genuinely didn't occur to Vasilyev that his judgment might be affected by his opinion of the artist.

Experience with dozens of helicopter flights in Chechnya told Grishkov this one was coming to an end, even before his eyes opened. Maybe the sound of the engine?

Grishkov couldn't have said why, but he cautiously opened his eyes, only a sliver. He didn't like what he saw.

Vasilyev was still awake and looked like he hadn't slept at all. He was holding Neda's drawings and looking at them. That wasn't the problem.

Every now and then, Vasilyev looked back and forth between the drawings and the still sleeping Neda. The look on his face was . . . very much like the one on Neda's when she had looked at Vasilyev on the flight to the border post.

Not good. Not good at all.

Grishkov made a production out of yawning and stretching himself awake. Vasilyev started like the proverbial child caught with his hand in a cookie jar but quickly recovered.

By the time Grishkov asked whether they were close to their destination, Vasilyev answered, "Yes, less than five minutes," smoothly enough that Grishkov could almost forget what he had seen.

Almost.

Grishkov had never had to deal with this problem before. Women served in the Russian Army, but none had been deployed in front-line combat in Chechnya, serving only in rear area support functions such as medicine and communications. The Vladivostok police force had female officers, but none were homicide detectives.

Neda and Vasilyev were both intelligent, sensible people. However they felt about each other, neither would do anything that could affect the success of their mission.

Grishkov told himself this and believed every word.

So why did he have such a strong feeling of impending disaster?

Ten Kilometers North of Jalalabad, Afghanistan

Captain John Rogoff looked at the small metal building dubiously. Mikhail Vasilyev, Anatoly Grishkov, and Neda Rhahbar were all in the Joint Light Tactical Vehicle (JLTV) with Rogoff, and none of them liked the look of the building either.

A radiation reading from the Okhotnik drone assigned to them in support had been sent to Vasilyev over his satellite phone, as well as a poor quality image of a vehicle, probably a truck. Vasilyev had then given the target location to Rogoff only as based on "new intelligence."

But nothing about the building or its location made sense. It was big enough to house the small truck that they expected to be used to transport the weapon to its target. But there was little room left over for any significant force to defend it.

The building had front and back doors that could swing up and allow the entry or exit of a vehicle. On each side, though, there was only a single window fitted with translucent glass. Excellent for admitting light, but no one inside could see out unless a camera system was present they'd failed to spot.

Of course, it also meant they couldn't see inside without someone getting close enough to punch a hole in the building's metal walls.

And why park the vehicle they thought was here away from Jalalabad, a city of over three hundred thousand people that could have served as a significant target on its own? Particularly since it was also home to Forward Operating Base (FOB) Fenty, next to Jalalabad Airport, where they had obtained this JLTV.

Come to think of it, wasn't it remarkable that in all of Afghanistan, the vehicle happened to be parked conveniently near one of the few FOBs the U.S. had left in Afghanistan? Almost as though someone wanted to be sure American soldiers would come to investigate.

So, this vehicle was probably a trap. And they were most likely the mouse about to bite on the cheese. But they couldn't ignore it, because the truck could be the real thing.

There was good news. This brand new JLTV, the successor to the HMMWV, was equipped with an M-153 Common Remotely Operated Weapon Station (CROWS) system. Rogoff had explained that it allowed him to direct fire from the Browning .50 caliber machine gun attached to the JLTV without leaving the vehicle.

Rogoff had deployed the other men of his unit on all sides of the small building. Neda had suggested to Rogoff in robust terms that his soldiers be placed in positions as far away as possible, consistent with carrying out their mission. Rogoff had shrugged and told her he'd already ordered his men to do just that.

The truth was that even more than most soldiers, Rogoff, and his men, had long since made their peace with the concept of a sudden and violent end in combat. A lengthy, lingering death from radiation poisoning though- that was another matter.

Fortunately, truck wheels were easy to hit from a considerable distance. Rogoff was confident his men would be safe from anything short of the warhead's detonation.

From what Neda had told him, if that happened, anyone within visual range of the building would never feel a thing.

Rogoff looked at the CROWS II system display, zoomed in on the small metal building, and frowned. No movement.

After some discussion, Rogoff had agreed to let Neda place a small sensor patch on the hood of the JLTV. It communicated wirelessly with a small tablet that Neda was examining, with a frown even deeper than Rogoff's.

"No, no, this is not right! Cobalt, iridium, strontium, caesium . . . these are the radioactive elements found in medical waste, not a nuclear weapon! This is a trap! We must leave . . ."

Before Neda could finish her sentence, the door on the building side in front of them flew open, and a small white truck roared toward them.

It didn't get far. Just as at the border post, multiple rounds hit all of the truck's tires as well as its engine, bringing it to a shuddering halt. Three bearded men carrying rifles jumped from the back of the vehicle and began to aim them at the JLTV.

None of them had the opportunity to fire a single round. Each fell in a crumpled heap as multiple shots struck them.

Rogoff spoke calmly into his handset, "Hazard, hazard, hazard. Exit best possible speed." Then he zoomed the CROWS II display on the driver, who sat alone in the truck's cab. However, Rogoff made no move towards the trigger that would have sent rounds from the Browning .50 caliber machine gun it controlled in his direction.

Rogoff then pointed at the driver's hand, which was visible resting on the truck's dashboard. He said softly, "Deadman switch."

From the backseat, Grishkov grunted. It seemed like months ago, but it had been just a few days since he'd been holding one just like it.

Neda whispered in Russian to Vasilyev, "Doesn't he understand that this is a trap? Why are we still sitting here?"

Vasilyev replied in Russian, "He's giving his soldiers as much time as possible to escape. They don't have the protection of this vehicle's metal walls."

Then he smiled and said, "My kind of officer."

Grishkov nodded approval as well.

Neda looked at both of them in disbelief and asked, again in Russian, "But what happens when that man realizes we're not coming any closer?"

A flash of light where the small truck had been an instant before, and a shock wave that flipped the JLTV upside down, answered Neda's question.

CHAPTER TWENTY-EIGHT

En Route to Bagram Airfield, Afghanistan

Mullah Abdul Zahed scowled as he looked at the text message on his satellite phone. It was a relatively cheap and straightforward model that could neither make calls nor access the Internet. All it could do was send and receive texts, and it was one of the very few possessed by anyone in the Taliban.

The expense of even a relatively cheap satellite phone, as well as the monthly bills that came with it, were one reason few besides Abdul had one. It was not the main reason, though.

No, over the years, the Americans had repeatedly demonstrated their ability to track down phones, in one case even launching a Hellfire missile from a drone before the hapless Taliban satphone user had finished his call.

So, Abdul was using the standard Taliban strategy to minimize this risk. The lead Taliban agent at Bagram Airfield would send a single number to Abdul based on a list of possible outcomes Abdul had prepared weeks ago.

258 · TED HALSTEAD

The number Abdul had been hoping for was "1". That would have meant all the Americans who had appeared to capture the decoy weapon had become casualties. Instead, he got "5". The decoy weapon had exploded, but none of the enemies had been killed. Though some had been injured, the force attacked with the decoy would still be able to pursue the real weapons.

Abdul had given the other satellite phone to their agent in Bagram in part because he knew that any Americans injured by the decoy weapon would almost certainly be taken to the hospital there.

Abdul was also counting on the agent to inform him of increased security measures in or around the base. Another number-based list Abdul had prepared ranged from "airfield has been closed to all incoming traffic" to "armor deployed on all approaches to the airfield." Abdul had also given the agent discretion to send him a more extended message if nothing on the list matched what the Americans did, and he believed Abdul had to know.

Abdul sighed. Well, it could have been worse. "6" would have meant that the decoy weapon had failed to detonate, or had failed even to injure the Americans.

The truth was, Abdul had been lucky to get the decoy weapon in place in time. Ironically, the death of Khaksar Wasiq is what had made it possible. The collection of radioactive materials from hospitals and clinics in Pakistan had taken years, and Khaksar had agreed to the project only because Abdul had promised the "dirty bomb" made with the materials would be used in Afghanistan. Abdul had been completely sincere in that promise.

But after the dirty bomb had been built and smuggled to Afghanistan, Khaksar got cold feet. He wanted a guarantee that the weapon wouldn't be traced back to the Pakistani Taliban, and Abdul had no idea how he could give that to him. There were only a few medical facilities in Afghanistan where radiation treatment was available, and they were under very tight security.

Abdul suspected it would be easy to prove the dirty bomb had been built using radioactive materials from the over two dozen hospitals and clinics using them in Pakistan. He could hardly say that to Khaksar, though.

Ignoring Khaksar's concerns wasn't an option either. The men who were guarding the bomb were loyal to Khaksar. Also, finding men to replace them wouldn't be so easy. The Taliban had plenty of men ready to fight against impossible odds to free their homeland.

The number ready to face certain, imminent death was much smaller.

The number ready to spend their last days close to radioactive materials that would make them progressively sicker every day was . . . even smaller.

When Abdul had learned of Khaksar's death, he had immediately sent word to the men guarding the bomb that they would be used to trap the Americans who were seeking the stolen Pakistani nuclear weapons. Since they had already learned of Khaksar's passing, they didn't question the order.

Well, it hadn't been a total waste of effort. The Americans had been both distracted and delayed.

And he had one more diversion left, more distracting than all the others.

High Energy Materials Research Laboratory (HEMRL), Pune, India

CL-20 was first developed by the U.S. Navy's China Lake facility in the 1980s, but due to its expense was used primarily as a propellant. With an explosive yield higher than either Semtex or RDX, terrorists had been interested in obtaining CL-20 for bomb manufacturing ever since its existence had been made public. However, as long as its only production source was the U.S. military, it remained out of their reach.

That changed once CL-20 production began at the High Energy Materials Research Laboratory (HEMRL) in Pune, India. A substantial research and production facility established in 1960 with over a thousand scientists on staff, HEMRL didn't stop with simple CL-20 production.

Instead, scientists at HEMRL took advantage of research first published in 2012, showing that a cocrystal of two parts CL-20 and one part HMX kept most of CL-20's explosive power while gaining HMX's stability. HEMRL became the first facility in the world to produce the new explosive in quantity.

Akshay Roshan was one of the senior scientists at HEMRL. He had expensive tastes, ones that even a salary generous by Indian standards were unable to meet. It took him several years to smuggle out a quantity of the CL-20 compound sufficient to meet his needs and to locate a buyer.

That second part had been especially time-consuming, and it led to Akshay having even more of the CL-20 compound to sell than he'd initially planned. Akshay was determined to sell only to a buyer who would not use the explosive in India.

This determination was in part because Akshay didn't want to see his countrymen hurt. But only in part. The more important reason was that he thought outside India its use was much less likely to be traced back to HEMRL—and to him.

Akshay had many clever ideas for verifying the identity and motives behind potential buyers. In the end, though, it was just dumb luck that the buyer for the explosives was neither an undercover government agent nor a member of one of India's plentiful domestic terrorist groups.

The Taliban agent who made the purchase was clean-shaven, slender, and had light brown, curly hair. Akshay thought he looked Arab, which made sense. The man said the explosives would be used to attack Syrian government offices in Damascus.

That was better than fine for Akshay since if true, that would put the explosion over four thousand kilometers away. Even if it was a lie, Akshay was certain the buyer wasn't Indian.

And Akshay was right. He wasn't. And in the days after the sale, the explosives were, in fact, not traced back to him.

Unfortunately, that generous payday whetted his appetite for more. Just months later, he had another batch of CL-20 compound ready for sale.

By now, though, Akshay's superiors had finally noticed missing quantities of controlled materials and notified the Central Bureau of Investigation. Akshay knew nothing about money laundering and had simply deposited the money from his last sale in his bank account.

That made it easy for the special unit within the CBI that dealt with threats to national security to focus on Akshay without delay. He was the sole scientist with access to the missing controlled materials to have a sizeable unexplained bank deposit.

Akshay had just concluded an expensive but delightful evening at an exclusive club with many attractive women on its staff. He was reflecting on one woman in particular, and how she had genuinely seemed to like him, as he walked to his car well after midnight.

A black van pulled up next to him, and Akshay found himself pulled inside before he knew what was happening. As the vehicle sped forward, the CBI agents inside identified themselves.

Terrified, at first, Akshay tried to insist on speaking to a lawyer.

The CBI agents handcuffed Akshay and told him that since he was being charged under national security statutes for providing material aid to terrorists, he had no right to speak to anyone.

Except, of course, them.

The CBI agents told Akshay that his only chance for leniency was to tell them everything he knew before the explosives he had sold could be used.

At first, Akshay attempted to be indignant, saying he knew nothing about any sale of explosives.

Then one of the CBI agents mutely handed Akshay a printout of his bank account, with the huge deposit from the explosives sale highlighted.

Akshay was taken to a secret facility near Mumbai used solely for the detention and questioning of individuals who had been determined to be a threat to national security. Thanks to the late hour, there was relatively little traffic. An excellent toll road connected Pune with Mumbai, so it took less than four hours to place Akshay in his cell.

Akshay had told everything he knew long before then.

In fact, not only had he already given up the location of the storage locker where he was keeping the CL-20 compound for his next sale. CBI agents were already there with bomb disposal experts to collect it.

Without his cooperation locating the CL-20 compound would have been quite difficult since the locker was part of a strictly cash-only operation that asked no questions about identity. Akshay had learned about it from another patron of the exclusive club he frequented when the man had consumed one drink too many.

That person, as well as many others, were due for a rude surprise once the CBI agents assigned to Akshay's case had time to pass the storage operation's location on to other agents in the CBI.

Akshay had given a detailed description of the man who bought the CL-20 compound, and even worked with a CBI agent qualified as a sketch artist to produce a likeness Akshay called, "as good as a photograph."

Unfortunately, it didn't matter much. The CBI agents correctly believed it was likely that the buyer and the CL-20 compound were no longer in the country.

Akshay eagerly repeated the story the buyer had told about his intended use of the explosives and asked whether the fact that they would not be used against India or its allies would help reduce the charges against him.

This was a question none of the CBI agents considered worthy of a response, since by then they were both near the secret detention facility, and were convinced Akshay had told all he knew.

Of course, that didn't mean the dedicated staff at Akshay's new home weren't going to do their very best to make sure there was no detail he had forgotten to mention.

CHAPTER TWENTY-NINE

Kandahar, Afghanistan

Khaled Tanha had been fighting with the Taliban since he was old enough to hold a rifle. Wounded twice, once seriously, he had never once thought about any other life. American, British or other NATO soldiers-they were all the same to him. Just like the Afghan Army men who fought beside them.

Targets.

Like any Taliban fighter who had been in the war as long as he had, several times, he had thought he would not survive.

Today was different, though. Today Khaled knew he wouldn't.

Khaled grinned fiercely. That didn't mean he would sell his life cheaply. Far from it.

He and three other experienced Taliban leaders had been recruited by Mullah Abdul Zahed months before for a mission that he promised would help free Afghanistan of foreign invaders once and for all. To help achieve that goal, he had promised them a new and extraordinarily powerful explosive.

Abdul had been plain and direct. They and the men they would recruit for this mission had practically no chance of survival.

As a religious leader with the title of Mullah, Abdul had always despised others who motivated fighters by promising them Paradise if they fell in battle. Fighting the enemy did not excuse all past sins, and only God knew who he would decide to have join him after death.

But Abdul didn't have to make any elaborate promises to Khaled. They had the chance to return Afghanistan to Taliban rule, expel the foreign invaders, and end the fighting that had lasted as long as anyone alive could remember.

If that didn't get Khaled into Paradise, he couldn't imagine what would.

Craig Joint Theater Hospital, Bagram Airfield, Afghanistan

Neda opened her eyes and immediately realized she was in a hospital, though she had no idea where. A slim female doctor with her blond hair pulled back in a severe bun was looking at a chart Neda assumed was hers, and quickly saw she was awake.

"Ms. Rhahbar! Good to see you awake! How are you feeling?" the doctor asked.

Neda paused before answering. She experimentally moved her arms and legs, which appeared to be intact and working. No pain that she was aware of . . .

"As far as I can tell, I'm fine. Though I don't know whether there are painkillers in there that might account for that feeling," Neda said, nodding towards the IV line leading to her arm, connected to a clear plastic bag.

"Also, please call me Neda," she added.

The doctor smiled and said, "I am Doctor Holt, and this is Craig Joint Theater Hospital at Bagram Airfield. There's nothing in that bag but saline. You took a blow to the head, but we've done a CT scan, and there's no sign of either internal bleeding or swelling. The fact that you're not feeling any pain is another excellent indicator. We're going to keep you overnight for observation, but I expect to discharge you tomorrow morning."

"How are . . .". Neda's question was cut off by the familiar faces of Anatoly Grishkov and Mikhail Vasilyev. But their hair!

Pointing at each of their bald heads, Neda asked, "What happened to . . ."

Vasilyev finished for her. "Our hair. Well, though we were the closest to the explosion, the vehicle's air filtration system protected us from most of what was a very nasty radioactive mix inside that truck. But to be extra sure, the doctors here recommended that we discard not only our clothes but everything else we could."

Grishkov made a face. "Arisha keeps telling me she wants another child. Not my preference, but I didn't want the choice being made for me."

Vasilyev smiled. "And though I'm not married, I agree with our friend that it's best to leave one's options open."

Neda's hand flew to her head, which she felt with relief still had hair on it.

Looking at Dr. Holt, Neda asked, "So in my case why did you . . ."

The doctor nodded and said, "You were wearing a scarf. It was made of tightly woven silk, which served as an excellent shield against radioactive particles. We've also washed your hair and body twice with a special decontamination soap. Once we've finished talking, I'll ask you to take a shower with it to be safe. But we've checked you thoroughly, and your readings show no trace of radioactivity."

Vasilyev asked, "Doctor, is this soap something you normally have on hand?"

Doctor Holt shook her head. "Good question. No, we don't. You have Captain Rogoff to thank for that. He had a friend of his at Ramstein send us a case of the stuff. I didn't understand why at the time, but it sure came in handy."

Neda asked quietly, "And how are Captain Rogoff and his men?"

Dr. Holt smiled. "They've all been treated and discharged. He asked me to notify him when you woke up, so I expect you'll see him later today. Now, if you have no other questions, you need to get in the shower and then back to bed. We'll be running a few more tests before evening."

Then Dr. Holt turned to Vasilyev and Grishkov. "As for you two, you're both supposed to still be in bed. Let's give this lady her privacy."

Seconds later, the doctor and Neda were alone. Frowning, Neda said, "You were a little harsh. I think they were just worried about me."

Dr. Holt grinned and shook her head. "Worried about you? That's what we call an 'understatement.' So, Grishkov is a good friend who deeply respects you, and Vasilyev is your boyfriend, right?"

Neda's eyebrows flew up. "What in the world makes you think that about Vasilyev?" she asked.

Dr. Holt cocked her head and took a moment before replying. "I've been on shift for over twelve hours, so I guess I let my mouth run away from me. Not the first time it's happened."

Then she looked at Neda and sighed. "But look, woman to woman, if you'd been awake like I was when Vasilyev was looking at you when we weren't yet sure about your condition- well, you would have known how he feels about you. I'd have guessed he was your husband, but I didn't see rings on your fingers, so that's why I thought boyfriend. Now, I will apologize and butt out of your personal life."

Pointing at a door on the other side of the room, Dr. Holt said, "Time to hit the shower. I'll stay here while you take it, in case you need help or feel dizzy. Take it slow, getting out of bed."

Neda had no trouble, and with her hand on the shower's door turned and said, "Thank you for your honesty, Doctor. You've given me a lot to think about."

CHAPTER THIRTY

Kandahar, Afghanistan

People were creatures of habit. Khaled Tanha had consulted weeks before with the Taliban leaders who were about to assault the other girl's high schools in three other cities, and they had all agreed. The best use of the new explosives would be to use them to approach the schools in sedans.

Guards were trained to be on the lookout for trucks because the quantity of ordinary explosives needed to level a building usually required one. That didn't mean they were supposed to ignore cars. But, habits formed over time, and people could only stay on their guard for so long.

There had been a time when, even so, this plan would have never worked. American troops used to guard all the girl's high schools. Then, when their numbers dropped, they were replaced with Afghan Army soldiers. Finally, private security contractors took their place. Armed, to be sure, but without much in the way of training or motivation.

This lack of training showed in the defense plan for all four schools, which all had the same security contractor. A wall surrounded each school with a single entry point, a vehicle gate next to a pedestrian gate. There was a guard inside who controlled the operation of both entrances.

So far, so good.

But, there was also a guard outside the gate. The thinking was, let's have a man on the outside who can see a truck bomb coming. All of the schools were on side streets in residential areas where ordinarily few large vehicles would go. If a truck was spotted headed for the school, the outside guard could duck inside and provide a warning. If the vehicle was approaching at high speed, the inside guard could call for backup.

The guard deployment wasn't totally without merit. But it depended on the idea that only a truck could carry a bomb big enough to threaten the school.

Khaled was about to show them that wasn't true.

Everything depended on a coordinated attack since once one school was attacked the others were sure to be warned. Khaled was in contact with the other Taliban assault team leaders through group texts.

No one was to text until a goal was being attempted. Using the standard Taliban security method, they had a simple prearranged code that would ensure they all moved at the same time. Each step had a number.

The first step was to get rid of the guards and enter the schools.

Khaled texted the number one and waited for each of the other team leaders to check-in before his sedan turned the corner and began moving towards the school. Khaled was in the passenger seat, so he could roll down the window and talk to the guard.

Khaled smiled to himself as he saw the school guard's reaction to his approach. They had stolen government license plates weeks before and placed them on the sedans they would use that morning. Because of their distinctive color, the plates were identifiable from a distance and worked as Khaled had intended.

The guard visibly relaxed.

Khaled's sedan moved at average, slow speed down the quiet residential street towards the school and the guard standing in front of its gate. Early in the morning, when the staff and girls arrived and again later in the afternoon when they left, the street was full of cars. Now, though, theirs was the only vehicle in motion.

Khaled and the other Taliban fighters with him had all shaved off their beards weeks before and had their hair trimmed to the short length required by police standards. Shaving every day was a genuine nuisance, but it was critical to making the guard at the gate believe they were plain-clothes police officers.

As the sedan reached the school and its guard, Khaled lowered his passenger side window and gestured for the guard to move closer.

"We are a special security unit," Khaled said, injecting what he hoped was the right tone of authority and impatience to his voice.

Pointing at an SUV parked about a hundred meters away and on the other side of the street, Khaled asked, "Have you seen that vehicle before, and if so, do you know its owner?"

Immediately hit with a question, the guard didn't think to ask Khaled for identification. That was good since Khaled had none.

Khaled also knew the guard's answer to his questions before he spoke, since his men had placed the SUV where it was now the previous night.

"No, sir," the guard said with a shrug.

"Very well," Khaled said. "Come with us to inspect the vehicle. We have been told it may contain explosives timed to detonate when parents come to pick up their girls this afternoon."

The guard wanted to refuse, but Khaled had struck precisely the right tone of command. Besides, if he said no, he'd look like a coward, and he couldn't have that.

"Very well," the guard said and trotted along beside them as the sedan moved slowly towards the SUV.

When they were alongside it, Khaled exited the sedan holding a small bag. The guard looked at it, puzzled.

"My tools," Khaled said, knowing he'd really explained nothing. "Come over to the other side of the SUV with me while I check to see if the doors are booby-trapped."

Nodding doubtfully, the guard did as Khaled told him. Now they were both out of view of the school's gate, and any camera that might be there.

"Now, listen very carefully," Khaled said, as he pulled first a pistol and then a small grayish cube from his bag. "Smell this," he said, lifting the cube to the guard's face.

Confused, the guard did as he was told. Though he said nothing, Khaled could see that the guard could smell the plastic explosive's distinctive odor.

"This is a new and very powerful plastic explosive," Khaled said calmly.

The guard reached for the pistol on his hip, but Khaled's gun was already in his right hand.

Shaking his head, Khaled said quietly, "None of that. We want you going back home to your wife. You have children, right?"

The guard nodded miserably.

"OK. We're not here for you or the guard inside the gate. You're just employees, doing a job for a salary to feed your families. Do as I say, and you'll walk away. If you think about it, if I'd wanted to kill you, I could have done it already."

The guard slowly nodded. "What do you want me to do?"

"First, hand me your pistol—carefully," Khaled said.

Once the guard had done that, Khaled put the pistol in his bag. Next, with his left hand, he pulled out first a strip of adhesive and then a small detonation device. Khaled quickly put the adhesive strip on the SUV's driver's side door. Then he pressed the small grayish mass of explosive into it, and next inserted the detonation device's probe into the cube.

"Come with me to our car's trunk," Khaled said next.

Once they were standing in front of the trunk, Khaled opened its lid. The trunk's interior was nearly filled with the same grayish material Khaled had the guard smell earlier and had a larger detonation device inserted in its top. An identical and much stronger odor emanated from the trunk. No one could doubt it was the same substance.

"We are going to drive back to the gate, and you are coming with us," Khaled said. "Then, I'm going to set off that small charge you saw me attach to the SUV. When you see what it does, you will understand that if I set off the explosives in the trunk, neither you nor the guard on the other side of that gate will be going home to your wives."

The guard looked like he was about to vomit.

Khaled smiled and said in a reassuring voice. "Remember what I said. We're not here for you. Once the SUV explodes, get on your radio and tell the other guard the school is under attack. Tell him that you're here with the police, and he needs to open the gate so we can enter and secure the school."

The guard shook his head. "Then you'll just kill us both."

Khaled frowned impatiently. "No, I won't. I want both of you alive to tell the real police how much explosive we have. We're going to demand the release of Taliban prisoners, and the police need to know that if they try to storm the school, our bomb will level it and kill everyone inside."

The guard still looked uncertain.

Khaled sighed. "Look, once you see what the small amount I put on the SUV can do, you'll know that it wouldn't have taken much more to blow down your gate. And if you don't make the radio call, that's what

I'll do, and then you and the other guard will indeed be killed. But again- that's not what I want."

The guard slowly nodded.

"Good. Now, get down on this side of our car. You can't make the ra- dio call if you get killed by shrapnel," Khaled said.

This time, the guard didn't hesitate. Very quickly, he was hunched down behind the bulk of the sedan.

Khaled pushed the button on the small remote control for the deto- nation device attached to the side of the SUV. At the same moment, he said a silent prayer. He'd tested a small quantity of the explosive as soon as he'd received it but still wasn't sure it would work as well now as it had then.

It was one of the very few times in Khaled's life where his concerns turned out to be completely groundless.

The small explosive mass Khaled had used had been shaped by one of the Taliban's explosives experts, who had made more bombs just like it for the team leaders sent to the girl's high schools in the three other cities. He had also given them precise instructions for where and how to apply the explosives to the SUVs.

The expert had explained why it was essential to follow his instruc- tions, but Khaled had barely listened. All that mattered was that follow- ing them was critical to the success of the mission.

The force of the bomb's explosion both lifted the SUV in the air and flung it down the street, fortunately away from them.

Khaled shook his head ruefully. No, that wasn't right. There was nothing fortunate about it. He recalled now that was why the explosives expert had been so insistent that his instructions be followed precisely.

Khaled looked at the guard and was gratified by his reaction. Not only was he impressed, but he was also lifting his radio to his mouth, and saying exactly what Khaled had told him to say.

The gate swung open.

Seconds later, Khaled's sedan and the guard were inside the school's courtyard, and the gate had swung closed.

A small, squat structure occupied the space directly adjacent to the exterior wall, and next to the gate. It looked new and sturdy and had one-way glass all around it, except the side it shared with the exterior wall. Cameras on all sides meant it could see everything that happened in the courtyard.

When the Americans drew down their forces in Afghanistan and had to reduce their activities, they had decided to improve security at the girl's schools they were no longer going to guard with their troops. The contractor picked for the job was American.

But many of the actual workers were Afghan.

After the projects were completed, it wasn't difficult to find one who was willing to share details of the security upgrades, for the right price. Of course, once he had told everything he knew, he had to be silenced, and his body buried where it would never be found. It wouldn't do for the Americans to be alerted to the fact that someone was interested in their security upgrades.

And in the daily chaos of the never-ending war in Afghanistan, people disappeared all the time. Here, there was no Missing Persons Bureau.

So, Khaled knew that the one-way glass was bulletproof, and the walls reinforced with steel plates that would protect the guard inside from even a high-velocity rifle bullet.

But the guard was facing a much greater threat today.

The guard booth was also equipped with exterior speakers, which the guard inside now used.

"Kader, what's going on out there? How many attackers are there?" the guard asked.

Then, without waiting for an answer, he said in a low and suspicious voice, "And I want to see ID from everyone in the car."

"Ali, these are the men who planted the bomb that blew up the SUV outside," the guard whose name Khaled now knew was Kader said.

The response was a stream of invective as detailed as it was colorful. Khaled found himself hoping, half-seriously, that none of the girls inside the school could hear it.

"Ali, listen to me. These men have a trunk full of the same explosives they used to blow up the SUV. You saw what it did to the SUV. What you didn't see is that they used an amount no bigger than my thumb. You're not invulnerable inside that shack."

Shack, thought Khaled. It was clear there wasn't a great deal of love lost between Ali and Kader.

There was a long pause. Finally, Ali asked, "What do they want?"

"They are going to demand the release of Taliban prisoners in return for freeing the girls. Look, I know we were hired to protect them. But against this kind of firepower, we have no chance. They want us to leave and tell the police how much explosives they have," Kader said.

Khaled pressed a button on the sedan's dashboard, and the trunk lid swung up, revealing its contents. With all the cameras he had, Khaled knew Ali would have no trouble seeing what was inside.

Another long pause. Then, Ali asked, "How do I know that as soon as I open this door, they won't shoot us both?"

Kader shook his head in exasperation. "Because they could have killed us both by now if that's what they'd wanted. If we don't tell the police how much explosives they have, the police will try to rush them, and then all the girls will die for sure. And if we're going to tell the police, we have to leave now."

Khaled added, "Before the police show up, and that's going to be pretty quick after that SUV explosion. Once they get here, I'm not going to open that gate."

That seemed to make up Ali's mind, because the gate swung open, and then Ali stepped out of the "shack's" door.

Ali looked like he expected to be shot on the spot. The truth was if that would have helped achieve the mission, that's just what Khaled would have done.

Fortunately for Ali and Kader, he'd been telling them the truth. Khaled gestured with his pistol for both of them to walk through the open gate.

Neither wasted any time in obeying.

Khaled stepped inside the guard booth and was glad to see all the control buttons neatly labeled. He pushed the one that closed the gate, just as he could see approaching flashing lights. As he'd thought, there'd been no time to spare.

The phone in the booth was buzzing. With amusement, Khaled saw that the digital readout next to the phone identified the caller as the principal's office. Yes, Khaled imagined she would have questions about the rather loud explosion she had just heard outside. Well, she'd have to wait a moment.

Next, Khaled touched a button that a Taliban communications specialist had programmed on each of the leaders' cell phones. Using something he called a "macro" the button sent texts and e-mails to multiple Afghan government offices throughout the city containing their demands and warning of the consequences of an assault.

There had been quite a bit of argument over the entry plan that Khaled, at least, had brought off successfully. The other Taliban leaders had said they had explosives—why not use them on the gate and the guard booth?

Khaled had pointed out that their goal was not just to take the girls at the school hostage. It was to keep the girls' hostage, and the American soldiers they were sure would be sent to free them occupied for as long as possible.

That was the point of the mission, not to free Taliban prisoners. Khaled and the other Taliban leaders all knew the Afghan government would never agree to such a demand for a simple reason. If they did, hostage-taking would increase dramatically.

A gate smashed flat by explosives would give those American soldiers an obvious and easy way in. An intact guard booth gave Khaled, and his men, access to external and interior cameras that would make an assault far easier to spot.

Finally, reluctantly, the other Taliban leaders had agreed with Khaled's plan.

Now to see whether the others had been as successful in implementing it. Khaled texted the number two to the rest of the assault teams. Within a few minutes, answering texts with the same number came in from two of the other teams.

From the third team, there was only silence. Khaled would never know it, but that team had the bad luck to assault a school where that morning, an Afghan Army squad had been sent to check on its security precautions.

In the firefight that followed, four soldiers were killed, and all of the Taliban fighters except the team leader. He set off their team's bomb, but it only killed him and the remaining soldiers. Though the school building was damaged, the explosion was too far away to do more than injure a dozen girls from flying glass when multiple windows were shattered.

Khaled and the two remaining team leaders in the other cities set about their next task. Taking control of the school building.

All of the schools were in old buildings that had been initially built for other purposes. For many reasons, none of the buildings would have passed an American fire code inspection.

From Khaled's point of view, one of those reasons was excellent news for him. Each building had only a single entrance.

Khaled took one of his men with him and walked across the courtyard to that entrance. Time to answer the principal's questions.

Khaled had ordered one man to monitor the displays in the guard booth and the other to stay at the gate in case the police were foolish enough to attempt an immediate assault. He thought, though, that was very unlikely.

A large sign in front of the first door to the right of the school entrance announced it as the principal's office. Neither the entrance doors nor the door to the principal's office was locked. Khaled smiled to himself. With armed guards at the front gate, why would they be?

Khaled told the fighter he had brought with him to stand watch at the building entrance. Then he didn't bother knocking but walked right into the principal's office.

The principal's secretary was in the outer office and had a phone pressed against her ear, trying no doubt yet again to reach Ali, the guard who was already gone. She had just looked up to see Khaled enter when the inner office door flew open.

Now Khaled noticed that the same bulletproof one-way glass that had been used for the guard booth filled the top half of the principal's inner office. Seeing the angry, self-important expression on the face of the woman approaching him, Khaled was sure that was her idea.

Well, it did explain how she'd been so quick to react to his appearance.

"Who are you, and what are you doing here?" the principal demanded.

Without waiting for an answer, she turned and yelled at her secretary, "Why can't you get Ali on the phone?"

That question, at least, Khaled could answer.

Pulling his pistol out of his jacket and pointing it directly at the principal's face, Khaled said, "Ali and Khader have both left. I have men at the gate and the entrance. We set off the explosion you heard earlier. If, and only if, you follow all my instructions to the letter, we will leave all of you unharmed. Are you ready to listen to what you need to do?"

When Khaled had pointed his pistol at the principal, her initial reaction had been precisely what he hoped to see. Her eyes widened, and her face paled. By the time he had finished speaking, though, she had already regained her composure.

Though, Khaled saw with some pleasure, she no longer looked quite as self-important.

"First, what do you want me to do? Next, what should I call you?" the principal asked.

Khaled thought with satisfaction that he'd learned quite a bit from those questions. The principal had apparently been given at least basic training in how to deal with a hostage situation. One of the first lessons was getting the captors to think of you as a person, which is why she'd asked for his name.

It certainly wasn't because she genuinely wanted to know it.

On the other hand, she wasn't nearly as smart as she thought. She should have also told him her name.

Well, he didn't care what her name was, and had less than no interest in thinking of her as a person.

The truth was that the smug, makeup-wearing woman with uncovered face and hair in front of him was a perfect example of the perversion of the natural order caused by the American invasion.

Keeping an American special forces team busy might be why he had been sent on this mission.

But for Khaled, the death of this woman and the teenage girls she sought to recast in her image was worth just as much. They were a cancer on Afghan society, and there was only one cure for a tumor.

You cut it out. Or the whole body would grow sick and die.

Khaled knew that there were Taliban who drew the line at killing children but also knew that those men were soft and weak. The girls at this high school were all old enough to have children, and that meant they should be married and doing exactly that.

Khaled would have died to protect his mother and his two sisters. They were all married, and they all had children. Raising children and caring for them and their husbands was honorable work, and it was work that Afghan women had been doing for as long as anyone could remember.

None of the teenage girls at this high school had been forced here by their parents. They were all here because they thought they were too good to follow their mother's path. That instead, they would pretend to be men.

As far as Khaled was concerned, they all deserved their fate.

All these thoughts went through Khaled's mind in a flash.

Then, at first, the habits of a lifetime made Khaled hesitate until he had a small smile at his own expense.

Why not give his real name?

"My name is Khaled. You will first get on the school's public address system and announce that there is a security emergency and that the police are about to enter the school and search it. For the protection of students and teachers, you are going to lock the doors to all classrooms. You will promise another announcement later when the emergency is over, and you can unlock the doors," Khaled said.

The principal was silent for a moment, clearly thinking over what Khaled had just said.

Finally, she appeared to have remembered the other part of her train-ing and said, "My name is Fereshtah Saheb."

Meanwhile, a glance at the secretary showed Khaled that she wasn't thinking about anything, and was simply terrified.

Turning back to Fereshtah, Khaled asked, "You do have a master key that locks all the doors in this building, correct?"

Fereshtah nodded.

"Good. Now, time to get on the public address system," Khaled said, waving her towards the microphone with his pistol.

Fereshtah wanted to find some way to object or delay, but one look at Khaled's expression told her that would be a bad idea.

Once she finished making the announcement, Fereshtah rummaged in a desk drawer, while Khaled watched closely. He thought it unlikely Fereshtah's hand would emerge with a pistol rather than a key, but he hadn't lived this long by being careless.

It was a key.

"Are there others?" Khaled demanded.

"Yes," Fereshtah said. "I keep a duplicate in my car's glove compart-ment for emergencies. That's the only other copy."

Khaled waved Fereshtah towards the door with his pistol and then turned to the secretary. "You too," he said.

The secretary looked like she was about to faint. Fereshtah walked over to her and said something in a low voice Khaled couldn't hear, but was evidently reassuring, because the secretary straightened up and walked with Fereshtah into the hallway.

Khaled put away his pistol and followed them as Fereshtah walked down the front hallway, quickly locking each of the classroom doors. Fi-nally, on the way back to her office Fereshtah walked past a door marked "Library" without locking it.

"Why didn't you lock that door?" Khaled asked.

"There's nobody in there," Fereshtah replied. "You can check if you don't believe me. My secretary staffs the library just before and just after classes finish. While classes are going on, it's empty."

Khaled nodded. "Good." Gesturing to the secretary, he said, "Get in there."

The secretary didn't like that idea at all. Again, though, Fereshtah leaned towards her and was able to calm her fears.

Once the secretary entered the library and closed the door, Khaled nodded towards Fereshtah and said, "Lock it." Then he put out his hand for the key, which Fereshtah silently handed over.

After that was done, Khaled pointed towards the principal's office. "Let's head back."

As they walked into her office, Fereshtah shook her head. "You know, you're not going to be able to keep them all locked up for very long. Even if you give them nothing to eat or drink, sooner or later, you'll need to let them use the restroom."

Khaled nodded noncommittally. Lack of bathroom breaks was the least unpleasant thing awaiting these girls and their teachers, but there was no need to go into that now.

"Before long, your phone is going to ring. Whoever from the police or military is calling will ask for me. Give them this number," Khaled said, handing Fereshtah a slip of paper on which he had earlier written his cell phone number. "Tell them I will answer calls only at this number."

Calling a landline phone like the one in the principal's office and trying to keep the hostage-taker on the line was an old police trick. At a minimum, it let the police know exactly where one of the hostage-takers was, and in a different setting could have let a sniper set up a shot at leisure. Fortunately, here, the high walls surrounding the school and its courtyard made that impossible.

Khaled still wasn't going to give government forces any advantage if he could avoid it.

His cell phone buzzed, and a glance at its screen told Khaled that all was well outside. Each of his men had cell phones and a regular check-in schedule. All they needed to do was key a single digit, and everyone on the team received a group text with their status.

Khaled despised almost everything Western. For cell phones, though, he made an exception.

His prediction proved accurate. Minutes later, the phone rang in the principal's office, and Khaled watched as Fereshtah recited his cell phone number.

As soon as his phone rang, Khaled answered it. Without waiting for the voice on the other end to speak, Khaled said, "I have information to give you. Are you ready to receive it?"

There was a pause, followed by a slow, "Yes . . . ."

"Good. Listen carefully because I will not repeat myself. The girls and the staff are uninjured and will remain that way as long as our demands are met. By now, you should have received our demands. Confirm this, please," Khaled said.

Another slow, "Yes . . ." followed.

"Good. You have twenty-four hours from this moment to meet our demands. After that, we will begin executing one student every hour until our demands are met," Khaled said.

A soft gasp from Fereshtah made Khaled send an annoyed glance in her direction. How did the woman think hostage-taking worked?

"Any action taken against us, including cutting power to the school, interfering with the exterior cameras, jamming our cell phones or assembling attack forces anywhere within our view, will be met by the immediate execution of a student. The moment any policeman or soldier attempts to set foot in the school or its courtyard, we will detonate enough explosives to destroy the school and everyone in it," Khaled said.

Another gasp from Fereshtah. Well, fair enough, Khaled thought. He'd told her nothing about the explosives.

Khaled continued, "We will be notified directly by our superiors if our demands have been met. If they are, we will surrender peacefully. In the meantime, we are not interested in food or anything else you may try to offer."

The Red Crescent, the equivalent of what the West called the Red Cross, had resumed its charity lottery in Afghanistan once the Taliban were overthrown. Khaled grunted with amusement as he thought to himself that the chances of their demands being met made a Red Crescent lottery ticket look like what the Americans would call a "sure thing."

The Taliban fighters at Parwan Prison would only be freed if their brothers came to power. If his mission was successful, that just might happen.

Khaled concluded, "So, any other call to this number will result in the execution of a student. Meet our demands."

Then Khaled pressed the button ending the call and turned to Fereshtah.

She looked very different now than when he had first seen her.

Good.

Khaled walked over to the landline phone and casually yanked out the cord connecting it to the wall, then stuffed it in his jacket pocket.

"You keep all cell phones for both the staff and students here in the office during the day, correct?" Khaled asked.

Fereshtah nodded dully. She had endless arguments with the teachers about this policy. Now she regretted enforcing it.

And realized that Khaled and his men had been preparing this attack for some time.

Khaled saw a backpack sitting in a corner and pointed to it. "Put your cell phone in there first, as well as all the others. Then, give it to me."

While she carried out his orders, something kept nagging at Khaled. He was forgetting something. Then it came to him.

"Your secretary's purse. Give it to me," Khaled said.

Khaled could see from Fereshtah's expression that she had not forgotten the sole remaining cell phone in the school was there. It quickly joined the others in the backpack, which now could barely be zipped closed.

"Now, there is a storage area on the second floor. It is up the stairs at the end of the hallway, correct?" Khaled asked.

Fereshtah looked confused. "Yes, but we don't use it. The stairs aren't safe, and there's been no money for repairs. Besides, it's a small, useless space anyway. Most of it is unfinished."

Khaled nodded. "Let's have a look anyway."

Fereshtah shrugged and walked with Khaled to the stairs.

The stairs were wood, old, and visibly unsafe. Khaled gestured for Fereshtah to precede him. They made it to the top, but the loud creaks along the way had made it clear it was only because each of them weighed less than the average adult.

Khaled had been expecting a door he could lock, but there was none. The top of the stairs opened to what Khaled could now see was really an attic, with just a small portion near the stairs covered by floorboards. The only light came from a small window set high in the wall, that Khaled was pleased to see was too small to admit a person.

The only items on the floor visible in the dim light were a few short stacks of dusty textbooks, evidently placed there and forgotten years ago. Most of the attic was bare wooden beams, with something that Khaled guessed was insulation between them.

No American special forces would be coming this way.

"Very well. Let's go back. I see why no money has been spent to fix the stairs," Khaled said.

Fereshtah shrugged. "I've visited the girl's schools in other cities. They were all built like this."

A few minutes later, they were back in the principal's office.

"I will need you to make more announcements later to keep the girls and staff calm, so you will remain in this office, which I will not lock. I will return here from time to time," Khaled said.

He expected this siege to last for hours, ideally most of a day. It would be stupid to exhaust himself by staying on his feet during the first hours, and the principal's office was as good a place as any other to rest in the meantime. Khaled smiled to himself. It would take the Americans at least that long to get here.

"If I find you out of this office for any reason, I will shoot you. Tell me if you need to use the restroom," Khaled said.

"Now, please," Fereshtah said sullenly.

Khaled nodded. Sensible. Take every opportunity offered.

As he walked down the hall with Fereshtah, Khaled thought to himself that he was looking forward to dispensing with her. He wanted to put off hysteria from the girls and their teachers inside the classrooms, which might make them try to break out. More announcements from Fereshtah would, Khaled was sure, at least buy him some time.

But no matter how this turned out, Khaled was sure he and his men would die.

And he was going to keep that woman close and make sure she died with him.

CHAPTER THIRTY-ONE

The White House, Washington DC

Air Force Chief of Staff General Robinson walked into the Oval Office, and President Hernandez could see from his expression that the news wasn't good.

Well, the good news didn't require him to do anything. So, maybe not a surprise that wasn't what made people come to see him.

"Sir, I know you've already been briefed on the situation at the girl's schools in Afghanistan," Robinson began.

Hernandez nodded. "So, now we have a formal request from the Afghan government for assistance?"

Robinson frowned. "Yes, sir, and specifically asking for both special forces and drone support. Normally, we'd let the commander of forces in Afghanistan make the call on this request. However, the assets requested are fully occupied carrying out your order to search for the stolen Pakistani nuclear weapons. That's why I'm bringing this to you for decision, sir."

Hernandez nodded. "You've done the right thing, General. Your recommendation?"

"I don't think we can say no without explaining why, and doing that would lead to a panicked exodus from Kabul that could threaten the government almost as effectively as a nuclear strike. Also, those girl's schools symbolize everything that makes the Afghan government we're supporting different than the Taliban."

Robinson paused. "So, I'd suggest leaving the special forces team going along with the Russians in place. That's the one nearing Kabul. We should divert the other teams and their drone support to free the girls being held hostage. I do, though, suggest we also keep a drone flying watch over the approaches to Bagram Airfield."

Hernandez shook his head. "I'm sure it's occurred to you, General, that a certain Taliban mullah was expecting precisely the reaction you just outlined? And that if I do as you suggest, it will be much more likely that one or more of the stolen nuclear weapons will make it to their target?"

Robinson nodded. "Yes, sir. But I still think we can stop both stolen nuclear weapons, even with reduced assets. On the other hand, we have the certainty of the death of dozens of Afghan girls whose only crime was seeking an education. The Afghan government will never meet the kidnappers' demand that they release the Taliban prisoners being held at Parwan, nor do I think that would be an acceptable outcome."

Hernandez sighed. "Agreed. Very well, carry out the plan you just outlined. I want updates as soon as anything happens at one of those schools. I also want those troops and drones redeployed as soon as the girls have been freed."

Then Hernandez paused. "But I suppose you would have done that anyway, right?"

Robinson smiled. "Sir, one of the first things we teach new officers is never to assume that your troops know what you want. This time the answer to your question is yes. But it's never a bad idea to tell me, or anyone else who works for you, exactly what you want."

Hernandez nodded, and Robinson left.

Leaving Hernandez to wonder just how much he was going to regret this decision.

Bagram Airfield, Afghanistan

Commander Dave Martins had just been informed of his pending promotion, which meant this would be his last mission commanding SEAL Team Six. As he looked over the mission brief in the ready room, his emotions were decidedly mixed. On the one hand, he dreaded the very immediate prospect of being shackled to a desk stateside.

On the other, if his team could pull off this mission, it would be quite a way to end his time commanding in the field.

Martins was inclined to recommend that Lieutenant Commander Mike Lombardy take over command of Seal Team Six. This mission would serve as his final exam for the position.

Lombardy had proved up to the task, no matter what, on every previous mission. He also understood technology in a way Martins was honest enough to admit he never would.

Looking over the mission brief had convinced Martins of one thing. They were going to need every trick they could think of to pull this off.

Lombardy put down the briefing folder and looked up. Martins could see from his expression that he had some ideas already.

Martins decided to start with what he saw as their biggest problem.

"So, now all the security upgrades we put into those schools are going to bite us in the butt. How do we get to the girls without the Taliban setting off their bomb as soon as they see us?" Martins asked.

Lombardy frowned. "My first thought was to use a device we have that will dampen cell phone and radio wave signals for a several block radius. That way, any remote trigger that depends on either one will fail, and we know the technology works."

Martins nodded. "But . . ."

Lombardy's frown deepened. "Everything these guys have done so far is smart. Especially taking over the schools while leaving the gates and guard booths intact. And leaving the guards alive, so dead bodies in the street didn't prompt an immediate assault."

"Yes," Martins agreed. "Plus, they gave us first-hand confirmation that the Taliban really do have powerful bombs at each school."

"Right. So, anyone that smart is going to have a trigger device with a lit indicator, telling them the connection between the bomb and the device is active. They're sure to have a manual trigger attached to the bomb as well, and once they see that light is off, they'll use it," Lombardy said.

"Makes sense. OK, do you have a second thought?" Martins asked with a smile.

"And maybe a third, sir," Lombardy said with an answering grin. "We've got two problems to solve. First, we have to find out exactly where all of the Taliban fighters are located. Second, we have to keep them from setting off that bomb."

Martins nodded. "I'm with you," he said.

"OK, the recon problem I think we can solve with a new micro drone I've worked with enough to be sure it will do the job. We've never used these drones on a mission before, but I've been training one operator on each of the other teams, and I think we're all ready to go with it," Lombardy said confidently.

Martins grunted. His early years in the military when even basic tools such as radios had failed in the field had taught him skepticism about technology.

"So, how do these things work? And how will we be sure they're not spotted?" Martins asked.

Lombardy shrugged. "As we know, nothing is certain. But you tell me. If this flew past you, would you think it's a drone?"

Lombardy then handed Martins a small piece of plastic and metal only a little bigger than a bee.

Martins stared at it in amazement. "If I saw this on the floor somewhere I'd think it was a dead bug if I noticed it at all. How does something this small have the power to fly?" he asked.

"Well, on its own, it can't get very far. Most of the way it gets its power from a laser, which operates at a wavelength invisible to humans. Ideally, we'd direct the laser from a nearby building, but since that won't work here, we're going to use another drone built for that purpose," Lombardy replied.

"OK, so why won't the Taliban spot that drone, then?" Martins asked.

Lombardy tapped a few times on the tablet in front of him and then turned it towards Martin.

"The first image you'll see is the power drone. Note that it also carries a camera, but because it will be about one hundred meters from the target, we're not expecting the feed from it to help much. We need to see areas where we expect the Taliban to be, like inside the school and just inside the wall, and the power drone won't be able to see those," Lombardy said.

Martins nodded. "So, I suppose that odd paint job is supposed to make it harder to see?" he asked. "Odd" was the right word for it, Martins thought. The pattern was irregular, multi-colored, and strangely iridescent.

"Yes, sir. Now, here's a video of the drone flying at a distance of one hundred meters in a clear blue sky, and supplying power to one of the micro-drones," Lombardy said.

Martins looked at the tablet intently and frowned. "Are you sure this isn't something staged by the manufacturer? After all, nothing would be easier than shooting a few minutes of empty sky on a nice day."

"That's true, sir," Lombardy said, nodding. "But I shot that video. Now, I'm going to show you the whole clip, starting with me standing in front of the power drone as it rises, and then walking backwards to the one hundred meter distance."

Martins had to admit he was impressed. He could still make it out up to about fifty meters away, but much of that time only because he knew exactly what he was looking for, and about where it was. At one hundred meters, it was effectively invisible.

"OK, sold. Now, what happens when these micro drones have to go inside the school, and there's no more laser power?" Martins asked.

"They have a tiny battery that will keep them going for a matter of seconds while still sending images, and then they'll make a soft landing on any available surface. Enough power is conserved to let us request and receive at least one still image when we need it. Since failure in any one unit is always possible, I plan to use multiple micro drones on the target. We're lucky we have so much time to prepare on this one," Lombardy said.

Martins shook his head. "Luck has nothing to do with it. Whoever's leading the Taliban teams gave us twenty-four hours for a reason. To keep us busy with something besides looking for those stolen nuclear weapons."

"Yes, sir," Lombardy said, nodding. "The next video shows the drone that should let us get back to that mission."

After the video finished playing, Martins shook his head. "Two questions. First, does it really work as well as in that video? Next, how many have we got?"

"Well, I talked to one of the guys at DARPA who tested it, and he swears it never failed in their tests. As you can see, I can't test it here," Lombardy said with a smile.

Martins grunted. No, certainly not. But the Defense Advanced Research Projects Agency, DARPA, had a good reputation out in the field. If they said this thing would work, he could go with that.

"As for how many we have, that's our only real problem. We have exactly enough for the job, with no backups. I wish we had time to get more, but we don't," Lombardy said.

"Very well. So, another problem I see is getting that drone inside the school without being seen. It's way too big not to be noticed. Have you got another drone that will do that for us?" Martins asked.

Lombardy grinned. "Sir, it's the same drone you saw earlier feeding power to the micro drones. But now it has a new trick."

The video played for several minutes, and again Martins was ... skeptical.

"OK, have you tested this yourself?" he asked.

"Yes, sir," Lombardy said, nodding. "It works just as fast as you saw here. The drone only has enough power on board to do it once, but that's all we'll need."

"What about the guy in the guard booth? How are we going to deal with him?" Martins asked.

"Well, the good news is that the panel with the displays from the security cameras and the gate controls carries plenty of power," Lombardy said.

Martins interrupted him. "Say, can't we hack into that security system? It would make this all a lot simpler."

Lombardy nodded. "Yes, sir, it would. However, the security system was designed by pros and is strictly closed circuit, so we can't access it from outside. Electrical power, though, we can get to."

"I see where you're going. We overload the control panel, and then cut the power and turn on the cell phone and radio dampeners. Are you sure the panel has enough power to knock out whoever's in the guard booth?" Martins asked.

"I think so," Lombardy said. "It would be ideal if he were in contact with the panel, but even if he isn't, that's a really small space. With the amount of power we're sending through, the panel should explode and send glass and metal fragments flying at high velocity. There's no way to be certain the explosion will render the man inside unconscious, but I think it's our best shot at keeping him away from that manual bomb switch."

"So, if all these tricks and gadgets work, next we go over the wall and into the courtyard. Then, mission complete. Do you really think it will be that easy?" Martins asked.

Lombardy shrugged. "Well, sir, I think our biggest advantage is nobody knows we have this tech. That means the Taliban shouldn't be ready for it. But you're right. If any of it fails, it won't be pretty."

CHAPTER THIRTY-TWO

Kandahar, Afghanistan

Khaled Tanha turned his head at the sound of pounding on one of the classroom doors. Fereshtah had made two announcements at his order, telling the students and staff to wait quietly, since the security emergency had not yet ended.

But, as Fereshtah had told him, now that several hours had passed, it appeared that some of those in the classrooms were no longer willing to sit quietly. Whether it was hunger, thirst, or a desire to relieve themselves didn't matter to Khaled.

All that mattered was that he didn't have the men it would take to watch these girls once they were out of the locked classrooms. Khaled, though, already had a plan for this moment.

He called for Fereshtah to join him in the hallway. She left her office, hesitantly.

Good, Khaled thought with a small smile. *She remembers what I told her would happen if she exited without permission.*

Khaled gestured towards the classroom door, where the pounding had still not stopped. There was a small window set in the upper third of the door, and to Khaled's disgust, the unveiled face of a teenage girl was visible through it.

"You know who the teacher is in this classroom, correct?" Khaled asked.

Fereshtah nodded.

"Good. Use the public address system to tell the teacher that the girl who is at the door should stand back. We are about to open the door and let her, and only her, leave the classroom. Everyone else in the room is to remain seated. Also, tell everyone that one and only one girl should come next to their classroom door as well. They should stand, so they are visible through the window. Once you make the announcement, come back here, and I will give you the key so you may open the door to that classroom," Khaled said, pointing at the door where the pounding had still not stopped.

Fereshtah nodded. "So, you are going to have me escort them one at a time to the restroom?"

Khaled glared at her. "Follow my orders," he said flatly.

Fereshtah pursed her lips, but said nothing, and walked back into her office. Shortly Khaled heard Fereshtah giving the instructions, and the pounding on the nearby door stopped.

Fereshtah came back out, and Khaled handed her the key.

Once she unlocked the door, a wave of excited chatter came from the girls who had crowded around the door's window. Khaled could hear Fereshtah reassuring them, and telling them everything would be fine soon. Seconds later, a girl came out of the room, and Fereshtah locked the door after her.

Fereshtah started to walk with the girl towards the restroom, but Khaled shook his head.

"Bring her here," Khaled said.

298 · TED HALSTEAD

Fereshtah wanted to object, but one look at Khaled's expression was once again all it took to convince her that would be a bad idea.

The girl stood in front of Khaled, her eyes downcast. Khaled looked up and down the corridor, and it was clear he had the attention of all the girls standing on the other side of the classroom door windows.

Khaled walked behind the trembling girl, and then in a single fluid movement, put one hand around her neck and pulled it backward, while his combat knife appeared in the other hand so quickly it seemed like magic.

This particular skill was one of the reasons Khaled had lived long enough to become a Taliban leader.

In a loud voice, Khaled said, "Everyone watching! This is what will happen the next time any of you make a sound or come near a door!"

"No!" Fereshtah screamed. "Kill me! The girls will be much more frightened if you kill me!"

Khaled considered the offer momentarily. In fact, he was impressed with her unexpected courage.

Then he noticed the sobbing and wailing coming from each of the classrooms.

Perhaps there was a better solution.

Khaled roughly shoved the girl towards Fereshtah. "Put her back in the classroom. Then, lock the door, and bring the key back to me."

Fereshtah did as he ordered and handed him the key.

"Now, go back to the office and make this announcement. We are going to come together to this hallway at random intervals until you tell them otherwise. If I hear any noise or see anyone at the classroom door windows, I will cut your throat," Khaled said.

The look of loathing Fereshtah gave him made him smile.

"Remember," Khaled said, "you volunteered."

As Fereshtah made the announcement, Khaled nodded, pleased with his solution. He couldn't have left the girl's dead body in the hallway where it fell. Khaled also knew from experience that after such a killing, he couldn't have moved the corpse without getting covered in blood.

The announcement complete, Khaled looked up and down the hallway. All the classroom door windows were clear, and the silence was absolute.

This was much neater.

Kandahar, Afghanistan

Commander Dave Martins looked doubtfully at the micro drones arrayed on the small table. The Afghan military had summarily evicted the residents of the home they were now using as their base. Just as Martins had requested, it was right across the street from the girl's high school.

Even though it was night, thanks to the security contractor's work, it might as well have been daytime. Lights blazed from the high wall surrounding the school, and a glow extending into the sky announced that the same was true for the school's courtyard.

The Afghan Army captain who had welcomed them had told Martins about the eviction by way of saying he would not have to worry about the home's residents returning and interfering with their operation. Martins had asked carefully whether those residents had been informed they would be compensated by the U.S. government for their inconvenience.

The captain had said yes, but with an evasiveness in his expression that told Martins he was lying.

Thinking back on the exchange made Martins sigh. He knew his history. Anger at homes being seized for the use of British troops was one of the colonial grievances that had led to the American Revolution. The U.S. Constitution, which consisted of four parchment pages, included a prohibition of such seizures.

Martins was convinced that the heavy hand used by the Afghan government in this and many other matters had helped to increase popular support for the Taliban. He was also certain that made his job a lot harder.

Lieutenant Commander Mike Lombardy was putting the finishing touches on a considerably larger drone, which Martins recognized from the briefing as the one that would supply power to the micro drones for most of their flight.

"So, are we about ready?" Martins asked.

"Yes, sir," Lombardy said. "I've just heard from the other teams, and in a few minutes, we'll all be ready for launch."

Martins glanced at the laptops set up on what had been the family's dining room table. Their displays were blank now, but with luck that would soon change.

"We're sure that their man in the security booth won't be able to spot the drone you're working on now?" Martins asked.

"I'm sure, sir. I'm not just counting on the paint job. We know exactly where the security cameras are because an American contractor did the work, and this baby's going to hover on autopilot where there's zero coverage," Lombardy replied.

Martins nodded. More than the words, Lombardy's total confidence was what convinced him.

A soft whirring and a "beep" announced the activation of the power drone, which rose slowly and then proceeded to the wide-open window. Through it, the wall surrounding the school was clearly visible.

Martins knew where to look, but seconds later, even he wasn't able to spot the power drone. Seeing the paint job's performance on video was one thing, but now in the field was another.

Martins had to admit, he was impressed.

"OK, now let's see what we're up against," Lombardy said, as he gently tossed the first of the micro drones out of the window.

One of the laptop displays immediately activated, though at first, the image was spinning and unstable. Then a "beep" sounded from the laptop, and the image stabilized.

"Power drone connection achieved," Lombardy said calmly, as he used what looked like a large video game controller to steer the micro drone. It took only a minute for it to pass over the school wall, and now they could see a man armed with an automatic rifle standing watch near the gate.

Lombardy gently moved the joystick, and now another man with an automatic rifle came into view near the entrance to the school. He was standing next to a sedan that had been backed up to the school entrance. Its trunk was open.

Martins pointed at the car's open trunk and said, "I'll bet that's where they had the bomb. I hope one of these gadgets will be able to spot where they put it."

Lombardy nodded but said nothing. Seeing his intent look of concentration, Martins kicked himself. Of course, Lombardy needed to focus on controlling the micro drone.

Moments later, the image of the armed man at the gate grew larger, as did the guard booth. Martins could see what Lombardy was aiming for as a landing spot and nodded with approval. The planter next to the gate was the same dark color as the micro drone, and once there should be practically invisible.

Martins found he was holding his breath as the micro drone slowly lowered itself onto the planter. There was no reaction from either of the men in the courtyard. The image stabilized, and then cut out.

Then Lombardy drew in a deep breath, and Martins realized he hadn't been the only one worried about detection.

Scrolling back through the images they had just collected, Lombardy stopped when he reached the one showing the open trunk. Then he zoomed in the small part of the trunk's interior that was visible.

"Sir, I think the bomb is still in the trunk," Lombardy said. "I don't want to risk flying a micro drone any closer with that guard standing right there until I have to, but I think that makes sense. If the bomb is made with enough explosives to fill up the trunk, as the school guards said, it's probably too heavy to move safely. Plus, from what we saw of the wreck of that SUV, there's no need to move it. It can level the school from right where it is, especially since they left the entrance door open right behind the trunk to admit the full force of the blast."

Martins grunted. It all made sense. It would also explain why, unlike the man near the gate who they had seen patrol from one end of the wall to the other, the one near the car hardly moved. It was probably because he was in charge of setting off the bomb manually if the Taliban leader couldn't do so by remote control.

Martins said none of this because there was no need. He just nodded agreement.

Lombardy then gently tossed another micro drone out of the window and repeated the process until only two were left on the table.

"I'm going to try to get one as far inside the school as I can before its battery fails, and the other I'm going to place closer to the entrance," Lombardy said.

Martins tensed because he thought the chances of the micro drones being spotted would be much higher inside the school than in the courtyard. But Lombardy deftly maneuvered the first one around the man standing guard at the entrance and then sent it sailing down the hallway.

Though he had been worried about finding a good landing spot, there was one practically calling Lombardy by name. It was a bit of dirt and dust that had accumulated in a corner at the very end of the empty hallway. No bigger than a large coin, it could have been designed to conceal the micro drone.

Lombardy's only real challenge was orienting the micro drone so that it faced down the hallway, rather than towards the wall, before it ran out of power. That done, he put down the control and ran his fingers through his hair.

"Last one," Lombardy said quietly, as he tossed the final micro drone out of the window. Once again, he had no trouble evading the guard at the school entrance, whose attention was firmly focused on the wall at the other end of the courtyard. Lombardy couldn't blame him since that was indeed where they were planning to make their entry.

The last micro drone rounded the corner into the hallway and nearly ran into a scowling man standing nearby. Thinking fast, Lombardy decided the only thing to do was to continue straight ahead. He punched two keys on the laptop keyboard in front of him with one hand while using the other to keep the micro drone flying.

Hitting the two keys activated the micro drone already at the end of the hallway. As programmed, it sent a single image that now filled the laptop's screen.

It showed the man running after the micro drone.

Unfortunately, the micro drone only had one speed. Which was not very fast.

Making matters worse was that Lombardy had no idea how close the man was to the micro drone.

He saw only one chance. Lombardy angled the micro drone's flight upwards, and then sent it up a flight of stairs he had seen at the end of the hallway.

There would be no image worth seeing, but at least he could keep the micro drone out of the hands of its pursuer. Because of his post inside the school, Lombardy suspected he might be the Taliban leader.

At the top of the stairs, the micro drone's camera showed only blackness.

And then the signal was lost.

Lombardy put down the controller and pressed the laptop keys that should have summoned at least one image from the micro drone. But there was nothing.

"What do you think happened?" Martins asked quietly.

"Well, sir, there are many possibilities," Lombardy replied. "It may have run out of power because of that altitude increase I did there at the end to try to put it out of reach of the man chasing it. If it dropped from a height onto a hard surface, it could have disabled the camera."

Martins nodded. "And then the guy chasing it could have picked it up, and be looking at it right now. Or he could have caught it, and smashed it."

"Yes, sir," Lombardy replied with a frown. "It's also possible that it made it far enough up the stairs that the guy wouldn't be able to find it. It looked pretty dark up there."

Martins shrugged. "That's assuming there's no nearby light switch. Or a flashlight. I think we have to face the possibility that the Taliban know we're here."

"Maybe so, sir. But the Taliban had to know we'd come at some point. As you said, they were probably even counting on it. Besides, even if they did find the micro drone and recognize it for what it is, would that be enough to make them set off their bomb?" Lombardy asked.

He had a point, Martins thought. Aloud, he said, "Very well. How do you think we should proceed?"

Martins genuinely wanted Lombardy's input. But he also wanted to see if he'd be right to recommend that Lombardy take over his team once he was gone. It was moments like this that were often the difference between success and failure.

"I think a short pause, sir. We keep our heads down and see if the Taliban do anything, like issue more threats. If everything stays quiet, we proceed as planned," Lombardy said.

Great minds think alike, Martins thought.

Aloud, he said, "Very well. Let me know when you're ready to proceed."

And for the sake of those girls, Martins thought, I hope I'm making the right call.

Chapter Thirty-Three

Kandahar, Afghanistan

Khaled Tanha had just finished a walk up and down a totally silent school hallway and entered the principal's office, where Fereshtah was sitting and doing her best to avoid looking at him. The look of contempt on her face was apparently harder to control.

He ignored it and sat down, thinking about how pleasant it would be to wipe that expression off her face permanently. They were over halfway to the deadline, and Khaled's orders were to keep it no matter what.

Besides, he was sure the Americans would get here before then.

What was that?

Khaled was sure he had seen something move in the hallway out of the corner of his eye.

Hadn't he?

Or was he getting tired and starting to see things?

Only one way to find out.

But when he got to the door and looked down the hallway, there was nothing. He walked back to the end of the hall, and even put one foot on the first step of the stairs. The loud creak that greeted his effort made Khaled shake his head.

No, there was no way someone could have walked up those stairs without making noise, and plenty of it.

But he was sure he had seen something.

There was only one thing to do. Stand in the doorway of the principal's office, and see if the motion happened again.

Minutes dragged past, and Khaled was almost ready to convince himself that he'd been imagining things.

Then, an insect came flying right past him! Khaled didn't get a good look at it, but maybe a bee?

Or maybe something sent to spy on them by the cursed Americans.

It was flying straight down the hallway. Khaled started to run after it and grinned. He was sure he'd be able to catch it.

Just as was about to reach out and grab it, whatever it was flew up out of his reach.

Khaled snarled a curse and ran even faster. The thing was flying up the stairs! Khaled knew that if it made it past the floorboards, he'd never be able to catch it. Abandoning all caution, he raced up the steps.

He made it to the third one.

The step cracked in half, sending his right leg plunging through to impact painfully on the floor below. Khaled fell forward, spreading his arms in an attempt to distribute his weight well enough that his entire body didn't follow his leg.

It worked. Slowly, Khaled was able to extract his right leg from the broken step and made his way off the stairs.

He looked down the hallway and saw Fereshtah's head duck back into her office.

Well, Khaled thought, she was right to hope something had happened to me.

He moved the injured leg experimentally. It hurt, but he didn't think he'd broken a bone.

Next, he took a few steps down the hallway. Yes, nothing serious. He wouldn't be running again soon, but at this stage, he thought, that shouldn't matter.

Khaled pressed the group text number asking each of the men on his team for a status update. All three reported promptly by return text that there was no activity to report.

Khaled did the same thing with the teams at the other schools and received the same reply. Nothing happening.

Though he thought about asking his men if they'd seen any flying insects, Khaled stopped himself. If they had seen anything they'd considered suspicious, they would have said so.

At this point, asking them about tiny drones the Americans had sent to spy on them would only make his men wonder whether they should continue taking his orders.

The truth was, Khaled was starting to wonder himself. Couldn't it have just been a flying insect?

Khaled shook his head. No. He hadn't stayed alive this long by doubting his instincts. The Americans were out there, and they were up to something.

Well, he and his men were waiting for them.

Khaled resolved that nothing was going to take his attention off that entrance door.

Kandahar, Afghanistan

Lieutenant Commander Mike Lombardy scrolled through the series of images that had been collected by the micro drones, while Commander Dave Martins joined him in looking for any hint that the Taliban were about to take any action other than continuing to watch.

One after the other, the two men in the courtyard looked at their phones and punched in a number. Other than that, nothing happened.

"Sir, I think we're ready to move forward," Lombardy said.

Martins nodded and pointed at the images on the screen. "You mentioned that you were feeding power to the micro drones in the courtyard just now to get those images without running down their batteries. Don't you need to bring back and recharge the power drone before you send it on this next mission?"

Lombardy shook his head. "The drone's power level is still high enough." He tapped a few keys on the nearest laptop, and a digital gauge appeared reading "87%."

"That should be plenty. Besides, it's a tiny window," Lombardy added.

Martins shrugged and gestured for Lombardy to proceed.

Special forces teams spent a lot of time thinking about good ways to enter a structure without making noise. Solid glass windows that were designed to admit light but never to be opened, like the one on the school's upper level, were a particular problem.

Smashing in the window was out. Cutting the glass was quieter, but still made some noise.

The power drone's laser offered a better option. Melting the glass.

This approach had one drawback. It left a residue of molten glass.

However, DARPA scientists had come up with an aerosol compound at a very low temperature in a handheld container, double-walled to protect the soldier's hand from the cold. Spray from the container rendered the residue safe in seconds.

For this mission, though, that wouldn't be necessary.

Lombardy maneuvered the power drone into position and tried to remember to breathe.

It was one thing to do this as a practice exercise, where each time it had worked perfectly. It was another to do it when the entire mission depended on glass of unknown thickness and composition melting completely before the drone's power supply gave out.

The small hole in the center of the window began to grow, and Lombardy relaxed a bit.

He had to be careful to adjust the laser's focus to hit the remaining glass, and had found that an outward spiral from the center gave the best results. Lombardy needed to be sure the laser hit only the glass and not the probably flammable materials beyond.

Yes! There was still a bit of glass remaining around the frame, but there was more than enough space to admit the drone that was going to help them finish this mission.

"Ready to proceed with the taser drone, sir," Lombardy said.

"Excellent," Martins replied. Then he leaned towards the laptop display and squinted.

"Isn't that smoke?" Martins asked.

Lombardy paled as he realized Martins was right.

"Sir, some of the molten glass must have dropped on the floor and come into contact with something flammable. I don't think there's anything we can do except finish this mission as quickly as possible," Lombardy said.

Then he immediately added, "That's not true, sir. Please ask our Afghan Army liaison to get firefighting equipment here ASAP."

Martins nodded, pleased. He'd already planned to do just that, but it was good to see his prospective replacement had thought of it too.

Lombardy maneuvered the power drone to the school's roof to save time. They could pick it up later.

Next, he sent the taser drone on its way.

Originally the taser drone had been designed solely to incapacitate its victims. Special forces troops ordinarily wanted to take the enemy captive if possible to question them. A remote-controlled taser was perfect for that purpose.

For this mission, though, Lombardy had adjusted the voltage that would be used on the target to the maximum possible. There were two limitations.

The first was that exceeding the design voltage too far risked damaging the drone itself.

The second was that using too much power on the first two targets risked too little being left to disable the third.

Lombardy believed the result of his adjustments would be, at a minimum, ensuring all tased men would be incapacitated long enough for the team to scale the wall and secure the school.

The increased charge could also very well kill its target, depending on where the electricity happened to be applied, and the target's physical condition.

Usually this would have been a problem since dead men couldn't provide actionable intelligence. In this case, though, the priority was making sure nobody could trigger the bomb.

Now Lombardy would see whether his calculations and adjustments were correct. He had carried them out on the taser drones being used by the other two teams as well, so this would determine mission success or failure.

As he passed the taser drone through the window, Lombardy winced. The fire had spread, and even with the drone's night vision capability activated, he could barely see the stairs leading down to the main level through the smoke.

Could the Taliban fighter, probably the leader, inside the school smell the smoke?

Lombardy tapped a key on a nearby laptop keyboard, which activated the micro drone at the end of the downstairs hallway. The image that shortly filled the laptop's screen showed the man who had chased one of the micro drones earlier standing at the other end of the hallway.

Thankfully, his attention appeared to be completely focused on the school entrance.

Well, that made sense, Lombardy thought. That's the way the micro drone he'd chased came in before.

"Please tell Jack to get ready to overload the power to the guard booth," Lombardy said.

Martins nodded and spoke quietly into his radio to the team's electrical specialist, Petty Officer Jack Collins. Like everyone else in the unit, Jack had more than one role. He was also the team's explosives expert.

Then Martins moved his hand towards the switch that would activate the equipment shutting down cell phone and radio transmissions for a three-block radius. He would hit it the moment he saw on the screen that the first taser target was down, and the security booth overload accomplished.

Lombardy maneuvered the taser drone down the stairs and lined up his first shot.

CHAPTER THIRTY-FOUR

Kandahar, Afghanistan

Khaled Tanha frowned. What was that smell?

Was it smoke?

Khaled first looked out the open entrance door into the courtyard, where he saw both of his men on watch as they should be. He nodded to the one a few meters away next to the sedan's open trunk.

No smoke out here.

Khaled went back in and looked down the hallway towards the stairs.

At first, his mind wasn't sure how to process what he saw. A metal shape was floating towards him, with nearly silent propellers on both sides. Though small, it was much larger than the insect-looking thing he had chased before.

This was definitely an American drone!

It only took Khaled a few seconds to complete those thoughts and pull out his pistol.

But it was a few seconds too long.

Khaled found himself down on the floor, his pistol out of reach beside him.

The pain was agonizing.

Khaled struggled to move, but couldn't. He was completely paralyzed.

Out of the corner of his eye, Khaled saw Fereshtah's head poke out of her office.

Then he heard her move closer.

Khaled tried as hard as he could to move his hand, which was inches away from his pistol.

Nothing.

Khaled felt his heart beating faster in his chest as he could just barely see Fereshtah's hand close around the pistol.

He still couldn't see her face. But he could hear her breathing.

Then, Fereshtah walked around him, so that now Khaled could see her face. She had no expression Khaled could decipher, but her eyes looked . . . as though she were lost in a dream.

Slowly, she said, "God has placed this weapon in my hand. I will send you to his judgment now."

Then, she began to lift the pistol towards his head.

At that moment, Khaled could hear gunfire in the courtyard. The Americans! He felt a sudden rush of hope. They would want to take him prisoner and question him!

Khaled wanted so much to tell her so. But he couldn't make a sound leave his mouth.

The gun pointed at his head looked so big. He had been ready to die. Khaled had even expected it.

Why did he now feel such terror?

There was an instant of intense pain, and then everything went black.

Kandahar, Afghanistan

Lieutenant Commander Mike Lombardy had to suppress a grin, which under these circumstances would have been hard to explain. After the millions of dollars worth of technology that had been applied to this point in the mission, their method for scaling the wall surrounding the school dated back at least three thousand years.

Ladders.

Well, Lombardy thought, it didn't matter how old the tech was as long as it worked.

First up one of the ladders was the team sniper, who didn't need a scope to give a quick "thumbs up" confirming that all terrorists visible were down. He stayed on the top of his ladder with his head just over the wall. The sniper kept his rifle balanced on the wall's edge so that it protected everything but his head. Placing his eye to the rifle's scope, he stayed focused on what mattered most.

That was the man who, for the moment, was down next to the sedan's open trunk.

The rest of the team raced over the other ladders set up against the wall. They then dropped down to the courtyard in a procedure rehearsed in countless exercises.

Two soldiers quickly bound the man lying prone on the courtyard floor next to the gate. It was only a precaution though since they could find no pulse.

No sooner had they finished when the guard booth door opened, and a man with a rifle emerged. Cuts and scrapes on his face and a dazed expression made it clear that the electrical overload had not been pleasant to experience.

Multiple rounds hit the Taliban gunman, who spun around and fell face first. Two soldiers ran forward to make sure he was as dead as he appeared, while the rest of the team moved to the school entrance.

The man on the ground was breathing. But in spite of his best efforts, he was unable to move. They had just finished securing him when they heard what they had been dreading most, next to the bomb's explosion.

A gunshot inside the school.

Was the remaining Taliban gunman shooting the girls?

Martins and Lombardy were first through the door, expecting to come under fire immediately. What they saw instead was . . . unexpected.

A woman, holding a pistol loosely in her right hand, standing over the body of a dead man.

It appeared that they now knew the whereabouts of the last Taliban gunman.

"Ma'am, we're American soldiers. Are there any other Taliban in the building?" Martins asked.

The woman shook her head slowly. She appeared to be in shock. "No. Some outside, but you must have seen them," she said.

"We have to get the girls out of the school. There's a fire upstairs," Martins said.

This news snapped the woman out of her daze. Though there was blood all around the man's body, it didn't appear to concern her as she went through his pockets, finally holding up a metal key.

"He locked all the girls inside the classrooms. We must hurry," the woman said. With that, she opened the door to the nearest classroom.

The girls inside were all huddled together with their teacher in the back of the classroom.

The woman said, "You are all safe now. I have American soldiers with me. They will take you out of the school."

Lombardy and two other soldiers, in the meantime, moved the body out of sight into a nearby office.

In minutes the school had been evacuated and checked for any hiding Taliban fighters. Then, Afghan firefighters moved in to extinguish the fire, which had not yet spread beyond the upper level.

Martins and Lombardy next joined the team's explosives expert, Petty Officer Jack Collins, who was looking down at the bomb filling the trunk of the sedan. They both immediately noticed a strong odor.

Collins nodded. "Stinks, doesn't it? Never smelled anything like it before, and I'd remember. No good for anything you'd want to hide away because of the smell. I'm betting somebody's military uses it, but I've got no idea which one."

Martins shrugged. "We'll let the intel guys worry about that. Can you defuse it?"

"Maybe," Collins frowned. "But I think a better idea would be to find the nearest vacant lot as far away from all these houses as possible and drive this car there. I've checked, and no wires are going from the bomb anywhere outside the trunk, so it should be safe. Or at least, safer than defusing it in the middle of a residential neighborhood."

"I thought you might want to do this elsewhere," Lombardy said. "I've identified a suitable location less than a kilometer away. I'll get our Afghan Army liaison to clear the way of traffic, and block off the location."

Martins was impressed. Preparing for this aspect of the operation had never occurred to him.

He had made the right choice for his successor.

Martins keyed his radio and made his initial report to headquarters. From his expression, Lombardy immediately knew things hadn't gone as well for the other teams, but waited patiently until Martins signed off. He knew he wouldn't need to ask.

318 · TED HALSTEAD

Martins looked at each of them and shook his head. "Bravo Team had the same outcome we did. All Taliban killed or captured, no civilian casualties. Alpha Team though . . . the bomb went off as they were going over the wall. We're not sure yet what went wrong, but a report from one surviving soldier makes it sound like one of the Taliban was able to recover from the tasing, and set off the bomb manually."

Lombardy nodded bitterly. He'd always known that was a possibility, especially if the Taliban gunman had been wearing something like a flak jacket that could absorb part of the shock.

Collins asked quietly, "How many of the team made it?"

Martins shook his head. "Too soon to say for sure. Three are en route to hospital at Bagram with critical injuries. One is confirmed dead at the scene."

Lombardy asked, "And the school?" Even though he could guess the answer.

"They're still searching through the rubble. But I don't think there's much hope. The entire building collapsed. There are even reports of injuries from homes nearby struck by debris ejected from the explosion," Martins said.

Lombardy frowned and gestured towards the bomb in front of them. "I sure hope they can find whoever sold these explosives to the Taliban."

CHAPTER THIRTY-FIVE

CBI Secret Detention Facility, Ten Kilometers South of Mumbai

Before now, Akshay Roshan had no idea life could be this miserable. From the moment the van had entered the unassuming single-story cinder block structure, things had steadily gone from bad to worse.

Though land this close to Mumbai was generally sought after, government documents showed that a chemical spill had made it hazardous pending cleanup. Somehow, the cleanup had dragged on for years, with no completion date in sight.

Akshay had been hustled out of the van through a small door. Once unlocked, it led to a small room with only one feature—an elevator door.

The elevator seemed to go down forever. In fact, it was passing the floors containing administrative offices and sleeping quarters for the guards and staff, who often worked consecutive shifts. One of the best ways to keep the facility secret was to keep its staff as small as possible.

Another excellent way was to promise that any security leaks would result in the offender becoming a guest of the facility.

Akshay was questioned at length using drugs and sleep deprivation. Though he had dreaded being beaten or waterboarded, neither ever happened. Not because his interrogators had any moral qualms over such methods, but because they considered them ineffective.

Eventually, they were satisfied that Akshay had nothing useful left to tell them, and he was left alone in his cell.

Until today.

Two unsmiling men led Akshay to a room with three dark wooden tables. Each had a single chair behind it. One table was set in front of the far wall. The other two were set back halfway between that wall and the door, with about a meter between them.

There was a man sitting at the far table, and another at the right-hand table. Both were middle-aged, and each was wearing a dark suit and tie. They both had manila folders filled with papers in front of them. Each had been looking through their contents but stopped when Akshay was led to the sole remaining table.

There was nothing on Akshay's table.

The floor was white, and the walls and ceiling black. Because of that, until now Akshay hadn't noticed the black LED display mounted on the far wall, directly above the head of the man sitting at the table there.

Now, though, the LED display switched on. It showed the image of a robed, blindfolded woman holding a pair of scales.

Once Akshay had been seated, the two men who had escorted him from his cell had taken up station standing on either side of the door. Now, one of them said, "This court is now in session, the honorable Judge Bachchan presiding."

The judge looked at the man seated at the table beside Akshay and asked, "Is the prosecution ready?"

The man nodded and said, "We are your honor."

The judge nodded back and said, "Good."

He then turned to Akshay. "You are charged with selling explosives that resulted in the deaths of dozens of innocent children in Afghanistan. How do you plead?"

Akshay could feel all the blood drain from his face. "Your honor, I never intended for the explosives I sold to be used in such a way! I was told they would not be! I was promised they would be used in a war thousands of kilometers away . . ."

The judge interrupted Akshay, saying, "Your beliefs and suppositions are irrelevant. Are you pleading not guilty?"

Akshay's head bobbed up and down. "Yes, your honor. Not guilty."

"Very well. The prosecution may present its case," the judge said.

"Excuse me, your honor! Am I not entitled to have a lawyer to represent me?" Akshay asked.

The judge nodded. "Ordinarily, yes. We have a staff of defense lawyers with the necessary security clearance to handle cases such as this, with their fees paid for by the government. However, once they learned of the charges and evidence against you, they all refused to represent you."

The judge paused. "This has never happened before in all of the cases heard at this facility. Those cases have included other charges of mass murder. Perhaps the lawyers were unwilling because so many of the victims were children. In any case, we offered to double their fee. They all still refused. So, that left compelling one of the lawyers to represent you."

The judge shrugged. "I decided not to do that for two reasons. First, I thought it unfair to the lawyers, who, in any case outside this facility, could not be forced to represent you. Perhaps more important, given their reaction to the evidence against you, I thought it highly unlikely any of them would provide effective assistance in your case."

Akshay shook his head stubbornly. "It's still not right."

The judge nodded. "Perhaps. But life is not always fair, as those Afghan children discovered. We can only do our best."

After looking down at his notes, the judge continued, "You do, however, have full rights in representing yourself. That means you can raise objections to any evidence presented by the prosecution, and offer any testimony you choose on your behalf. Now, before we proceed, do you have any questions?"

Akshay wished desperately he could think of any, but instead found himself saying slowly, "No, your honor."

The judge turned to the prosecutor and said, "Present your case."

The image of the blindfolded woman disappeared from the LED screen and was replaced by a frozen image of Akshay under interrogation.

"Your honor, as you know, the defendant was subjected to interrogation under the influence of pharmaceuticals immediately after his detention. This was done due to the threat posed by the explosives he had already admitted to having sold. However, the video the court is about to see was made a full day after administration of the last dose. I have a certificate from a doctor attesting to the fact that the defendant could not have been under the influence of the drugs by that time. I request that this video be admitted into evidence, and to play it for the court at this time," the prosecutor said.

"Objection!" Akshay said frantically. He remembered everything he had said, both while he had been drugged and later when he had not. "These statements were made under duress!"

The judge looked at Akshay coolly. "Were you beaten or threatened with violence?"

Akshay shook his head.

The judge said, "Overruled." Turning to the prosecutor, he said, "Proceed."

The video clip played for about half an hour, long enough for Akshay to describe in detail how he had smuggled the CL-20 compound out of HEMRL, and subsequently sold it.

When the clip finished, the screen went black. Into the echoing silence that followed, the judge asked Akshay, "Was that you speaking in the video we have just seen?"

Akshay nodded mutely.

"Do you have anything you wish to add or retract from the statements we have just observed?" the judge asked.

Akshay shook his head.

"Very well," the judge said. Turning to the prosecutor, he said, "Proceed with your case."

A still image with over a dozen mangled bodies filled the screen.

"Your honor, this is a picture showing some victims of a Taliban attack on a girl's high school in Afghanistan. Analysis by our scientists of the explosives used confirms the conclusion of the Americans that the explosives were identical to those sold by the defendant, as shown here," the prosecutor said, holding up several stapled pieces of paper.

"Request that these documents be entered into evidence," the prosecutor said.

"Objection!" Akshay said, and then stopped, clearly at a loss for words.

"Yes? What is your objection?" the judge quietly asked.

"Your honor, I knew nothing about the planned use of these explosives. If I had, I would have never sold them. The men who bought them lied to me. Surely that must count for something!" Akshay said.

The judge shook his head. "You knew very well that what you were selling was the most powerful conventional explosive ever produced. You knew that was why it was valuable. And you knew that the men buying it were planning to use it to kill people. Even the lie you were told admitted as much. So no, your ignorance of the actual planned use of the explosives counts for nothing at all," the judge said.

The judge turned to the prosecutor and said, "Your documents will be entered into evidence. Do you have any further exhibits to present?"

The prosecutor shook his head. "No, your honor. The prosecution rests."

The judge turned back to Akshay. "Do you have anything further to say in your defense?"

Akshay felt as though the room was spinning around him. Finally, he said in a near whisper, "I wish I could have it to do all over again. I would have never sold those explosives."

The judge nodded and said, "I believe you." Gesturing towards the image that was still on the screen, he added, "If they could speak, I'm sure they would wish you had never sold the explosives as well."

Leaning back in his chair, the judge said, "This court finds you guilty. I am ready to render my verdict."

The judge frowned and looked down at his notes.

"Many countries have abolished the death penalty. India is not one of them. However, it is applied only rarely, in fact, in only ten cases in the past twenty years. The circumstances must be beyond the simple taking of a life. Those circumstances could include, for example, the undoubted innocence of the victims. Such as helpless children."

The judge paused to glance at Akshay, with no readable expression.

"Naturally, the law provides the death penalty as an option for cases where more than one person has been killed. We do not yet know the exact count of how many died due to your actions. But we do know the number is in the dozens."

The judge looked again at Akshay, who seemed ready to faint.

The judge appeared to be anything but concerned.

"The record will reflect that these two considerations are the ones that have led me to pronounce the death penalty in this case."

Akshay shook his head violently. "This is not proper. India is not a country that kills its citizens in secret. This is a democracy, and Indian citizens have rights!"

The judge nodded. "This court shares your concerns. Our strong preference would have been for a public trial, which along with the charges already discussed, would have included your betrayal of the oath you swore at the time you became an employee of the Indian government."

Now the judge fixed an icy stare on Akshay. "The democracy that guarantees you the rights you feel have been violated."

The judge continued, "This court believes the Indian people should know the crimes you have committed, and the punishment you will receive. Both because the people have the right to know, and as a cautionary tale that would help prevent others from going down the same path."

Akshay felt a glimmer of hope. "So then why not give me a public trial? I want people to hear that I didn't want to kill those children!"

The judge shook his head. "As you pointed out, India is a democracy. The people's elected representatives have recently passed laws providing, under extreme circumstances, that trials may be held in secret. The President himself has determined the shame that would fall upon India if our role in this crime were to become known cannot be borne."

The judge nodded towards the two men who had escorted Akshay to the courtroom. They had been standing silently on either side of the door ever since.

The judge knew from his file that Akshay was, at least nominally, a member of India's small Christian minority. This probably inspired his next words.

"The sentence will be carried out immediately. May God have mercy on your soul."

CHAPTER THIRTY-SIX

U.S. Cyber Command, Ft. Meade, Maryland

Carol Banning had been an analyst with U.S. Cyber Command for five years now, coming on board not long after its elevation to the status of a "unified command." Co-located with the National Security Agency, it had only a small fraction of the over fifty thousand employees who worked in one capacity or another at Fort Meade.

There had been many critics of the decision to keep USCYBERCOM at Fort Meade, especially after it had become a unified command. One undeniable advantage, though, was that it made it easier to share information and cooperate on programs of common interest.

Like Sapphire. Though NSA resources were used to collect data, store it, and perform the initial assessment, anything flagged for further review was assigned to analysts at both NSA and USCYBERCOM. Which one depended on the data's content, and which organization had the analyst with the greatest relevant expertise.

Carol's best three languages were Dari, Pashto, and Arabic, though she was fluent in several others, including Uzbek, Turkmen, and Urdu. This ability made her one of the very few analysts fluent in all the languages spoken in Afghanistan, and one of the analysts in highest demand.

As a result, she had a rare privilege. If Carol thought an intercept assigned to her by an initial review wasn't worth her time, she could pass it on to a more junior analyst. It was a privilege Carol never used to shirk work. There were always more intercepts to review. Instead, the point was to use her talents where they were most needed.

That decision process began before she even opened an intercept file. Carol immediately noted that the Sapphire software had grouped three video files, based on the place and time of their upload. Simultaneously, from the Afghan-Pakistan border region.

Then she saw the keywords that had resulted in the files being flagged for an analyst. "Taliban" was pretty common. "Bagram" wasn't.

And Carol didn't think she'd ever seen "nuclear" before.

OK, these were going to be worth a look.

As soon as she clicked on the first file, Carol froze.

"What in the world … that looks like Mullah Abdul Zahed," Carol thought to herself. A few seconds later, the image on the screen identified himself as precisely the man she'd thought she recognized.

"There hasn't been a confirmed sighting of him in years," Carol thought, as the Taliban leader continued to speak.

"They've done what?" Carol thought in near panic, as Abdul calmly explained why it had been necessary to destroy Bagram Airfield with a nuclear weapon.

Carol turned up the volume on the nearby TV, which was already tuned to a cable news network. It was reporting on yet another wildfire in California. She turned to two other news channels … nothing about Afghanistan.

OK. So, this was a recorded announcement for something the Taliban had planned. And the other two video files?

Carol opened the next file and found it was once again Abdul, this time taking responsibility for a nuclear attack on the Green Zone in Kabul.

The last file was Abdul, speaking even more solemnly, explaining why the Taliban had destroyed both the Green Zone and Bagram Airfield.

Carol's fingers blurred as she typed a verbatim transcript in both the original Pashto and an English translation for all three messages.

The same thought kept running through Carol's head again and again as she typed.

How long would it be before the attacks described in these messages happened?

The White House, Washington DC

President Hernandez frowned as he saw the large LCD display at the other end of the Situation Room was on, though so far it just showed the logo of USCYBERCOM. A woman Hernandez had never seen before stood next to the screen. She was doing her best to conceal her nervousness and mostly succeeding.

Understanding a person's true mental state was a talent that had served Hernandez well in business, and even better in politics.

General Robinson, the Air Force Chief of Staff, was the only other person in the room, and he stood as soon as Hernandez entered. Hernandez impatiently waved him back down.

"So, General, Chuck told me he agreed with you that we should be the only three to see these videos. Will the reason be clear by the time we finish watching?" Hernandez asked.

"Chuck" was Chuck Soltis, the White House Chief of Staff. Among his many duties was deciding who else got to learn what the President did. That often meant deciding who would be in the room when the President was briefed.

"Yes, sir, I think so," Robinson replied. "I should also add that Ms. Carol Banning here is the analyst who flagged the importance of these short clips, and is the one who prepared the English subtitles, which were not present in the originals."

"Right," Hernandez said. "Now, do I understand correctly that these videos were intercepted by us, and have not yet been broadcast anywhere?"

"Yes, sir," Robinson replied. "When you watch them, you'll understand why."

Hernandez nodded and gestured for the videos to start playing.

As soon as the first image came on the screen, Hernandez gestured for Robinson to stop the playback.

"That's Mullah Abdul Zahed. I thought the CIA believed there was a good chance he was dead, and that the Taliban was keeping his death quiet because he was the last surviving member of the Afghan Taliban regime we forced from power in 2001. Then they thought they'd found him, but it turned out to be a trap that a SEAL Team barely escaped. Are we sure this is a new video?" Hernandez asked.

Banning glanced at Robinson, and he nodded.

"Sir, I did the technical review of the video files. There is metadata embedded in them that shows exactly when and where they were recorded. That's because the recording was made using a cell phone with GPS enabled. Normally the Taliban are much more careful about that. Based on the videos' content, I think it's likely they were recorded by one of the Mullah's relatives. He probably didn't trust anyone else to broadcast the right one," Banning said.

Hernandez almost asked what "right one" meant, but instead realized that it would probably become clear once he watched the videos, and gestured for playback to resume.

This time Hernandez sat stock still until all three of the short speeches had finished.

"Great work on this, Carol," Hernandez said. "It's a big help in making sure we stop the planned attacks."

"Thank you, Mr. President," Carol said. She correctly understood she was no longer needed and left.

"Well," Hernandez said slowly, "now we know we were right. Bagram and the Green Zone in Kabul are definitely the targets. And we also know the Taliban think they're going to hit at least one of them."

Robinson nodded. "I think there's also a good chance that at least one of the weapons will be traveling under Mullah Abdul Zahed's command. That's why he decided he had to record these speeches in advance."

"Well, none of these little speeches are ever going to be broadcast, because we're going to make sure none of these attacks are successful. Have we increased drone coverage over Afghanistan, as we discussed earlier?" Hernandez asked.

"Yes, sir," Robinson said. The fact that this topic would almost certainly come up was one of the main reasons that Chuck Soltis had decided the Air Force Chief of Staff needed to be at this briefing.

Robinson added, "We have deployed not only every unassigned drone but pulled more from less urgent missions in the region. The Ranger and SEAL teams are being redeployed from the girl's schools back to searching for the stolen weapons. This mission is our absolute top priority."

Hernandez nodded. He had expected nothing less.

"Good, General. Let me know as soon as there's progress to report," Hernandez said.

Hernandez added to himself silently, and I hope I don't hear about a successful attack on cable news first.

CHAPTER THIRTY-SEVEN

Forty-Five Kilometers South of the Town of Bagram, Afghanistan

Mullah Abdul Zahed shook his head with disappointment as he reviewed the American media reporting on the outcome of the attacks on the girl's high schools. Such an expenditure of time, money, and Taliban lives for such a poor result. He had been hoping to land a blow on American special forces so heavy they'd never be able to recover in time to follow either advancing nuclear weapon.

Instead, just two soldiers killed, and a few others injured.

Well, at least two of those accursed girl's high schools had been damaged or destroyed.

As his small truck and its two escorts bounced over the rough secondary road, though, Abdul shook his head again.

He was wrong and needed to ask God's forgiveness in his next prayers, probably the last ones he would make before going to see Him in person.

Abdul was making steady, unimpeded progress towards Bagram Airfield. The Afghan Army troops he had paid in advance to let them pass had stayed bribed, with only the expected small additional top-up payments before they were allowed to proceed.

Did Abdul think this would have gone so smoothly if the American soldiers hadn't been occupied at the schools?

Certainly not.

Abdul sat back in his seat, nodding. Yes. He needed to have more faith that he was indeed an instrument in God's plan. He was close. So close to the goal he had spent more than two decades planning.

And it would all come true before the day was out.

Seventy Kilometers South of Kabul, Afghanistan

Mikhail Vasilyev looked at the code on his satellite phone that indicated another radiation signature location report by the Okhotnik drone, along with a poor quality picture. It showed a truck, which though not large, was a bit bigger than the one used as a decoy at Jalalabad.

A few minutes later, another beep from his satellite phone told Vasilyev that there was an updated location report on the same target. So, this vehicle was moving.

Each of the first two messages had provided coordinates from the GLONASS system. Another beep announced the arrival of a new image, this one displaying a dot indicating each location tracked, as well as a timestamp. This image allowed Vasilyev to see the direction the truck was traveling.

Straight to Kabul.

Vasilyev had two conflicting thoughts almost simultaneously. The first was satisfaction that such useful information could be delivered to him this quickly by Russian technology. Though his country had been the first to put a satellite into orbit, Chernobyl, the sinking of the nuclear submarines *Komsomolets* and *Kursk* and many other disasters had shaken his generation's faith in Russian technical prowess.

That faith had not been reinforced by learning that their Mil-8 helicopter had been grounded by technical problems.

It was nice to see they could still do some things right.

Vasilyev's second thought was that the vehicle, now only fifty kilometers south of Kabul, had to be stopped immediately.

Looking around the Sikorsky UH-60 Black Hawk filled with Captain John Rogoff and his heavily armed men, Vasilyev thought to himself they had the tools necessary to do just that.

Vasilyev had been ordered to keep the Okhotnik drone's radiation sensing capabilities secret unless "operational necessity" required sharing them with the Americans. For the static, unmoving vehicle that had turned out to be a decoy, Vasilyev had decided to do no more than pass on the coordinates.

Now, though, Rogoff and his pilot needed access to the continuously updated location track fed to Vasilyev on his satellite phone. Vasilyev didn't hesitate, tapping Rogoff on the shoulder.

"Captain, our drone has located a vehicle with a radiation signature that makes it a likely transport for one of the stolen weapons," Vasilyev said. He made sure he was speaking loudly enough that both Neda Rhahbar and Anatoly Grishkov could hear as well.

Vasilyev then handed Rogoff his satellite phone, showing the last two reported positions.

"The vehicle appears to be a truck, and it is headed straight for Kabul. It is fortunate we decided to travel to Kabul ourselves. I believe its last reported coordinates are about twenty kilometers from us," Vasilyev said.

Rogoff looked at the screen and nodded. Then he leaned forward and keyed a microphone in his helmet that from the conversation that followed connected him to the pilot. Shortly after that, their Black Hawk as well as the other two banked slightly right and then increased speed.

Leaning now towards Vasilyev, Rogoff said, "Of course we guessed that drone of yours was the source of your intel, but every tech guy I talked to at Bagram insisted you couldn't have instruments more sensitive than ours. Glad to see they were wrong."

Vasilyev nodded, impressed. Not a word of reproach for holding back the source of their information. Instead, a compliment for Russian technology. If this was the sort of officer who rose to command an elite unit in the American armed forces, then this would be a bad day for their common enemy.

The next thought was inevitable. Let's hope we can avoid going back to the Cold War days when men like this would be my enemy.

Vasilyev looked ahead, where what Rogoff called "the DAP" flew in the lead. The American military's love of acronyms had been mentioned several times in Vasilyev's briefings. "DAP" stood for "Direct Air Penetrator." It had sincerely puzzled Vasilyev when he saw it on the ground at Bagram Airfield because while its airframe was identical to the one he was in now, the DAP was a gunship.

Armed with two fixed M134 miniguns, four AIM-92 Stinger air-to-air missiles, a single M230 30mm chain gun, and an M299 launcher holding two AGM-114 Hellfire missiles, the DAP carried enough firepower to quickly destroy whatever escort force the stolen nuclear weapon might have.

What puzzled Vasilyev was why the Americans had gone to the trouble of creating the DAP version at all when they already had far more capable combat helicopters such as the Apache. When he had asked Rogoff at Bagram Airfield, at first, Vasilyev thought he wouldn't answer.

Finally, Rogoff shrugged and gave him two answers that made a surprising amount of sense. The first was that American special operations forces had their dedicated air squadrons, and limiting helicopter types simplified planning and maintenance.

The second was more of a surprise. Rogoff had already told Vasilyev that the DAP had no room for passengers because it was full of ammo. He said to Vasilyev now that under truly urgent circumstances, like the loss of one or more Black Hawks during a mission, the ammo could be jettisoned and the DAP used for troop transport.

Rogoff had also said he was glad that he'd never had to do it.

The DAP . . . Vasilyev asked for his satellite phone back and then pressed the necessary keys to bring up the drone's image of a truck.

"I know this isn't the best quality image, but I think it shows a truck. If I had to guess a color, I'd say white. The drone is programmed to focus solely on the source of radiation, so any escorts aren't on camera. Please ask your men, especially the crew of the DAP, not to use any heavy weapons on the truck in this image," Vasilyev said.

"Understood," Rogoff said. "I get that setting off the nuke would be a bad day all around." He then keyed his helmet microphone and began giving orders.

Vasilyev saw that several of Rogoff's men within earshot grinned and nodded at Rogoff's "bad day" comment. He noted that neither Grishkov nor Neda had been amused.

Neda . . . Vasilyev had been surprised by the depth of his feelings when he had seen Neda lying unconscious in a hospital bed. He should have been concerned first and foremost with the impact of her death or serious injury on the mission. Though he had studied Neda's drawings and instructions diligently, and he knew Grishkov had too, he also knew neither of them was likely to defuse one of the jury-rigged nuclear weapons successfully. There were just too many ways to go wrong.

But when he saw Neda in the hospital, he wasn't thinking about any of that. All Vasilyev could think about was how unfair it would be for such a beautiful, intelligent, talented woman to die at the hands of the Taliban.

A small part of Vasilyev's thoughts were about how much he wished he could spend time with Neda, get to know her . . . But he pushed those thoughts down almost savagely as selfish.

Now Vasilyev wasn't sure what he would do after this mission. Ask Neda out? Since joining the FSB, he'd been so busy that he'd only gone on a few casual dates that had led nowhere. Would dating Neda end the same way? Would it be better to keep their relationship professional, and keep Neda as no more than a friend?

Vasilyev rejected the last option almost as soon as it came to him as dishonest.

He smiled to himself wryly. Maybe he should wait until they both survived this mission to wrestle with these questions.

Rogoff helped make the point by gesturing out the windshield and saying, "Target vehicles should be in view shortly."

He was right. Seconds later, a large white dot was visible, as well as two smaller black dots. All three rapidly got larger.

Then several things happened simultaneously. A harsh, pulsing buzz filled the helicopter's cockpit, and they banked sharply left, while rapidly losing altitude.

Vasilyev could then hear the pilot report to his base that they were under missile attack.

Next came a hard impact and explosion, and the helicopter began spinning. At the same time, it filled with smoke, a combination that made Vasilyev nauseous.

Then everything went black.

CHAPTER THIRTY-EIGHT

Forty Kilometers South of Kabul, Afghanistan

Ibrahim Munawar had been pleased with their progress since crossing the border into Afghanistan. Ironically, though he had always considered himself Afghan and was now in charge of a weapon that could free Afghanistan from the American invaders, it was the first time he had been there.

Yes, both his parents might have been Pakistani. But his mother had drilled into him as long as he could remember the need to free Afghanistan, and to keep their plans from his father. She celebrated his outstanding work in high school as another step on the road to victory. When he had graduated from university at the top of his class, she had thrown a party in his honor.

Ibrahim would always cherish the day he had been assigned to duty as a technician in Pakistan's nuclear program. It was the first time he could remember receiving a hug from his mother.

Ibrahim had been impressed with Afghanistan's natural beauty, especially in the mountains. Of course, the circumstances had something to do with his feelings about the landscapes they were passing. No matter how this journey ended, Ibrahim had no illusions about surviving it.

Though that reality would have depressed many others, Ibrahim felt more exultant the further they traveled. Mullah Abdul Zahed had carefully mapped out a route using secondary roads that had so far seen them progress towards Kabul without incident.

Abdul had taken another precaution that had eased Ibrahim's path, though he had told him nothing about it. Secondary roads or not, ordinarily by now, they would have encountered at least two roadblocks. Abdul had arranged payments to local Afghan officers to make sure that while Ibrahim and his cargo traveled on these roads, the roadblocks were placed elsewhere.

Of course, these officers had no idea what sort of weapon they had allowed to move towards Kabul. They believed they were allowing a shipment of American dollars to reach Kabul, to then be used to pay for drugs. It was a plausible story since much of the Afghan economy depended on opium exports. As the Russian agents had discovered at the border, since many considered electronic banking payments too risky, large quantities of cash were often required.

Though an occasional Afghan officer over the years had tried to steal such cash shipments for themselves, the retribution eventually visited on both the officers and their families had made such thefts rare. As Abdul had expected, the payments worked.

"Helicopters!" one of the Taliban fighters called out.

At first, Ibrahim hoped they might have nothing to do with them, and would continue flying past. As the helicopters continued straight towards them, that hope faded rapidly.

Men had already piled out of both of the black vans that had joined them shortly after they crossed the border. They had two anti-aircraft missiles, which they were readying to fire.

Abdul had told him that these were SA-24 Igla missiles. The extent of Ibrahim's curiosity extended to asking what "Igla" meant. Abdul had explained that it meant "needle" in Russian and then looked at him, expecting more questions.

When none came, Abdul had been annoyed, saying that the missiles had been quite expensive and were their only hope if attacked from the air. Ibrahim had then done his best to pay attention, but now that their lives really did depend on the missiles could only remember three facts about them.

Their warheads carried about four hundred grams of explosives. Ibrahim only remembered this because as a nuclear technician, he thought in terms of kilotons, and found a quantity less than a single kilogram somewhere between quaint and amusing.

They traveled at nearly twice the speed of sound, which again Ibrahim found less than impressive. The Nasr missile he had worked on reached Mach 6.

The Russians were replacing the Igla with a more capable model. Abdul had explained this was why some SA-24s had come on the market. Ibrahim had been smart enough not to say aloud that he wasn't excited to be getting obsolete Russian castoffs to defend their most important weapon.

At this point, though, one non-technical detail seemed more important than any of those facts. They had two Iglas.

Ibrahim could now see there were three helicopters.

In spite of this, Ibrahim was still reluctant to begin the triggering sequence for the weapon for several reasons. The first and most important was that there were no people or structures anywhere in sight. All of the effort that had gone into bringing the nuclear weapon this far would have been for nothing.

Next, it was at least possible that one missile might damage or destroy two helicopters. Ibrahim might not know much about anti-aircraft weapons, but he knew that when they exploded, they produced a cloud of shrapnel that could travel a considerable distance.

Ibrahim was also honest enough to admit to himself that the chances of this happening were small.

Looking at the men getting ready to fire the missiles, though, gave Ibrahim some real hope. Big, strong, capable, and heavily armed, Ibrahim thought to himself ruefully that they were everything he was not. If the Americans landed their helicopters, Ibrahim thought they'd have a fight on their hands.

One "woosh" and a trail of smoke was quickly followed by another. Each missile went straight as an arrow towards one of the approaching helicopters, which immediately scattered.

One missile scored a hit, and all the men around Ibrahim cheered. After a moment, Ibrahim realized he was too. The stricken helicopter was smoking and spinning and then hit the ground. Hard. But, disappointingly, there was no fire or explosion as there always was in the movies.

The other two helicopters were still moving around frantically, and apparently successfully. Ibrahim couldn't see what had happened to the other missile, but it hadn't hit one of the helicopters.

Then two small dots that quickly grew bigger leaped from one of the helicopters and moved straight towards them. Ibrahim realized it had to be answering missiles and dove for the ground.

Just in time. Both black vans disappeared in a roar of fire and smoke, and many men whose reflexes weren't as good as Ibrahim's were no longer there.

Through the pounding in his head, Ibrahim wondered dully why only two missiles had been fired. Why not a third one to destroy the truck with the weapon?

Like a bucket of ice water, the realization hit Ibrahim that it was precisely because the white truck held the weapon that no missile had struck it. Not only was this no random anti-Taliban patrol, they even knew which vehicle held the nuclear device.

Abdul's fear had been correct. The enemy did have better radiation detection equipment than anyone knew.

Looking around him at the few other survivors, he felt a rush of anger. They weren't going to make it to Kabul.

But at least he could take this bunch of assassins with them.

Ibrahim strode towards the white truck.

No sooner had he done so than he could hear weapons firing, and a glance backward revealed that the few men left were all on the ground. None of them were moving.

Ibrahim began to run.

It felt as though a giant hand had shoved him face-first to the ground. And it happened so quickly.

That was Ibrahim's last thought before consciousness fled.

Forty-Two Kilometers South of Kabul, Afghanistan

Mikhail Vasilyev opened his eyes to see nothing but clear blue skies. That was quickly replaced by a face he didn't recognize wearing a concerned look. The face turned and yelled, "He's conscious, sir!"

Captain Rogoff. Now, that face he recognized.

"Glad to see you're still with us," Rogoff said. "Think you can sit up?"

A good question, Vasilyev thought, and only one way to answer it. He grabbed Rogoff's outstretched hand and was soon sitting upright. Rogoff sat down next to him.

Vasilyev took stock. Head was spinning and throbbing a bit. He'd felt worse after drinking too much celebrating a friend's birthday.

Ready to complete the mission.

"How are my friends, Captain?" Vasilyev asked.

"Well, I'm glad to say our bomb expert came through OK. She's getting bandaged behind you," Rogoff said, pointing.

Vasilyev turned, and could now see Neda Rhahbar getting a white cloth bandage applied to her forehead.

"She needed some stitches, but says she's OK," Rogoff added.

Vasilyev nodded. "And my friend Grishkov, and your men?"

Rogoff frowned. "There, I'm afraid the news isn't so good. Grishkov took shrapnel damage and is unconscious. We think he's bleeding internally. We've got him stabilized, and a medevac chopper is en route. It should be here in less than ten minutes. The rest of us got lucky, with no serious injuries."

"Any remaining enemy forces?" Vasilyev asked.

Rogoff shook his head. "Not that we can see. We've seen a couple of twitches, but I have a man on that," he said, pointing at a soldier with a sniper rifle who was slowly and methodically sweeping the area around the distant white truck.

Rogoff added, "Normally, we'd try to take prisoners to get intel, but I figured anybody still alive would try to set off the bomb, so . . ."

Vasilyev nodded vigorously enough that his head started spinning again.

"Agreed, Captain." Pointing at Neda, he said, "We need to get to that bomb."

Rogoff nodded. "Figured you'd say that." Gesturing towards the smoking helicopter to his right, he said, "We're lucky the pilot was able to get our bird down in one piece. It's not going anywhere."

Pointing at the helicopter on his left, Rogoff said, "This one's still in good shape. We're going to hop you two over to the truck once the corpsman's done bandaging Neda."

Right on cue, the corpsman working on Neda looked towards Rogoff and lifted up his right thumb.

Rogoff stood up and extended his hand again. Grasping it, Vasilyev was shortly standing.

More spinning, a bit more throbbing. Rogoff handed him a canteen, and Vasilyev swallowed from it gratefully.

Better.

Vasilyev walked over to Neda. She looked pale but determined.

"How are you doing?" Vasilyev asked.

"Well enough," Neda replied. "And you?"

"The same," Vasilyev said.

"Have you heard anything more about Grishkov?" Neda asked.

"Just that a medevac helicopter is on its way. At least we know he will be in competent hands," Vasilyev said.

While he was at Bagram Airfield, he had heard that the hospital there boasted a very high survival rate, so high that nearly all combat deaths in Afghanistan happened before the victim reached the hospital.

Even thinking that felt like bad luck.

As Vasilyev had that thought he could hear an approaching helicopter, and fractionally relaxed.

Neda's head followed his towards the sound, and he could see her relax slightly as well.

"They say they've moved all of my tools to the other helicopter. Are we ready to go?" Neda asked.

Rogoff had stood off to the side while they were talking, but walked towards them once Vasilyev looked in his direction.

"We are ready," Vasilyev said.

344 · TED HALSTEAD

Rogoff nodded and gestured to the pilot that Vasilyev could now see was already seated in the helicopter.

As they walked together towards the helicopter, Vasilyev saw that several soldiers were boarding as well.

Seeing Vasilyev's questioning look, Rogoff shrugged.

"I said I thought we got all of them. Better safe than sorry," Rogoff said, as they all entered the helicopter and strapped in for takeoff.

Just as they did so, they could see the medevac helicopter touch down, and corpsmen race to where Grishkov lay unmoving on a stretcher.

Their helicopter rose, but to a much lower altitude than before. The pilot pitched it forward, and the truck quickly grew larger in the helicopter's windshield.

As the pilot lowered the helicopter to the ground, it kicked up a cloud of dust so thick that visibility outside was close to zero. Some of it found its way inside so that Vasilyev's eyes burned, and he began to cough.

Vasilyev thought to himself that he would be delighted to be finished with this mission.

CHAPTER THIRTY-NINE

Forty Kilometers South of Kabul, Afghanistan

How am I still alive?

Ibrahim had no sooner asked himself the question than he knew the answer. Abdul had insisted he wear body armor under his clothes, even though Ibrahim had complained that it was uncomfortable and unlikely to make a difference.

Well, Abdul had been right, Ibrahim thought. Too bad I'll never have the chance to thank him.

Ibrahim started to get up, but some instinct made him stay still. Seconds later, the *craaak* of a rifle came to him at nearly the same instant he heard a dull thud not far away.

Ibrahim correctly guessed that movement would make him the target of that rifle. Gritting his teeth, he realized that he could do nothing but wait face down in the dirt.

It seemed like his wait went on forever, but Ibrahim knew that only minutes had passed when he heard a new sound. A helicopter. And it was rapidly getting closer.

Ibrahim was smart enough to build a jury-rigged nuclear weapon. It took much less intelligence to realize that if the helicopter landed nearby, it would probably kick up enough dust to obscure his run to the truck.

Sure enough, in less than a minute, dust started to swirl around him, as the sound of the helicopter went from loud to deafening.

Ibrahim quickly discovered that the dust was a double-edged sword, as it stung his eyes and clogged his throat. But it didn't matter. This was his chance.

Ibrahim rose and, bent double ran as quickly as he could to the truck. As he dove inside the back, he could hear a *craaak* that was immediately followed by something hitting the truck's metal side with a loud clang.

Too late, Ibrahim thought exultantly as he hurried to the weapon he had labored for so many hours to build.

He had given a lot of thought to how to set off the device, in particular how to do it as quickly as possible while making accidental arming as difficult as he could. Ibrahim believed the design he'd chosen was the best possible.

Anyway, it was undoubtedly the best he could do, he thought wryly.

Ibrahim had thought about trying to defeat the Nasr nuclear core's built-in detonation delay, a design function that guaranteed a regular missile firing would have time to clear the launch area before detonation. Since it appeared reshaping the core's nuclear material would have been required, it seemed impractical.

Ibrahim knew that he had already received fatal radiation exposure. If he put his hands on the core, even with lead-lined gloves, he knew he might not make it to Kabul.

Abdul had already been forced to put the men who had removed the cores from the warheads and carried them to the trucks in Pakistan out of their misery. As well as the men who had helped Ibrahim build the finished weapons, which again required repeatedly handling the cores.

In the end, he had decided against trying to defeat the delay, because the risk just wasn't worth the reward. The Nasr's range was short enough, and its speed sufficiently high that the core's detonation delay could be only a few minutes.

In an attempt to prevent detection, Ibrahim had put heavy shielding around the core in both of his finished devices. He was bitterly disappointed that his effort had failed.

In truth, though, the shielding had failed only partially. The Okhotnik drone would have detected his device far more quickly without it. And in the meantime, Abdul's weapon continued towards Bagram Airfield.

Ibrahim was proud of the arming switch he had devised. It depended on a piece of metal with a small electrical charge making contact with another. This meant moving the metal piece protruding from the case within a groove cut into the casing. First up, and then to the right.

Ibrahim was sure that no matter how much the weapon was jostled within its elastic lattice, that precise set of pressures would never be applied by accident. Whether or not that was true, he thought, didn't matter now.

His design had made it this far. Now to see if it worked.

Ibrahim's hand moved forward to the switch, and did what he had been born to do.

Up, and then to the right.

Ibrahim was immediately rewarded with a steady "beep" that repeated every few seconds. He almost hadn't bothered to add this feature but had reluctantly concluded that whether or not he believed accidental arming was possible, he should have some way to know if it happened.

The next step, Ibrahim thought, was to delay the enemy in the helicopter long enough to let the arming process finish. Not that he thought there was a real chance someone could disarm the weapon in the few minutes available. Just to be thorough.

The simplest way to have achieved this would have been to lift the cloth flap separating the truck bed where he was now and the front seats, followed by sitting in the driver's seat. The keys were still in the ignition.

Granted, he wouldn't have made it far. But certainly far enough to ensure there would never be enough time to defuse the warhead.

Instead, Ibrahim's background betrayed him. He had gone through military training as an officer, but as a college graduate destined for Pakistan's nuclear forces, combat infantry skills got little emphasis.

On the one hand, Ibrahim's education and skills meant better pay, better housing, and better working conditions than nearly anyone else in Pakistan's military.

On the other, Ibrahim knew that behind his back, a lot of the others in the Pakistani military didn't consider him a "real" soldier.

Well, that was going to end today.

There was an AK-74 lying in the truck bed. Ibrahim checked to make sure the clip was seated correctly, and a round chambered. Then he checked that the rifle was set to automatic fire. He knew the helicopter was close enough that even an average marksman like him could hardly miss it.

Ibrahim was going to empty the rifle's entire clip into the helicopter before they killed him. That ought to slow them down enough.

Ibrahim took a deep breath, and then leaped through the cloth flap in the back of the truck and landed outside on his feet. In a single smooth motion that took less than a second, he had the AK-74 aimed at the helicopter. It was close enough that he had no trouble seeing the people inside, including two who were just starting to exit the helicopter.

Ibrahim pulled the trigger.

Nothing happened.

He had forgotten to take off the safety.

Everything went black.

Forty Kilometers South of Kabul, Afghanistan

The American soldiers who had climbed aboard the helicopter with Captain Rogoff had said nothing within Mikhail Vasilyev's earshot during the entire trip. Vasilyev wasn't sure but suspected this was due to orders they'd received from Rogoff.

Now, though, one said laconically, "Remind me to buy Pete a beer when we get back."

The soldier he was speaking to nodded. Both of them looked out the windshield at Ibrahim's body and prepared to follow Vasilyev, Neda, and Rogoff out of the helicopter.

Vasilyev guessed correctly that "Pete" was the American sniper who had stayed next to the damaged helicopter.

The Americans took up position outside the truck in case any more Taliban appeared, while Vasilyev and Neda began work inside it on defusing the bomb.

The beeping they heard as soon as they climbed into the truck bed made it clear that the weapon had been armed, and they probably had only a very few minutes.

Fortunately, there were only a few screws to remove to get at the weapon's interior. Vasilyev had feared that it would be welded shut, but now realized that would have made access impossible for its creators too if something went wrong.

Neda hissed in dismay. Vasilyev saw that the needle nose pliers she was holding were hovering over a complex mass of circuits and wires that he didn't recall from any of Neda's sketches of the weapon's likely layout.

Then Neda's expression cleared, and was replaced with a small smile. She thrust her left hand towards Vasilyev and said, "Your knife!"

Vasilyev really wanted to ask what use his combat knife could have in disarming a nuclear weapon, but swallowed the question and mutely placed it in her hand.

Vasilyev was astonished when Neda next lifted the entire mass of wires and circuits and began vigorously sawing through them with the knife. Finished, she tossed the jumble of plastic and metal back over her shoulder.

The beeping continued.

Neda saw Vasilyev's concerned look and smiled. "A decoy. Put there to buy time."

Her hands had never stopped moving while she spoke. Vasilyev recognized all of the steps she had tried to teach him and was profoundly grateful their lives didn't depend on his memory.

Less than a minute later, Neda stepped back, satisfied. "That should do it," she said.

The beeping hadn't stopped.

Vasilyev was about to point that out when Neda's smile stopped him.

"Yes, I know. The beeping. All it means is the weapon was armed. I could stop it, but the designer could have tied in another detonation circuit to activate if someone did that. Why take the chance?"

Vasilyev nodded. "So, there's nothing to do but wait?"

Neda stepped towards him. "Exactly."

Vasilyev stood paralyzed as he looked into Neda's eyes, struck all at once by the depth of his feelings for her, in what could very well be their last moments.

Neda frowned and said something under her breath in Russian that made Vasilyev's eyes widen, and then grabbed his face in both hands.

Their kiss seemed to go on forever. Vasilyev was dimly aware of the smell of smoke that permeated their clothes and hair from the helicopter fire, and how the bandage on Neda's forehead scratched his where it pressed against him.

It was wonderful.

Finally, they broke free and looked at each other.

The beeping hadn't stopped. But they were still here.

"So, it would probably have gone off by now, yes?" Vasilyev cautiously asked.

Neda shrugged. "I won't tempt fate by saying yes," she replied.

Vasilyev laughed. "An excellent answer! We may make a Russian out of you yet!"

Then, instantly serious, he held both of Neda's hands.

"There is a great deal I wish to say to you. But I want to do it away from this bomb, and our American audience," Vasilyev said.

Neda smiled and squeezed his hands. She nodded, her eyes shining.

They both climbed out of the truck bed and saw that the Americans were all still holding station right outside. Unless they were deaf, almost certainly within earshot of everything they'd said.

If they'd been listening, Rogoff gave no sign. "So, mission complete?" he asked.

Vasilyev shrugged. "We certainly hope so. Of course, the device should still be handled with extreme caution."

Rogoff nodded. "We've got nuclear weapons experts in the air, who I've been told should get to Bagram later today. A relief force will be on its way as soon as I advise the weapon has been disarmed. They'll guard it in the meantime, and provide security for its transport."

"Good," Vasilyev nodded. "I didn't think you'd leave it here for anyone to find."

Rogoff smiled. "Right. Just one more question."

"Yes?" Vasilyev replied.

"Are we invited to the wedding?"

CHAPTER FORTY

Town of Bagram, Afghanistan

Mullah Abdul Zahed looked out of the truck's windshield with little interest as it passed through the town of Bagram. It looked like dozens of small towns scattered across Afghanistan, though a bit larger than most.

As a child, Abdul's father had made him study Afghanistan's history. At the time, he had hated it, but now he was grateful for what his father had made him learn. As with much else, he thought wryly.

His father had lived to see Afghanistan's liberation from the hated Russians, and died before the Americans came to take their place. Not for the first time, Abdul thought that he was glad his father had not lived long enough to see Afghanistan once again under foreign occupation.

Or the price they were about to pay to free it once again.

Abdul knew that Bagram had a recorded history dating back over two thousand years. It had been the capital of the Kushan Empire that had controlled Afghanistan and parts of modern Pakistan and India for three centuries until finally succumbing to foreign invaders.

Truthfully, Abdul didn't care. He was proud of Afghanistan's history, and it was good to remember that Afghans had sometimes ruled others, and not always been ruled by outsiders themselves.

But Afghanistan was full of other towns and cities with rich histories. Abdul knew that destroying Bagram Airfield would, at best, kill many of the nearby town's residents. At worst, it could do more than devastate the town. Radioactive fallout might make it impossible to rebuild for many years to come.

So be it. The past was the past. Abdul had to concern himself with Afghanistan's future.

Creech Air Force Base, Nevada

Captain John Pettigrew looked over the mission brief and nodded with satisfaction. He couldn't have managed the prep work better if he'd done it himself.

The Avenger drone had been landed at Bagram Airfield, refueled and loaded with another R9X model Hellfire missile to replace the one he'd fired. Pettigrew hadn't even known that model Hellfire was stocked at Bagram, and so was pleased he would still have it available as an option for the next mission.

Now the Avenger was again in the air with Senior Airman Evans back at the controls.

An update flashed across Pettigrew's display, and his eyes widened.

Pettigrew stood up and quietly asked Evans to put the Avenger on autopilot for a moment.

Then Pettigrew gestured for attention, and every eye in the drone control center turned towards him.

"A few of you know what the mission is about today," Pettigrew said.

"I think you all deserve to know. We're looking for a nuclear bomb headed towards Bagram Airfield. I've just been advised that a second nuclear bomb has been located and defused outside Kabul."

Pettigrew paused. "We'd already been focusing our search efforts on the area around Bagram. The good news is that now we're sure we're looking for just one bomb. The bad news is that our drone's sensors aren't very likely to detect its radiation signature. Not anyone's fault. Just not a job that the sensors were designed to do."

Looking around the room, Pettigrew saw nothing but grim expressions. Nobody liked to think that they were doomed in advance to failure.

Pettigrew smiled. "But after that bad news, there's more good news," and waited for the expected relieved laughter to die down.

"Believe it or not, we're getting help from the Russians. They have a drone headed our way that should get to us in minutes with sensors capable of detecting the bomb. The Russians have been given the Avenger's altitude, so they should be able to avoid our drone. Evans, you'll want to keep an eye out in case they forget," Pettigrew said.

"Yes, sir," Evans said, nervously looking at his display.

"This is the drone that spotted the bomb that was just defused near Kabul, so we need to be ready to strike the vehicle carrying the other weapon as soon as it's identified. I've been advised the team that carried out that successful mission will need more time to reach Bagram than we probably have," Pettigrew said.

Then he turned to Evans, who looked like he had a question. "Go ahead," Pettigrew said, gently.

Pettigrew had gone out of his way to make it clear to Evans he harbored no ill will over the previous day's events, but he was clearly still nervous around Pettigrew.

"Sir, is there any chance we could get a special forces team out of Bagram Airfield to deal with the weapon?" Evans asked.

Pettigrew shook his head. "It's a good question, but from what I hear, the answer is no. You all heard what happened to one of the teams trying to free hostages at one of the girl's high schools."

Everyone nodded soberly.

"Well, the others had to secure their schools. For example, making sure the Taliban didn't leave any presents behind. Now they have to make it back from across Afghanistan. Even by helicopter, that's probably going to take more time than we've got. Command thinks these attacks are synchronized so that if one bomb was close to Kabul, the other one is close to Bagram," Pettigrew said.

Everyone nodded. They were all familiar with the terror tactic of simultaneous attack.

"OK, let's get back at it," Pettigrew said. "With luck, we'll be hearing from the Russians soon."

It was, in fact, only minutes before a set of coordinates flashed across Pettigrew's monitor, which were quickly superimposed on a map of the Bagram area.

Pettigrew didn't need to ask whether Evans had the same information. He could hear Evans' heartfelt, "Oh, no," from where he was sitting.

Pettigrew looked at Sergeant Alonzo Johnson and asked, "Johnson, are we still tied in with Bagram Airfield's operations center?"

Johnson nodded.

"OK, cut our link to Bagram Airfield at this time. When they ask you what happened, tell them we're having technical difficulties. I'll explain why later. There's no time now," Pettigrew said.

Johnson frowned, but nodded and began to carry out the order.

Pettigrew walked over to Evans and put his hand on his shoulder. "Evans, this time, I'm going to relieve you because I'd never ask someone else to do this. But we both know it has to be done."

356 · TED HALSTEAD

Evans nodded and stood. He whispered, "Thank you, sir," and sat in the nearest vacant chair, while Pettigrew took his place at the drone control console.

Town of Bagram, Afghanistan

Mullah Abdul Zahed had been happy. The last roadblock before reaching the main entrance gate at Bagram Airfield was behind them. They had driven through most of the town. Only a handful of kilometers remained between him, his weapon, and his glorious destiny.

After so many years of waiting, Abdul was finally allowing himself to imagine what life would be like without the American occupiers. He knew that there were many, including even men who had been fighting in the Taliban cause their entire lives, who believed he and those who would follow in his place would be content to return to life as it had been before the Americans came.

But they were wrong. So very wrong.

Time had dulled the memory of so many. But not the memory of Abdul's faithful followers, the ones who would ensure Afghanistan followed the one true path.

During the decade the Taliban had been in power in Kabul, resistance to their rule had never stopped. Warlords with their soldiers sprang up everywhere. Some were supported by foreigners, like the cursed Americans. Others made their money from control over a portion of Afghanistan's opium production. They only had one thing in common.

They all hated the Taliban.

So, Abdul and his followers believed the solution was simple. Some thought the Pashtun people, led by the Taliban movement, consisted of a mere forty percent of Afghanistan's population.

Abdul knew that the correct number was over sixty percent.

One fact, though, was clear. Many of those who lived in Afghanistan were not Pashtun.

That would have to change.

The solution would not be death camps of the sort the Pol Pot regime had used in Cambodia, or the Serbs had used in Bosnia. History had shown repeatedly that, sooner or later, governments using such methods were overthrown by outsiders.

No, they would have to be more subtle. Encourage settlement in the worthless border region with China, much of it now a nature reserve, by non-Pashtuns. Then, cede the territory to China in return for a large cash payment, including its hapless inhabitants.

The Chinese had shown they could turn even the most troublesome minorities, such as the Uighurs, into productive assets. Why not the Hazara and the Tajik as well?

Non-Pashtun ethnic groups near the Pakistani border could find themselves cut off from opium production income. Many had fled to Pakistan before. They could be encouraged to do it again.

There were so many solutions to the problem. It just took being creative.

Reversing the so-called "progress" of women was simple on its face. Make sure that the women elected to the illegitimate "National Assembly" as well as the surviving girls who attended high school quietly disappeared. No ISIS-style public beheadings. In fact, no bodies at all.

Just unmarked graves in the mountains that would never be found.

But that would be just the beginning. Female literacy, female education in any form, and female employment outside of a family farm or family-run business would be illegal. The penalty for violations would be death.

Abdul had spent over twenty years working quietly behind the scenes to make sure that once he was gone, the Taliban would continue on the correct path. The key was making sure that the leaders in critical positions, the ones with real power, thought as he did.

Of course, he had opponents. Some thought he was dangerous.

Others thought he was mad.

One after another, over many years, they fell by the wayside. Some Abdul outlived. The Americans took care of many others.

For those opponents who remained, some were discovered to have kept opium money that should have gone to Taliban operations for themselves. Others were found to have sold their Taliban brothers to the Americans for money. Yes, many scandals had been discovered about Abdul's opponents over the years, and he had taken care of a few more using this method just before settling out on this final journey.

Some of the scandals were even true.

Certain opponents had accidents, always somehow without witnesses. Some fell from heights. Others had their brakes fail. One unlucky man stepped on a mine.

Well, everyone knew Afghanistan was a dangerous place.

Abdul was roused from these happy thoughts by the realization that the truck had stopped moving. When the driver gestured helplessly at the gridlock before him, Abdul called for one of the men in the truck bed to come forward. Instructing him in simple and clear terms, Abdul sent him to discover what had halted their progress.

When the man returned with the explanation, Abdul didn't know whether to laugh or cry. A glorious future for the country he loved, put on hold by a donkey.

Well, it seemed that the donkey's cart had been righted, and they were about to resume their way forward.

What was that sound?

CHAPTER FORTY-ONE

Creech Air Force Base, Nevada

"From this moment on, no one is to leave this command center without my express approval. Is that understood?" Pettigrew asked.

A chorus of "Yes, sirs," several of them sounding puzzled, and others resigned, followed.

Well, at least some of them understand what's about to happen, Pettigrew thought.

"Sir, I'm passing you a message from the Russian drone operator. It's on your screen now," Johnson said.

Pettigrew read the message, and nodded. So, there weren't going to be any position updates from the Russian drone. The operator had been ordered to fly back their drone to base in Tajikistan to preserve "valuable Russian government property." The operator wished the Americans good luck in carrying out the remainder of their mission.

Well, Pettigrew couldn't say he blamed them. He'd been surprised to get any help from the Russians, and hoped someday he'd learn why they'd bothered.

Right now, though, he had a very unpleasant duty to perform.

Pettigrew ordered the sensor operators to focus the Avenger's optics on the coordinates provided by the Russians. They had obviously anticipated the order, because the target came into focus almost immediately.

The mission orders specified that the vehicle carrying the bomb was believed to be a small truck, probably white. Sure enough, there it was. Though several minutes had passed since the Russians had provided the coordinates, it was still right where it was supposed to be.

Why wasn't it moving?

Pettigrew told the sensor operators to pan the camera a short distance ahead, both to check on what could be causing a delay and to see whether there were other small white trucks nearby.

It turned out that there were no other trucks of any color or size nearby. But the reason the truck was stationary was now clear.

The Bagram street the white truck was on was hemmed in on both sides by buildings, which were lined with stalls immediately outside them covered with canopies. Judging from the volume of the traffic, it was probably market day.

Most of the traffic was composed of sedans, along with a number of scooters and motorcycles. Not far ahead of the small white truck, there was also a bus.

And just ahead of that, there was a donkey cart.

The cart had overturned, and Pettigrew couldn't see but correctly guessed that the donkey's harness had become tangled in the cart and its overturned cargo.

As he watched, the cart's driver succeeded in enlisting the help of several other men to right the cart, untangle the harness and get back underway. It looked like people passing by had already helped themselves to much of the cargo, which looked like a fruit of some kind. The rest was scattered in the street.

It looked like traffic could get moving again any minute.

Pettigrew still hesitated. Shouldn't he try Bagram, and see if a special forces team could somehow get to the truck in time?

Another look at the map told him that idea wasn't going to work. In a matter of minutes the truck would be close enough to Bagram Airfield to inflict casualties.

If it wasn't already. The mission brief had stressed that command's information on the bomb's potential yield and blast radius was only an estimate.

Every second Pettigrew hesitated he was risking the lives of service members and civilians from both the U.S. and Afghanistan who were at Bagram Airfield.

Plus, there were a lot more of them at Bagram Airfield than there were people living in the town of Bagram.

Pettigrew still wondered if he'd be able to live with doing this.

It seemed as though he was watching someone else go through the next steps of designating the small white truck as a target, locking an R9X model Hellfire on the truck, and announcing, "Missile launched."

But Pettigrew knew it was all him.

He had seconds to hope that the truck didn't have the bomb after all. Though another part of his mind immediately chided him for that thought, since it would mean the bomb was still out there.

OK, then Pettigrew would hope that the R9X's kinetic warhead wouldn't set the bomb off. That was possible, wasn't it?

In fact, it was possible. An explosive warhead would have made the bomb's detonation much more likely. A detailed analysis performed later estimated that the choice of the R9X warhead had reduced the likelihood of the bomb's detonation by over half.

It had also reduced the proportion of fissile material that would be consumed, if the bomb did detonate.

But luck was not on the side of the town of Bagram that day.

The bomb detonated. Only about half of its fissile material was used, so if it had been detonated as designed, the explosion would have been even more devastating.

This mattered for Bagram Airfield, and the adjacent Parwan Prison. It meant no casualties for the airfield instead of mass deaths and injuries at and near the gate, and far fewer for the prison.

It did not matter much for the town of Bagram. It was simply too small.

Software had saved the Avenger's optical sensors. They were programmed to cut off automatically when an event like a nuclear explosion occurred.

The Avenger itself was saved by several of Pettigrew's decisions. He had fired the missile from high altitude, and several kilometers away. Just as important, he had set an oblique course at top speed away from Bagram, and executed it as soon as he'd fired the missile.

For a moment, Pettigrew thought none of this would be enough as the shock wave from the explosion hit the Avenger, and he had to fight for control. It passed quickly, though, and he was able to regain level flight.

In the meantime, the sensor operators had refocused the optical data feed on the town of Bagram. Once Pettigrew regained control, the picture came into focus on all their monitors.

There was no mistaking the distinctive mushroom cloud. Any doubt about what had just happened was immediately erased.

"Johnson, advise Bagram Airfield that there appears to have been a nuclear detonation in the town of Bagram. Reestablish our data link with Bagram, and get me General Robinson ASAP," Pettigrew ordered. Johnson nodded, and immediately got to work.

"OK, everyone, listen up. There are to be no communications of any kind with anyone outside this room unless I give you my direct authorization. What I said earlier about not leaving this command center now goes double. I am going to ask General Robinson to designate everything that happened today as Sensitive Compartmented Information," Pettigrew said.

Everyone in the room nodded, since they all had an SCI clearance for the Avenger, both systems and operations. They understood that today's events would be a separate "compartment" with its own code word designation.

They also knew that the already severe penalties for divulging Top Secret information were increased for SCI. That was because two steps were taken before an SCI clearance was granted.

First, the already thorough background investigation for Top Secret clearance was done again, this time in more detail. As a result, many who had been granted TS clearance were denied it at the SCI level.

An unlucky few also had their TS clearance revoked.

Next, anyone who was granted an SCI clearance was given a briefing on its implications and requirements, including penalties for either inadvertently or deliberately disclosing SCI information.

"Once General Robinson decides whether or not to agree with my SCI recommendation, we will proceed accordingly. If he does agree, you will all receive a briefing on your responsibilities with regard to safeguarding this information. Is that all clear?" Pettigrew asked.

The expected chorus of, "Yes, sirs," followed.

"Very well, carry on," Pettigrew said.

"Sir, General Robinson's office is on the line," Johnson said.

Pettigrew nodded and picked up the handset. Now he'd see whether he'd be considered the savior of Bagram Airfield and its forty thousand personnel, or one of the greatest mass murderers in American history.

He wasn't sure himself.

CHAPTER FORTY-TWO

The White House, Washington DC

President Hernandez looked up as General Robinson, the Air Force Chief of Staff, walked into the Oval Office.

"So, General, that was the last nuclear weapon the Taliban had. Do we have a casualty count yet?"

Robinson shook his head. "No, sir. Not for Afghan casualties from the town of Bagram. I've had confirmation from Bagram Airfield's commander that they did not sustain any casualties, and are following all anti-radiation protocols. We have a specially equipped team from Landstuhl Regional Medical Center en route from Ramstein Air Base to assist."

Hernandez nodded. "I'm old enough to remember the bad old Cold War days. I'm not surprised we had the necessary equipment to deal with a nuclear incident at a base in Germany. I suppose we didn't send it earlier because of concern about causing a panic?"

Robinson rocked his hand back and forth. "That was only one consideration, sir. There was also the possibility we might need to send the team and their equipment to Hamid Karzai Airport in Kabul if the strike against the Green Zone had been successful. Also, if we had been unable to prevent the strike against Bagram Airfield, we could have lost the team as well."

Hernandez winced. "Yes, I see your point. Glad you thought all that through. When will we be able to start helping the Afghan government with rescue and recovery?"

"A matter of hours, sir. But from initial reports, I have to be honest. We expect few survivors and even fewer who we can successfully treat. Ironically, the largest number may be from the Parwan Detention Facility, which primarily holds captured Taliban," Robinson said.

It was easy to see this news didn't please Hernandez. "Please explain, General."

"Well, sir, we built the prison. That means the structure held up better to the blast than the civilian buildings in the town, which were built to local construction standards. Also, the prison was almost directly adjacent to Bagram Airfield, which means it was relatively far from the blast," Robinson said.

Hernandez shook his head. "We turned Parwan over to the Afghan government in 2014. Any word from them on its status?"

Now Robinson looked uncomfortable. "Yes, sir. They confirm that there are survivors at the prison, including prisoners, guards, and administrative staff. However, the Afghan President himself has asked us to give priority to assisting people in the town of Bagram, and only once that has been done to help survivors at Parwan."

Hernandez grunted. "Parwan holds the same prisoners who the Taliban were demanding be released when they bombed one girl's high school and took three others hostage. And then bombed another one, and would have bombed the last two if they hadn't been stopped by our troops, right?"

Robinson nodded and said, "Yes, sir."

Hernandez looked thoughtful, and asked, "What do you think our assistance team would do, in the absence of guidance from us?"

Robinson shrugged. "Once they deplane and organize, Parwan would hold the closest group of survivors to Bagram Airfield, so that's where they would go first."

"That's what I thought. Here's what we're going to do. Tell the Afghan President that we have heard his request, and will do as he asks. The Landstuhl medical team goes to the town of Bagram first. Now, I hope that the team will be bringing enough equipment to let our medical people at Bagram assist?" Hernandez asked.

"Yes, sir. They'll be bringing additional protective gear, but I've been warned that our medical staff at Bagram Airfield should not attempt to accompany them to the town since they've had no training for operations in a high radioactivity environment," Robinson replied.

"That's fine," Hernandez said. "What I have in mind is that at the same time the Landstuhl medical team is assisting in the town of Bagram, we have a well-armed security team with proper protective gear go to the relatively lower radiation threat environment at Parwan. They should be accompanied by Afghan officers we can trust. We have such liaison officers in place at Bagram Airfield, correct?"

"Yes, sir," Robinson said.

"Good. Those Afghan officers will help us identify all surviving Parwan guards and administrative staff. We will evacuate them to our hospital at Bagram for treatment. Our soldiers will then secure the Parwan facility until that task can be taken over by the Afghan government. Once the Landstuhl medical team's work in the town of Bagram has been completed to their satisfaction, they will redeploy to assist the prisoners at Parwan," Hernandez said.

"Yes, sir," Robinson said doubtfully. He hesitated, and then said, "Sir, what if we're accused of leaving the Taliban prisoners to die at Parwan?"

Hernandez looked at Robinson coldly. "You tell anyone who says that we're following the instructions of the duly elected Afghan government. And remind anyone who is asking who set the bomb off that's killing those prisoners."

Robinson now looked even more uncomfortable than he had before. "Sir, about that. It turns out we set off the bomb."

Hernandez, for a moment, was at a complete loss for words.

"You're going to have to explain that one, General," he finally said.

"Yes, sir. We had a Predator C Avenger drone monitoring the approaches to Bagram Airfield operated from Creech Air Force Base in Nevada. Data from a Russian drone in the same area advised that a vehicle in the town of Bagram exhibited a radiation signature consistent with one of the stolen Pakistani nuclear weapons," Robinson said.

"So, the Russians have a drone that can sniff out nuclear weapons more effectively than anything we've got. And didn't feel like telling us until now," Hernandez said acidly.

"Yes, sir. Well, as soon as that data was sent to Bagram Airfield, it was also available over our dedicated defense network, including Creech Air Force Base. The drone operator's supervisor took command of the Avenger, and launched a Hellfire missile at the vehicle identified as the source of the threat," Robinson said.

Hernandez shook his head. "And the bomb detonated," he said.

"Yes, sir. Preliminary analysis from our experts suggests that the weapon failed to achieve its full yield. Still, it appears that at least half of the fissile material in the weapon was consumed in the explosion. So, if the Taliban had been allowed to detonate the weapon undisturbed, the damage would have been even greater," Robinson said.

"Maybe so, General. But I understand those Russian agents successfully defused the other stolen weapon. Couldn't they have done the same with this one?" Hernandez asked.

"No, sir. The Russians were too far away. At the speed the vehicle was traveling, Bagram Airfield would have been within the weapon's blast radius in a matter of minutes. For the same reason, the drone commander decided a ground assault on the vehicle was impractical," Robinson said.

"And so this officer decided to make the call on his own? Without involving anyone else in the chain of command? Like, say, the Commander-in-Chief?" Hernandez asked.

Then Hernandez held up his hand. "Hold on a second. You said Creech Air Force Base. This isn't the same officer who saved that SEAL team, is it?"

Robinson sighed. "It's the same officer, sir. Captain Pettigrew. It's not really a coincidence, sir. We run armed drone operations for the region out of Creech, and both incidents took place in Afghanistan."

"Fair enough," Hernandez said. "Continue."

"Sir, Pettigrew believed there was no time to seek higher authority. Based on the facts as I now know them, sir, I agree with his judgment. Besides his duty to protect the lives of American service members and U.S. government property, Pettigrew also pointed out to me that there are far more people at Bagram Airfield than in the town of Bagram. He also noted that many Afghan military personnel, as well as Afghan civilian contractors, work at Bagram Airfield as well," Robinson said.

Hernandez grunted. "So, this wasn't a straight trade-off between American and Afghan lives, and we would have lost more lives if he hadn't acted. OK, good points. Now, how many people besides us know about this?"

"The service members at the drone control center, who were all directly or indirectly involved in the attack. Pettigrew knows me and so decided to bypass the chain of command and call me directly. I have approved his request to designate all information regarding this incident as SCI," Robinson said.

"That's all very well, General, but do you think none of them are going to talk?" Hernandez asked.

"Sir, everyone at that drone control center already has an SCI clearance. If we didn't think they could keep their mouths shut, they wouldn't be there," Robinson replied.

"OK, but what about Bagram Airfield? How many people there know?" Hernandez asked.

"Fortunately, Pettigrew cut off Bagram Airfield's data feed before firing the missile. So far, at my order, there is no formal written report of this incident in any military computer system," Robinson replied.

"What about that Russian drone? Couldn't it have seen what happened?" Hernandez asked.

Robinson shook his head. "I've asked our experts, and they all think that's unlikely. The drone had set course for its base in Tajikistan well before the Hellfire was launched, and was headed there at its top speed. So, it was probably too far away to see what happened."

Hernandez still looked skeptical. "This is the same Russian drone that was able to detect a radiation signature our drones couldn't find. How can we be so confident its cameras and sensors aren't better than we thought too?"

"The truth is we can't be sure. But the Russians' priority had to be getting that drone back to base, not looking behind them. Our intelligence says they only have a few drones that advanced, so they sure wouldn't want to lose it. Plus, we haven't heard a peep from the Russians since the explosion," Robinson said.

Hernandez nodded. "So, do you think we can keep a lid on this? What about the Afghans? Would they have been able to see the Hellfire strike?"

Robinson shrugged. "It's certainly possible. But any Afghan close enough to see it . . ."

Hernandez finished for him. "Almost certainly died in the explosion."

"Yes, sir," Robinson said softly.

"So, right now, the Afghan government is blaming the Taliban, and the Taliban are denying responsibility as loudly as they can," Hernandez said.

"Yes, sir," Robinson said, obviously puzzled. Why restate what they both already knew?

"That video from the Taliban mullah we intercepted. You remember I said we were going to make sure it was never broadcast?" Hernandez asked.

Robinson nodded.

"Well, I've changed my mind. I'd like first to plant the portion claiming credit for successful attacks on Bagram Airfield and the Green Zone in Kabul on a website known to be used by the Taliban. Then, as soon as we can confirm copies have been downloaded, remove it and replace it with the one only claiming responsibility for the attack on Bagram Airfield. Can we do that?" Hernandez asked.

"I'm not sure, sir, but probably. Cyber Command will either have the capability or will coordinate with any other agency necessary. So, you think we can let people know the Taliban were planning to attack the Green Zone in Kabul, and successfully blame the Bagram explosion on the Taliban?" Robinson asked.

"Blame, General? I'd say more like set the record straight. We didn't steal that warhead from the Pakistanis, rig it to explode, and put it in a populated part of Afghanistan next to an American military base with the intent to attack it. We didn't fake those videos. Technical experts can poke at them all day long, and they will still come up as the real deal because they are just what they appear to be—a full confession," Hernandez said.

"Yes, sir. If people believe the videos, and since as you say being real they should, then I think they will do real damage to the Taliban's reputation," Robinson said.

"I think they may do more than that, General. How important would you say popular support has been to the Taliban's battlefield success?" Hernandez asked.

"Well, critical, sir. With the people on their side, they get warning of our movements. Afghan women and children willingly mingle with Taliban fighters to make our targeting more difficult. They provide food and shelter, bandage wounds, pass messages—sir, without their support, the Taliban would be finished."

Robinson paused. "A lot of people forget that Mao Zedong started as a guerrilla fighter against a Japanese occupation force. Mao compared guerrillas to fish and the people to the water in which they swim. He said take away popular support, and they'll have the same chance that fish do tossed ten kilometers inland by a typhoon's storm surge. None."

"Good," Hernandez said, nodding. "I want you to get the rest of the Joint Chiefs here to meet me in the Situation Room this afternoon. I'll have Chuck coordinate it with you because I want to keep it quiet. This opportunity won't last long, and I want to take full advantage of it. I'm going to hit the Taliban harder than they've ever been hit before."

"Yes, sir," Robinson said doubtfully.

Hernandez grinned. "I know. Everyone says victory can't be purely military, and they're right. What I'm going to do after the Taliban lose popular support and take some real battlefield losses is offer them a place in an Afghan coalition government. We both know that in a fair election, they'd get some votes."

Robinson shook his head. "I don't think you'll get the Afghan government to agree, sir."

"Oh, I think they might, General. If they know that the other option is the withdrawal of all our forces, so they'll be facing the Taliban alone. We did that before the same way we did it in Iraq, and just like in Iraq, the enemy was almost in sight of the capital when we were asked to come back," Hernandez said.

"Yes, sir, I remember that well," Robinson said grimly.

"This is our chance, General. One way or the other, this will be the end of America's war in Afghanistan," Hernandez said.

"Yes, sir," Robinson said as he stood, having correctly guessed that their meeting was over.

"General, if you see Fred Popel out there when you leave, please send him in," Hernandez said.

Robinson nodded. The Secretary of State? Yes, that seemed like a good person to talk to next.

CHAPTER FORTY-THREE

The White House, Washington DC

President Hernandez could see that Secretary of State Fred Popel looked worried. He mused that if he ever did a survey of the most common expression worn by officials coming to see him in the Oval Office, "worried" would probably win.

"Mr. President, I think the Taliban's attack on innocent civilians in the town of Bagram will have far-reaching implications for the entire region. I'd like to know how you plan to respond, and then I have a few ideas of my own," Popel said.

"Good," Hernandez said with an approving nod. "First, we've had on-again, off-again talks with the Taliban in Qatar for a while now. They really haven't come to anything, right?"

Popel nodded. "Correct, sir. Those low-level talks have led nowhere so far. It's been weeks since they last met, and no follow up meeting has yet been scheduled."

"Let's keep it that way. No announcement that we're ending talks, or anything like that. Just . . . no action. For your ears only, I'm planning a military strike against the Taliban with more resources than we've used in years. I think it will be effective after the drop in popular support I'm expecting for the Taliban," Hernandez said.

Popel frowned. "Are you thinking that military defeat will make them more inclined to negotiate?"

Hernandez shook his head. "Not by itself. But if we couple a new reality on the battlefield with an offer for participation in free elections and a place in a new coalition government, I think they might listen."

"They might, sir. But what about the current Afghan government? Many of them, including the President, may resist including the Taliban in their government in any meaningful way," Popel said.

Hernandez nodded. "You're right, Fred. And as a sovereign country, they have that right. Just as I have the right to pull out all U.S. forces."

Popel grunted. "Well, the trick would be to communicate that to the Afghan President, and only him. And then hope he stays quiet about it. If the Taliban learn we're ready to leave, they'll be as difficult as they can in the negotiations just to get that outcome."

"You see, Fred, that's why we have pros like you. I'm going to leave details like that in your capable hands. Now, let's talk about Pakistan," Hernandez said.

"Are we going to strike their nuclear weapons production facilities, sir? There's been a lot of speculation in the press that we'd do it if one of the stolen Pakistani nuclear weapons was used against U.S. forces. Everyone knows Bagram Airfield was their target. Of course, Pakistan still denies publicly that any of their nuclear weapons were stolen," Popel said.

"I'm not taking that option off the table, but for now, no. The hundreds of nuclear weapons they have now are dispersed, mobile, and so extremely difficult to target. Their production facilities would be much easier to hit, but it wouldn't take the Pakistanis long to replace them. So, Fred, any other ideas?" Hernandez asked with a smile.

Popel was visibly relieved. "Sir, I hope it's one you had too. Let's tell the Pakistanis we're shelving the idea of striking them, even though we came very close to losing a base with thousands of American troops to one of their weapons, on one condition. They begin good-faith negotiations with India to first freeze and then gradually reduce each side's stock of nuclear weapons."

Popel paused. "Now, that will be a hard sell. The Pakistanis have been saying from the outset that they're relying on their nuclear weapons to offset India's superiority in conventional forces. That superiority is already pretty glaring, and as India's economy keeps pulling ahead of Pakistan's they'll have the resources to make it even worse."

"All true," Hernandez said, nodding. "But what if next time it's the Pakistani Taliban that steals one or more nukes to use against, say, government offices in Islamabad? Wasn't their leader killed in something to do with this business?" Hernandez asked.

"Yes, sir," Popel said. "Khaksar Wasiq. We haven't heard yet who's going to succeed him."

"Right," Hernandez said. "And what if whoever that is, decides to make getting his hands on a nuke a priority? It's simple. The fewer there are, the harder that will be, and vice versa."

Popel shrugged. "That makes sense to me, sir. I'll do my very best to get the Pakistani leadership to see it the same way."

Hernandez smiled, and tapped the side of his head. "I just remembered something, Fred. The images Space Command linked to that so-called "chemical factory" explosion in Risalpur. I wonder how the Pakistani government would like it if that lie got revealed to their voting public."

Popel smiled back. "Probably not much, sir. I'll find a tactful way to include that in our discussions."

Hernandez nodded. "Good. That leaves India. Now, we've already passed on to the Indians what we learned about the explosives used to destroy those two girl's schools in Afghanistan, right?"

"Yes, sir. As you instructed, we said that we hadn't yet decided whether to make the discovery that the explosives originated in India public. They've already responded by telling us informally that they've discovered and dealt with the source that sold the Taliban the explosives, and that what they're calling an illegal sale won't be repeated."

Hernandez grunted. "Good as far as it goes. But that's not nearly enough. Tell the Indians that if they don't want their role in the bombings to become public, they need to engage in good-faith negotiations with Pakistan over their nuclear stockpiles."

Seeing Popel getting ready to object, Hernandez smiled. "I know, Fred. Their nuclear weapons mean more to them than embarrassment over their role in killing children. Suggest just a freeze for a start. Both sides already have enough to wipe out the other. Why not stop there for now?"

Popel merely raised his eyebrows, and now Hernandez laughed. "OK, Fred. I'll rely on you to put that in more diplomatically acceptable language."

Popel smiled and said, "Yes, sir. We'll give negotiations a try with both the Indians and Pakistanis. I agree with you that this may be a real opportunity to stop, or at least slow, the world's most dangerous arms race."

"While we're on the subject of things nuclear, Fred, let's ask the Russians for access to that technology they used to find both the bomb approaching Bagram Airfield and the one nearing Kabul. Of course, thank them first, though we both know this was more about the Russians helping themselves," Hernandez said.

"I agree, sir. The Russians don't want to see the Taliban running Afghanistan any more than we do. A Taliban with multiple nuclear weapons, which at one point looked like a real possibility, even less. Plus, if the security situation ever improves to the point the Afghan government can start mining operations, I think we can now expect a big Russian firm to be one of the participants. But do you think the Russians will agree to hand over that technology?" Popel asked.

"Not without an incentive. The Intermediate-Range Nuclear Forces Treaty that we withdrew from in 2019. Remember, I'd been thinking about opening talks on a new version of the treaty?" Hernandez asked.

"Yes, sir. But some big contractors have been developing missiles in the five hundred to fifty-five hundred kilometer range covered by the treaty in the years since 2019. That's a lot of jobs in a lot of states. It's also a lot of Congressmen and Senators lined up to support that spending. I thought you were going to wait until the next election to take this on," Popel said.

"Well, Fred, I don't think these new missiles are going to make us any more secure. In fact, once the Russians build the same number or more, the reverse. But that Russian nuclear detection technology, that will make us safer," Hernandez said.

Then he paused. "Let's tell the Russians we want the technology to help reduce the need for on-site inspections to ensure compliance with the terms of a new INF treaty. Make sure you're clear that we're saying reduce, not eliminate."

Popel nodded. "That just might work, sir."

"Oh, and one last thing, Fred. Please pass on my thanks to Embassy Islamabad for getting us the word right away on that intel from their Pakistani source. And at an ungodly hour to boot," Hernandez said.

Seeing that Popel looked surprised, Hernandez smiled. "I can read a timestamp, Fred. They sent that cable at three AM, their time. Not exactly the banker's hours so many people seem to think civilian government employees keep."

"Yes, sir. Happy to pass on the good word. I know it will be appreciated," Popel said and left.

That reminded Hernandez that there were a few more people to thank. The officer who spotted the nuclear explosion at Risalpur. The analyst who prepared the brief on what turned out to be Mullah Abdul Zahed's confession.

And especially the officer who stopped the bomb from getting to Bagram Airfield. Hernandez could well imagine living with the burden of that decision because if time allowed, it should have been his to make.

Maybe get him out of the pressure cooker of managing drone operations at Creech Air Force Base. Hernandez had just acted on a decision paper for the drone training about to start in the Baltic countries and Ukraine, designed to shore up their ability to stand up to the Russians.

It had come to him for decision because some thought Russia appeared to be backing off its aggressive designs in Europe. Others thought it best to be prepared, just in case Russia shifted its stance yet again.

Hernandez had always believed in being prepared. So, he had approved both the drone sales and the training package that went with them. But for the moment, at least, Russia seemed peaceful enough. In this last crisis, they'd even been helpful.

Yes, Europe should be a nice, quiet place for Captain Pettigrew to recover.

Hernandez made a note to bring all this up with General Robinson. Knowing him, he'd probably have already thought about at least some of these details.

Then he shook his head. Hernandez had made a successful business career by following a few basic principles. One of the most important was to reward outstanding performance. It astonished him how often he had to prod much of the federal government to follow that simple rule.

Well, Hernandez thought, as long as I'm in this chair, that's how it's going to be.

CHAPTER FORTY-FOUR

Pakistan Secretariat, Islamabad, Pakistan

President Hamza Shadid looked coolly at General Firoz Kulkari, who was standing at attention in front of his desk and sighed. The man looked just like his predecessor, right down to his neatly trimmed mustache.

Since his predecessor had just been executed for treason, this was not particularly a recommendation.

Hamza glanced again at the notes on his desk and realized there was no point in second-guessing himself now. He'd had to reach down far into the ranks of Pakistan's generals to find one who had no association with the one he'd just had executed.

Now to see if this one had any more sense.

"General, I need your honest military assessment on the question I'm about to ask you. What I don't want is for you to worry about how many of your fellow generals might be unhappy with your answer. Is that clear?" Hamza asked.

"Perfectly, sir. As far as I'm concerned, what you've just asked is the most important part of my job," Firoz said.

Hamza grunted and sat back in his chair. So far, so good.

"Would our national security be threatened if we agreed to freeze our nuclear weapons program at its current level, on condition that India does the same? Assume that we can work out the issue of verification to our satisfaction," Hamza said.

Firoz stood stock still for several moments, clearly considering the question.

Well, good, Hamza thought. Only an idiot would answer such a question instantly.

Firoz finally said, "I do not believe so, sir. India has more nuclear weapons than we do. However, our land-based missiles are on mobile platforms. We move our nuclear-capable air assets regularly. And we have successfully tested and deployed submarine-launched cruise missiles. A devastating response would still meet even the most effective first strike imaginable."

Hamza nodded. "Good. Do you have any concerns, then, with this freeze proposal?"

Firoz frowned. "Just one, sir. How likely is it that the Indians will agree to discuss the idea? Not only do they have more nuclear weapons than we do, but their production capacity and overall military budget is also superior to ours. Without a freeze, I would expect them to pull even farther ahead of us in the years to come."

Hamza smiled thinly. "Yes, and on top of that, we just lost eight of our nuclear cruise missiles."

And, Hamza thought to himself, no need to tell Firoz the Americans have proof that one of them exploded in Risalpur.

Firoz wisely stayed silent.

"Well, General, it turns out that's not a problem. The Indians came to us with the freeze proposal. They say they know the Taliban stole several of our nuclear weapons and exploded one of them in Afghanistan, though, of course, we continue to deny that publicly. They also say that a freeze is the best way to keep the numbers of nuclear weapons low enough that we can concentrate on not letting a theft happen again. What do you say to that, General?" Hamza asked.

Firoz was silent for several seconds, only a twitch from his mustache betraying his anger.

"I would say that the Indians are just as insolent as usual. For your information, sir, one of my first orders was that any nuclear weapon transport would only take place with a full escort of tanks and armored personnel carriers. Security for the convoy the Taliban attacked was inexcusably lax."

Firoz paused. "However, I have to admit that the basic proposition is sound. Fewer weapons are indeed inherently easier to guard. If we extended a freeze to not only weapons production but also the development of new missile systems, we would save serious money that we could put to far better military use."

Hamza was surprised and intrigued. "For example, General?"

"Well, the point of developing even longer-range missiles never made sense to me, since even the Shaheen-3 can reach any point within India, including the Andaman and Nicobar Islands. For that matter, the Shaheen-3 could even reach Israel. It was only after the arrest of the traitors that I learned of the ridiculous plan to ally with China against India and Russia, which would have indeed required even longer-range missiles. Once we freeze those development programs and suspend the production of additional units of current models, we could put the funds saved into our export program."

Hamza looked at Firoz blankly. "What export program?"

"Well, sir, we haven't given it much publicity. But we've already exported JF-17 fighter jets to Nigeria, Myanmar, Malaysia, and Azerbaijan. We've also exported unarmed surveillance drones to the American Border Patrol," Firoz said.

"Remarkable. Now, the JF-17 is a Chinese design, correct?" Hamza asked.

"Yes, sir," Firoz said nodding. "Thanks to our lower-cost but skilled labor, we can assemble them more cheaply than the Chinese. All of our customers are happy with the result, and with funds to expand production, we could sell more. But not everything we sell was designed in China," Firoz said.

"For example?" Hamza asked.

"Well, not only the unarmed drones we sold the Americans, but our armed drones such as the Burraq were developed in Pakistan. We also developed the laser-guided missile, called the Barq, which arms the Burraq. In fact, with the successful use of a Barq missile carried by the Burraq against terrorists in 2015, we became only the fourth country in the world to use an armed drone in combat," Firoz said proudly.

"Impressive," Hamza said, nodding. Then he cocked his head and asked, "Myanmar borders India. How did India react to our sale of fighter jets to the Myanmar Air Force?"

Firoz grinned. "An excellent question, sir. They didn't like it. Not at all. Myanmar is not and never will be a real threat to them. But a more capable Myanmar Air Force means, at a minimum, stepping up air patrols along their border. That draws away planes from elsewhere, including from our border with India."

Hamza nodded thoughtfully. "Perhaps we can use some of the money we'll save on nuclear weapons to offer a truly excellent deal on JF-17 fighters to Bangladesh."

Firoz's eyes widened. "An inspired idea, sir. The Indians wouldn't like that a bit. However, I suggest waiting until the freeze is in place, and we have a chance to build up our JF-17 production facility to meet the order if the Bangladeshis agree."

Hamza frowned, but then nodded. Firoz had a point. India remembered well that until 1971, Bangladesh had been East Pakistan, and was still very much a Muslim country. It just might end the nuclear weapons freeze if it thought "the two Pakistans" were forming an alliance against it.

He'd have to give that idea more thought.

Aloud Hamza just said, "Agreed."

"One other thing about the Indians, sir. The more I think about it, the less I believe that their real motive for proposing a nuclear freeze is concern over future weapons thefts. They aren't stupid and know we'll increase our security. So, why give up a numerical advantage that is set to grow larger in the future?" Firoz asked.

Firoz then immediately answered his question. "It doesn't add up. Something else is going on we need to understand. I suggest we ask our friends at ISI to look into it."

Hamza grunted. Anything that got the intelligence people looking at the Indian threat rather than, say, meddling with Pakistani internal politics sounded good to him.

"Good, General. Write up a proposal, and I will send it on to ISI with my endorsement," Hamza said.

"One last thought, sir. Many of the generals who were pushing so hard to advance our nuclear weapons program had ties to the companies that made components, wrote software or provided technical services for the missiles. I suggest we nationalize every company with any role in military production, to remove any incentive for generals to send us down the wrong path again," Firoz said.

"Interesting idea, General. It appears you've already given this problem some thought. I thought that Pakistan Ordnance Factories already had a monopoly on military production," Hamza observed.

"No, sir. While they are indeed the only source for the final assembly of military equipment, parts, software, and technical services are still being provided by private companies. A famous American General who later became President named Eisenhower warned about the danger of what he called the 'military-industrial complex.' Let us take this opportunity to bring it firmly under government control, sir," Firoz said.

"Thank you for some excellent suggestions, General. I will consider all of them, and get back to you soon," Hamza said.

Firoz saluted and left.

So, on the one hand, Firoz was embracing the idea of a nuclear weapons freeze, which came as a pleasant surprise.

On the other, he was quoting generals who had become President. Pakistan had spent much of its existence ruled by generals, and Hamza had no intention of giving up his seat to one.

And that very much included General Firoz.

He would definitely bear watching.

Creech Air Force Base, Nevada

Lt. Colonel Emmanuel Wainwright knew something had happened at the drone control center. Nobody he had asked had told him anything about it.

But Wainwright had pressed one young airman on his first tour hard. Finally, the airman had said he couldn't talk because it was Sensitive Compartmented Information. When Wainwright had told the airman he had an SCI clearance, he'd just said, "Not for this you don't, sir."

Wainwright had asked the airman how he could be so sure. When the airman said, "You weren't there, sir," Wainwright had his confirmation.

Something had definitely happened at the drone control center. If Wainwright could just find out what it was, maybe he could use the information to hang Captain Pettigrew and get his career back on track.

385 · THE END OF AMERICA'S WAR IN AFGHANISTAN

Just as he had this pleasant thought, the phone rang on Wainwright's desk.

Wainwright immediately recognized the caller's voice. It was Archie, the one friend who had been willing to give him a heads-up on Pettigrew.

"Great to hear from you, Archie!" Wainwright began.

"Look, Manny, I've got to make this quick," Archie replied.

Wainwright frowned. Whatever this was, it didn't sound like good news.

But Archie's next words seemed to contradict that impression.

"Manny, I know you've been looking for a pilot's job with an airline based out of McCarran Airport there in Vegas. That job is yours. The catch is you start tomorrow. That means you put in your retirement papers today. Agree right now, and I'll e-mail you the details," Archie said.

Wainwright had to think about that one a moment. He had the time in to qualify for immediate voluntary retirement. But why the rush?

"Archie, first, thanks a lot. Just one question. What's the hurry?" Wainwright asked.

This was met by silence at the other end of the line, long enough that Wainwright started to think they'd been cut off.

Then Archie finally replied. "Look, I'm in real trouble, and it'll be a lot bigger if you don't say yes. For you, too. They found out I talked to you about Pettigrew. They want you out right now. If you don't retire and take the job, they're going to bring you up on charges. Something to do with violating security regulations."

Archie paused. "Look, Manny, you're a good pilot, always have been. The pension plus the new job will give you more money than you're making now. This is a great chance for you, and you should grab it with both hands. You'll be saving both our necks."

Wainwright almost asked who "they" was, and then realized he knew the answer. General Robinson, or someone working for him.

Part of him wanted to blow the whistle on whatever Pettigrew had done. If "they" were willing to buy him off with a job to keep him quiet, it had to be something big.

Wainwright had many faults. One of his few virtues was that he cared about his family.

Say he was successful in finding the truth about what had happened at the drone control center. No outcome Wainwright could foresee after revealing that would work out well for his wife and children.

If he were convicted of violating security regulations, Wainwright might not just lose his job. He might forfeit his pension too.

This was an easy decision, Wainwright realized.

"I'll take the job, Archie. I'll look forward to the e-mail with details. And I'll submit my retirement papers today," Wainwright said.

"Outstanding!" Archie replied, with audible relief. "I'll send you the e-mail as soon as I hang up. Good luck to you, Manny," he said, as the line went dead.

Wainwright shook his head. On the one hand, this wasn't right. He shouldn't be shoved out the door like this after more than twenty years of service.

On the other, in his gut, Wainwright knew that the outcome for him and his family could have been far worse.

CHAPTER FORTY-FIVE

Gospital Fsb Na Shchukinskoy, Moscow, Russia

Anatoly Grishkov's eyes slowly opened, revealing a doctor looking at a chart and a nurse checking an IV line.

Which led to his arm. So, I'm in a hospital.

Now the doctor glanced his way.

"Ah, the stimulant worked! Excellent! My name is Doctor Kotov. First, let me give you some details about your condition, which I am happy to say is much improved."

Kotov looked down at his chart and then continued.

"American doctors successfully removed all of the shrapnel found in your body and repaired all internal damage. I must say I admire the quality of the work. I doubt there will even be much of a visible scar," Kotov said, smiling.

"Where am I, and how much longer will I be here?" Grishkov asked.

"You are at a military hospital in Moscow," Kotov replied and then shook his head.

"You've had major surgery, and we'll want to monitor you for at least several more days. That could be longer, especially if you develop complications such as an infection. However, so far, your progress has been remarkable, and we expect you to make a full recovery."

"How long have I been unconscious?" Grishkov asked.

"You were unconscious for several days, during surgery and transport to Moscow. However, it would be more accurate to say you've been sleeping during the past three days here. We gave you a light sedative to give your body a chance to heal itself, and so you wouldn't have to deal with the pain of recovery. I have been steadily reducing the painkillers administered, hoping that your body would still let you sleep. How are you feeling?" Kotov asked.

Grishkov frowned and took stock. There was an ache in his side, but not too bad.

Grishkov pointed at his right side and asked, "Is this where I was injured?"

Kotov nodded. "Yes. Still painful?"

Grishkov shrugged. "I can feel it, but it's bearable. What kind of painkillers are you giving me, and what dose?"

Kotov grinned in evident relief. "Truly remarkable! I had you taken off pain medication last night, and had you closely monitored in case pain woke you up. I had to argue with my supervisor to take this approach."

Then Kotov drew closer, and his voice dropped. "I'm tired of losing good men to addiction after we make such efforts to save them from their injuries. I'm glad that in your case, it worked."

Kotov hesitated, and then said quietly, "My supervisor made me promise to offer you pain medication once you were awake if your discomfort is too much to handle. So, your choice?"

Grishkov looked at the doctor thoughtfully. "I'll take two aspirin. I'm also going to use whatever influence I have with my boss to get you promoted, and your approach put in place more widely. I agree that we've lost too many good men to drugs, and we have to do something to stop it."

Kotov smiled. "Thank you. Speaking of your boss, he and two of your friends are waiting outside to see you, if you feel up to it."

Grishkov's eyes widened. "Director Smyslov is here? Please, show them all in!"

Kotov and the nurse left. The nurse was wearing a frown that, at first, he didn't understand. In fact, he'd wondered why she'd stayed during his conversation with Kotov.

Then he realized the nurse had been told to report back to Kotov's supervisor on whether he had offered Grishkov painkillers. Someone happy to make such a report would not like the promise he'd made Kotov to help advance his anti-painkiller agenda.

Grishkov sighed. Doing the right thing was never simple or easy.

Smyslov burst into the room and headed straight for Grishkov. Grishkov's head and shoulders were propped up in the hospital bed and were both quickly engulfed in Smyslov's embrace.

So, Grishkov thought, this is what the Americans call a "bear hug." Will I survive it?

It was only a half-joking thought, as Smyslov's arms seemed determined to squeeze the breath out of him.

Finally, Smyslov released him and boomed, "I'm so glad to see you're all right! Once you're out of here, we'll have a proper celebration!"

Now Mikhail Vasilyev and Neda Rhahbar approached Grishkov, at what he was grateful to see was a slower speed.

Vasilyev patted him on the shoulder, while Neda bent down and kissed his cheek.

Grinning, Vasilyev said, "Glad to see the Americans were able to put you back together. Sure you've still got all your parts?" he said, gesturing to Grishkov's waist.

Neda punched Vasilyev in the arm, and said something in Russian that made both Vasilyev and Smyslov gasp, and then roar in laughter.

Grishkov shook his head and asked, "Where in the world did a nice girl like you learn to talk like that?"

Vasilyev nodded. "Yes, and it's not the first time she said it," thinking about the first time Neda had kissed him.

Neda blushed, and said, "I didn't know it was that bad. It's what my Systema instructor said the first time I beat him."

Still smiling, Smyslov said, "Well, then he's a sore loser. Vasilyev will have to teach you more appropriate language."

Grishkov thought to himself, so. It seems the Director knows something is going on between those two.

Then he saw the ring on Neda's hand, and his eyes widened.

Neda, observant as always, sighed. She looked at Vasilyev and said, "Tell him."

Vasilyev smiled and said, "Neda has agreed to marry me."

"Congratulations!" was all Grishkov could manage through his astonishment.

Smyslov laughed and said, "But of course, first there is paperwork, reams of it. Even I as Director can only do so much to hurry it along."

Grishkov nodded and then asked, "What happened with the nuclear weapons?"

Smyslov held up his hands and smiled. "First, security," he said, nodding towards Vasilyev.

Vasilyev left, and a few minutes later was back. "As you requested, the floor has been cleared. The doors at both stairwells are locked, and guards are in place outside them. The elevator will not stop on this floor as long as we are here."

Smyslov looked at Grishkov soberly. "I will start with the good news. The Taliban targeted eight weapons. You destroyed four. The Pakistanis recovered one, and another partially detonated inside Pakistan, with casualties low enough that the government was able to pass it off as a chemical factory mishap."

Smyslov paused and pointed at Vasilyev and Neda. "These two defused another weapon inside Afghanistan, just after you were injured."

"Well done!" Grishkov said, with all the sincerity he could muster.

Vasilyev and Neda both smiled and nodded, but their eyes were still downcast.

Grishkov knew bad news was coming.

"And the last one?" Grishkov asked quietly.

"Another partial detonation, but this time more of the fissile material was consumed in the explosion. It happened in the town of Bagram, just outside the American military airfield," Smyslov said.

"Casualties?" Grishkov asked, even more quietly.

"The Americans appear to have escaped unscathed. Afghan casualties in Bagram number at least in the hundreds, and probably thousands. The Americans were quick to assist, and are still on site. Both they and the Afghan government are still saying that it's too early to give precise casualty numbers," Smyslov said.

"But," Smyslov added, "it's not too early to say who's responsible. The Taliban. Sentiment in both Afghanistan and Pakistan has turned against them with remarkable speed. The Americans have made video equipment from their nearby base available to the Afghans. They are broadcasting images of the devastation on national TV, which has been picked up by the Pakistanis. Few other countries have the stomach to air the images."

Grishkov nodded thoughtfully. "It would be a good time to hit the Taliban hard."

"Yes, not a simple policeman anymore," Smyslov said with a smile. "From our base in Tajikistan, we have been monitoring an increase in

American military activity in Afghanistan. I think our friends there have had the same thought."

"My wife and children? They are well?" Grishkov asked.

"Of course! They are here to see you, and will as soon as we finish here. Ordinarily, I would have had them come to see you first. However, we are also here to discuss matters of state security, and no matter how I feel personally, those must take precedence," Smyslov said.

It was the first time Grishkov could recall Smyslov looking so uncomfortable.

"So, first, I will share with you in more detail than I would for ordinary agents the consequences of your last mission. Why? Because I think it's important for you to understand that those results go far beyond saving lives, important though that goal may be," Smyslov said.

Smyslov gestured towards a thick file that Grishkov noticed for the first time had been placed on a table behind Neda.

"Details of what I am about to tell you are in that file. I'm going to give you the highlights, so you have the chance to ask questions. Vasilyev will return the file to headquarters later, but in the meantime, you may all review it," Smyslov said.

Vasilyev, Neda, and Grishkov all nodded.

"So, first, the President is extremely pleased with your performance. Your actions saved thousands of lives. At our request, the Americans have shared your role in defusing the weapon that nearly reached Kabul with the Afghan President, who says he will visit Moscow soon to convey his thanks in person," Smyslov said.

Vasilyev smiled. "So, we may not have a guaranteed role in Afghanistan's mining future, but at least we're on the field."

Smyslov nodded. "Just so. Also, at our request, the Americans have agreed to keep our role in this matter quiet otherwise."

Grishkov frowned. "If the Afghan President knows, surely it won't be long before he tells others, or am I missing something?"

Smyslov shrugged. "You may be right. The Americans asked him to keep our role to himself, but only self-interest will do so. I think it likely he will realize the degree of panic that would be caused by the realization a nuclear weapon was minutes away from exploding in Kabul. And perhaps blame his government for letting it get so close. There would be the plus of further outrage against the Taliban. But there is already plenty of that from news coverage from Bagram."

Neda said quietly, "I hope the Taliban reaps the reward they deserve."

"As I mentioned, the Americans appear to be working as we speak on making your wish come true. Speaking of wishes, you are now all in a position to fulfill them. The President has ordered that your previous award for completion of such an important mission be doubled to two million American dollars each. As before, the money will be paid from his private funds," Smyslov said.

Grishkov noticed again that Smyslov was doing his best to hide discomfort about . . . something.

"Now, I will explain the real reason he was so pleased with the outcome of your mission. Ironically, none of you were directly responsible. Our drone detected the radiation signature of the weapon once it reached Bagram and passed that information to the Americans. That drone was also able to monitor and record an American drone using a missile to strike the truck carrying the weapon, which then detonated," Smyslov said quietly.

Grishkov shrugged. "The town is almost directly adjacent to the base. If the Americans had allowed the weapon to proceed any further, the detonation would have cost them military lives and equipment. There would have been no time to organize a ground assault. We would have made the same decision."

Smyslov nodded. "For someone like you with military experience, that is the reaction I would expect. However, we believe the Afghans in particular and public opinion worldwide would hold the Americans at least partly responsible for the carnage in Bagram if their missile firing were to become known."

Neda said hesitantly, "Excuse me, Director, but did the Russian . . . I mean, our drone record the size of the blast? I ask because a nuclear detonation caused by an outside force should not have consumed all of the weapon's fissile material."

"You are correct," Smyslov said with an approving nod. "First, to catch yourself and call it 'our drone.' After what you have done for Russia, I consider you as much a citizen as these two," he said, pointing at Vasilyev and Grishkov.

Neda blushed and murmured thanks.

"Second, the drone did indeed record details of the blast and was nearly lost in the process. Fortunately, after detecting the weapon and transmitting its location to the Americans, the drone's operator realized it would be a good time to be elsewhere, and so was already on a course back to base in Tajikistan. Our scientists have analyzed the drone's data, and believe that only about half of the weapon's fissile material was consumed in the explosion," Smyslov concluded.

Vasilyev nodded. "Surely, then, people would recognize that it would have been worse to allow the weapon to proceed to its target. We saw many Afghans at Bagram Airfield, so it's not as though the only casualties would have been American."

Smyslov shook his head. "I don't think that's how most people would see it, and neither does the President. And that is why he is so pleased with this outcome. You have given the President a secret to use against the Americans, one they would go to great lengths to keep out of public view."

"Do you know what our President will ask the Americans to do?" Vasilyev asked.

"That's not how these things work," Smyslov said with a smile. "He will keep this secret in his pocket, and wait for the right time to use it for maximum effect. As you know, the Americans are by far the greatest threat to our security and our plans abroad, and so the importance of this new asset cannot be overstated."

Now Smyslov's smile disappeared, and he gestured again towards the file.

"Most of what you see in that file expands on what we have already discussed. And I sincerely wish that I could leave you with no more than that to study. I have loudly and repeatedly proposed exactly that. I regret that I have been overruled," Smyslov said.

Now we come to it, Grishkov thought. This is what's been bothering him.

"Your accomplishments have been most impressive, and the President seems to have fixated on you as the solution to all our most difficult problems. However, I have pointed out to the President that you are not the only three FSB agents. Also, that you are all human and do not wear capes. All of you, especially you, Grishkov must have time to recover from your last mission," Smyslov said.

Smyslov's voice had been rising with each word, and all of them were thinking the same thing.

They had never seen the Director truly angry before.

"I also showed him the analysis given to us by the Americans of the device that these two defused," Smyslov said, gesturing towards Neda and Vasilyev. "They said it was impossible to say precisely how much longer it would have taken the device to detonate if they had not defused it, but they could give a range."

Smyslov glowered, and they were all profoundly grateful that his anger was not directed at them.

"Between two and eight seconds! I asked the President, just how much more luck do you think these agents have left?"

Smyslov shook his head and sighed, deflated. "I even offered the President my resignation, which he rejected. Not at a time of national crisis, he said. Maybe after this is over."

Seeing their confused looks, Smyslov laughed sadly. "Yes, what crisis, you will want to know. First, I was able to win a reprieve by pointing out we can't send a man from his hospital bed early to take on a mission. Other FSB agents are working on the problem now, and if we're lucky will succeed before the doctors clear Grishkov to return to duty."

Grishkov shook his head. "And how far will we go this time?"

"That is the only good news I have to give you. Less than a thousand kilometers," Smyslov said.

All of them exclaimed with surprise. Vasilyev was the first to guess, "Kyiv? We are going to Ukraine?"

"Correct," Smyslov said.

Grishkov sighed. "So, with the Koreans, we had to worry about one nuclear weapon. The Iranians, three. The Taliban, eight. How many this time?"

Smyslov frowned and said, "First, I have to tell you that the prospect of a nuclear detonation, bad as it would be, is not our primary concern. It is that the Americans may feel obliged to react militarily. From my discussions with the President, I think it is likely that would end only one way."

Vasilyev said in a low voice, "Badly."

"Correct," Smyslov said, nodding.

Turning to Grishkov, Smyslov said, "Now, to give you a direct answer to your question, this time, there is just a single missing weapon."

Smyslov paused.

"Unfortunately, it is ours, and it is thermonuclear."

First, thanks very much for reading my book! I sincerely hope you enjoyed it. If you did, I'd really appreciate it if you could leave a review—even a short one—on Amazon.

If in spite of the best efforts of my editor (and me!) you found a typo or some other error, please let me know with details. I will fix it!

If you have questions, please send those to me too. You can reach me at my blog, https://thesecondkoreanwar.wordpress.com or on Twitter at https://Twitter.com/TedHalstead18

Or if all else fails, you can e-mail me directly at thalstead2018@gmail.com

I'll answer a few questions now that I received after my first two books. First, are any of the stories in the books from my own experience, and if so which ones?

You can apply common sense to answer that one.

In my first book, *The Second Korean War:*

Characters set mines, throw grenades, and attempt to defuse nuclear weapons.

None of that was me.

Characters describe kicking up tear "gas" powder on a Seoul subway platform and not enjoying the results, and dealing with poorly aimed golf balls hit by American military officers landing in their yard at Yongsan Army Base in Seoul.

Yes, that was me.

In my second book, *The Saudi-Iranian War:*

Characters fire rockets, and drive a truck off a pier.

Not me.

Characters in Saudi Arabia go through traffic experiences themselves, and recount others. They describe the treatment of women in Saudi Arabia. Hulk Hogan makes an unexpected appearance in the narrative.

All me, all true.

In the book you just finished . . . I think you get the idea.

Many readers have asked questions along the lines of "why would the Russians want to help." I think the answer is simple. Like citizens of all countries, Russians want first and foremost to help themselves.

In each book, I've tried to lay out what I believe is a compelling case for the Russians to take action. I think it's also important to remember what the Russians are actually risking in these books—the lives of a few agents, and a plane here, a drone there.

So, each time Russia may not stand to gain that much. But the risk/reward ratio is always very, very favorable. To me, that makes Russia's actions in the books credible.

I noted on the book listing page that all of my books are set in the near future, not the present. Please keep that in mind when deciding whether the technology described in this book is plausible. If you still think not, remember that not so long ago widespread GPS capability in cars and phones wouldn't have been just science fiction. It would have been not very credible science fiction.

Finally, some readers may believe that Rangers would not be assigned missions of the sort described in this book, or that they are not true "special forces." I would first note that Rangers fall under SOCOM, and participated in the raid that killed al-Baghdadi. If that's not good enough, I'll again remind readers that this book is set in the near future, when I expect Rangers to be called upon more and more to carry out such missions.

Thanks again for reading my book, and I hope you will enjoy my next one in 2021!

CAST OF CHARACTERS

Alphabetical Order by Nationality
Most Important Characters in Bold

Afghan Citizens
Amooz, fighter on the side of the Russians since the 1980s
Baddar, Taliban leader
Afan Malik, Mullah Abdul Zahed's nephew and videographer
Hashmat Mohebi, Taliban leader
Fereshtah Saheb, girl's school principal
Mamnoon Sahar, Taliban bomber
Khaled Tanha, Taliban leader
Mullah Abdul Zahed, Taliban leader

Pakistani Citizens
Nasir Cheema, nuclear technician
Colonel Azita Kamar, Senior Military Police Investigator
General Firoz Kulkari, Commander of Pakistani Forces
    (replaced Monir)
General Ehsan Monir, Commander of Pakistani Forces
Ibrahim Munawar, nuclear technician now working for Taliban
Hamza Shadid, Prime Minister of Pakistan
Khaksar Wasiq, Taliban leader

Indian Citizens
Judge Bachchan, CBI Secret Detention Facility, near Mumbai
Akshay Roshan, scientist, High Energy Materials Research Laboratory,
    Pune, India

Russian Citizens

Captain Igor Bronstein, 201st Military Base, Tajikistan

Anatoly Grishkov, FSB agent, former Vladivostok homicide detective

Dr. Kotov, Gospital Fsb Na Shchukinskoy, Moscow

Neda Rhahbar, FSB agent, former Iranian citizen

FSB Director **Smyslov**

Mikhail Vasilyev, FSB agent

American Citizens

Captain Walt Addison, U.S. Space Command watch officer

Carol Banning, U.S. Cyber Command analyst

U.S. President Hernandez

Sergeant Alonzo Johnson, communications technician,
    Creech Air Force Base

Lieutenant Commander Mike Lombardy, Deputy Commander,
    SEAL Team Six

Commander Dave Martins, Commander, SEAL Team Six

Captain Josh Pettigrew, Deputy Commander of Drone Operations,
    Creech Air Force Base

Fred Popel, Secretary of State

General Robinson, the Air Force Chief of Staff

Captain John Rogoff, Ranger unit commander

Chuck Soltis, the White House Chief of Staff

Lt. Col. Emmanuel Wainwright, Commander of Drone Operations,
    Creech Air Force Base